NASA, you h

"A novel you'll want to read twice before the movie is produced!"

—*Tampa Free Press*

"I have flown and tested fighters and I have been in space four times, including once to the Moon—and I can tell you that *Ignition* captures the fast-paced excitement of our quest for space and the struggle for the future."

—Thomas P. Stafford, Commander, Gemini 6, Gemini 9, Apollo 10, Apollo-Soyuz

"The really frightening thing is how plausible it is....I thought I had already imagined everything that could go wrong with the shuttle. I was wrong!"

—Kerry Joels, author of
The Space Shuttle Operator's Manual

IGNITION

KEVIN J. ANDERSON
AND
DOUG BEASON

TOR®

A TOM DOHERTY ASSOCIATES BOOK
NEW YORK

IGNITION

Copyright © 1997 by Kevin J. Anderson and Doug Beason

A Forge Book
Published by Tom Doherty Associates, Inc.
175 Fifth Avenue
New York, NY 10010

Forge® is a registered trademark of Tom Doherty Associates, Inc.

ISBN: 0-812-54548-6
Library of Congress Card Catalog Number: 96-29343

First edition: March 1997
First mass market edition: February 1998

Printed in the United States of America

0 9 8 7 6 5 4 3 2 1

To the men and women of NASA,
America's space program,
who continue to ignite
our dreams of
the future

ACKNOWLEDGMENTS

This book would not have been possible without the many contributions of the following: Milt Finger of the Lawrence Livermore National Laboratory; Tina Pechon, Manny Virata, and Bill Johnson of NASA Public Affairs at the Kennedy Space Center; Charlie Parker from NASA; Michael "Mini" Mott of NASA HQ; Dr. Kerry Joels; Lieutenant Colonel Chuck Beason; Major Lon Enloe; and Norys Davila.

Along the way, we also received valuable advice from Dean Koontz, Al Zuckerman, Richard Curtis, Patrick Nielsen Hayden, Joseph M. Singer, Brian Lipson, Amy Victoria Meo, Lil Mitchell, Scott Welch, Philippa Pride, Janet Berliner, Bob Fleck, Mark Budz, Marina Fitch, Kristine Kathryn Rusch, Dean Wesley Smith, Deb Ray, Inès Heinz, General Tom Stafford, Joe Domenici, and, as always, Rebecca Moesta Anderson and Cindy Beason.

AUTHORS' NOTE

While we have done extensive research on NASA, the
Kennedy Space Center, the Johnson Space Center, the
European Space Agency's Ariane program, and other
topics for this book, many specific details have been
intentionally changed. The locations of certain buildings and facilities—particularly the Vehicle Assembly
Building and the Launch Control Center—have been
moved, and some NASA security procedures have
been altered in order to preserve the integrity of these
national assets.

PROLOGUE

Arianespace Launch Center
Kourou, French Guiana

The thick humidity was a magnifying glass, amplifying the sun's heat in the coastal jungles of French Guiana. Just north of the small town of Kourou, security patrols locked gates and inspected chain-link fences in preparation for the launch of an Ariane 44L rocket, flagship of the European Space Agency.

On roads freshly bulldozed through the South American jungle, khaki-uniformed guards patrolled the swampy lowlands of the Guiana Space Center. One guard stopped to light a cigarette. Though armed, the guards were complacent—unaware of the sabotage team deep inside the complex.

The Ariane countdown continued.

Mr. Phillips sat on the springy seat of his camouflaged Jeep and raised binoculars to his eyes, carefully adjusting the focus. He wore an immaculate white suit and tie, despite the jungle heat. His movements were spare and meticulous, as if he planned each step down to the bending of a finger joint. He studied the towering launch vehicle on ELA-2, the pad for all Ariane 4 rockets.

Impressive construction, he thought. *Very impressive*. Mr. Phillips pressed a snow-white handkerchief to his forehead to absorb the perspiration that glistened there, and tucked a strand of his dark hair back into place. If he didn't pay attention to the small details, then the larger ones would defeat him.

The heat was oppressive, unlike the cool dampness in Connecticut where he'd spent much of his first life. He buried the momentary discomfort, moving past it as he had with so many other obstacles before.

Beside him in the Jeep, an eager young man with sunburned skin and a mop of coppery hair swatted an insect. "Damn bugs," he said, then slapped the same spot on his arm again and again, though the insect was most certainly dead. "After this humidity, Florida's going to seem like paradise. Definitely."

Mr. Phillips gave him a wry smile. "One mission at a time, Rusty. Please stop your fidgeting—you're ruining my focus." Even Florida had miserable humidity, but again, the discomfort would only be temporary.

He studied the rocket's contours as if it were a desirable woman. A tall spire with a bulbous rounded head, the unmanned 44L resembled a shining white lance with four smaller rockets strapped around its base.

Unfortunately, this particular rocket wouldn't make it to orbit. Not today—not ever.

In front of him, leaning against the hood of the camouflaged Jeep, stood Jacques, his hair so blond he looked almost albino, though his skin had achieved a golden tan. In one hand he held the detonator, a box no bigger than a pack of cigarettes. Jacques had always been good with explosives.

Mr. Phillips pulled out his pocket watch and studied the hour. *Patience*, he told himself. He straightened his tie, then reached into his pocket for a breath mint.

Mr. Phillips heard a rustling sound from the left and glanced up to see a khaki-clad security guard trudging out of the jungle from one of the narrow access roads. The guard, whose bronzed skin and long black hair showed his Amerindian descent, held his rifle loosely; mirrored sunglasses hid his eyes.

Taken completely by surprise, the guard stopped as he saw the short, formally dressed man sitting with his companions in a Jeep. Mr. Phillips's mouth drew tight at the guard's utterly dumbfounded expression.

The guard brought up his rifle and swept it around. *"Halte! Qu'est-ce que vous faites la? Je vous arrête!"* he barked in French. The entire restricted area had supposedly been swept clean of bystanders.

Mr. Phillips turned away from the intruder in annoyance. It had been hard enough slipping inside the secure area—first the bribe, then the unpleasant disposal of the official who had given them entrance. He disliked this additional inconvenience . . . but Mr. Phillips had allowed for such contingencies in his planning.

Jacques tucked the detonator into his pocket. Pretending to surrender, he lifted his hands above his head and translated. "He wants to know what we're doing here, Monsieur Phillips. His accent is very bad. He is placing us under arrest."

Mr. Phillips raised his eyebrows. "Oh, he is?"

Silent as a cobra, fluid as a deer, a lithe blond woman slipped out of the underbrush behind the guard. From her waistband she slipped out a thin stiletto so sharp and pointed it might have been an ice pick.

She moved without hesitation, crossing the ten meters without a sound. The guard stopped as if he suddenly heard something—then the woman struck, jamming the stiletto into the base of his back. Without a word, she rammed it up his spinal column all the way to the hilt, as if trying to dig crabmeat out of a shell.

The guard twitched and jiggled like a pithed frog. His fingers slipped from the trigger guard, and he dropped his rifle. The muscular blond woman jerked her wrist, and the stiletto slipped back out with a wet *pop*. The guard fell to the muddy ground as if unplugged.

"Thank you, Yvette," Mr. Phillips said. "Your timing, as usual, is impeccable." Nonchalantly she wiped the blood from her blade on the wide, glossy leaf of a rubber plant and glided the stiletto back into her belt.

Rusty paid no attention to the encounter, still staring toward the white rocket on the launchpad. "We should've just had Mory use one of his Stinger missiles, like we did in China. We could be back on the beach by now, having a swim. Definitely." He gave a short, high laugh.

Mr. Phillips spoke to him the way a patient father would. Unlike the other members of the team, Rusty was not a professional, and Mr. Phillips had to cut him some slack. "Different goals, Rusty. We proved in China that we can slip into a highly restricted area.

Here, we must demonstrate that we can plant an explosive surreptitiously and detonate it at our convenience.''

"But why not blow it up now, while the rocket's still on the pad? Why wait until it launches?" Rusty swatted at another bug.

Mr. Phillips shook his head. "By waiting, we *control* the situation. Much greater impact . . . much more exhilarating."

"Yeah, sure," Rusty said, obviously not understanding the nuances—but then, the redhead wasn't paid to think. "I just want to hear the kaboom."

As blond as Jacques, Yvette strode on her long legs over to meet him by the Jeep. Two sets of water-blue eyes, the color of ice melting in the heat, locked together. The pair spoke quietly in French; Yvette ran a hand up and down Jacques's arm. They then kissed each other long and hard, oblivious to the rest of the team. Breathing quickly, their mouths opened as they deepened the kiss with lingering tongues. Jacques let his fingers drift in a tightening circle around the swell of her right breast.

Mr. Phillips clapped his hands. "Time enough for that later!"

The two broke apart, glazed with perspiration and breathing shallowly.

"Let's keep an eye on the clocks, everybody," Mr. Phillips said. "Less than a minute to go."

The Toucan VIP Observation Site at the Kourou launch facility was designed to accommodate dignitaries, but Colonel Adam "Iceberg" Friese didn't see it as anything more than a set of bleachers shaded by a canvas awning. Dust, humidity, and glaring sun made sitting on the aluminum bleachers almost unbearable.

It didn't matter to him, though—he had been through far greater hardships as an astronaut. Now, he was more interested in seeing the spectacular launch of the Ariane 44L.

But what made him far more uncomfortable than the heat or the rustic conditions was the petite woman sitting next to him—a powerhouse inside a pretty, trim exterior. Her short brown-gold hair, though tinged with perspiration in the thick humidity, was still styled just so, her makeup perfect. In his memories of her, she rarely wore makeup. Now she looked every bit the administrator, working her way up the professional ladder.

"At least you're managing to keep a smile on your face, Iceberg," Nicole Hunter said quietly out of the corner of her mouth.

"I'm here representing my fellow astronauts," he answered, his voice cold. Like an iceberg. She herself had been one of those astronauts, and a Naval aviator, to boot—until her recent change of heart. "It's my obligation as a professional."

"Yeah, we're both such professionals." She wore a colorful but conservative cotton blouse and skirt, panty hose that must have been hot as hell in the Tropics—with *earrings* and a delicate gold necklace, for God's sake.

In the years he had known her, even in their most intimate moments, Iceberg had never thought of buying her jewelry. That had never been "Panther"'s style.

No, he pictured her in sweats, jogging with him for

their morning workout . . . or dressed in an astronaut jumpsuit in the simulators at Johnson Space Center, her dark eyes squinting at the controls, mechanically reacting as problem after problem was tossed at her in the sims. She and Iceberg had been the best: part of a team, confident of being selected for a shuttle mission . . . soon. It had been enough of a shock when she had resigned her Navy commission to become a civilian astronaut.

But then Nicole had changed her mind and gone "VFR direct"—visual flight rules—into NASA management, returning from a six-month special MBA program, and at Harvard, of all places! A new golden girl on a fast track to become Launch Director for an upcoming flight. And Iceberg had been picked to command the shuttle crew without her.

A staticky announcement in garbled French came over bullhorns mounted on towers near the bleachers. Iceberg couldn't understand a word of it, but he could watch the blinking numbers of the countdown clock as well as anyone. Not long now.

He fidgeted on the uncomfortable bleacher, sweating in his suit, but vowing not to let it show. At least he wasn't in his Air Force uniform; that would have been even hotter. And if Nicole could manage to look nice under these circumstances, he could do the same.

He ached when he looked at her, though he usually masked his deeper feelings. He just couldn't understand her copping out to join the desk jockeys instead of hanging in there, doing the real work for the real glory. Of course, neither of them had ever been very good at compromising. It wasn't in the blood.

From the Toucan Observation Site, Iceberg could make out launchpad ELA-2. The Ariane rocket stood

beside an enclosed gantry, a rectangular wafer shim-
mering in the heat. The facilities displayed the European Space Agency's logo, a blue circle design with
bold lowercase letters, **esa**.

In the nearby seats, well-dressed guests waited,
shading their eyes and staring east into the morning
sun. Some were local politicians, others celebrities,
and most looked bored in the sticky equatorial heat.

In the mountains above the coastal lowlands, the
locals had set up encampments, bringing fruit and picnic lunches to watch the launch. Iceberg had heard it
was a common pastime around the Guiana Space Center.

The clock ticked down. Tension built in the air. On
the bleachers, observers squirmed as if they could
somehow improve their view.

"Sure wish something would happen," Iceberg
muttered.

"Patience has never been one of your strong
points," Nicole said.

The walkie-talkie at Mr. Phillips's waist crackled. He
grabbed it in annoyance; the entire team had been instructed to observe strict radio silence, despite the en-
cryption routines the team had developed.

Mory's voice burst out, distorted from the descram-
bling routines. "We're blown, Mr. Phillips!" he said.
"Some guard spotted me and Cueball. He tore out of
here in his Jeep before we could kill him. I don't know
if he's radioed for help yet."

"Bother," Mr. Phillips said. "Less than thirty seconds to go." *A momentary inconvenience.*

Another voice came over the radio, laced with an

Australian accent. "Duncan here, Mr. Phillips. Not to worry—I got him. He's about to drive over the . . . dotted . . . *line*."

Muffled by the jungle underbrush, a small land mine exploded with a *crrump*.

Mr. Phillips squeezed the "talk" button. "Excellent work, Duncan." The other man acknowledged the compliment with two quick clicks on the speaker.

"Ten seconds left. I hope they don't go into a launch hold." Mr. Phillips turned toward Jacques, who stood caressing the detonator box, Yvette beside him. "Be prepared to detonate if the countdown stops. Otherwise, let's sit back and enjoy the show."

In front of him, a pair of sapphire blue butterflies flitted, oblivious to the monumental event about to take place. The air was as tense as a held breath.

On launchpad ELA-2, the countdown reached zero. *Ignition.*

Four Viking 5 first-stage core engines lit off simultaneously in the center of the Ariane 44L; at the same time, four additional strap-on Viking 6 booster rockets fired. Flames and white exhaust belched in a great fan across the launchpad. Clouds of smoke rolled away from the concrete apron, enveloping the rocket.

Finally, loud alarms began to blare far from the launch site, faded by distance and overwhelmed by the blast-off roar. Mr. Phillips heard a warbling siren, but the Guiana Space Center was so large he and his team would have plenty of time.

The white lance of the unmanned 44L rose into the air on a pillar of fire, clearing the top of its umbilical tower and heaving itself above its own toxic exhaust.

Jacques turned toward him, the detonator box in one

hand. "Now, Monsieur Phillips?" Yvette clung to his muscular arm.

Mr. Phillips continued to watch the marvelous rocket, astonished by the technological achievement, the sheer power of the engines. An inverted Roman candle, suspended by a glowing ball of white-hot plasma. "Exhilarating," he said.

The rocket climbed higher and higher, picking up speed as it struggled against the chains of gravity.

"*Now,* Monsieur Phillips?" Jacques asked again, anxious.

"Yes," Mr. Phillips whispered. "Now."

Jacques punched the button to trigger the explosives concealed behind one of the Viking 5 core engines.

As it rose, still gaining speed, the Ariane 44L blossomed into a fireball, followed several seconds later by a thunderclap that bowed the mangroves and jungle underbrush.

With complex emotions, Mr. Phillips watched the expanding cloud of debris and smoldering exhaust. *A shame to destroy such an engineering marvel.*

He stared transfixed for just a few minutes, then shook himself. "A perfect performance. I congratulate you all." He clapped his well-manicured hands. "Quickly now, call the team to the rendezvous point before we're discovered." He drew a deep ecstatic sigh. "So much for practice. Now we start planning for the main event."

Iceberg bolted to his feet, trying to determine what had just happened. An accident—or something else? He had heard the faint alarms just before the launch.

Unable to understand the overlapping French announcements blaring over the public-address system, he squinted into the hazy sunlight. Flames and smoke roiled up from the distant explosion. Images of the *Challenger* disaster raced through his mind. . . .

The crowd on the VIP bleachers moved about in an uproar. Emergency Jeeps and vehicles tore through the jungle along muddy access roads to penetrate the restricted area.

Iceberg squeezed his hand into a fist. Every instinct, all his training, told him to respond to the crisis. Astronauts were taught to *do* something, not just sit and let the world pass them by. But he was forced to remain where he was, a mere observer relying on the capabilities of others. The frustration of being reined in, of not being able to react, simmered inside him, but he ordered himself to cool down.

This wasn't his show, his mission, or his space program.

He didn't turn to Nicole as he spoke, trying unsuccessfully to keep his sarcasm under control. "Now that you're a hotshot manager, Panther, I suppose you'd never *allow* something like this to happen on your watch." He opened and closed his fist.

Nicole shook her head, staring fixedly in the direction of the explosion. "Damn straight," she said.

1

KENNEDY SPACE CENTER

Six Months Later

Zero-dark-early—3:00 A.M. on a launch morning, and the Kennedy Space Center was as busy as Times Square on New Year's Eve. Passing checkpoints, a steady stream of traffic crawled along the access roads—Kennedy Parkway, Phillips Parkway, NASA Parkway—the chain of headlights glittering like a sinuous caterpillar.

Away from the traffic, past the badge gates and barricades that blocked off the restricted area from all but authorized personnel, a beat-up old Pontiac Firebird pulled onto the scrubby grass beside the road, leaving tire tracks next to the many others there. From here, the guard shack was within easy hobbling distance.

"Thanks for the ride, kid."

"Sure, Iceberg. Be careful out there—don't break anything else."

Iceberg grunted as he swung his leg out of his little brother's car, moving far too slowly for someone who, up until a few weeks ago, had been in peak physical condition. The damned cast slowed him down as much as a ball and chain, covering his foot, his ankle— nearly up to his knee. And all for just a couple of broken bones, little ones at that. You'd think he was an old lady with arthritis, rather than NASA's hottest astronaut.

Ex-hottest astronaut, Iceberg thought sourly.

He gazed at the illuminated space shuttle on the nearest launchpad, three miles away. *Atlantis.* Under a brilliant glare of spotlights, white vapors vented from the shuttle's liquid oxygen and liquid hydrogen tanks. The launch gantry, the massive concrete flame buckets, and the rest of Launch Complex 39A looked surreal in the darkness three hours before dawn.

Only two days earlier another shuttle, *Endeavour,* had been rolled onto the second launchpad, 39B. But that was for another mission. Somebody else's mission, so it didn't matter to him.

The shuttle crew—*Iceberg*'s crew—would be suiting up, getting ready, eating their mission breakfast . . . the people he'd trained with for the past year, led, cajoled, prodded, and pushed into preparing for this launch. They were the world's slickest mission specialists. Now they would have to make do without the world's slickest mission commander.

His brother, Amos, pushed his heavy-rimmed round glasses up on his nose. "Birth control" glasses the astronauts called them, because no girl would be caught dead within a hundred feet of someone wearing the old-style spectacles. But then, Amos spent more time staring into video monitors than looking in mirrors. He leaned over from the driver's seat.

"Just try not to get me in any trouble, Iceberg," Amos said as a NASA security helicopter flew low over the road, drowning out his words. Wearing a goofy smile, he waited for the noise from the helicopter to abate. He removed one hand from the steering wheel to smear down his mussed, dark hair, though he didn't manage to knock a single strand back into place.

"I wouldn't risk you, kid—I'll just get myself in trouble."

Officially, Iceberg was supposed to be at home, resting. Fat chance. Iceberg had called Amos, the one person he could absolutely count on not to spill the beans.

A half dozen NASA choppers patrolled the launch area, hooking out over the ocean to deter curious maritime onlookers who bobbed on their crafts in the Atlantic. High overhead, an Air Force C-130 special operations plane flew in a tight racetrack pattern around the launch area, scanning for trespassers with sophisticated forward-looking infrared sensors. Somewhere out in the jungle surrounding the Launch Complex were security forces, but they could be miles away.

"Come to the Space Society meeting next week?" Amos said hopefully. "You could give your assessment of how the mission went. Besides, you owe me big-time for this."

"If that's the price I have to pay," Iceberg said. His thin lips formed his quirky smile that turned up first the left corner of his mouth, then the right.

"That's great!" His little brother sometimes reminded him of a puppy, wanting nothing more than to be loved.

Leaning into the front seat, Iceberg rummaged through his daypack. The tiny Walkman TV and his snack seemed surprisingly heavy. He'd rather have brought a small two-way radio to communicate with his crew, but that would have given NASA some extreme heartburn.

"See you after the launch, kid. And say hi to Cecelia for me. She's on shift with you this morning, isn't she? No hanky-panky."

Amos flushed crimson with embarrassment. "*Some* of us have duties to perform on launch day." He pushed his glasses back up his nose.

"Sure wish I did." Iceberg pulled the daypack out of the car and swung it over his shoulder. He wore a light cotton shirt and shorts in neutral colors for hiding in the underbrush. The temperature would rise quickly after dawn. Right now, the air felt cool on his bare, muscular thighs, but the supposedly lightweight plaster-and-fiberglass cast on his lower leg was going to get awfully hot before long. He had covered it with a moisture-proof "moon boot" as a precaution against the rough terrain he might have to cover. At least he could walk on it.

Shutting the door of the Pontiac behind him, he started hobbling toward the gate. The old car roared forward and stopped briefly at the guard shack before being waved into the launch area. In less than a mile Amos would turn off to the communications relay bunker nestled within the restricted launch area. The kid's job was about as essential as tits on a bull, but NASA procedures dictated that two warm bodies had to be present to oversee the video relay during each manned launch, even though everything was completely automatic.

A sign on a post read RESTRICTED LAUNCH AREA—KEEP OUT! Iceberg made his way carefully to the guard shack. Light from inside spilled to the ground through an open door. A three-wheeled all-terrain vehicle was parked next to the small structure. All around Iceberg, the swamp insects and frogs made a din as loud as a rock concert.

The guard would be busy this morning, after letting so many people through, checking so many extra badges. One might think the guards were more alert during the intense launch-day preparations—but Iceberg knew to worry most during the slow times, when guards were bored and apt to imagine terrorists in every bush.

As Iceberg approached, keeping to the side of the road, a uniformed man stepped out of the shack. The guard was nearly as tall as the door, thick-waisted, and sporting a bushy salt-and-pepper mustache. The outside light from the shack shone down on him. He put a hand on his hip holster as Iceberg's shadowy figure approached, drowned out by the lights.

"Keep where I can see you," the guard said.

Iceberg laughed and continued toward the guard shack. "Stay frosty, Salvatore, you old goat. Do they even give you any bullets for that gun?"

The guard relaxed, then called out with a thick Hispanic accent. "Iceberg! What are you doing way out here? You should have the best seat in the house on today of all days."

"The best seat is in the shuttle cockpit, Salvatore—and they don't let you fly with a broken foot." He scratched his dark brown hair, which he kept cut short to minimize the hassle when wearing various helmets.

Salvatore chuckled and fingered his chin. "No, I mean in the VIP area, with the rest of the important people at Launch Control."

Iceberg snorted. "That's my crew out there, and no way in hell am I going to watch this launch with a bunch of nonflying bureaucrats! You don't see any real astronauts inside those air-conditioned rooms." He could imagine all the TV cameras, the questions he'd have to field, the journalists with tape recorders urging him to tell the "sad story" of how he had missed his chance to command the mission through a clumsy accident. The reporters would spend more time looking at him than watching the launch. A great "angle" for their stories.

Salvatore lifted his eyebrows. "I didn't know you thought your Panther was a bureaucrat. This would be a good chance for you to see her."

"Just shows how long you've been alone in this shack, old man," said Iceberg. "These days she'd rather tear me apart than let me get close to her. Anyway, she goes by Nicole now, not Panther." Eight months out of the corps and she had become a true paper pusher, 100 percent. *The ice queen is in her element now.* She'd keep herself so busy with all the dignitaries at the VIP viewing area; she wouldn't even notice he was missing.

Salvatore motioned him into the cramped shack. "So you'll keep me company? I feel honored. Not many people come up the east road through Canaveral." He shook his head. "I'm glad I am not guarding the tourist gate today—what a mess!"

Iceberg grunted as he limped through the door. Salvatore had done the tiny security hut justice, transforming it into a comfortable place in which to sit and keep watch. Blue-and-white checkered curtains covered the windows; a cable TV tuned to NASA Select showed a close-up view of *Atlantis*; four monitors with a video feed from Amos's relay bunker lined one wall.

Salvatore had pinned two rows of shuttle crew patches over the door, his collection commemorating the numerous missions he had worked. The old guard had been here as long as Iceberg could remember; he was as much an icon as the old Redstone launchpads, now abandoned in place, rusted and overgrown with the Florida jungle.

"I appreciate the hospitality, old friend, but I'd rather be alone for this shot," Iceberg said. He set his daypack on the narrow counter next to the black telephone, rummaging among the items there. "I'm going to go deeper inside the site. I'll get a mile or so from the pad, find a comfortable spot."

He finally found what he was looking for. He pulled out a hand-sized patch with the embroidered picture of an eagle and bear reaching toward the stars. "You need one of these for your collection. It's one of the original crew patches, still has my name on it—only six in existence, far as I know."

Placing his coffee on the desk, Salvatore reached for the patch. He squinted, then grinned like a kid who had just found a rare baseball card as he spotted the names FRIESE, GREEN, BURNS embroidered at the top. "This is even more of a collector's item!"

Iceberg smiled back wearily. "Up until a week ago, they planned to make thousands of those. But now, my friend, you have one of the only such patches ever made. The rest have Dr. Marc Franklin's name on them."

The sound of NASA security helicopters droned in the background, scanning the grounds with infrared seekers; before long, the sun would rise and play havoc with the IR spotting scopes. High clouds over the launch area were tinged with pink, like cotton candy; in the east the ocean glowed a dull red at the horizon.

Iceberg struggled to his feet and shouldered the pack. "Got to get going."

Salvatore sipped his coffee, still admiring the rare mission patch. He nodded to the array of security TV monitors. "Be careful of my sensors. I'd rather you didn't trip an alarm and get me fired!"

"Don't worry." Iceberg laughed. "I know how to get around this place with my eyes closed."

"It's not just the sensors," Salvatore called after him. "Watch out for the alligators and wild pigs and snakes—they can creep up on you when you're off the road."

"They won't want to mess with me." Turning toward the shuttle, Iceberg saw the jungle spread out before him, dense and difficult to cross. He struck out toward the waiting behemoth, dazzling in the spotlights. Soon, the *Atlantis* crew would be taking their places, ready for launch. *His* crew.

Without him.

2

LAUNCHPAD 39A

Jacques felt sweat cling to his white "bunny suit" as he rode the elevator up the giant Fixed Support Structure on the launchpad. The humid Florida air remained cool before dawn, much more pleasant than the equatorial jungles of French Guiana. But he still felt as if he were in a pressure cooker.

He worked well under pressure.

Two other NASA technicians—real ones—shared the open-framework elevator with him, telling each other glory-days stories of previous launches. Jacques kept his white-blond head down, pretending to study a technical brief he had kept folded in one of the pockets of his bunny suit. His modified tool kit sat at his feet on the metal-grid floor.

He had been practicing this infiltration for the past two weeks, accustoming himself to the routine, doing dry runs. His badge and access codes were up-to-date, and with nearly a thousand technicians working on *Atlantis* during the frenzy of launch preparations, he knew he could slip through, so long as he didn't do anything to draw attention to himself. Security might look tighter, but the chaos and distractions of such a busy time actually made infiltration easier.

The elevator bumped to a stop at level 195, the crew entry. As the door opened, Jacques saw three technicians standing next to the elevator power box. He stiffened, not expecting anyone there, but he quickly realized they must be waiting for the astronauts to arrive. As the techs inside the elevator cage shuffled off, one turned and gave Jacques a thumbs-up, jerking his head toward the topmost levels of the external tank. "Good luck up there."

"Same to you," Jacques said stiffly, trying to smother his French accent. People might remember it.

He relaxed as the elevator rattled shut again. With a whirring sound, the lift continued up to the gaseous oxygen vent access arm. He placed his foot against the tool kit, guarding the ten-kilogram surprise inside.

In many ways this was much easier than sneaking into the Ariane launch facility. Even though NASA had more than fourteen thousand contractors working on the shuttle program, the Americans were so confident they rotated people in and out of the launch team a thousand at a time—too many faces for the security people to check personally, forcing them to rely on sophisticated video monitoring systems and badges.

He smiled at the thought of silky Yvette and her own part of the task; Yvette should just now be entering the TV relay bunker, and soon the surveillance cameras would no longer be a problem.

Clockwork. Mr. Phillips's plans always went along like clockwork.

The clanking elevator slowed to a stop much higher on the gantry. The metal frame doors creaked open, and Jacques looked out with an unobstructed view of the Kennedy Space Center from hundreds of feet above the huge, burn-streaked concrete pad. In the pre-dawn darkness, the area spangled like a Christmas tree, blazing lights all across the swamps in chains of light.

Some distance north, at launchpad 39B, another shuttle stood at another gantry, and even more distant stood the towering gantries for Titan rockets. "America's Spaceport," Jacques said to himself. It would never be the same after today.

Bathed in white glare from the spotlights, the gaseous oxygen vent access arm was a pathway two meters wide and extending in front of him to the top of the shuttle's rust-orange external tank. The spacecraft was already a giant bomb, filled with explosives. It needed only a small spark to set it off.

Jacques picked up his tool kit, stepped out onto the walkway, and glanced around, blinking in the glare. A lone technician worked at the end of the access arm, monitoring the flow of oxygen topping off the tank. A steel-runged ladder led from the access arm to a bank of open metal storage bins just below. A video camera monitoring the tank and the attached equipment watched from the end of the arm, pointing in the other direction; he saw no other cameras around.

Good. Then they were alone.

Jacques pulled on his respirator hood, as required to prevent workers from being overcome by fumes. He zipped it shut, then covered the zipper with a Velcro flap. NASA people were so concerned about safety. He turned on the oxygen flow and took measured breaths—timing was critical. Clockwork.

He waved a gloved hand at the technician at the end of the access arm until he got the man's attention. His voice sounded muffled inside the loose white hood, keeping his accent from being noticeable. "Excuse me, could you come here a minute? I've got a problem."

The tech twisted a safety valve and strode down the access arm toward Jacques, boots clomping. He glanced left and right behind his own respirator faceplate to see Jacques's badge as he approached. "Hey, you don't have access for this level. What are you doing up here?" The tech frowned.

Jacques motioned toward the storage bins below, out of range of the stationary video camera. "A problem came up. I need your help."

"What problem?" The tech leaned over.

Jacques quickly wrapped his forearm around the man's hooded neck and jerked as hard as he could. He heard a muffled *snap*, and the technician grew slack. "My mistake, *mon ami*," Jacques said to himself. "The problem is taken care of."

Next step.

Two hundred and twenty-seven feet above the launchpad—the top of the skyscraper—the long truss of the gaseous oxygen vent arm ended in a "beanie cap" at the tip of the external tank. Warm gaseous nitrogen was pumped into the beanie cap to prevent chilled oxygen vapor from condensing ice out of the damp Florida air, where it might collect on the shuttle and cause damage during launch.

Unrecognizable in his bunny suit, Jacques lingered at the top of the vent hood, casually bracing himself against a guardrail. In full view of the diagnostic cameras, he went through the motions of inspecting for clumps of ice.

Periodically stooping for better access, Jacques moved out of view of the cameras and reached inside his tool kit. He withdrew a plastic-cased box containing the explosives and the RF receiver wired to the detonator. The box had been painted the same rust-red as the foam on the external tank. He removed the adhesive strips and pressed the device into the thick insulation of the tank, securing it in place.

The vent arm was the highest swing arm of three attached to the Fixed Service Structure. One minute and forty-five seconds before launch, the vent arm would rise from the top of the rust-red tank and retract.

It would make the bomb totally inaccessible. And once the explosive detonated, the fuel reservoirs in the shuttle's external tank and solid rocket boosters would take care of the rest.

Satisfied that all was well, Jacques moved back down the access arm to the elevator cage. He glanced behind him at the storage locker down one level. From this vantage point, Jacques could barely tell it held a corpse.

The tech's body would be cremated by the intense heat—either during the launch or the explosion of *Atlantis*, whichever came first.

He reached into his pocket and squeezed a thin transmitter, sending a microsecond-long, encrypted radio signal to Mr. Phillips. Next step completed.

3

LAUNCH CONTROL CENTER

If **the adrenaline rush** wasn't so thrilling, Nicole
Hunter would never have put up with the hellish
chaos of running the Launch Control Center. But she
loved being in total control—like the conductor of an
orchestra, not just a musician.

The space shuttle *Atlantis* sat on launchpad 39A,
three miles away under brilliant spotlights, its countdown proceeding smoothly. Outside, the low swampland and thick foliage made the Kennedy Space Center
seem quiet and peaceful. Dawn was just about to
break.

But here in the LCC, Nicole had a hundred problems to take care of, a thousand details to watch, and
a million glitches just waiting to stall the countdown.
In other words, a typical mission—though her first as
actual Launch Director. In the public spotlight.

The secure firing floor housed a hundred highly

trained men and women at seemingly identical computer stations. Each station had a beige telephone, printer, dual CRT monitor screens, and a bank of indicator lights.

The place was a vastly scaled-down version of the old Launch Control Center during the Apollo moon shots. The reduced number of stations was partly due to superior technology and computer automation—that was the optimistic story she told the reporters, her smile emphasized with subtle lipstick. The primary reason for the shrinkage, though, was due to years of drastic budgetary cuts.

Nicole hated the word *downsizing*, but she'd had to learn a whole new language when she'd gone into management. Even as an astronaut she'd been taught to speak in carefully phrased sentences when dealing with the media, but upon moving into administration she'd learned how much more meticulous she had to be just to survive.

Nicole placed her hands on her slender hips and self-consciously brushed a strand of gold-brown hair back into place. Her job had never before demanded that she remain so aware of her appearance, makeup, hair, wardrobe. She'd had little respect for the NASA public relations handlers when she was an astronaut, and even less as a Naval aviator; but she wasn't running through training courses now, or making PR appearances at schools, or even pressing the flesh at shopping malls during community service events. The TV cameras were on and she had to *look* in control, as well as tend to her real duties on the firing floor.

Now she strode through the clusters of computer workstations, a general inspecting her troops. Clad in a white silk blouse and a rayon suit, navy jacket, and snug slacks, she felt duly presentable for the cameras. Nothing flashy, but *professional*, a step up from the hot-dog test pilots and cocky astronauts. She lived in emotional whitewater, and she rode it like an expert.

Though compact and petite, she was not a delicate flower but a dynamo—as she'd had to be to survive the rigors of astronaut training and to keep up with Iceberg. No one on the firing floor seemed intimidated by her presence, not that Nicole expected them to be.

She glanced up at the glassed-in VIP viewing area half a floor up, where a dozen or so special visitors and their guests watched the LCC activities, awaiting the launch. Though it was Nicole's job to treat each distinguished guest with respect, not all observers were particularly welcome.

With his back turned to the frenzied activities and computer checks as if they were irrelevant, Senator Charles Boorman lectured to the news cameramen he had brought onto the observation deck, choosing his words carefully to make certain he didn't end up mis-quoted. Being too far from the cameras seemed to make him uneasy.

Nicole fumed—normally it was against NASA policy to bring the media here, but the senator didn't think rules applied to him. "Surely, you don't have anything to hide?" he had asked with a tight smile, but with a look that she knew was dead serious. And so the Launch Control Center had scrambled to make facilities available to accommodate Boorman's paparazzi.

Boorman did not choose to sit outside in the bleachers over at the Banana Creek VIP viewing site—similar to the facilities where she and Iceberg had watched the disastrous Ariane launch down in French Guiana—nor did he accept one of the special roped-off areas on the NASA Causeway that looked east toward the pads. She suspected that Boorman wanted to schmooze at the LCC, complete with air-conditioning and hot coffee. He was not a vocal enemy of the space program. He simply afforded it no interest whatsoever, remaining firmly in the "let's solve all the problems on Earth before we look to the stars" camp of pipe dreamers. But his duties had brought him here for the *Atlantis* launch.

Nicole pulled her lips tight, watching the man's gaunt face lit like a revivalist preacher's. He waved his big hands at the end of long arms, and she thought he might be speaking on the perceived faults of the new treaty before his Senate committee, which required his recommendation before it could be ratified. Boorman had often expressed his doubts about continued joint ventures with the Russian space program, afraid that this treaty could open up a black hole of funding forever. He was much more interested in keeping the projects in this country, and in his own state.

The senator offered his opinions, well aware of the fact that here of all places, on launch day, his views about the space program were not welcome. But he was getting the attention, just as he wanted. And Nicole had to be nice . . . at least to his face. She had learned that during her intensive grooming for the Launch Director's slot.

She turned to the EE COM station tech and gestured with her chin toward the observation deck. "So what's the 'distinguished gentleman' talking about now?"

The tech tapped his earphone, staring distantly at the acoustic tiles in the ceiling as if he had been listening in all along. "Same old, same old." He reached

into a cubbyhole next to his monitor and pulled out a
roll of toilet paper—NASA Kleenex—and ripped off
a wad of sheets to wipe away the dust clinging to his
monitor.

Up in the VIP booth, the senator turned to look
toward Nicole, seeming to stare directly through her.
The TV news cameras followed. Nicole put on a dazzling smile and waved back at the reporters. She hoped
the cameras got that.

The big countdown clock blinked as each number
reeled down. Phones rang repeatedly—stations reporting in, checklists being verified. Another phone jan-
gled nearby; the Range Safety technician picked it up,
then began punching numbers into her computer monitor.

"Ms. Hunter," Ground Control called, holding up
a beige phone, "got a report for you from the video
relay bunker."

"I'll take it here." Nicole went to the nearest station
and picked up the phone, punching in the line.

"Hi, Ms. Hunter. This is Amos Friese down at the
relay bunker, Iceberg's brother."

"Stow that, Amos. I know who you are!" She
laughed in spite of her reluctance to think about Iceberg. Amos had always been quiet and shy, overwhelmed by the shadow of his brother. The shy kid
had tagged along on enough barbecues and launch
team parties that he should have felt more comfortable
talking to her. "What's your report?"

Amos said in a nervous voice, "Have you received
word from my backup, Cecelia? Cecelia Hawkins?
She was due here before me, but the blockhouse was
empty when I got in. Air-conditioning's turned up,
though."

Great, thought Nicole, groaning inwardly at yet another snafu. Scrub the launch because of a missing
tech. She kept her voice soft and calm, knowing how
easily Amos could get nervous. "What's her criticality
code?"

"Uh, she's Level Two."

Nicole felt relieved. That meant the person was
there as backup for an automated system. "You saw
the launch-day traffic coming in, Amos. She might be
stuck in a jam. We've still got plenty of time in the
countdown. Don't sweat it."

"Not to worry, ma'am," Amos said, as if gathering
courage. "Worst-case scenario, I can handle this
whole setup by myself. You can count on me."

"Thanks for checking in," Nicole said reassuringly,
then hung up the phone and turned to look for the next
item that demanded her attention. She felt uncomfortably warm in her suit, glad of the LCC air-conditioning. Outside it would be far worse as the sun rose.

Months, even years, of preparation had gone into
this morning's event. Every launch had its share of
complications and joys, but this flight had been a particular political hot potato. The Russian *Mir* space station, the new backbone of the International Space
Station—if it ever got off the ground before they
redesigned it for the fiftieth time—depended on the
U.S. space shuttle for regular resupply missions, and
this time nearly half the crew consisted of Russian
nationals. The Belorussian cosmonaut Alexandra Koslovsky, who had trained at Star City outside Moscow
and at the Baikonur Cosmodrome, was scheduled to
perform a space walk in an American Manned Maneuvering Unit.

It was particularly important that Amos had all his
video cameras up and functional with feeds piped in

to the LCC to record every aspect of the launch. It would make great publicity footage for next year's funding presentations.

Overlapping conversations became a droning buzz inside the center, growing louder as the countdown progressed and sequence after sequence was completed: CAPCOM, EGIL, DPS, INCO, MOD, and a dozen other Scrabble-nightmare acronyms.

"Open loop test with the Eastern Range checks out."

"Orbital maneuvering system engines read optimal."

"Conducting gimbal profile checks, all A-okay."

Nicole felt like a shuttlecock in a badminton match—but it was her job to answer every detail as it came up. She was the captain of the ship, and everyone looked to her.

She fingered her gold necklace, the tiny charm pendant her father had given her—an old-fashioned key. "The key to the future," he had told her solemnly. "Follow your dreams, and it'll unlock all the doors you need."

She had followed her true desires, first resigning her Naval commission, then changing course to go into Launch Control and the many NASA political duties she found so engaging. She could have been an average astronaut, or an excellent space program administrator. She had chosen excellence over mediocrity. Unfortunately, that little gold key hadn't been enough to unlock Iceberg's mind about her decision—for him, any career other than being an astronaut was a waste of time.

"Excuse me, Ms. Hunter," another technician called. "The roadblock vehicles are prepared and the guards are ready to stop traffic. The Crew Transfer

Vehicle is in front of the Operations and Checkout Building, and the astronauts have finished suiting up. They're ready to board the CTV for the launchpad."

"Good," Nicole said, snapping back to her duties. "Have they made their press statements yet?"

"Yeah, they read the cue cards," the technician said. "They've all departed the ready room. Oh, wait." She touched her earphones. "Lieutenant Commander Green wants to speak to you before we hand him over to CAPCOM." Johnson Space Center in Houston, CAPCOM, controlled all communications with the astronauts once they boarded the shuttle.

"Put him on." A video feed from one of the private NASA cameras appeared on the television monitor in front of her. The technician slid her rolling chair aside to give Nicole room to talk.

"Howdy, Panther," Lieutenant Commander Vick Green said. His face was a smooth chocolate brown, his eyes large, his cheekbones high, giving him a look of deep intelligence and a broad good humor.

"Yo, Gator," she said, bristling a bit. After years of astronaut training, everyone had gotten so accustomed to their call signs that it seemed second nature now—except that her old call sign of "Panther" reminded Nicole too much of the past. "Everything check out? How was breakfast?"

"Steak and eggs, as usual," Gator said, grinning. "But I feel light as a feather. Wish you were coming with us. We're having a great time—even without Iceberg. Don't tell him I said that."

Nicole had gotten good at masking any change in expression when it came to discussions about Iceberg. "It was his own hot-dog stunt that pulled him from the mission."

"That's our Iceberg," Gator said. "Hey, after we get down, how about we all go back to the Fat Boy's in Cocoa Beach? Just the three of us. Heck, bring Amos along, too. I hear they're still having their all-you-can-eat barbecue chicken special."

"Gator, you're thinking with your stomach again. I'll pass."

She recalled the times their training group had gone to the old astronaut hangout, a small building with white siding and a crumbly asphalt parking lot only a few blocks up from the oceanside strip. Inside, the barbecue joint was lined with dingy, heavily varnished booths. Folded paper menus carried sticky, greasy fingerprints like badges of honor, and a smell of smoke and sauce hung in the air like fog in the morning. Autographed photos of astronauts and test pilots hung on the paneled walls. Nicole and Iceberg, Gator Green and his latest girlfriend, and others often hung out to eat ribs and drink pitchers of beer.

Gator shook his head good-naturedly. "See what happens when you get two stubborn people too close to each other. I bet Iceberg would come along if I dared him. Maybe you two could arm wrestle."

Nicole leaned forward and said quietly, "Shouldn't you be concerned with the mission and not my personal life, Mister?"

"Sure, Panther." He seemed momentarily embarrassed. "Did Iceberg show up in the VIP area for the launch? I'd like to have the crew say good-bye to him."

Nicole forced a laugh. "You think Iceberg would show up here with all the reporters? So they can ask him embarrassing questions and make him look pathetic on TV? For once I agree with him. He's probably sleeping in, taking the day off."

Gator's eyes widened in utter disbelief. "Sleeping in? *Iceberg?* If you say so, Panther."

"I'm the Launch Director." Nicole smiled. "People listen when I say things."

"Right, boss," Gator said. "Too good for us lowly astronaut types. Hey, I'll have CAPCOM relay a message from the shuttle. The Crew Transfer Vehicle is ready for boarding."

"Good luck, and Godspeed, Gator," Nicole said.

She had just enough time to take a deep breath and collect her thoughts before someone else called. "Miss Hunter! Excuse me, Miss Hunter." She saw the EE COM station tech holding his headset and waving at her. "I think you'd better hear this—you won't believe what the senator's talking about now."

With a lump forming in her stomach, she grabbed the headphones, snugging them over her ears. Boorman's nasal yet ponderous voice plodded along as if in an attempt to add import to every word.

". . . have chosen to launch a routine investigation into the financial records of every member of the astronaut corps. To answer your question, though, just because Colonel Friese is no longer Mission Commander does not excuse him from my inquiry."

Nicole tore the headset off, losing her temper and barely managing to put the lid back on it. *Smile for the cameras*, she thought. "Excuse me. I'm going up to the VIP bubble."

"But, Miss Hunter—the astronauts are loading the CTV!"

Nicole fought to keep her voice steady as she looked toward Senator Boorman. "You know where to find me. This won't take long."

4

NASA TELEVISION RELAY BLOCKHOUSE

Inside the TV relay blockhouse, Amos Friese could sit back in his government surplus chair and watch the launch from every perspective, thanks to the array of video cameras. Next best thing to being there!

NASA Select and the commercial TV channels would cull the best footage from Amos's tapes and run it on a twenty-second spot in the evening news—unless they had something more important to show, such as a politician's cat mysteriously acquiring a limp, for instance.

With a wall full of TV monitors, this was the primo seat in the house. He was such a space buff he loved to watch it all . . . even though it meant he had to stay inside a clammy old blockhouse rather than experience the earth-shaking roar directly within sight of the pad.

He wondered how close Iceberg had managed to get.

Amos thought of his brother, the big shot astronaut. The former Mission Commander had spent months in training, running simulators, memorizing control panels and subsystem linkages and backup computer programs—yet only last month Iceberg had secretly invited his little brother over just so Amos could hook up Iceberg's new direct broadcast satellite dish! As a management major at the USAF Academy, Iceberg was great at memorizing procedures, but someone had to hold his hand to get him past the technical details. Amos had laughed at his brother's quandary, and Iceberg had threatened him with dire embarrassments if Amos ever told a soul about it. Not that he ever would.

Alone in the bunker, Amos sat back in his old chair. It was comfortable enough, but it squeaked like a miser's wallet—standard gray government-issue, left over from the Apollo days, as was this mildewy old blockhouse that connected the launch-control monitoring systems, the video cameras on the gantry, and those positioned around the launchpad itself.

His desk was cluttered with cryptically marked videotapes, a chain of paper clips, an orange windup space shuttle toy, and a big jar of colorful jawbreakers, one of his vices. The jawbreakers didn't taste very good, but at least they lasted a long time.

He gulped from a can of Jolt Cola, checking his watch. His reflexes needed to be sharp, and he had to be wide awake. As if sneaking Iceberg inside the restricted area wasn't enough of an eye-opener! In fact, most of the thrills in Amos's whole life had to do with ill-advised schemes his big brother talked him into. But he wouldn't have traded them for anything.

He just wished Cecelia would show up. He could cover for her without much trouble, as he had told

Launch Director Hunter. The cameras knew what they were supposed to do; the videocassettes were already recording. He was a relatively useless cog in the system, though NASA did not waver in its "man in the loop" philosophy.

But Cecelia had never been late before, and he was worried about her.

He glanced over at the other desk, saw her coffee cup, her plastic plants. Thinking about Cecelia sent a chill up his spine—which embarrassed him a great deal.

Cecelia was full-figured with black hair, dusky features, generous lips, and the sweetest voice he'd ever heard. She was a video tech like himself . . . they had so much in common and they worked so closely together, how could he *not* like her? Amos had been terrified Iceberg would figure it out, would tease him mercilessly about the budding romance or use his bulldozer personality to force his little brother into proceeding too swiftly. But Iceberg had sensed the attraction and had been supportive, nothing more—much to Amos's relief. Sometimes his brother proved that even he had soft spots.

The air conditioner blasted on, making the refrigerated air inside the bunker even more tomblike. Amos felt cold to the bone, with an added shiver caused by concern for Cecelia. He went to the coat rack and pulled on a thick white cable-knit sweater, letting it hang loose, then went to double-check his video feeds from the remote cameras.

Down the corridor, the heavy blockhouse door swung inward on its recently oiled hinges. He jumped, startled, as Cecelia Hawkins bustled in, looking sheepish and somewhat uneasy. "Hi, Amos. Sorry I'm late." She feigned a smile.

"I was getting worried about you!" he said. She was dressed in a magenta-and-green flowery top with black slacks. The flush to her cheeks only made her more beautiful.

He had often wondered what Cecelia might look like with a skirt snug against her ample hips—but Amos would have to ask her out to see that. NASA policy allowed for no uncovered legs, no shorts or skirts, because of the danger of injury out in the processing areas. He still thought she looked nice in slacks, though.

Cecelia shot a nervous glance over her shoulder. Amos finally noticed two other figures entering behind her, a man and a woman negotiating a cart through the equipment-crowded corridor. Both stood tall and muscular, wearing nondescript Kennedy Space Center jumpsuits. The pale-blond woman was built like a mud wrestler, and she was a *knockout*; the word leaped to Amos's mind. His attention was drawn to her like a magnet, even with Cecelia there.

The exotic woman's cheekbones were broad and flat, her face so tanned the color looked artificial. Her short hair was nearly white, matching bleached-pale eyebrows that stood out like bright blazes on her bronzed forehead. Her eyes were a watery blue, as if she had stared directly into the sun and had faded the color out of them.

The man accompanying her had carrot-orange hair and a face so spattered with freckles it seemed as if the skin coloring had been scrubbed raw. Together, the two of them pushed a cart laden with video components and diagnostic tools, wires, and extra videotapes, each carefully labeled with cryptic coding.

"Hey, what's this, Cecelia?" He nodded to both of them. "Howdy, I'm Amos Friese. A little late to be running an unscheduled check, isn't it?"

"They're just here to help out, Amos." Cecelia stepped forward, flicking her dark brown eyes from side to side and not meeting his gaze. Suddenly he felt very warm in his thick sweater, despite the air-conditioning.

The two workers brought the cart into the small central room of the blockhouse. The rusty-haired man picked up three coded tapes and shuffled them, checking his watch and selecting one of the black plastic cases.

"Cecelia, we don't need any assistants," Amos said. "The station is so automated we could sleep through the launch."

Cecelia lowered her voice, and a shadow of panic fluttered across her eyes. "Amos, just be quiet."

Carrot-top chuckled. Amos blinked, momentarily confused enough to wonder if he should sound an alarm.

Cecelia gripped his arm so tightly he could feel each of her fingers even through the sleeve of his thick sweater. She said in a hushed, awed voice, "They're here from the *CIA*, Amos—they've got badges and everything. We have to cooperate with them."

Amos blinked in surprise, turning to look at the two strangers.

The redhead nodded with a serious expression that seemed somehow mocking. "You bet. Because of the international ramifications of this mission, Russian crewmembers and all, we're here to increase security monitoring, check for encrypted signals. All in our nation's best interests.''

"*Oui*," said the blond woman.

"I thought CIA people always wore suits and ties," Amos said lamely, not sure what to do, how to react in this remarkable situation.

"That's the FBI," Carrot-top answered. "Just relax."

"I even called the number they gave me," Cecelia said. "They checked out."

The beautiful Amazon woman selected a narrow metal pipe as long as her forearm. She held it to her face, studying its two polished ends. "Perhaps this will help you relax." Her thick French accent sounded like melted chocolate in her mouth.

She lifted the tube to her mouth, then blew a sharp puff. Amos instinctively flinched as a bright red dart shot toward him. He stumbled backward, but the dart struck him in the chest. He felt a prick through the thick sweater.

"Ow!" He slapped the red tassel-tailed dart off him. The point where the needle struck him burned. "What's the big idea?"

His vision became blurry. Everything smeared with fog . . . losing focus, and he knew he had been drugged. *I always hated shots*, he thought. Then his knees melted and flowed like water beneath him. He slumped to the concrete floor of the blockhouse.

Yvette watched as Cecelia Hawkins knelt beside her nerdy co-worker, glaring at her. "Why did you do that?" The fat bitch held the geek's hand with her pudgy fingers, then stroked his cheek. He breathed deeply like a kid asleep with a teddy bear. She carefully removed his round glasses, then stood uncertainly, indignantly. "He wouldn't have caused any trouble!"

"Just couldn't take that risk," Rusty said.

Yvette slipped the blowgun back onto the tray. *Humor the bitch for another minute. That's all we need.* "Are all the sensors functioning properly?" she asked, not bothering to hide her accent anymore. When Cecelia hesitated, Yvette snapped, "I asked you a question!"

"Uh, yes, they've been double-checked for the launch," Cecelia said, looking nervously down at Amos.

Ignoring her, Rusty stepped up to the control panel and scanned the readouts, knocking Amos's clipboard aside. He selected one of the videotapes they had brought with them. "This is a good loop," he said. "Right weather conditions, right time of day—the sun will be up in minutes."

Yvette leaned over the controls, looming over Cecelia, who seemed to grow more uncomfortable with each passing second. "Explain how these systems work."

"It's—uh—it's all quite simple," Cecelia stammered. "H-how much do you need to know?"

"Everything."

Cecelia looked longingly down at the geek's sleeping form, then shuffled in front of the console. Carefully, but quickly, she led them through the routines, growing more terrified by the minute. Her skin had a moist, grayish appearance. "Look, maybe I'd better help Amos."

Rusty interrupted and pointed to a small color

screen, ignoring the plump woman entirely. "It's all pretty standard—everything's relayed through here. These banks monitor the motion and sonic sensors, these ones do the video cameras. They've even got separate banks for the LCC and other stations."

Cecelia forced a nervous laugh. "Yes, they tell us that a chimpanzee could probably do it."

Rusty snorted again. Yvette considered it only one of the many unpleasant sounds he often made.

She picked up the silvery blowgun and fitted another dart into its end. "I'm afraid we'll need a bit more privacy, Mademoiselle. My apologies."

Before Cecelia could move, Yvette touched the blowgun to her lips and with a quick burst of breath, sent a stinging red needle into the soft flesh of Cecelia's arm.

"What did you do that for?" Cecelia swatted the dart. "I cooperated—"

Yvette turned away, disgusted at the bitch's weakness. She gathered her material as she heard Cecelia take a few stutter steps. "My God. I can't breathe—"

Yvette didn't turn as she heard Cecelia crash to the floor.

Less than five minutes later, Rusty turned from the control systems. "The loop tape's in place. Motion detectors disabled, sonic sensors off, IR feeds scrambled. We're ready to rock, if Jacques is finished with his part on the gantry."

"Don't worry. By now he has the explosives armed," said Yvette with an edge to her voice. Rusty should have known better than to question Jacques's dependability.

Yvette stood up from the frame of the blockhouse's

blast door that led outside, adjusting the wires she had installed. She placed the delicate contact sensors on the hinges and the open gap of the door. "If anybody tries to enter without disabling these sensors, they'll find an unpleasant surprise."

Rusty indicated the motionless forms of Amos and Cecelia on the floor. "Think I should put a bullet through these two in case they wake up from their nap too soon?" He started to pull out a pistol from his jumpsuit.

Yvette raised her white eyebrows, annoyed at him for questioning *her* actions now. Rusty forgot who was in charge. "Each of those darts contained enough tranquilizer to knock out an elephant. Quite a fatal overdose for humans. See for yourself—the bitch is dead. They will sleep until hell snows over."

"Until hell freezes over," Rusty corrected.

She said softly, her words like weapons, "Is there a difference?"

Rusty saw the pure edge in her gaze. "Definitely not," he said, returning his pistol to his jumpsuit.

"Let us go." She glanced at her watch. "Monsieur Phillips is waiting."

They left the blockhouse as Yvette clipped arming sensors to the wired explosives. Pulling the blast door shut, they engaged the booby trap.

A white OFFICIAL USE ONLY sedan drove up with a front-seat passenger already inside. Yvette and her partner climbed into the back, slamming the doors behind them.

The car roared off to the next stop.

5

LAUNCH CONTROL CENTER

Storming to the exit of the firing floor on level 3, Nicole Hunter slid her badge through the reader and gained access to the LCC's outer corridor. She ran up to the mezzanine observation deck and burst in on where Senator Boorman continued to speak to his cadre of reporters.

His aides and several other VIP attendees watched their boss's soapboxing with varying expressions. One aide had brought a copy of the *Wall Street Journal* and casually skimmed the listing of stock prices.

"Excuse me, Senator," Nicole said breathlessly, trying to keep a sweet sound in her voice. "Could I have a word with you in private?"

Boorman looked shocked, but he quickly composed himself. He followed Nicole, smiling pleasantly back at the reporters. "Certainly, Ms. Hunter. Yes, indeed."

Holding his elbow, she eased him away from the

reporters. When they were alone out in the hall, she said in an exaggeratedly relieved tone, ''I hope I caught you in time to save you from potential embarrassment. About these investigations—''

He held up one of his big hands, cutting her off. ''I know what you're going to say, Ms. Hunter. But as a United States senator I have every right to look into the spending records of the space program, including its personnel. Even astronauts must be held accountable—if I find any misbehavior.''

''I quite agree, Senator,'' Nicole said, fighting to keep her tone neutral. In her earlier days with the astronaut corps, she would have just knocked him to the floor with a punch in the gut—but here she had to calm herself, use her wits. Negotiate. ''Nevertheless, I believe you were about to gravely misspeak yourself in front of those reporters. You should reprimand your staff for providing you with faulty information.'' She nodded at the senator's aides, who plainly couldn't hear her.

Boorman's look hardened. ''Faulty information? What are you talking about? My staff isn't known to make mistakes.''

''They should have told you that the tax and financial records of these crewmembers have already been investigated and cleared. Any questions raised were dealt with in follow-up interviews. NASA certainly doesn't want any embarrassing financial misdeeds either, Senator.''

''I wasn't aware of any such prior investigation.''

''It's part of their security clearances and fitness-for-duty reviews. Full documentation is easily available from the NASA press office. Any redundant investigation—especially one without prior evidence of wrongdoing on the astronauts' part—would merely waste the taxpayers' money, at best . . . or look like a vindictive witch hunt, at worst.'' She blinked at him calmly, helpfully.

Feigning an interruption, Nicole snatched the pager at her waist and looked at it with a furrowed brow, though she had not felt it vibrate. It provided a good pretext to escape from the VIP area, now that she had said her piece. ''If you'll excuse me, Senator, launch day is very busy for all of us. Thank you for your time. If there's anything else I can do to help, please feel free to let me know.''

She walked back into the VIP observation area, toward one of the phones, covering a half-restrained sigh. All this politicking gave her a different kind of thrill than the astronaut training procedures, flying aircraft, pushing her reflexes to the red edges. More of an intellectual rush. Here, acting as Launch Director, Nicole had to fight with dialogue instead of controls, using people instead of subsystems to accomplish what she needed done.

Out of the astronaut corps for only eight months, Nicole Hunter had become NASA's new golden girl. After winning her MBA, she had been hustled into important positions, receiving the ''Sally Ride,'' as one of her colleagues said. Nicole already knew the procedures, knew the stations, knew the personnel, and knew the astronauts themselves. After working back at Houston for three launches as CAPCOM, she now faced the morning as Launch Director for *Atlantis*.

The sour smell of coffee simmering too long on the burner caught her attention, and she gestured to one of the KSC runners. ''Make a new pot, would you? When it's done, see that I get a cup. Two sugars, no cream. I've been up since one A.M. and I need all the caffeine I can get.'' The runner nodded eagerly and disappeared.

A large man heaved himself out of his chair and came over to her as Boorman huddled with his aides, seemingly chewing them out. Florid-faced and with nondistinctive brown hair cropped into a crew cut, Ambassador Andrei Trovkin, the cosmonaut liaison from Russia, waved a wide hand to catch her attention.

Blinking his dark eyes behind black-rimmed government-issue glasses, Ambassador Trovkin lowered his voice into a comical stage whisper. ''Bravo, Miss Hunter! Even in Russia we have foolish politicians. I am sure you 'let him have it,' as you say.''

Nicole stood straight and touched her short golden-brown hair, smoothing it in place just behind her ears. ''Why, I never meant to imply the senator was foolish, Ambassador Trovkin. He's chairman of the Senate Foreign Relations Committee, a very important man. It's up to him to decide on the new treaty for future cooperation in U.S.–Russian space missions.''

''He seems to be 'tough customer.' Not friend to space programs of my country or yours.''

Nicole looked at him seriously. ''Senator Boorman is a powerful man, but he has never been a particular threat to us before. Depending on how he votes, he *could* be a threat. That's why we have to be nice.'' Her lips curved in a broad, sweet smile that *almost* looked sincere.

''He needs to be convinced this treaty is best for both of our countries,'' Trovkin said.

The KSC aide came up to her with a plastic foam cup of coffee. ''Here, Ms. Hunter,'' he said. ''Found a fresh pot down on the firing floor.''

She took a sniff, thanked him, then sipped the hot liquid. Nothing worked better than coffee to wash away headaches, and this morning she had already encountered plenty. She drew a deep breath, then turned back to Trovkin, who grinned broadly at the NASA Select television monitor, showing a gap between his front teeth.

Garbed in their orange pressure suits and carrying their helmets, the *Atlantis* astronauts filed aboard the camper-van that would take them out to the launchpad.

Traffic inside the Kennedy Space Center had been cleared along the Crew Transfer Vehicle's path. Imagine the embarrassment of delaying a countdown because the astronauts got caught in a traffic jam on their way to the gantry—and with all the spectators hanging around for every launch, a traffic jam wasn't such a ridiculous possibility.

The Belorussian cosmonaut, Alexandra Koslovsky, stepped up to the camper-van and glanced directly into the camera. Her strawberry blond hair hung behind her in a neat braid. She wore sunglasses, which she would no doubt leave in the van before the team climbed out onto the gantry elevator that would take them up to the shuttle's crew access hatch.

"Ah, look at her," Trovkin said, his dark eyes fixed on the image, the lenses of his glasses glinting in the fluorescent lights. "See the sinuous way she moves? The strength of her character? She is magnificent!"

Nicole glanced at the ambassador. "Yes, she is beautiful."

"That much is obvious, my friend," Trovkin said, his eyes sparkling. "Wait until she walks in space. Then you will see true grace."

Nicole had heard rumors of the two of them; Trovkin and Koslovsky didn't keep their relationship terribly secret. The pair had much in common. Trovkin himself had gone through cosmonaut training but had been forced to step out of the program due to a heart murmur. He seemed not to resent the fact that Alexandra would spacewalk from the American shuttle. Instead, he seemed enthusiastic about the opportunity she had.

When the astronauts had boarded the van and the news cameras backed off to watch the CTV lumber into motion, Trovkin finally managed to tear his attention away. Nicole studied the man, broad shouldered, square jawed. *A stereotypical hero type*, she thought.

"So, Launch Director Hunter," Trovkin said, "has your friend Colonel Friese come to observe launch? This was to have been his mission."

"I'm afraid not, Ambassador Trovkin," she said simply.

"A pity," he said. "I had looked forward to meeting famous 'Iceberg.' "

"Yeah, well," Nicole said, looking away and fumbling for some excuse. "I think he had other training to do. With his qualifications, he's naturally expected to be assigned to a different crew and—"

Trovkin chuckled. "Of course I understand. I would never have wanted to be on display, poignant reminder of how fragile we all are, hobbling about with foot in cast. He is more Russian than American—unflappable."

"Oh, is that what he is?" Nicole said, raising her eyebrows. "I suppose unflappable is as good a word as any . . . but I must get back to my duties, Ambassador. Please enjoy the launch."

"I intend to, my friend."

Carrying her coffee carefully to keep from sloshing on her white silk blouse, Nicole started to leave the VIP observation deck, when the reporter from channel 7 caught her arm. "Could I get a statement, Ms. Hunter?"

"Sure."

As she waited for the cameras to come on, she understood fully why Iceberg didn't want to be here for the launch, for all the reasons Gator Green and Andrei Trovkin had stated—but also the big show-off probably felt intimidated to be with his old flame in a place where she was clearly in command.

Though they had their differences, they'd also had marvelously strong ties to each other, and now Nicole felt true disappointment for him. Iceberg had lost his chance to command the mission because of his crazy stunt for the cameras.

Supposedly in quarantine, taking care of himself, making sure he didn't get exposed to any cold virus—Iceberg had been jogging along the beach to the hoots and catcalls of reporters from a local television station. Iceberg had then proceeded to do the quick, resilient backflip that had become his trademark performance. Iceberg had competed as an all-American gymnast in college; he had done the trick hundreds of times—but here, in front of the cameras, his own damned showboating had done him in. He had landed wrong and broken his left foot.

And now, on launch day, replacement commander Dr. Marc Franklin sat in the *Atlantis*'s left-hand command seat.

Nicole didn't dare express how sorry she was. Iceberg's ego was already as big as a refrigerator, and it might serve him good to be taken down a notch. If

Iceberg couldn't sit at the head of the table, he didn't want to come to breakfast. That was just his character.

But today, while he could sleep in and ignore the countdown chaos, Nicole had a thousand important duties to attend to. As the light above the TV camera winked red, the phones in the main firing floor continued ringing. The numbers on the countdown clock decreased steadily.

Step by step, the shuttle prepared for launch.

6

TWO MILES FROM LAUNCHPAD 39A

E and E: Escape and Evasion. At daybreak.
Iceberg used the techniques he had learned at the Air Force Academy nearly twenty years ago. Enjoying the challenge, he worked his way from Salvatore's guard shack deeper into the restricted area, to where he could watch the launch undetected.

He crouched low and avoided the open paths, keeping an eye out for the multiple motion, sonic, and video sensors hidden in the underbrush. He knew where the devices were, how to find them, and—he hoped—how to avoid setting them off. He just had to keep cool, nerves of ice, frosty control.

Iceberg thought about a course called SERE he'd taken at the Academy—Survival, Escape, Resistance, and Evasion. The E and E part had been a major component during the Cold War, and even when peace broke out, knowing how to evade the enemy had saved pilots like Captain Scott O'Grady when he had been shot down over Bosnia.

As he E and E'ed across the swampy turf, Iceberg found himself having fun keeping out of sight from the distant roving NASA patrols, even with his broken foot. He hoped the cast would hold up in its protective moon boot covering. It would really be a bitch if sand got inside the cast where he couldn't scratch.

Iceberg crept onto a small rise and spotted the shuttle, perfectly visible in the spotlights and the competing dawn light. This would be a good place to establish his base. *Endeavour*, ready for its own launch within the next month, stood on the other pad farther in the distance. He flopped down, out of sight from the launchpad and, more importantly, out of view from the LCC building and the rest of Kennedy Space Center operations.

His foot throbbed like crazy, but he had managed to keep the cast dry. He rubbed the skin around the cast just below his knee, annoyed at the deep-seated itch within his bones that he couldn't reach. With a sigh, he distracted himself by concentrating on the activity around him.

NASA security helicopters flew low over the brush-covered ground as they searched for anyone attempting an illegal entry—such as Iceberg. But now that the sun had splashed over the horizon and added the warmth of dawn to the swampland, the aircraft had to rely more on sight and less on the sensitive infrared detectors to detect any people below them.

Effective launch-day sweeps were nearly an impossible task, more difficult than the Coast Guard searching for a person bobbing in the ocean, because in the ocean people didn't have bushes, sand dunes, hollows, and trees to hide them. Iceberg had ridden in the NASA security helicopters once during astronaut training as they had skimmed over the site, searching for imaginary terrorists. They hadn't found any, of course, but he still remembered the thrill of zipping above the sparse vegetation, popping up over a small rise, and startling an alligator crawling through the swamp toward the wide, sluggish Banana River.

Iceberg looked over his shoulder as he settled into his private little viewing area. From here, if he stood above the vegetation level, he could still barely make out the guard shack, though he had taken a circuitous route across what must have been two miles of swamp.

He glanced at his watch. The shuttle crew would have ridden the Crew Transfer Vehicle out to the pad by now. *His crew.*

One morning, more than a month before the scheduled launch date, Iceberg had used his clearance and his badge to enter the Orbiter Processing Facility, where *Atlantis* was being outfitted for the mission. In the hangarlike building, teams of workers combed the giant orbiter, testing every minuscule system, every connection, every stress point.

The doors yawned open in the back; the shuttle was so tall that a separate notch had been cut above the doors to allow the tail fin to slip through. Sunlight spilled in from outside, brighter than the garish naked bulbs shining from catwalks far above. Jumpsuited workers passed back and forth, carrying clipboards, comparing checklists.

Iceberg had stood under *Atlantis*, admiring the craft, watching technicians test every one of the specially shaped ceramic heat tiles on the bottom of the hull, replacing those in need of repair, approving the undamaged pieces. They installed gap fillers between the tiles, designed to keep the searing heat from reaching the aluminum hull. He had walked around silently staring, watching, feeling like a kid in a toy store. One of the shift supervisors asked if he needed anything, but Iceberg waved him away, wanting only to look at the craft, to "kick the tires" before launch.

He had been so confident then.

After Iceberg's injury, NASA had put that strait-laced idiot Marc Franklin in as commander. Besides being a civilian, Franklin didn't have the right stuff to be a shuttle commander. Sure, the guy had flown a couple of missions before, and he'd actually done a pretty good EVA on that last flight when they hauled in the Wake Shield. But there was one hell of a difference between following orders as part of a crew and running the whole shooting match. It was a matter of mind-set. Why else did the military spend so much time grooming its people for the particular demands of command?

Iceberg tried to push the sour thoughts out of his mind as he settled in. No changing it now. *He* had broken his own foot, and he couldn't blame anyone else for that. His people knew their stuff. They could pull off the mission, even with Franklin as commander.

He opened his pack and dug out a bottle of buffered aspirin, double strength. He debated for a second, then dry-swallowed three tablets to cut the pain in his foot. He didn't want to be bothered in case he had to high-tail it back to Salvatore's shack in a hurry.

Iceberg pulled out his binoculars and a TV Walkman. Leaning back, he extended the antenna and tuned to the launch coverage from channel 7. He saw a picture of *Atlantis* sitting on the pad, a feed from Amos's TV relay bunker. On television, though, the shuttle looked brighter, with a high scudding of clouds above. Iceberg glanced up—the sky was absolutely clear. He frowned. *That's funny*, he thought. Were the TV cameras picking up something he couldn't see, or was he getting a ghost reflection on the screen?

Iceberg tried to get better reception. The talking head from channel 7 came on and explained that the launch was in the middle of a built-in hold. He lay prone, setting the miniature TV to the side as he got out the binoculars. He surveyed the area. Ants marched along the sand, upset at his presence. With a sharp gust of breath, he blew them away from his face, then focused the binoculars.

Technicians in white bunny suits moved around the launch structure. Nearly a mile in front of him sat the nearest M-113 Armored Personnel Carrier, ready to roar into action at the launchpad if called. The seven safety lines—the emergency exit system—fanned out from the 195-foot level of the Fixed Service Structure to a safety bunker twelve hundred feet away.

Iceberg was situated perpendicular to the flame trench, part of the flame deflector system that bisected the hardened launchpad. The trench divided the pad lengthwise, five hundred feet long, sixty wide, forty deep. Nearby, a water tower stood ready to dump its contents down onto the pad in the first seconds of launch for cooling and noise suppression. During ignition, flames from the shuttle's main engines and solid rocket boosters blasted down the trench and out the sides. The deadly orange cloud from the solid rocket booster's fuel would drift harmlessly out to sea.

But Iceberg figured his position was safe enough.

On the launchpad the final checkout crew was making their last rounds. By now the countdown should be within T minus twenty minutes.

Iceberg rolled over on the rise and adjusted the volume on the Walkman. Nicole Hunter's smiling, professional face took up most of the small TV screen. The words LAUNCH DIRECTOR were set at the bottom of the screen, but instead of Nicole's voice, the reporter from channel 7 gushed over the audio. "So do you think your past training as an astronaut gives you more credibility with the crew when you have to make tough calls?"

"Tough calls? Give me a break," Iceberg snorted at the TV. "She has a checklist, doesn't she?"

"Absolutely," said Nicole. "I even have a checklist. And the astronauts know they have one of their own calling the shots. Since I've been out there on the pad myself, I know what thoughts are rolling through their minds right now."

"Yeah," Iceberg muttered. He turned away from the small TV set and looked through his binoculars at the launchpad. "I bet my crew's thinking 'Let's cut the PR bullshit and light this friggin' candle.' "

Iceberg studied the shuttle as Nicole's interview continued. Her voice brought back the memory of her being on the training team with them, and the fun they'd had with so many things in common, when she was part of operations, not management and fluff.

He supposed the world needed those kinds of people—the maintenance crews, the launch infrastructure, even the PR flacks and lobbyists that ran interference before Congress. But Nicole had been an *astronaut*, one of the chosen few who had actually slipped the earthly bonds and—as corny as it sounded—touched the face of God. Then she gave it up.

Nicole claimed she had to look at her long-term career goals. It sounded like a line from some self-help tape she had listened to. Now, though, she was sitting in the limelight, along with Franklin, Gator, and the rest of his crew.

And here he was, hiding in the dirt, swatting mosquitoes.

For now he'd just sit back and relax, let the others enjoy the thrills while he laid low and kept out of sight. He'd always wondered what the tourists felt like at a launch.

7

SWAMPS,
NORTH BANANA RIVER

Air bubbles churned the surface of the still, tepid water. Biting flies buzzed angrily up from floating weeds at the surface. The half-submerged heads of two alligators cut through the water like dark boats as they swam away from the bubbles, grunting. The alligator-infested water served as a natural barrier to stop curious onlookers from approaching the restricted Launch Complex.

Unless the intruders were prepared.

A dark blue trail of dye extended from the bubbles, diffusing into the water, barely visible as the low sun filtered through the trees. The alligators avoided the foul-smelling repellent, crawling onto the soggy shore to get away. A fat bull alligator opened his mouth in frustration but made no attempt to reenter the water.

The small tributary ran inland and stopped between the shuttle launchpads and the massive Vehicle Assembly Building. To the north, *Atlantis* stood prepared on its gantry, lit by morning light.

The bubbles in the water grew more intense, and two masked faces broke the surface at the same time. The men wore black wetsuits and scuba gear, the dark blue repellent foaming around them. Once on land, they would have to watch out for snakes and wild boars. Surmountable problems.

The frogmen swam silently toward shore, scanning for NASA helicopters above. But the dawn had driven the aircraft high, spotting for obvious intruders.

The two men stood in the shallow water, their flippers sinking into the muck. Behind them they dragged a black waterproof satchel that looked like a body bag, heavy with weapons. The first man dropped the air hose from his mouth and raised his face mask. His scraggly beard dripped water as he sniffed the sour-smelling air. ''Ah, sightseeing in the swamps—eh, Cueball?''

The second, larger man raised his mask as well but did not speak. His ebony head was smooth and hairless as a black billiard ball. He looked quizzically at Mory, the first man, and made a hand signal.

Mory sniffed again, scowling at the stench of rotted vegetation, searching for a hidden human presence—gas fumes from patrolling Jeeps, rifle oil from foot patrols, human body odor.

Looking behind him, Mory saw that their alligator repellent had quickly diffused through the water. Good—it certainly stank. After being let off from a private, hidden yacht six hours earlier, they had timed their arrival on shore perfectly. Any sooner, and the IR sensors on board the NASA helicopters could have detected them; any later, and the blue dye would have been clearly visible in the sunlight.

Mory spotted a small depression under a tangled canopy of creeper-covered mangroves, framed by palmettos. There they could remain hidden from the Vehicle Assembly Building and the launchpad. Perfect. A little camouflage and they would be completely invisible as they set up. They quickly removed their flippers and hung them from their belts.

Mory tugged on the floating satchel, gesturing toward the depression with his other hand. "We'll hide the equipment there." Cueball nodded and picked up the rear of the bag. Their feet made squishing sounds in the muck as they climbed onto shore and into hiding.

Mory sniffed the air and turned just as another alligator slipped into the water with a surprisingly graceful splash. He smoothed the weeds and soft ground around the equipment bag so that he could open it on a flat surface. His hand struck hard, thin metal embedded in the ground.

"Lookee here." He dropped to his knees and started digging carefully around the device. Scooping sand from around the metallic pipe, he uncovered a thin whip antenna and several sophisticated sensors ending in a bulbous cavity that held a battery.

Cueball's eyes widened. The hairless man pounded his fist to get Mory's attention and used sign language.

Mory grinned. "You're right. It's a sonic sensor—probably has a motion component as well. But it's not doing our NASA friends much good now, is it?"

Cueball glanced at his watch; then a slow grin spread across his face. He pantomimed someone being hit by a blow dart.

Mory tossed the deactivated sensor to the side. "Come on, we've got a timetable to follow. Keep your eyes open and your weapon ready in case we have to take out one of NASA's roving patrols, though I'd prefer to save the excitement for later."

Cueball struggled to remove his wetsuit. The bald man's chest rippled with muscles, his massive arms as thick as Mory's legs.

Under the wetsuits the men wore swimming trunks. Mory broke the watertight seal on the equipment bag and pulled out mottled, sand-colored camouflage and a pair of boots. He tossed Cueball the larger set of camouflage and footgear. In moments the two had transformed themselves from scuba divers to camou-flaged militia.

Mory unzipped the heavy equipment bag the rest of the way, peeling back two different waterproof layers to pull out the weaponry. Cueball bent to help him, unfolding a pair of 7.62-mm Valmet M78 long-barrel automatic rifles with scopes, armor-piercing shells, a pair of FAMAS G2 assault rifles, high-power binoc-ulars, two radios, backpacks, a shoulder-mounted Stinger missile launcher, and six small missiles. "Enough for a real party," Mory said.

He brushed back wetness from his scraggly beard, then crouched at the top of the rise, pressing binocu-lars against his face. He caught a faint whiff of heli-copter fuel, oily exhaust—but the fumes were stale by now, no threat. He slapped at a mosquito that landed on his face. Damn bugs. At least they were better than the alligators.

He felt a tap on his shoulder. Cueball had buried the scuba gear inside the equipment bag, but left their weapons exposed and available. He snatched a few broken branches from a nearby deadfall to cover the disturbed sand.

"Good," Mory said. "Let's start hiking. Half a mile straight ahead will put us well within range. I don't want to risk shooting from this far out."

Cueball nodded, then turned to pick up his share of the weaponry—which was far more than half. Each man hung an assault rifle over his shoulder while carrying a sniper's rifle. He grabbed the shoulder-mounted missile launcher as Mory pulled on a sleek backpack.

Crouching and loaded down, Mory led the way, weaving around small clumps of vegetation and sand, keeping as low as possible. His boots crunched on the underbrush and slurped in the muck. Behind him Cueball looked around like a machine programmed to perform a search-and-destroy mission.

They made the distance in little more than twenty minutes. *Atlantis* loomed on its launchpad like a sacrificial lamb; Mory caught glimpses of the Armored Personnel Carrier nearest the gantry. Good. They'd be able to cover Jacques from here as well.

Mory stopped and shrugged off his pack. The nearest road was a quarter mile away, so they'd be invisible from an unexpected vehicle patrol. He motioned for Cueball to set up post. The silent man reconnoitered the area and positioned himself where he had a view of both the shuttle complex and the Vehicle Assembly Building. No one would be able to get in or out without being seen.

Mory joined his companion, then glanced at his watch. It was not yet six o'clock, and they had minutes to spare. He found himself breathing hard, and sweat rolled down his face, more from the damned humidity than the physical exertion. He used his camouflaged sleeve to brush away the perspiration, then fumbled in his pack for a portable beeper.

Cueball remained vigilant, inspecting the territory they had taken.

Mory punched in the Skypage number and entered a code in the small transmitter. Mr. Phillips needed to be kept apprised of their progress.

Satisfied that the message had been sent, Mory settled back to wait for the show.

8

LAUNCHPAD 39A

Navy Lieutenant Commander "Gator" Green stepped out of the NASA camper-van that served as the Crew Transfer Vehicle at the base of *Atlantis*. He felt his heartbeat increase. This was even better than running onto a lighted football field.

This was it—two hours before launch and no more practicing. No more of the endless NASA drills to get him as comfortable as possible with his first real flight as pilot of the shuttle. He just wished Iceberg were here.

His bird stood on the pad, beautiful and white, blessed by thousands of engineers. Named for the Woods Hole Oceanographic Institute's research ship in service from 1930 to 1966, OV-104, *Atlantis* towered 184 feet from the bottoms of its two solid rocket boosters to the top of the rust-red external tank. White fumes of liquid oxygen and hydrogen vented from their tanks.

Technicians stopped their work and applauded as Gator and his fellow astronauts stepped from the Crew Transfer Vehicle. NASA television cameras and flashbulbs lined the walkway; Gator paused as a dozen hands reached out to pat him on his back. He'd come a long way from when he was a boy growing up in the Atlanta ghetto. Luckily, the Navy had been open to an ambitious, good-humored black kid with excellent grades . . . and a kid who kept trying and trying until someone said yes.

A Russian voice spoke behind him, deep but very female. "Are you stopping for portrait painting, Lieutenant Commander Gator? You are holding up the rest of us."

Gator joked, "Not at all, Comrade. After you." He knew the Russians were sensitive about using the outdated communist title.

Cosmonaut Alexandra Koslovsky stepped past him, grinning. Since the orange pressure suit hid her lithe features, she did not look like so much of an athlete, but Alexandra was one of the stars of this flight, scheduled to perform the first U.S.–Russian tandem space walk.

"I didn't expect so many gawkers," said Gator. "They must have shown up to see our Russian friends."

"Then maybe I should stop for portrait instead of you," Alexandra said over her shoulder.

Gator laughed and turned back to the cordon of applauding NASA and contractor personnel. *Now, this is the way it should always be*, he thought. He started toward the elevator that would take the crew up the gantry to the White Room, where they would board the shuttle.

He shook hands with more well-wishers, technicians from KSC's operations contractor, NASA contractors, even a few high-level managers distinguished from the rest by the ties beneath their work overalls. The seven astronauts crammed into the elevator, grateful for the relative silence.

"I prefer this sendoff to what Belorus gave us," Alexandra said. "Our press does not get as excited as yours."

"The difference is our press never even knows of launch," said Orlov, one of Alexandra's fellow cosmonauts. Gator and the other Americans chuckled politely. Only recently had the Russian press even been allowed to attend space launches.

The elevator began its rattling climb. Gator said, "It may not seem like a big deal to you Eastern Europeans, but our press loves 'firsts'—like last year's resupply mission to *Mir*, or this joint U.S.–Russian space walk. We made such a big deal over Sally Ride, our first female astronaut, although *your* first female cosmonaut, Valentina Tereshkova, upstaged her by two decades."

Dr. Marc Franklin, the replacement mission commander, interjected, "You should have seen the sendoff they gave the guys back in the Apollo years, when we won the moon race."

Open mouth, insert foot, thought Gator. Having to get used to a new shuttle commander in the past week and a half had been difficult for the crew. It didn't help that Franklin came off as an inflexible, humorless horse's ass. Franklin's intentions were right on, and the man had a reputation for being a solid worker. But he was certainly not a leader.

Orlov appeared offended by Franklin's comment, but Alexandra took it with grace, leaning over to stage-whisper into Gator's ear. "Dr. Franklin has not been given vodka and caviar initiation. We can hold nothing against him."

Gator covered a snicker. Back at one of their outings during the first months of training with the cosmonaut crew, Alexandra had reverently brought in a gift she'd carried in her personal possessions, a small jar of Beluga caviar and an oily gray-green bottle of state-produced vodka from one of the distilleries in her home city of Minsk. Alexandra had stored the vodka in the freezer, then carefully spread the caviar like tiny black pearls on crackers, adding chopped white onion. She passed the crackers out to the crewmembers like a priest distributing the host.

Gator had looked strangely at the stuff, sniffing. "If it weren't for the onions, it would smell just like fish eggs. Now at least it smells like fish eggs and raw onions together."

Alexandra nodded, then ate her cracker with obvious delight, as did the other two Russian mission specialists. The two American specialists, Major Arlan Burns and Frank Purvis, were not so enthusiastic. Frank Purvis ate his delicately, making polite comments, and Arlan Burns gulped his in one bite, as if taking medicine.

Gator had looked at Iceberg, both waiting for the other to pop the caviar in his mouth. With unspoken assent, they bit simultaneously. Luckily, Alexandra's shots of vodka scalded away the taste while bringing tears to Gator's eyes. He was very glad when they switched back to drinking beer. . . .

"I watched news conference before getting in Crew Transfer Vehicle. Your Senator Boorman," Alexandra said into the brief, awkward silence. "I am surprised at lack of support a political figure gives space program in public, especially while at launch center. What do financial records have to do with astronaut accomplishments?"

Gator made a raspberry sound. "Haven't you heard that astronauts are all private millionaires?"

"In Russia politicians understand importance of space flight, and public's need for heroes," said Alexandra. "Even with end of Cold War and fragmentation of Soviet Union, we have cooperation among independent nations for our space program."

Gator said, "Unfortunately in our society, a lot of Neanderthals go into politics."

"Then our countries are actually not so different." Orlov laughed.

The elevator bumped to a stop at level 195 and the White Room chamber. Franklin pretended he had never made his clumsy comment, or perhaps did not even notice. "Okay, kids—leave the politics back on Earth. It's time to rock and roll. We've got a mission to accomplish."

White-jumpsuited technicians lined the orbiter access arm that led to the White Room connected to the shuttle. The five-foot-wide, sixty-five-foot-long access arm looked like a gladiator tunnel. The last few techs applauded as Gator strolled toward the shuttle. *Yep, I could get used to this real fast*, he thought. *And everybody said I had a big ego when I was just a Navy football player.*

He reached the circular hatch on the orbiter's left side, which led directly to the mid-level of the craft. A tech stood on either side to assist him; another waited just inside the shuttle. "Good luck, Lieutenant Commander," said one of the techs as she held out a hand to help him through the access way. "My daughter wants to be an astronaut, just like you."

Gator shook the woman's hand and saw a lot of his mother in her eyes. His mother had pushed him never to accept the mediocre. "Make sure your daughter goes to Annapolis, then," Gator said, "and not any of those other two dinky schools that try and pass for military academies."

"I heard that, Gator! Don't lead that young lady astray." Major Arlan Burns was the crew's sole remaining Air Force officer—now that Iceberg had been pulled from the mission.

Gator waved the comment aside with a laugh. Stooping down, he climbed into the shuttle, using the mid-deck wall as the floor. He walked in a low crouch, stepping over hand and foot grips, and made his way to the flight deck. There the pilot's seat was on the far right, its back to the floor.

The front section of the flight deck was covered with lighted panels, old screen displays, and switches masked by metal guards—technology straight from the seventies, but it *worked*, virtually guaranteed not to fail. Gator stepped over the mission specialist's chair and climbed into his seat on his back in a sitting position.

Commander Franklin followed, and they both strapped into their seats up front. Gator scanned the console, concentrating on focusing his mind on the mission. Just like the simulator. He glanced at the panels—front, left side, next to the commander, center, right, next to the pilot overhead—and at the upgraded flatscreens. All there, no surprises.

They had another few minutes before it was time to remove the Velcro-backed cue cards from the flight-deck file and attach them to the instrument panel. He put on his headset and plugged into the console. This would be the last time in the two-week mission he had a moment to himself to collect his thoughts.

So here he was, Annapolis's smallest football player on top of the biggest Roman candle in the country. He glanced over at Franklin. The new commander looked over his shoulder at the white-suited techs helping the astronauts climb aboard. Alexandra strapped in directly behind him in the mission specialist's seat; her Russian comrades were on the mid-deck with Burns and Walker, out of sight. Franklin allowed everyone to spin up their stations by themselves.

Even with the well-rehearsed routine, Gator still thought it would be comforting to have Iceberg's cool hand guiding them. He started to wonder about his friend, but Franklin's voice came over the intercom. "Voice check, kids. On my count."

Gator turned his attention back to the flight. A little more than one hour to go. From here on out it was by the book, no surprises.

9

GUARD FENCE— RESTRICTED AREA

As the commandeered NASA car drove away from the video-relay blockhouse, Mr. Phillips lounged in the front passenger seat, studying his handheld personal data assistant. He adjusted the brightness on the small liquid crystal screen and squinted at the list displayed by the computer.

Things to Do Today.

Using a blunt stylus to scroll through the data file that detailed every point in the shuttle countdown sequence, he ticked off the events that had already occurred. He rubbed one finger along his clean-shaven upper lip and studied the parallel timeline for his team, marking each activity his people had completed and the tasks in which they were presently engaged.

He cleared his pager of the message that had appeared just moments before: PACKAGE PLANTED—

JACQUES. "Good." He used the stylus to check that item off on the touch-sensitive screen.

As Duncan drove the car north along the narrow grass-lined road, puffing on a menthol cigarette, Mr. Phillips fumbled in his front pocket and withdrew the pocket watch. He looked up from the watch and the open PDA to note their location and allowed himself a warm, satisfied smile. "Precisely on time." He twisted in his seat to see Yvette and Rusty sitting in the back, both flushed with excitement. "Success comes through careful planning," he said to them. "And we have been careful indeed."

"You always are, Mr. Phillips," Rusty said.

Duncan tossed long gray-brown hair out of his eyes and glanced away from the road toward the passenger seat. "We're about half a mile from the guard shack, Mr. Phillips," he said in his cheery Australian accent, tossing the cigarette butt out the window.

"All right, pull over to the side of the road, please. Yvette, my dear, would you care to drive? We'll need your expertise in a few moments."

"*Oui*, Monsieur Phillips," she said.

Duncan pulled off onto the flat damp grass beside the road, leaving fresh tire tracks among others already pressed into the soft sandy ground. Shifting the government car into park, he opened the squeaking door and climbed out, holding it open for the pale-blond Amazon.

Mr. Phillips scanned the area as Duncan and Yvette exchanged places. The road was deserted. The NASA vehicle had allowed them to gain access to the eastern security road, which they had driven up from Cape Canaveral earlier that morning. The terrain lacked the rugged, rocky features Mr. Phillips had known growing up near the New England coast; here in the lowlands they were sure to be spotted if they acted out of place.

Yvette slipped behind the wheel and slid the seat back as far as it would go. She adjusted the mirror, then clicked the left turn signal before pulling back onto the deserted road. She drove the white government sedan at precisely the posted speed limit, never straying over the divider line.

Mr. Phillips turned back to the PDA and pointed the stylus to the other items on the list. "Rusty," he said, "you're sure all the motion sensors are disabled? The video loops playing in the TV bunker are a perfect substitute?"

"Definitely, Mr. Phillips," Rusty said. "I picked a video to match the weather and time conditions for this launch. NASA will keep watching their screens, but they'll be seeing last year's launch. Sooner or later somebody's going to notice the difference—but they'll be snowed long enough."

Mr. Phillips checked that item off as complete, then straightened the gold-and-white cloisonné space shuttle pin at his lapel. The pager in his pocket went off, and he pulled it out to scan the brief message on its tiny screen. "READY—MORY."

"Ah," he said with a smile, "our aquatic friends are in position. Good." He used the charcoal-gray stylus to check off the next item on the list, then clicked shut the lid on the handheld PDA. "Only two more steps in phase one. Everything is proceeding with remarkable efficiency."

"Approaching the gate, Monsieur Phillips," Yvette said, slowing down.

"Onward and upward," he said. "Just like a bull market."

From the backseat, Duncan said, "After today we won't need to do any more working for the rest of our lives, mates."

Mr. Phillips frowned and turned to him. "Let's not get ahead of ourselves, Duncan."

Not much larger than a telephone booth, the guard shack stood alone by the road. Bright red letters on a white signboard admonished, "Warning, Restricted Area."

An older, mustached man sat outside the shack in a colorful folding lawn chair, the kind one could buy for a few dollars at a discount department store. Seeing their white NASA car approach, the guard stood to wait for them. From the casual way he moved and the friendly expression on his face, it was apparent that he expected no trouble. They were probably the hundredth car to pass through in the last few hours. This old man would pose no problem at all.

Yvette brought the car to a gentle stop as the guard came around toward the driver's side window. She carefully turned the crank to lower the glass, then shifted the car into park so she could use both of her hands.

"Excuse me, my good man," Mr. Phillips said, leaning close to Yvette, "isn't this the way to the rocket?"

Yvette whispered, "Monsieur Phillips, I will need room—if you could lean back?" He pressed himself against the passenger door, out of the way.

"Sorry, folks," the guard said with a Hispanic accent as he stooped to Yvette's window. He was swarthy and potbellied. "This area is restricted for the launch. Everybody's been cleared beyond this point. The last van hauling the remaining workers from the launchpad is due out here any minute. You'll have to drive back to the causeway and park your car there to watch the launch, or you can drive around to the Banana Creek VIP viewing site." He frowned. "Could I see your passes, please?"

"No, I'm afraid not," Mr. Phillips said quietly.

The guard raised his eyebrows. "Excuse me?" He leaned into the car, unable to believe what Mr. Phillips had said.

Yvette struck in one fluid motion. She whipped her left arm over the old guard's neck. The man struggled. He gasped as Yvette tightened her grip. Pulling his head sharply down, she viciously twisted his head and slammed him down against the door again, crushing his larynx. A loud snapping sound reverberated throughout the car, and the guard fell slack, his eyes bugging out in astonishment, rapidly growing dull with death.

"Something caught in your throat?" Mr. Phillips said. He reached over, planted his hand on the guard's head, and shoved, toppling the old man away from the driver's door to prevent messy stains on his suit.

Mr. Phillips found it amazing that Yvette could move so well in such a cramped space. Exhilarating! She was so professional, and so entertaining. The only other person remotely comparable was her dear lover, Jacques.

Duncan scrambled out of the car as Rusty holstered the silenced pistol he had taken out, just in case Yvette ran into difficulty. Yvette remained behind the wheel while the others did their duties; she had already done hers.

Mr. Phillips waited primly beside her. "Pop the trunk for them, Yvette," he said.

Duncan came around and bent over, gripping the fallen guard under the armpits. He relieved the old man of his side arm, then dragged him through the thick grass into a bog of weeds and underbrush behind the shack, hiding the body from the main road. He wiped his hands on his nondescript jumpsuit, then shucked out of it to reveal a gray NASA security uniform. Kneeling, he unfastened the guard's badge and pinned it on himself. He then folded the jumpsuit and stuffed it behind the body. Sooner or later, some animal would take care of the details.

From the trunk, Rusty lifted the box of carefully packed land mines and carried them around behind the shack next to an old, empty watercooler. A three-wheeled all-terrain vehicle sat parked behind the shack, like a grown kid's toy. Rusty returned to haul out the tripods, tripwires, motion sensors, and five FAMAS G2 automatic assault rifles, piling them beside the shack for Duncan to set up once they had left him in position.

Mr. Phillips took a moment to step out of the car for a stretch. Curious, he peeked into the guard shack, wondering what kind of man would just sit there in boredom all day long waiting for something to happen . . . and then be completely unprepared for it when it did. He shook his head.

Numerous mission patches adorned the walls, like poor man's trophies. On the speckled Formica counter lay a new cloth patch for this morning's *Atlantis* launch, colorful and embroidered, showing a bear and an eagle. How patriotic. Mr. Phillips picked it up, fingering the rough, regular texture of fine threads.

His lips formed a gentle smile as he pocketed the patch, smoothing his suit jacket. "It'll make a fine memento . . . might even be worth something someday." This launch—or lack thereof—was sure to go down in history.

Mr. Phillips turned to view the distant shuttle on the launchpad. The orbiter waited like a bridled stallion, ready to leap into the void of space. He stared in awe, slowly shaking his head. Such a magnificent machine. A technological marvel. The pinnacle of mankind's engineering achievements. Elegant, sleek, fantastically complicated . . . yet deceptively simple.

He sincerely hoped he wouldn't have to blow it up.

Rusty brushed his hands on his coveralls and came back to the car, jumping into the open rear door. "Ready to go!"

"All right, Duncan, take your position in the shack," said Mr. Phillips. "The technicians' van is due out from its last routine checks on the launchpad. Be sure to wave to the driver, since we're all friends here. Then close the gate and plant your land mines and set up your targeting systems."

"Aye, Mr. Phillips," Duncan said, settling down into the colorful folding lawn chair. He yawned, just like a real security guard, and placed his assault rifle under his chair.

Yvette shifted the car into drive. Mr. Phillips glanced at his pocket watch again as he slammed the passenger door and buckled his seatbelt. "Now we double back and get to the Launch Control Center," he said. "We've got a schedule to keep."

10

LAUNCHPAD 39A

Jacques didn't blink when the Klaxon on the pad gave a startling blast, announcing the planned hold at T minus twenty minutes. Spooked by the sudden sound, a group of snowy egrets beat their wings in unison and flew gracefully away from the mangroves next to the Launch Complex. Activity heightened around the pad as the last teams of technicians prepared to leave.

A voice echoed over the intercom. "Technicians, clear the area. We're ready to continue the countdown. I say again, all technicians clear the area. Once clear, the countdown will resume at T minus twenty minutes."

The army of white-suited techs moved away from the shuttle in an orderly fashion; some waited for the elevators in the Fixed Service Structure; those already on the ground hustled over to waiting buses.

Whistling with satisfaction, Jacques picked up his tool kit and moved along, just as a NASA tech was expected to do. His tool kit weighed ten kilograms less without the explosive device and detonators.

Standing in the elevator as it began the long descent, Jacques took one last glance at the gaseous oxygen vent access arm. The plastique was out of sight from the main gantry, blending into the insulating foam encasing the massive external tank. As the countdown continued, the access arm would retract, leaving the bomb behind, and unreachable.

The elevator bumped to a stop at level 250. A pair of technicians walked in and ignored Jacques. One carried a clipboard and spoke with the other, obviously a trainee from the symbol on the person's badge. They were in deep discussion about the final checklist procedure.

Jacques turned so they couldn't see his face. He acted as calm as when he and Yvette had been hustling johns on the streets of Cahors, aloof as they sold their bodies, disconnected from the reality around them. It was the only way to survive, the same now as it was then—disconnect flesh and mind. Do what was necessary.

When he was younger it had been difficult to take the strangers' money, to do whatever the men wanted. He did not try to understand what pleasure they drew from their acts, because he knew he would always return to Yvette's arms, where she would hold him, rock him gently, then make love in her attempt to cleanse him and herself of what they had gone through. It was the only way for them to survive on the streets.

As the elevator rattled down the gantry, Jacques felt

disconnected from his body again as he ran through
Mr. Phillips's plan. The technician he had already
killed was just a small sacrifice for what they had to
accomplish. An "investment," Mr. Phillips would
have called it. Jacques held the man's electronic badge
tightly in his fist; the badges would be read by computer scanners at the exits to ensure that everyone had
left the pad. NASA would not resume the countdown
until the area was cleared.

He spotted the Armored Personnel Carrier at the
edge of the launchpad complex. A technician walked
out to the vehicle to give a new water bottle to the
guards stationed there. Good. No one would suspect
anything.

The last banks of spotlights on the gantry spilled
bright patches of light on the ground, brighter than the
morning sunshine. Jacques watched the stream of technicians exit the area. It was difficult to see all of them
as they walked in and out of the glare. Security guards
stood around the gates, but they all looked *outward*.
Jacques felt warm with satisfaction, knowing that no
one suspected the threat coming from within.

The elevator bumped to a stop at ground level, and
the other two technicians walked off. Jacques passed
a computerized checkpoint, sliding his badge through
a magnetic-strip reader. Intentionally fumbling as if he
hadn't succeeded at first, he swapped his own badge
with that of the dead tech's, then slid it through the
reader again. All personnel accounted for.

One group of people filtered off to the right, toward
the first bus. Jacques joined the end of the crowd, and
as they stopped to file into the vehicle, he slowly
backed up to the massive flame trench, in the deep
well of shadow out of the spotlights. In the dark shelter

Jacques immediately began to unzip his white bunny suit. He looked from side to side as he stripped off the uniform, exposing a sand-camouflaged jumpsuit. No one approached.

Balling it up, he stuffed the suit in his nearly empty tool kit; it was too risky to leave the suit lying around. Grasping the kit, Jacques crouched low and slipped toward the Armored Personnel Carrier. Since the security cameras were broadcasting only a continuous loop of landscape visuals, thanks to the work of Yvette, he would be safe from electronic surveillance.

The APC sat in a strategic position nearly a mile from the shuttle, close enough to the escape slidewires that it could roar in to rescue the astronauts in case of an emergency.

But Jacques had an entirely different purpose in mind for it.

11

LAUNCH CONTROL CENTER

When Yvette pulled the white NASA car into the crowded parking lot of the Launch Control Center, Mr. Phillips pointed to the left. "There—an empty space up front. They must have known we were coming."

Yvette eased past vans, pickups, and cars, most of which bore *Challenger* memorial license plates, though a few said SAVE THE MANATEE. Mr. Phillips squinted to read painted words on the curb, black letters on a scuffed white background. "*Government Vehicle Parking Only*," he said. "Ah, then we've got the right place. Wouldn't want to do anything illegal."

From the backseat Rusty guffawed. Mr. Phillips turned and raised an eyebrow toward him. The redhead shut up.

Rusty frequently got on his nerves, but Mr. Phillips restrained himself from getting rid of him. For old times' sake . . . but tolerance was getting harder.

After the crash of his investment portfolio, and after he had vanished from the trading floor, he had needed to commit "physical suicide." He would disappear with a hefty profit even though his own investments had proved disastrous and had wrecked a once strong family fortune. He would reemerge from the ashes as a new person, leading a new life, with no strings attached.

But after he had rigged his Porsche convertible to go over the cliff on the rugged New England coast, sending it down into an automobile graveyard of jagged rocks and crashing surf, he had turned around in the last moment to see Rusty pull up in a battered pickup truck, watching the entire spectacle and grinning at Mr. Phillips's misfortune.

Rusty had understood exactly what Mr. Phillips was up to—and burst out laughing. The redhead had taken him home, wanting a piece of the cloak-and-dagger lifestyle. He'd had absolutely nothing to lose in his own life, and since that time Rusty had proven a valuable compatriot, someone who didn't mind getting his hands dirty, someone who could vanish into a crowd in places where Mr. Phillips wouldn't demean himself. What he lacked in sophistication, Rusty made up in enthusiasm.

After today, everything would pay off . . . or nothing would.

The three of them climbed out of the car, and Mr. Phillips slid his PDA into the pocket of his suit jacket, then popped a breath mint in his mouth. "Everybody ready? It's show time."

He looked up at the tall white building. The Launch Control Center was a "mid-sixties modern" structure, four stories tall with white siding and curved corners. Banks of narrow vertical windows faced toward the launchpads, covered with long black shields that had been put in place during the Apollo days, when immense Saturn V rockets lifted off with such a powerful blast that debris from a launch explosion could conceivably pelt the LCC more than three miles away.

Rusty opened the trunk of the car and removed their weapons. He checked the thumb safety and tossed a Colt OHWS handgun with a flash-and-noise suppressor to Yvette, who caught it smoothly and slid it into her clinging jumpsuit. She took her FAMAS G2 automatic assault rifle and extra magazines of ammunition. Rusty pocketed his own Colt OHWS and took another assault rifle for himself. He extended a 9-mm Beretta toward Mr. Phillips, who politely waved it away. "Suit yourself, Mr. Phillips." He stuck the Beretta in his other pocket. His freckled face was flushed with excitement. He shouldered a backpack of ammunition.

They had left one more guard dead in his shack just outside the LCC parking lot, and this time they had not bothered to use a disguised replacement. Part of him was disgusted that each step had proven so easy thus far—it had been only six months since they had sabotaged the Ariane rocket; he would have thought NASA's heightened security awareness might have lasted a bit longer than that. He supposed after today some jobs would come under serious review.

The time for subtlety was over. Now their plan called for brashness and quick thinking. They had to get inside the building without drawing attention to themselves—TV cameras and the press bleachers lay half a mile to the south, and they could turn the LCC into an armed fortress filled with hostages.

"Let's move inside," Mr. Phillips said. He adjusted his tie and the space shuttle lapel pin. "I don't want to depend too heavily on our grace period." He held the glass door open for Yvette. She nodded at his politeness.

The lobby was decorated with dark blue cushioned chairs, courtesy telephones, and a Plexiglas-encased model of the entire Kennedy Space Center. Rusty held his pistol with the silencer up in the air; Yvette hung her assault rifle over her left shoulder.

A lobby guard turned as they entered. Another creaked forward in his chair behind a security desk, standing up in surprise as he saw the weapons. "Excuse me! You can't—" The other guard fumbled for his side arm clipped into its holster.

Rusty brought down his handgun and squeezed off two shots, rapidly moving from one guard to the other. Thin coughing sounds came from his silencer. The two guards dropped onto the linoleum floor.

"Like shooting sitting geese," said Yvette.

"Ducks," Rusty corrected. "Sitting ducks."

Mr. Phillips pointed to the rest room doors. "Drag the two bodies into the ladies' room. It's probably used less than the gentlemen's, unless NASA hired a great many more female employees since I last checked."

"What about the blood?" Rusty said, motioning to the floor.

"We'll have to leave it for the night custodian," Mr. Phillips said. "Quickly now."

Rusty and Yvette each took a guard by the arms and dragged the bodies across the linoleum floor. The guards' black shoes squeaked on the tiles. Yvette kicked open the door to the rest room and hauled the first man inside, while Rusty followed.

Waiting, Mr. Phillips inspected the educational models on display, like a tourist. Pursing his lips, he studied the mockup of the cube-shaped Vehicle Assembly Building, launchpad 39A, and the Orbiter Processing Facility where the shuttles were reconditioned and prepared for each launch. The left-hand wall was lined with wooden plaques, each bearing the mission patch design for every shuttle launch. Beneath each plaque dangled two small metal tags, engraved with the launch date and landing date for each STS mission.

He heard a high-pitched cry and then another muffled gunshot in the ladies' room. Frowning, he pulled out his pocket watch. He forced himself to be patient, but time was running short. What had Rusty stumbled into now?

Yvette and Rusty stepped out of the bathroom, letting the wooden door sigh shut on pneumatic hinges. Rusty brushed his hands together as if proud of a job well done. Yvette breathed deeply, her cheeks flushed with excitement. She glided her handgun back into her pocket. "A woman fixing her makeup in front of the mirror," she said.

"She looked such a mess!" Rusty laughed. "Definitely!"

Mr. Phillips flashed a disgusted look; the redhead had no tact whatsoever. Although Rusty had helped him in the past, he would have to reevaluate the redhead's terms of employment after they were finished.

"How unfortunate," said Mr. Phillips. He drew in a deep breath, feeling elated at clearing the last obstacle before entering the control center. "All right now, double quick."

He led the way across the lobby, knowing exactly where to go. He had spent the same amount of time preparing for this mission as NASA normally spent preparing for a shuttle liftoff itself. He knew the floor layout of the LCC as well as he knew the interior of the Connecticut house where he had grown up. Even better. Because he had dreamed of coming here, to the nerve center of the space program, while he had hated his mother's cold, old mansion. Mother's house had been dark and lonely; the LCC was vibrant, full of energy, a taste of the future.

He took the corridor to the left. The building was an artifact of the sixties, with thick coats of beige paint on the cinderblock wall, a brown vinyl baseboard against a linoleum floor. Mr. Phillips shook his head, distressed at the austere conditions. A high-tech agency such as NASA should have the sleekest, most modern facilities . . . but much of their facilities looked like something out of an old television rerun. *Inexcusable*, he thought, *but telling*.

"Launch Control itself is on the third floor," Mr. Phillips said. "Provided we can get up to the mezzanine VIP viewing area before anyone discovers our handiwork, we should be home free." He used his fingers to brush down his lapels.

"Should we take the stairs?" Rusty said.

Mr. Phillips pursed his lips and shook his head. "No, we'll use the elevators. No sense getting out of breath. We'll need our stamina for . . . other things." He felt the adrenaline surge through his veins. The excitement reminded him of stepping out onto the trading floor for the very first time. He was about to make a killing.

Rusty began to laugh again, and this time Mr. Phillips ignored him.

12

LAUNCH CONTROL CENTER

Returning to the main firing floor of the Launch Control Center, Nicole Hunter slid her badge through the magnetic-strip reader to gain access.

"The crew has boarded the shuttle, and the hatch is sealed," one of the station chiefs told her. "Pad is cleared and safed."

"Right on time," Nicole said, with a glance at the countdown clock on the wall. Though Commander Franklin had a conscientious crew, as Launch Director she was the one responsible for making sure everything happened down to the precise second. *Remember the six Ps,* she thought: *Prior preparation prevents piss-poor performance*—and nobody did it better than NASA. She ran a hand quickly through her brown-gold hair, then moved along, keyed up . . . and loving it.

One of the women station chiefs looked up and announced, "The last bus has returned from the launch-pad. Beach Road, Kennedy Parkway, and the crawler access road are now closed."

"Copy that," said one of the other technicians.

"Perimeter gates six T, four, and two C are green. Aerial surveillance reports the area as secure," announced another.

"APCs in place for emergency rescue. Standing by."

Nicole looked down at her own checklist, watching the items. The information flew at her like water spraying from a fire hydrant. One station after another checked in. Nicole glanced down at a TV monitor from the launchpad cameras, seeing the gantry and the stately shuttle with its rust-brown external tank and tall solid rocket boosters like fat white pencils tacked to each side. The Rotating Service Structure had moved aside, but the venting "beanie cap" remained firmly in place atop the external tank. Wisps of cirrus clouds drifted across the screen.

Nicole looked out the window; the morning sky shone perfectly clear, no clouds. *That's odd.* She slurped the dregs of her sweet dark coffee and tossed the plastic foam cup in a wastebasket. She dismissed the discrepancy as someone else demanded her attention.

"Guard gates checking in for their final report," said a station tech. "Everyone gives the clear—" The man frowned, spoke into his microphone again, waited. "Everyone checks in except for one guard gate."

Nicole felt a wash of concern. "One of the perimeter gates?"

"No, perimeter gates are all green," the man said.

"It's the station directly outside the LCC. Right next door, nowhere close to the launchpad."

Nicole heaved a short sigh of relief. "He's probably out gawking at the shuttle with his binoculars. Call Security Control. Have them cover the gate and admonish the guard for leaving his station. Proceed with the countdown."

She looked around, saw teams intent at their stations, some speaking into telephones, others studying computer displays. Dot-matrix printers documented each step. The entire LCC was a whirring, smoothly running machine in high gear.

She touched the tiny gold key on her necklace and smiled, totally satisfied with her position and her responsibility.

Nicole called her deputy over, a quiet, older man with a short crew cut. "Handle the floor for a few minutes," she said. "I'm going back to the VIP area to hold some hands and coddle a barracuda."

Securing the glass door with her badge, she trotted up the mezzanine steps to where the honored guests looked down at the activity like spectators at a zoo. The technicians had by now become accustomed to performing their daily routine under a magnifying glass.

Ambassador Andrei Trovkin, the Russian liaison, stood with his hands clasped behind his back, staring out the narrow windows toward the launchpad. On a low hill to the right stood press stands crowded with TV crews and newspaper photographers. They would get a breathtaking view of the launch across the Banana River toward Cape Canaveral. Separate white-sided buildings bore the logos of major networks, ABC, NBC, CBS, and CNN. Behind them sat the old trailers of NASA's Media Relations Bureau. On a tall flagpole an American flag hung limp in the morning stillness. The digital numbers on the large countdown clock winked down for the press.

"Feeling the suspense build, Ambassador Trovkin?" she asked the Russian.

He turned to her with a preoccupied smile. "I am astonished how wonderfully public American launches are," he said. "In Russia they never used to be announced at all. Oh, and call me Andrei, please."

"Then you must call me Nicole."

"Thank you." He nodded to her.

She turned to one of the runners. "Would you get me another coffee please? Two sugars—"

The young man nodded. "—and no cream. I know, Ms. Hunter." He turned to dash down the steps just as the elevator chime rang.

The doors slid open, and three strangers emerged, blocking the runner's way. One of the newcomers—a statuesque woman with close-cropped hair so blond it looked white—shoved the runner into the cinderblock wall, as if batting a fly out of the way. The strangers jogged briskly up the mezzanine stairs and spread out.

With the freeze-frame vision brought about from adrenaline, Nicole saw that the blond woman carried a compact automatic assault rifle. One man who emerged with her—bright orange-red hair and a coppery spattering of freckles across his face—brandished two handguns, one with a prominent phallic silencer screwed to the barrel. A compact assault rifle was strapped across his chest.

The dapper man between them looked calmly in charge. He was quite short, no more than five feet, dressed in a dark pinstripe suit that sported a gold-

and-white space shuttle pin on the lapel. His demeanor and appearance reminded her of a comically polite English butler.

"Excuse me, who are you?" Nicole said, feeling a tightness in her chest. She stepped back to push the silent alarm that would summon the security guards from the lobby.

"That alarm won't be necessary," the nattily dressed man said, his lips drawn together into a flowerbud frown. "I'm afraid no one is available to take your call downstairs."

The redhead chuckled, but the short man silenced him with a sharp glance before he turned to the others gathered in the observation deck. "May I have your attention, please? My name is Mr. Phillips. I believe we have about five minutes before the first of your security forces arrives, so I would like to lay down a few ground rules. They'll be most useful. Yvette, Rusty—would you join me?"

Trovkin, Senator Boorman and his aides, and the other guests stood up with a mixture of indignation and uncertainty, looking at the ominous weapons. Boorman's crew of four cameramen turned. Sensing news in the making, they pointed their video cams at Mr. Phillips and his two companions.

Nicole froze, her mind spinning. She couldn't sort out the procedures she had learned for dealing with a situation like this.

"I apologize for the intrusion," the dapper man said, "but unfortunately I have found it necessary. There will be a slight modification to the launch plans today, but I'm fully aware of your launch window, Ms. Nicole Hunter." His direct use of her name startled her, although the identity of the Launch Director was certainly no secret. "So I will make every effort to prevent a delay. I know how costly scrubbing a shuttle launch can be."

Nicole blinked. This was crazy—unless this Phillips character had an army of people covering him, literally hundreds of NASA, military, and state police would be here within the next few minutes. "Whoever you are, I think you underestimate the defenses of the space center." She stepped forward but stopped when the freckled man leveled one of his pistols at her not more than five feet away.

"Thank you, Rusty," said Mr. Phillips. He turned to Nicole. "Should your security people charge in here like a bunch of superheroes, they may encounter some unexpected obstacles."

Squaring his broad shoulders, Andrei Trovkin strode next to Nicole, his face florid with rage. "How dare you bring guns here? This mission has half Russian crew! You are causing international incident!"

Mr. Phillips pulled his lips tight, as if annoyed at the interruption. He studied the badge on Trovkin's chest. The urbane man barely came up to the Russian's sternum. "Ah, my foreign friend, let's make good use of the few minutes until NASA Security rears its ugly head." He pulled out a gray-cased Personal Data Assistant, flipped open the liquid-crystal screen, and withdrew a stylus. Touching the screen and selecting names, he called up a file and studied the words on the screen.

"Here we are!" he said triumphantly. "Andrei Ivanovich Trovkin, born in Belorus, received a degree in engineering and aerospace science, completed Air Force and cosmonaut training, but was *excused*"—he said the word slowly, as if with distaste—"from fur-

ther cosmonaut service due to a·heart murmur. Pity.''
Mr. Phillips shook his head. ''Just like Deke Slayton—
but he finally got a chance to fly on the Apollo-Soyuz
mission, so don't give up hope.''

As Trovkin sputtered, Nicole turned to Phillips,
calm and professional. All they needed were a few
more minutes and security would be here. She wanted
to keep him talking. ''So you've done your homework.
What is it you want?''

Senator Boorman stepped up, his face stormy and
indignant, putting on an air of command he must have
used often on the Senate floor. ''Our nation has a
clearly stated policy of refusing to negotiate with terrorists. Whatever you have planned is hopeless.'' The
news cameras quickly pointed at him, capturing every
moment of the tableau.

''Ah, Senator Boorman,'' Mr. Phillips said with ill-
concealed distaste, ''let me see.'' He glanced down at
his PDA screen, calling up new data. ''My, what a
long file you have. But one thing stands out.'' He
raised his eyebrows curiously. ''Why exactly were you
arrested wearing woman's underwear coming out of
the sorority dorm in nineteen sixty-five? May twenty-
fifth? Do you recall that incident, Senator Boorman?''

The senator gasped, then turned red with anger. ''I
won't be intimidated—''

Mr. Phillips cut him off. ''I've *already* intimidated
you, and I've got condensed files on every person here,
so maybe we'll have a show-and-tell for the television
audience. But that will have to be later, since we need
to move rather quickly on this—I have only another
minute before your cavalry arrives. And I fear I may
need to make my point, unless NASA Security is willing to take my assurances at face value.'' He stepped

up to one of the video cameras positioned high in a corner. Looking up, he cleared his throat and spoke directly to the camera.

"First, I know we're being monitored by security personnel. Let me assure you that if any attempt is made to enter this building, we will shoot our hostages. All of them. It's as simple as that." He snapped his finger at the tall blond woman, the one he had called Yvette.

Holding her assault rifle on the crowd of VIPs, Yvette withdrew a small respirator mask from one of the green satchels she carried. She handed it to Mr. Phillips, who dangled it up to the camera. "Second, we have gas masks, and our hostages don't. If any gas comes in, the hostages die. Need I say more?" He tossed the mask back to Yvette; she caught it with a casual flick of her wrist. "So, do *not* attempt to enter this building. I also have numerous colleagues stationed at strategic positions around the entire launch site, and they have orders to severely punish any misbehavior."

Stepping away from the camera, Mr. Phillips folded his hands together and raked his gaze over his audience. "Ms. Hunter, you are the person with whom I wish to speak." He glanced sidelong at the senator. "I've always had little respect for . . . that man and his narrow-minded politics."

Nicole kept her expression stony, but inside she felt a horrid fear. She had to play him out, take this carefully.

Mr. Phillips glanced at the security video cameras in the ceiling. "Rusty, could you remove those please? Leave one, but shoot the rest. I prefer to have more direct control over the images broadcast from here."

Rusty pointed the pistol in his right hand at the observation cameras. ''Definitely!'' With short hisses of silenced gunshots, glass, metal, and black plastic flew as the cameras blew apart.

The news reporters pointed their own lenses at the spectacle.

Just for effect, Rusty fired two more times into the acoustic ceiling panels. Boorman's aides drew around the senator. Most of the others cringed, but Nicole made a great effort to stand stock-still, without flinching. Everyone would be looking to her, and as much as she felt like cowering, she had to be strong.

''Now, if you will all be patient,'' Mr. Phillips said quietly, ''I will issue my demands and explain the consequences if you do not meet them. Let us keep the shuttle astronauts unaware of the situation for the moment. We wouldn't want them to overreact.''

He checked his pocket watch, then snapped it shut again. ''I assure you, everything is under control.'' He smiled pleasantly. ''And I do very much enjoy being in control.''

13

ATLANTIS FLIGHT DECK

Gator Green reached down to the center console on *Atlantis*'s flight deck and flipped through the laminated checklist resting on his leg. Same as in all the simulations—only this time it was for real. It should have made no difference, no matter that he was decked out in a pressure suit and wore his helmet. He stopped just before touching the switch and read from the checklist. "Orbital maneuvering system pressurization check."

"Check," Marc Franklin said in a flat, professional voice. Franklin read from an identical checklist in the mission commander's chair on the left-hand side of the compartment.

Gator flipped both switches marked OMS ENG. "Armed." He swung his attention to the overhead panel, near Franklin. "Increasing cabin pressure to sixteen point seven psi."

Franklin watched the results carefully. "Cabin leak check complete."

Gator clicked his mike. "Control, *Atlantis*. OMS pressure on, cabin vent check complete."

"Roger that."

Atlantis vibrated with internal pumps, relays, and switches groaning under the constant contracting and expansion from the cryogenic fuel in the external tank. The shuttle seemed alive and anxious to go as Gator went methodically through the rest of the checklist.

He completed the voice check as Franklin reached down to close both cabin vent switches. As they completed the sequence, the voice from CAPCOM came over the radio. "Change of plan, *Atlantis*. We are continuing to extend our hold. Please stand by."

Gator sighed and clicked his mike. "Copy that." He wondered how long the delay would be this time.

He looked over at Franklin. Although it was the commander's fourth space flight, the older man looked as nervous as a rookie but capped it off with a brittle, forced stoicism that only increased the tension for Gator. On his other flights, Franklin had been a mere mission specialist. *It must make one hell of a difference knowing you're responsible for the entire crew*, Gator thought. He wondered if Iceberg ever felt that way.

If this mission had gone off as originally planned, Gator knew that Iceberg would probably have been fast asleep in the commander's chair during the extended hold, catching a few winks. The man oozed coolness, and his calm attitude infected every member of the crew so that no one had any doubt the mission would be a complete success.

He remembered being with Iceberg and Nicole at a

cookout on the patio of his rented bachelor pad in Canaveral City, flipping burgers on a smoking Weber grill, horsing around to show off for Monique, a woman he had ended up dating for only two months. He splashed Tabasco sauce on the burgers as they sizzled over the flames, urging his guests to drink more lemonade. He had gotten it into his head that he wanted to try to make some fresh-squeezed lemonade the way his mother had done it once, and so he spent the afternoon making a godawful mess of his kitchen, massacring a whole bag full of lemons—and, dammit, Iceberg and Nicole were going to drink the stuff, no matter how much sugar they needed to add.

Monique had told him later that night how much she envied the stability apparent in Iceberg and Nicole's relationship. . . .

Now, up on the flight deck, he and Franklin had an indefinite amount of time to kill. Gator tried to loosen some of the tension that permeated the cabin. He turned off his mike so that his voice would not be broadcast over the shuttle, much less over the radio. He leaned close to Franklin. "Hey, Marc—once we dock with *Mir*, it'd be easy to remain connected; let us stay up there awhile. You know, continue glasnost by giving some of their crew a break. We could have a poker game."

Franklin looked up from studying the flight checklist again. His eyes were red, tired through the helmet. "You must be kidding."

Gator fought to keep a straight face. *Of course I'm kidding.* "They might want to take a vacation on board *Atlantis* while we explore their station. Every nook and cranny. Nobody else needs to know."

Alexandra Koslovsky leaned forward from her mission specialist seat, situated just behind the pilot and mission commander's position. Her long straw-colored hair was stuffed inside the fabric Snoopy headgear. "Discussing travel plans, Lieutenant Commander Gator?"

Franklin stiffened. "We're just going over the post-launch checklist, Cosmonaut Koslovsky." He didn't sound convincing.

Gator gave Alexandra a wink. "And to think we could have opened up a new frontier for international relations."

Franklin snorted, realizing his leg had been pulled. He turned back to the checklist. "You've had your fun, Gator. No more, understand?"

"That's a rog," said Gator. "Just trying to lighten things up." He turned to the next item on the checklist: Load flight plan OPS-1 into the computer. He'd have to load the program after the hold. Whenever it ended.

From here on out it was following a set schedule of checklists. It reminded him of preparing for a game at Annapolis, with the play strategy laid out days in advance. All he had to do was to run on the football field, with four thousand midshipmen yelling their heads off, waving their white wheel caps in the air— and execute the plan without errors.

At the back of his mind, as had probably happened with every single astronaut in the past decade, was the image of the *Challenger* disaster, the shuttle passing through max q with all readouts indicating complete success—until that gut-wrenching moment when it all went wrong. How could anyone sit aboard the shuttle on the launchpad and *not* think of that while waiting for the countdown to commence?

Gator pushed the image out of his mind. He couldn't afford to dwell on it. With or without Iceberg as commander, this mission was going to go. Nothing could stop them now.

With Franklin, he ran though the post-launch checklist again, all the time glancing at the mechanical switches, old cathode-ray tubes, LED switches, and computer pads. Gator reached to his right and re-attached the checklist to a Velcro pad, then stretched. He glanced at the countdown clock and frowned in concern. "Hey, Marc—we're pushing up against the hold limit."

Franklin scanned a row of lighted buttons, double-checked the countdown clock himself. He clicked the microphone. "CAPCOM, *Atlantis*. You're keeping mighty quiet out there. What's going on? Give us some good news."

It took a disquietingly long moment for Houston to come back. "*Atlantis*, CAPCOM. We are still in an indefinite hold. Standby one."

Gator raised his brows and looked at Franklin. "What do you think? Are they looking for an abort? What could it be?" The ground crew had a perfectionist reputation before okaying a launch.

Franklin looked grim, then disgusted. He flicked the comm switch again. "CAPCOM, can you give us details?"

"That's a negatory. No data at this time, *Atlantis*."

Gator clicked his own mike, letting disbelief trickle into his voice. "Come on, you don't have an indication of the problem? Are we scrubbing the launch?"

"The hold was directed by the Launch Director herself. We'll feed you more information as we get it from KSC."

Gator shifted in his seat. Lying on his back staring up into the sky was getting damned uncomfortable. "CAPCOM, put me through to Panther—uh, Ms. Hunter, I mean."

"Sorry, *Atlantis*. We're having comm problems with Launch Control. We'll keep you updated."

"Comm problems?" Gator sounded incredulous.

"We've got to shut down, *Atlantis*—we'll be out of communication with you for a while. Relax while we deadstart the comm link."

Gator clicked his microphone twice to signify that he understood the directions. He frowned. *Deadstart the system*? That's weird. He shrugged. Somebody probably found a hangnail somewhere.

"Not much we can do," Franklin said. "You heard CAPCOM."

"How about letting us unbuckle and get some blood back in our feet, Marc? No telling how long these clowns are going to keep us waiting."

Franklin looked grim. "Our launch window won't allow more than a half hour hold before we have to reschedule." He started to unfasten his straps while speaking over the in-board intercom to the rest of the crew. "Okay, let's take a short break, helmets off—but be ready to strap back in."

Now unbuckled, Alexandra Koslovsky leaned forward. She grasped the back of his seat to support herself. "What do you think the problem is, Lieutenant Commander Gator?"

Gator twisted and looked at the pretty Russian cosmonaut. He gave her a disarming grin. "Who knows—gremlins, probably. No launch ever goes without some kind of hitch."

14

SECURITY CONTROL, KSC

Emergency Klaxons blared throughout the main NASA security complex. Many buildings were empty, with workers camping out in folding lawn chairs in the parking lots or gathered on viewing stands to watch the impending launch. But the alarms screamed on.

Khaki-and-black uniformed guards poured from Security Control, carrying automatic rifles and struggling to tug on flak jackets. They wore thick black boots with steel-plated insoles and head-mounted microphones with tiny speaker earplugs. The guards ran for their black all-terrain vehicles, slammed heavy doors, and started their engines.

Radios mounted inside the ATVs spat out sharp voices: "All teams, this is a priority one alert. This is not an exercise—repeat, *not* an exercise. Hostage situation at LCC and possible danger to pad thirty-nine

A. Sensors and video cameras have been neutralized, situation unknown.''

Team members scrambled to fall in as the crisp voice continued barking orders. ''Employ scenario G for Golf. Teams switch to respective buttons: Team One, switch to button one; Team Two, button two . . .''

Each five-person security unit changed to a preset channel in addition to the coordinating frequency used by Security Control. Cool excitement permeated the teams; they had trained for this moment for years, but no one had really thought they would be called into action. Who would have the nerve—the *gall*—to attack the Kennedy Space Center?

Seven ATVs squealed out of the parking lot. Three headed for the guard gate at the southeast point of the restricted launch area; the other four raced up State Highway 1, toward the threatened Launch Control Center.

On the Gulf shore across the Florida peninsula, U.S. Central Command Headquarters at McDill Air Force Base was notified of a potential national emergency unfolding. The message percolated through the command's enlisted force, the first line of administration that monitored the launch. Several minutes passed before the news reached someone with the authority to take direct action. The Air Force special operations C-130 aircraft that had earlier been routinely monitoring the vicinity from high above was diverted from its standoff area.

Twenty miles south at Cape Canaveral Air Force Station, a team of elite Air Force security policemen charged into action. News of the alert spread from the Federal Emergency Management Agency to the Department of Defense crisis-management network as military personnel methodically prepared for a decisive response.

Back at Kennedy Space Center, whining sounds came from two helicopters squatting on the center of a concrete pad as the pilots revved onboard auxiliary power units. It would take two full minutes until they could start their rotors, and the required time seemed to take forever to the pilots and guards that had rushed on board and strapped themselves in, ready to go. Four helicopters already patrolling the skies tipped their rotors toward the LCC.

The first black all-terrain vehicle screeched up to the white Launch Control building. The five-person security team poured out of the armored vehicle and, using the bulk of the ATV as a shield, readied their weapons while crouching.

The team leader raised her fist. "Team One, check in. Alpha here."

Each person keyed his head-mounted microphone. "Bravo."

"Charlie."

"Delta."

"Echo."

Satisfied that her team was ready, the leader gripped the cool muzzle of her M-16 automatic rifle. "Orders are to surround the building only. Do not get closer than fifty feet. Execute."

The team spread out as the backup ATVs roared up from Security Control. The team leader keyed her mike. "Team one is in position and the situation is in hand. Waiting for your instruction."

"Proceed with caution, Alpha," said Security Control. "We have a hostage situation in there with some VIPs."

As Team 1 sprinted for the perimeter of the tall white building, a barrage of automatic rifle fire rang out from the stairwell on the third story. Instantly, two members of Team 1 fell to the ground as if they had been struck with baseball bats; a third spun in his tracks, hit in the arm.

Team 1 Leader dove for cover behind a parked car as she screamed into her microphone. "Back off, back off! Security Control, live fire—abort G for Golf." She huddled beside the parked car and gasped for breath. Bullets showered all around the vehicle. Adjacent windshields burst, and glass shattered, falling to the ground like broken icicles. The other ATVs spun their wheels in an effort to back away.

Team 1 Leader tried to get a glimpse of her team members, taking a tally of casualties. She spotted two of the four members lying on the ground, their blood seeping onto the black pavement. She shouted into her headset. "Team One, report! Alpha here."

"Echo. I'm okay under cover behind a red pickup truck."

"Delta," came a weaker voice. "I'm hit. Bleeding. I can last a little while, though."

A voice came over her head-mounted earphone. "Team One, this is Security Control. What is your assessment?"

"We're still under fire. Three team members hit." Breathing deeply she looked at the second hand on her watch and counted the number of bullets she heard smack into the ATV and around her. "Things have tapered off, but there's still plenty of action."

"Can you spot where the firing is coming from?"

"I think there's only one gunman, but he means business. Appears to be shooting from the third-floor stairwell, a perfect strategic position."

"Offer medical assistance to your team members, if you can do it safely. Reinforcements on the way. Do not proceed with the assault."

She sat back to wait while the bullets continued to rain around her.

Three black ATVs roared up to Salvatore's guard shack at the far southeast point of the restricted launch area. The security personnel inside the vehicles gripped the sleek barrels of their weapons as they listened to the updates coming from their colleagues in Team Alpha outside the LCC.

"Sounds like they got a war going on over there!"

Just as they approached the guard gate, the first ATV drove over a tripwire, triggered a land mine, and flew up into the air.

Mounted on tripods hidden in the brush at the side of the road, remote-controlled assault weapons opened fire. A volley of bullets ripped into the sides of the black ATVs. Glass shattered, metal punctured by the armor-piercing rounds. Screams from the jumpsuited guards quickly died out. The first ATV rolled over in the ditch and groaned, a molten hulk.

Twenty yards down the road, just outside the guard shack, a lone man clicked his radio. "Yo, Mr. Phillips—Duncan at checkpoint one. No survivors for the first wave. Three vehicles down. A beauty."

It took only an instant for the answer from the LCC. "Very good, Duncan. Thank you. Perhaps our NASA friends will listen more attentively from here on out."

Satisfied, Duncan turned back to watch for more incoming traffic. Plenty of land mines remained scattered around the area, and he could easily pick off anyone who tried to disarm them.

He strode forward to reload the expended magazines of ammunition. He lit a menthol cigarette, rifle in hand, and went back to his lawn chair to wait.

15

ONE MILE FROM LAUNCHPAD 39A

Iceberg sat behind the brush-covered rise, well hidden from the routine search patterns and confident that he would remain undiscovered. The launchpad was in the distance, its access road more than a mile away. He heard sirens behind him, probably the last warning blasts of security personnel to clear the restricted area. Under other circumstances, this might have felt like a picnic.

But he should have been up there in the cockpit right now.

Iceberg watched NASA's coverage of the launch on the Walkman TV. He didn't waste much time worrying about politics, but he thought Senator Boorman had dominated the news for far too long. Didn't the reporters have their priorities straight on launch day at least?

Now, the only thing on the screen was a distant shot

of *Atlantis*. The technicians had cleared the launch area before the T minus twenty hold, which had been extended for some reason Nicole hadn't yet bothered to explain. Maybe she just needed to touch up her makeup, or maybe she had found a green card that wasn't on a checklist.

Iceberg leaned back, propping the miniature TV in the soft dirt so he could have an unobstructed view of the pad. *Atlantis* looked beautiful in the clear morning sky. Daylight caught the top of the gantry as cryogenic oxygen and hydrogen boiled faint wisps of steam into the muggy air.

The TV replayed an earlier interview with the Launch Director. Here, alone with his thoughts where no one could see him, Iceberg had to admit that Nicole looked good on the tube. Damn good, in fact. She'd kept her cool dealing with numb nuts from Washington and those pestering reporters. Of course, if she could put up with *him*, then an antagonistic senator would have been a piece of cake. Iceberg never had the patience for all those dances with words. He wanted to *do* something, not explore how many different ways one could talk about it.

But talking and planning had always been Nicole's style. Stand up against the odds and fight it out, finding some political compromise that let both sides feel they had won. She didn't give up easily.

Except when it came to being an astronaut.

Iceberg shook his head. He dug his fingers into the dirt, wishing the launch would hurry up and happen. Get that shuttle up into the sky! He hated just sitting here with nothing to do but think.

He caught a glimpse of the countdown clock superimposed on the lower right corner of the TV picture, and frowned. The extended hold had been going on for quite a while. Of course, unplanned delays happened all the time. Maybe the NASA bureaucrats couldn't make up their minds about what type of toilet paper to put on board.

The scene switched from a far-off view of the shuttle to an image from a camera on top of the Fixed Service Structure, showing the oxygen vent access arm partially retracted. Then another view, this time of the shuttle's main engines. The pad looked deserted, as it should have been.

Iceberg leaned forward and turned up the sound. Something still didn't seem right. On the TV those cirrus clouds above the shuttle were still there, but it must be some kind of ghost image on the screen. He saw no clouds for miles around.

The sound of a low-flying helicopter startled him. The copter suddenly burst over the brush-covered rise, flying like a bat out of hell. Its downwash threw up debris and toppled the small Walkman TV.

"Shit!" Iceberg scrambled away, hopping on one foot to get to cover. A streak of pain shot through his foot where the healing bones ground together like fingernails on a chalkboard. The helicopter wheeled in the sky and headed to his left, as if it were searching for something. Him, probably.

Iceberg cursed. He must have set off some kind of alarm, tripping one of the motion or sonic sensors. And now they were out looking for him. Maybe *he* was the reason for the extended hold in the countdown. He knew he was going to look like a fool.

The helicopter made another pass, but Iceberg wasn't sure whether they had spotted him. Then the craft roared off, straight for the launchpad.

He felt a sour feeling creep into his stomach as he realized that the guard Salvatore was probably being harassed this very minute. The poor guy had worked at KSC for years without getting into trouble; now Iceberg had involved him in something that just might get the old guard fired.

Iceberg could BS his way through whatever reprimands might come his way. He'd get a slap on the wrist, and he'd have to kiss some nonflying puke's rear end. But they'd let him off. After all, he *was* a modern-day hero—shuttle commander and senior member of the astronaut corps.

He just hoped that he'd be able to sweet-talk the bureaucrats into letting Salvatore off as well.

Well, if they were out looking for him, they'd eventually find him. Especially with this broken foot. Better to surrender now and cut his losses, let the countdown continue, get his crew up into space during the launch window.

Iceberg gathered up his TV and binoculars, then trudged gingerly toward the guard shack, ready to make up a good story.

16

LAUNCH CONTROL CENTER

Inside the LCC, Nicole watched a NASA security helicopter chop its way through the air, thundering across the sky toward the launchpad where *Atlantis* waited, its countdown frozen. Three other copters swept low over the restricted launch area, hunting for additional terrorists.

A firecracker sound of gunshots had echoed down the hall, coming from the stairwell that looked out on the LCC parking lot. Far away, Rusty shot repeatedly, letting out whoops of delight every time he hit his targets.

Nicole moved over to the wall beside Andrei Trovkin, peering through the vertical observation windows. She placed her hands against the thick glass as the dark insect shape of the helicopter pounded away, skirting the LCC toward the swamps. Her heart pounded with instinctive relief that help was on the way . . . yet she felt an inner dread of what might happen. The terrorists seemed to have few compunctions about murder.

"Do helicopters really think they can stop this madman?" Trovkin snorted with a glance back at Mr. Phillips, who studiously inspected his fingernails, oblivious to his precarious hold on the situation.

Rusty returned from down the hall, wiping sweat from his freckled forehead and grinning. He shouldered his automatic assault rifle. "Bull's-eye! I think I won myself a stuffed teddy bear. You should have seen those security troops running like ants under a hot magnifying glass!"

With a disappointed sigh, Mr. Phillips shook his head. "Duncan tells me we've had some excitement out by his guard shack as well, and now these pesky helicopters. NASA doesn't seem to be taking our threat seriously, which I find quite exasperating. Don't they even want to hear what I have to *say* before they come blasting in? Talk about short attention spans."

He picked up his walkie-talkie and tuned to the chosen frequency. "Mory, are you there? How would you like to do a little duck hunting?"

With a squelch of static a man's thin, nasal voice came back. "Ready and waiting, Mr. Phillips. Any problem with Cueball doing the honors? He's pretty anxious for some action, and he needs the target practice."

Mr. Phillips sounded impatient. "I asked *you*, Mory. I don't want to risk missing, not with the television networks watching. That would be most embarrassing."

"No problem. Does it matter which helicopter I take out?"

Mr. Phillips pursed his lips. "Just make it spectac-ular for our viewers out in TV land."

"Stay tuned for the Fourth of July," Mory an-swered, signing off.

Mr. Phillips wore a smug smile that Nicole wanted to wipe off his face with a hot iron. Her stomach tight-ened as she forced down her hot-tempered reflex. "Let me get on the radio, Mr. Phillips. I'll tell the security teams to back off so you can issue your demands."

"I think I'd prefer a more dramatic demonstration," he said. "Watch."

A white finger of fire erupted from the swampy low-lands as the unseen sniper launched a deadly projec-tile.

"A Stinger missile," Mr. Phillips said. "Light-weight, portable, easily fired, easy to aim. A thousand and one uses."

The missile targeted the NASA helicopter closest to the LCC. The pilot swerved his aircraft, but the ground-launched rocket moved at intercept speed. The Stinger struck the helicopter, and both exploded in a huge flash displayed on the TV screens.

"Not as great a technological marvel as the space shuttle, but still exhilarating, nonetheless," Mr. Phil-lips said, then grabbed the walkie-talkie. "Good shot, Mory."

Nicole found herself hyperventilating, her heart pounding. "You just killed those men!"

"Let us not be sexist here," Mr. Phillips said. "One of the crew could have been a woman. And you're forgetting the three security vehicles out by the gate—there could have been women on that security team as well. And who knows how many Rusty shot out in the LCC parking lot? I'm sure it wasn't just men. We believe in equal opportunity.''

He grew suddenly serious. ''The stakes are *required* to be high, Ms. Hunter. NASA must realize this is not a game.'' He punctuated his words by jabbing a slender finger in her direction. ''I needed to establish that at the outset, so my demands will be heard with due consideration.''

He handed her one of the telephones. ''However, you have made a good suggestion. Before we cut off the outside phone lines, if you would be so kind as to contact NASA Security, perhaps you could prevent further loss of life if they agree to back off.''

Nicole hesitated. What else could she do? Phillips lifted an eyebrow as she raced over the options in her mind. . . . The little man had the upper hand. She took the phone, desperate to salvage the situation. Her hands were sweaty. ''What do you want me to say?'' She felt defeated.

''Just tell them to restrain themselves, stay out of the restricted area. I also know about NASA's roving security patrols around the swamps, so tell them to sit tight and keep away from the Launch Control Center. My people are infiltrated throughout the site, as you've just seen. I call the shots here, no pun intended, and Security will have to sit on their hands until they receive further instructions from me.''

Nicole's mind whirled, trying to focus. Her thoughts threatened to cascade over into panic—but she fought the confusion down. She had to handle this situation delicately, pretend it was one of the crash simulator routines in which Iceberg had always excelled. This would be the crisis of her career, and there were numerous lives at stake, as Mr. Phillips had so clearly demonstrated.

The sooty stain in the sky from the helicopter explosion dissipated, but its memory would leave a scar in her mind forever.

She gripped the phone and made the call.

Beside her, Mr. Phillips flipped through the pages of the *Wall Street Journal* Senator Boorman's aide had left on the table. Flicking frequent glances at Nicole and the other hostages, he scanned down the tiny print on the stock pages, scowling distastefully.

Struggling out of his chair, Senator Boorman cleared his throat, as if he considered it part of the process of making any sort of important speech.

Mr. Phillips turned to him and brightened. "Ah yes, Senator, I believe it's time we had a talk. As chairman of the Senate Foreign Relations Committee, you must be very well connected with powerful people. I may need your assistance to negotiate my demands."

The senator scowled. "Cooperation wasn't exactly on my mind, sir."

"It's in your own best interests to resolve this situation."

Boorman grudgingly nodded. "If that's the best way out of this mess."

Mr. Phillips looked thoughtfully at him. "How heroic, Senator," he said. "Just what I expected of you. We'll see to you later, though. I haven't yet even *made* my demands."

Nicole looked up sharply from the phone. "Let's get on with it before anyone else dies."

"Don't rush me, Ms. Hunter. It's my fifteen minutes of fame," he said simply. He rubbed his upper lip again. "I'm going to bask in it."

17

GUARD SHACK

Iceberg had hobbled to within a half mile of the guard shack—still keeping a low profile, miserably wondering the best way he could surrender to minimize the problems for Salvatore—when the NASA helicopter exploded overhead. A ball of fire roiled in the air; the sound of the blast came like a thunderclap.

Iceberg dropped to the muddy, weedy ground, heedless of his cast and the sharp increase of pain that shot from his toes to his knee. "Holy shit!"

Swallowed by the weeds, he frantically looked around, scanning the sky. The fireball diffused into a low red glow, but the detonation had left a purple afterimage in his sight. Burning debris fell from the air, raining down on the thick vegetation, and a dull quietness hung over the swamps as heavy as the humidity.

He was sure he'd seen the curving trail of a ground-launched *missile* just before the explosion.

"Chill out, cool, frosty..." he muttered, hoping the repeated words might calm him. "Now, more than ever." He dug his hands in the soft dirt while lying still, trying to make sense of what he had witnessed. It was some sort of IR missile, launched on the ground and guided by an infrared sensor.

Years ago as part of his Air Force training, he had brought down an unmanned target drone with an IR missile, but at the time he had been strapped in an F-15 and flying over the Gulf of Mexico, safely shooting on a test range. This was friggin' *serious*. Iceberg dismissed any notion of the NASA security detail looking for him. Something else was going on, and he had blundered smack into the middle of it.

Without raising his head, Iceberg shrugged off his daypack. He fumbled through the canvas bag and pulled out the Walkman TV. The network reporters from the press stands broadcast long-range shots of the exploding helicopter and jabbered about some other SWAT operation over at the LCC building, but nobody seemed to know anything.

Here, inside the guard gates, Iceberg sure as hell wasn't going to hide like a field mouse, not with his friend Salvatore possibly in danger, not with his crew out there on *Atlantis* . . . and not with Panther in the Launch Control Center. Although he was still an active-duty Colonel in the USAF, it had been years since he'd participated in war exercises. As an astronaut, he lived in a different world entirely. He wasn't sure he was ready for this.

Well, he'd just have to refresh his memory.

Iceberg crawled toward the guard shack and made a hundred yards before he reassessed the situation. His foot hurt like a son of a bitch, but after the destroyed copter, NASA Security might shoot first and ask questions later. He had to be slick and quiet, a snake in the grass until he knew what was going on.

He kept in the lee of the small dunes, crouching beneath and behind the thick underbrush, Georgia pines, tangled creepers intent on breaking his other foot. His clumsily rushed evasion tactics weren't good enough to thwart a full-fledged search, but at least he wasn't calling attention to himself.

Still hidden, Iceberg came to an abrupt halt, astonished.

Down the road from the guard shack, black-and-white smoke rolled up into the sky from three motionless security ATVs. One rested on its side, where it had blown up. Bodies of the security team lay sprawled half out of the vehicles; bullet holes looked like starbursts on the black ATVs. The men and women had been mowed down, a total slaughter.

He listened, straining for the sounds of sirens, but he heard nothing. No rescue vehicles, no backup troops. Everything was too damned quiet!

He started crawling forward again, his inner alarm bells ringing. Far ahead, he saw a lone figure step out of the small, metal-walled shack. At least Salvatore would be able to tell him what was going on. . . .

Iceberg rose, intending to wave, when he noticed that this rangy man was smaller and thinner than the old guard's tall figure. The stranger wore the uniform of a NASA security guard, but he made no move toward the scattered bodies, the smoldering ATV wreckage. He took a long drag from a cigarette, then walked around the shack by the off-road motorbike, kneeling to inspect some wires in the grass. He reminded Iceberg of a Doberman on patrol in an equipment yard.

Iceberg dug out his small field glasses, straining to see what the man was doing. He had intended to use the little binoculars to watch the shuttle lift off, to see the solid rocket boosters ignite—now he watched a terrorist's preparations instead.

The strange guard looked small and shifty, out of place, with long hair tied back in a ponytail. He tucked down the collar of his security uniform. Iceberg turned the focusing knob until he spotted cables running from the man's position to a battery of . . . *rifles* mounted on tripods?

Iceberg discerned a dark clump propped against the back of the hut. He swung his binoculars over toward the weeds and squinted. With a sharp intake of breath, he recognized Salvatore. The old guard's head hung on his chest at an unnatural angle, as if he had been carelessly dumped there.

The impostor guard seemed satisfied with the cable connections. He surveyed the area again, then flicked the butt of his cigarette off into the long grass. He lit up another one, then sat down casually in the colorful folding lawn chair, holding an assault rifle, waiting.

18

LAUNCHPAD PERIMETER

Sitting in an Armored Personnel Carrier a mile away from the launchpad was the ultimate job for a firefighter.

The APC's heavy armor would shield the two-person crew from the ignition blast or unexpected debris; the top hatch was required to be closed during the countdown ever since, contrary to NASA regulations, one crew had been caught sitting exposed on top of their armored vehicle gawking at the launch.

If something went wrong with the shuttle before it lifted from the pad, the astronauts would try to escape. As the crew rode emergency baskets down the long escape wires, the APC would roar toward the terminus to pick them up. The astronauts could hole up in fortified bunkers, but if the danger was great enough, and if the firefighters had time, the astronauts could scramble inside the APC and rumble away in relative safety.

Standard emergency procedures, frequently reviewed, but hopefully never required.

The two-person rescue crew sat inside their vehicle, routinely ready but not expecting problems. In all previous launches, the APC had roared into action only once—when a computer glitch had shut down the shuttle main engines after ignition, but before the solid rocket boosters had lit. In that instance, the emergency procedures had worked perfectly, as expected.

So when the sirens blared, distant gunshots rang out, and the helicopter exploded overhead, the rescue crew was justifiably startled.

The APC commander grabbed her radio. "Launch Control, APC here. I'm picking up sirens, and we've detected an explosion. Is there a problem? Should we evacuate the crew?"

Launch Control sounded tense. "Negative, APC. This is part of a, uh, planned exercise. No further data at this time."

"Planned exercise? We haven't been notified! A helicopter just exploded!"

"I say again, keep on hold, APC. Take no action. Control out."

The commander frowned and picked up her checklist, then tossed it aside in disgust. She unbuckled from her seat.

"How can they have a planned exercise without reading us into it?" Her crewman turned as she struggled to stand in the cramped compartment. The adjoining compartment had enough room to hold the astronauts, but the command alcove was jammed with radios, computer screens, and high-tech video systems.

The APC commander started to undo the upper

hatch. "I'm going to take a look-see. 'Take no action'—give me a break!"

"But the checklist—"

The commander ignored her partner as she swung the hatch up with a grunt. The muggy air mixed with the metallic, air-conditioned clamminess of the vehicle. She pushed her shoulders out to look around.

She never felt the bullet take off the back of her head.

Jacques shot the bitch between the eyes before she had a chance to cry out. Moments earlier he'd been wondering how he would get the rescue team to open the APC hatch—but they'd done so without even being asked.

"*Merci*," he said.

As the bitch slumped down, he shoved her body back inside and clambered on top of the opening. A frightened voice squawked from within the APC.

Jacques bent down into the armored vehicle, knocking the corpse aside. A helmeted head turned toward him, and Jacques saw a young man, quite good-looking. Too bad to have to waste good meat. The crewman tried to disentangle himself from his commander's bloodied body that had toppled onto him, and groped for his side arm.

Jacques pumped two quick shots into the young man's chest. He hoped the bullets wouldn't rattle around the closed compartment, where a ricochet might damage the equipment. The young man gurgled and tried to catch himself, sliding down onto the metal floor.

Jacques leaned back out of the APC, turned around,

and descended the ladder into the vehicle. Pulling his small tool kit inside, he closed the hatch.

He picked up the dead crewman by his shoulders and dragged him to the adjoining compartment meant to carry rescued astronauts. He ran a hand over the young man's cheek, now lolling against the chest. Such nice, soft skin . . .

Straightening, he pulled the bitch's body by an arm and tossed her on top of the young man, out of his way.

Now, to assess the situation. He took a moment to familiarize himself with the APC instrumentation, smearing blood away from one digital readout; the interior of the vehicle looked like a wall-to-wall video-game. Everything was in place, just as Mr. Phillips had promised. Good. Jacques fumbled in his pants and pulled out a portable beeper and pushed the button several times, sending the next expected signal.

He squatted, opening his tool kit to reveal a jumble of metal parts. Working patiently and methodically, he assembled a 7.62-mm FR-G2 high-powered sniper's rifle. After wiping the barrel with a cloth, he carefully attached a laser bore sighter to zero in the rifle. It took a few precious minutes, but it was worth it for the increase in accuracy. He'd wait here, a mole in their safety net, as the rifle's eight-hundred-meter range was well within the astronauts' terminus point.

No one would suspect a thing.

19

LAUNCH CONTROL CENTER

Mr. Phillips used a pocket mirror that he had borrowed, at gunpoint, from one of Senator Boorman's aides. He stroked his eyebrows with a fingertip, then took his comb to straighten his hair. He wanted to be sure he made a good first impression.

He brushed the front of his suit jacket, dismayed at the rumpled quality it had acquired from his exertion in the humid air outside. Now, in the heavily air-conditioned LCC, he felt uncomfortably clammy. He hadn't planned to perspire so much. The careful organization of his entire scheme should have allowed him to pull it off without breaking into a sweat—but he had to be flexible.

"Very well," Mr. Phillips said and handed the mirror back to the terrified aide. "Thank you." When she seemed afraid to retrieve it, he snapped, "I don't have all day!" Like a skittish rodent she grabbed the mirror

and tucked it back into her purse. Mr. Phillips regained
his composure and turned to Rusty. "How do I look?"

"Definitely ready for TV, Mr. Phillips," the redhead said with a grin.

"Just as I thought." He pulled out the short step
stool one of the LCC workers had retrieved from an office down the hall and climbed up to stand an additional
foot taller. "The camera never knows the illusion,"
he said sotto voce. He smiled self-deprecatingly at
the hostages, then popped another breath mint in his
mouth.

Andrei Trovkin glared coldly, furious at him, as he
expected; Senator Boorman held his mouth tight, as if
he were trying to figure out how to cut a deal somehow.

The Launch Director herself seemed a mass of conflicting impulses. Most of the archival pictures he had
seen of Nicole Hunter had been taken during astronaut
training events, and she looked quite different now in
her navy suit and pants, white silk shirt, delicate gold
necklace. He knew from his research that she had been
one of the VIP observers at the Ariane explosion in
French Guiana, so when he announced his own connection to that spectacular explosion, she would be
well aware of what he could accomplish. It would be
quite amusing to watch her reaction.

Down the half flight of stairs Yvette paced in front
of the badge-locked door to the main firing floor, keeping the stymied engineers at their stations, not knowing what to do with the launch countdown on hold.

Mr. Phillips stood on the step stool and peered
around, running his well-rehearsed speech over in his
head. Rusty's stock videotape of old shuttle-launch
footage would soon run out in the TV relay bunker,

letting the NASA televisions see the real *Atlantis* again now that his team had secured their objective. If the government would just accede to his demands, everybody could live happily ever after.

"Show time! Cameras on me, please," he said to the captive reporters. "I have the announcement you've all been waiting for." He whispered conspiratorially over at Nicole. "I'm a little nervous, so wish me luck."

"You'll need it," she said with an edge to her voice.

One of the cameramen panned around the VIP deck, focusing on the nervous expressions of the hostages. Mr. Phillips clapped his hands like a gunshot. "I said cameras on *me*! Rusty, if you could provide a reminder the next time anyone diverts their attention from the real story?"

"Definitely, Mr. Phillips," Rusty said, and waved his pistol around.

Mr. Phillips sniffed at the wayward cameraman. "Mr. Channel Seven—make sure you get the focus right. This is real news for once in your life." Embarrassed and angered, the reporter ducked behind his video cam.

"Good morning, and thank you for your attention," Mr. Phillips began. It wasn't the Gettysburg Address, but he had worked hard on the speech. "You may call me Mr. Phillips, since we are about to enter into business dealings.

"The space shuttle is mankind's flagship into space, our vehicle to take us to the future. But some of you have forgotten how precious, how complex . . . how *expensive* our shuttle is. Many have grown bored with the near-flawless performance of this marvel of technólogy. Today, the American people must decide how much it is worth to them.

"Because I believe the space shuttle is so precious, I'm going to sell you its safety. My colleagues and I have planted explosives on *Atlantis*, and if you agree to pay my very reasonable price, I will *not* blow it up." He smiled sweetly for the camera.

"My team has secured the entire area around the launchpad for the purpose of these negotiations. We have already demonstrated our resolve in numerous ways, as NASA can attest.

"This"—he held up a small remote control device—"will detonate the explosives, if I so choose. I know numbers are tiresome, but let me explain that there are over a million pounds of propellant in each of *Atlantis*'s two solid rocket boosters, plus one point six million pounds of liquid hydrogen and oxygen in the external tank. Enough to make quite an explosion.

"We all recall the *Challenger* disaster. Another such occurrence—especially a preventable one— would be a devastating blow to American prestige, not to mention the loss of the brave astronauts who are even now waiting in the shuttle pending the outcome of our discussions. I'm sure my hostages here at the Launch Control Center would be equally disappointed. I'll ask the cameras to pan across our distinguished visitors, so you can see the guests I have with me."

Rusty prodded the cameraman, who turned his video cam on Nicole, Trovkin, and Senator Boorman. They looked grim-faced into the lens.

"The problem with gold, or even paper money, is that it tends to get very heavy in large quantities, and I am unfortunately limited to the amount I'm able to carry conveniently. I must get the most value per pound of ransom,'' Mr. Phillips continued. ''Therefore, I'm asking for a single sturdy briefcase, dimensions not smaller than twenty inches wide by fourteen inches tall by four inches thick, stuffed chock full of diamonds and other precious gems. Rubies, emeralds, sapphires . . . oh, and I have a particular fondness for alexandrite. Each gem in an individual packet marked with carat, color, and clarity, the way they come at diamond wholesalers. No gems smaller than one carat, please, and no larger than two. Decent quality stones, of course.''

He knew that world-class gems were frequently traceable, and that their true worth would be severely devalued when he had to sell them through various black-market outlets, but he had no doubt he could still turn a decent profit. Gems he could liquidate for ready cash anywhere in the world, while Swiss bank accounts did not always remain secret. Besides, after the debacle he had personally witnessed on Wall Street, he wanted nothing more to do with electronic transfers of funds.

''I have a loupe, a Mohs' scale, and gemology expertise, so don't play games with me. I intend to select fifty stones at random and test them for authenticity. If I find any fakes—and I *will* find them—then I would have no choice but to void our transaction.'' He frowned sternly.

''While it's impossible for me to assign an exact dollar amount for such a suitcase full of gems, you'll realize that the price is quite a bargain, regardless. The replacement cost of a new spacecraft is close to two billion dollars, not to mention the amount of time it would take, since our country has foolishly mothballed the production facilities for additional orbiters.''

Mr. Phillips folded his hands in front of him. "These are my terms: You have four hours for the suitcase to be delivered here, along with a rescue helicopter for myself and my team; then we will be on our way. If everything goes smoothly, *Atlantis* can even blast off tomorrow to meet its launch schedule with the *Mir* station."

"How do we know you're not bluffing?" Senator Boorman said.

Rusty swung the heavy handgun directly at the senator, who turned gray and held his big hands up in surrender. The cameraman from channel 7 wavered the lens toward Boorman, then remembered Mr. Phillips's threat and swung the focus back to where it was.

"Excuse me, Senator, but I have not yet yielded the floor." He frowned. "However, since I've been so rudely interrupted—by a man who should know better, being thoroughly familiar with Roberts Rules of Order—if you check your records you will find that an unmanned Chinese Long March rocket was destroyed at its launch complex eleven months ago. We were responsible for that. Also, we exploded an Ariane 44L rocket in Kourou, French Guiana, some six months ago, and can offer proof." He held up the remote. "Don't make us prove our skills again, please."

From her seat, Nicole Hunter looked at him in amazement. "The Ariane! You did—" Then she cut herself off, as if to deny him the pleasure of her surprise.

He reached into the front pocket of his suit and removed the mission patch he had taken from the hapless security guard where Duncan now held the perimeter. He tossed it on the counter and gestured toward it.

"Focus in on this," he said quickly and quietly. The cameras crowded closer. The new mission patch, not yet released to anyone but the astronauts themselves, showed a colorful design collaboratively chosen by the Russian and American crew—an eagle and bear reaching toward the stars. Mr. Phillips waited a moment as the cameras zoomed in on the original three astronaut names written across the top: FRIESE, GREEN, BURNS; the other four names were written on the bottom.

"The choice is yours," Mr. Phillips said. "Do you want to lose a two-billion-dollar spacecraft, as well as the lives of seven heroic astronauts, for the sake of a few shiny rocks?" He pulled out his pocket watch, flipped it open, and paused for effect. "You have four hours. Please don't make me destroy this marvel of engineering. Thank you for your time."

He smiled. "I now return you to your regularly scheduled programming."

20

GUARD SHACK

Iceberg ducked out of sight of the impostor guard, the man who had murdered Salvatore. He drew in several breaths, trying to clear his head, but his pulse wouldn't slow.

Armored ATVs blown up, a whole NASA security team wiped out, a helicopter detonated in midair. And his friend the old guard was dead! The bastards. Iceberg drew in several more breaths, trying to stay calm, to keep his hands from shaking in rage.

Cool.

Chill.

Frosty.

It had always sounded good before, but now he had to put it into practice.

Okay, he thought. What to do? He switched his priorities from finding out what was going on to just trying to survive. But no way was he going to hide under a bush until someone else took care of the problem. The SERE training he'd taken at the USAF Academy sure as hell hadn't covered this—but it *had* taught him to react. The leathery-faced sergeant who had instructed the cadets had insisted that these techniques were applicable in a wide variety of situations. Time to prove it.

Iceberg tried to restore his cold facade while going over the options. Think! He had to find out for certain if Salvatore was really dead, or if the old man needed medical attention . . . and he sure couldn't waltz up to the shack and take the motionless guard's pulse.

But earlier this morning he *had* scrambled to within a mile of the launchpad without being detected by NASA's most sophisticated sensors; sneaking close to one guy at a guard shack should be a cakewalk by comparison.

Iceberg scooted on his hands and knees across the thick weeds and vines, careful to avoid bumping his foot cast. The mosquitoes found him easily; small animals rustled through the underbrush. He just hoped he didn't spook a snoozing alligator.

Iceberg counted off paces as he moved. Every time he reached a hundred, he peeked over a small rise or peered between bushes to check his progress. The impostor guard sat in his lawn chair, arms crossed over his chest as he surveyed the carnage, a thin smile on his face. The man stretched, then got up and went back inside the shack to watch his TV monitor.

Iceberg ducked and continued moving. Slide and scoot, keeping his tender foot protected, careful not to make any noise. It infuriated him that he couldn't just rush to the shack and see if he could help Salvatore.

He lost count of the minutes, but finally Iceberg

found himself within twenty yards. He saw little or no cover on three sides of the shack and the road—only short, scrubby grass and sandy-muddy dirt torn up in patches from the nocturnal rootings of the prevalent wild pigs.

He rose to a crouch and starting jogging through the tall weeds as fast as his broken foot and its dragging cast would allow him, gaining momentum in a strange, hippity-hop stride. He hid, panting, beside the three-wheeled vehicle Salvatore had used to patrol the KSC backroads.

Inside the shack, with his back turned, the pony-tailed thug rocked back in his chair as he watched the TV monitors. The image of *Atlantis* filled one of the screens while Nicole Hunter and Senator Boorman showed on another. Even with the quick glance he got, Iceberg could tell Nicole looked visibly upset.

Iceberg crept around the side of the hut. His heart yammered, his hands grew slick with sweat. The sounds from the TV were louder now. The thug laughed at something on the broadcast, then tossed a cigarette butt out the door of the shack.

Finally reaching Salvatore's slumped form discarded like a piece of garbage, Iceberg found that the old guard's chest didn't move at all, and his head lolled at an impossible angle, as if his neck had been snapped. Dead—no question about it.

Iceberg felt his anger mount. With an icy determination hardening in his gut, he quietly patted down Salvatore's body but found no weapon. The impostor guard must have stripped the old guard of his gun.

Inside the shack, the thug stood up. He turned down the sound on the TV, stepping cautiously outside.

Iceberg cursed, having lost his element of surprise

without even developing a plan of attack. He desperately wished he had some sort of weapon, anything. He flexed his hands, knowing he'd run out of time.

The long-haired impostor popped around the corner of the shack, Salvatore's pistol drawn. "Gotcha, mate!"

Iceberg plunged into the leafy underbrush to one side of the guard shack, ducking, tearing vines out of the way. He stumbled on weeds and interlocked bushes that smacked against the hard shell of his cast and its protective moon boot.

"Yo!" the impostor shouted. "Bad idea." With sharp cracks, he began firing his pistol. Iceberg watched a branch splinter less than a foot away from his head; another bright tan gouge suddenly appeared on the trunk of a pine. He ducked and weaved, Escape and Evasion, unable to traverse a straight path through the swamp forest even if he had wanted to. The thick underbrush and his broken foot prevented him from moving quickly.

Iceberg dropped to his hands and knees, making progress through the thicket toward the road where the wrecked NASA security vehicles lay. If he could just manage to get there, take brief shelter behind the ruined ATVs, he could find a weapon inside, even if he had to tear it from the hands of dead NASA security personnel. At least he'd be able to shoot back.

The impostor fired again, and a bullet tore through the weeds behind him. He had gotten ahead of where the long-haired man thought he was.

Iceberg finally reached a spot even with the nearest smoldering ATV, but he would have to cross at least fifteen feet of open terrain to get to the vehicle. He'd be a sitting duck if he tried to cross the clearing.

No more wasted time thinking about possibilities. He had to make a run for it. *Three, two, one . . . go!*

Instinctively, he wanted to give a battle yell, but Iceberg clamped his lips shut. Silence might gain him an instant more time. He charged out of the underbrush straight toward the vehicles. His foot screamed in pain, but he told it to shut up. Cover, shelter . . . weapons.

The impostor spun toward him, running full out, cursing and trying to aim his pistol.

Iceberg put on extra speed with his strange, lurching gait. His foot felt as if a bear trap had just closed about it.

The impostor shot once. The bullet grazed past him, just missing. That was too close.

Iceberg saw another glint of metal out of the corner of his left eye, the dark blue steel of three rifle barrels. In the bushes next to the road he saw the unattended weapons mounted on tripods, automatic assault rifles. And tripwires.

"Holy shit!" he cried, then spun about, diving to the ground in the opposite direction. Iceberg skidded across the scrubby grass just as the automatic weapons fire spat out, criss-crossing the air where he had just stood.

Now he lay out in the open, in the middle of the grassy clearing, with no shelter in sight.

The impostor ran forward, his pistol waving. "You're making this too easy for me, mate!"

Iceberg covered his head with his hands, squeezing his eyes shut, trying to sink into the ground. He couldn't just lie here and be shot. He'd have to run, crawl, do anything. But there was no cover, no weapons, no way in hell of surviving. . . .

The next sound was a *boom* as loud as a cannon shot.

Chunks of turf and dirt rained around him, and Iceberg looked up to see a dissipating explosion, as if a small volcano had erupted out of the ground. He saw no sign of the long-haired impostor, only a crater in the grass. The mud pattering all around had a decidedly reddish tinge.

A land mine! The thug had stepped on one of his own land mines! Iceberg got to his hands and knees, stunned and disbelieving.

Iceberg stood up on shaky legs, looked around him at the rough grass, the patches of muddy dirt, the numerous gouges that he had thought were caused by the common wild boars . . . but now might simply be the marks of buried land mines.

Buried explosives all around.

Swallowing in his dry throat, Iceberg very gingerly made his way back to the guard shack. . . . Of course, the impostor guard's gun had also been blasted somewhere, lost in the underbrush . . . even if it did remain serviceable. He needed a weapon, but he had no intention of prodding around in a minefield looking for it.

Finally reaching the shack, he felt as if he had participated in a marathon gymnastics meet back at the Academy in Colorado Springs. Still gasping for breath, he straightened Salvatore's chair and flopped down, barely keeping himself from passing out. His foot throbbed like a pile driver.

From the small building he had an unobstructed view of Phillips Highway, the north-south road coming in from Cape Canaveral, as well as the east-west access road. The terrorists must have considered it a good place to set up an ambush. Smoke still rose from the shot-up and burning security ATVs.

Panting, he glanced around the shack. Everything on the monitors looked serene, no movement.

But the main screen showed some smartass effete twerp. Iceberg caught his name as Phillips. As he listened, it dawned on Iceberg that the space shuttle was being held for ransom. *Atlantis*—his crew! That's what all this was about.

Iceberg felt as if a ton of gravel had been poured on him. The smoking ruins of the security ATVs, the downed helicopter, and Salvatore's murder confirmed that these people were not jokers. Whoever the slimeballs were, they held the upper hand.

For now.

The dapper man disappeared from the TV, leaving a shot of Nicole, Ambassador Trovkin, and Senator Boorman. They all looked worried.

Mr. Phillips returned and threw something onto a counter; the camera focused on a crew patch—and on the names FRIESE, GREEN, BURNS embroidered at the top. It was the patch Iceberg had given Salvatore that morning.

He felt his face grow red, pissed off beyond words. He glared at the monitor. Mr. Phillips looked as if he were speaking directly to Iceberg, taunting him. Iceberg turned up the volume.

"—four hours. Please don't make me destroy this marvel of engineering. . . ."

After the little man finished his speech, the radio on the counter sputtered. "We've got NASA on the run. All sites please check in."

He recognized the voice he had heard on TV!

Clipped voices came over the radio. Mr. Phillips's

voice acknowledged them, until he repeated something about a guard shack—then it hit Iceberg that the voice was talking to *him*. He felt a sudden chill. If he didn't answer, they would know something had happened to the fake guard.

Mr. Phillips's voice came again, this time with an edge to it. "Duncan? Are you still at the guard shack? Check in."

Iceberg picked up the microphone and clicked it twice. The international signal for "okay." That seemed to satisfy Phillips and the radio fell silent. He slumped back against Salvatore's old desk. "Chill, chill, chill," he said. He ran a hand through his short dark hair. "Have I just given this Phillips guy a green light?"

He picked up the telephone in the shack, but the line was dead. The impostor had smashed all of Salvatore's radio equipment. Aside from the fixed-frequency walkie-talkie that was tuned to Phillips alone, Iceberg had no communications gear at all.

Which meant no one knew he was out here. Including Mr. Phillips.

He felt sick to his stomach. Phillips had NASA over a barrel. Iceberg wasn't sure what he could do, but he had to do something.

He could never let Gator Green and the rest of his crew on *Atlantis* wait for bureaucrats to negotiate the hostage situation. Knowing this Administration, they'd be more concerned about being politically correct than stopping the terrorists. Iceberg had to take matters into his own hands. It might be the only way to save his crew.

Part of him realized it might be the only way to save Panther, as well.

21

GUARD SHACK

Iceberg yelped as he forgot himself and put his full weight on his left foot. He hopped up and grabbed his heavy cast, drawing a breath through his teeth. "Can't let that happen again." He had more important things to worry about, like a bunch of terrorists.

But what should he do? He gripped the door frame of the guard shack. Phillips had finished his tirade on the television, and now commentators excitedly chattered about what it all meant. Iceberg tried to think calmly, get hold of his senses. He swung into "checklist" mode, that detached state where he put his body into autopilot while his mind raced ahead.

He took a long, full breath. He had to think clearly, plan every move, be calm. Frosty.

He had to get through to NASA Security, let them know that this strategic point was no longer held by the bad guys. A sufficient force could easily pass through the gate.

But what would that accomplish? The shack was miles from the Launch Control Center as well as the launchpad. If Phillips really did have his people stationed throughout the restricted area, then it would do no good for security to show up here. They'd just provoke Phillips to push the button. The counterstrike would have to be more subtle than that, quieter—something a single man could accomplish.

NASA should have been able to control the TV relay bunker, cutting off the little twerp's grandstanding. A chill ran through Iceberg. *Amos*. Was he okay? What if his little brother's bunker had been overrun like Salvatore's guard shack?

Then Iceberg remembered that the bunker was protected well enough to withstand a direct explosion: thick walled, reinforced, one of the old blast observation shelters from the Apollo launches. Since the communications lines were still open, Amos must be all right. Maybe Phillips had insisted on making a televised speech. Terrorists loved to hear themselves talk.

Meanwhile, Iceberg's crew were trapped as hostages on board *Atlantis*, sitting ducks on the launchpad. Knowing NASA bureaucracy, they were probably given no reason and thought they were waiting on an indefinite hold—and all the while they were pawns for a ridiculous ransom.

Maybe if Iceberg could get in touch with Gator Green directly, he could convince the crew to exit the shuttle, take cover in the emergency bunkers. That would remove one of Phillips's major bargaining chips.

The thought of getting the crew out of danger—*his*

crew—gave Iceberg a renewed sense of hope, and a motivation that he could somehow strike back. He couldn't ask for more.

Dragging his cast, he limped behind the shack to where the three-wheeled all-terrain buggy had been parked. He set his mouth at the sight of Salvatore's body, slumped against the back wall. Iceberg knew the space program had been the old man's life; every memento in the small shack reflected Salvatore's enthusiasm for NASA—the shuttle patches, a picture of Salvatore and his wife with the crew of Apollo 10.

Reverently, feeling queasy in his stomach, Iceberg hauled the old guard into the shack and laid him on the floor. Panting, breaking into a sweat from the pain and his own grief, Iceberg straightened Salvatore, then reached up to turn off the TV monitor, which continued to replay ''news analysis'' and sound bites. ''No need for you to have to listen to that garbage.''

One of the news broadcasts replayed the ransom demand while hastily conscripted ''experts'' discussed other hostage crises. Like Nicole, everybody wanted to talk the situation to death. But that was typical nowadays—they'd rather flash a Vu-graph showing the possibilities than make a commitment. At least Iceberg intended to *do* something.

Limping, he grabbed his daypack and thought again about obtaining a weapon, but he didn't dare risk running the gauntlet of buried land mines to reach the tripod-mounted rifles, which were themselves wired to motion sensors. He'd look mighty stupid if he got himself mowed down with nobody else around to shoot at him.

No, he wasn't planning to get into a shootout. He was just going to make a call to the shuttle cockpit.

Next procedure, just like going through a "Dash-One." One thing at a time on the checklist.

He limped around back to the small three-wheeler. With its fat balloon tires and putt-putt engine, the little ATV was the only way he could get around fast enough to make a difference. He'd have to chuck the E and E'ing, and hope that Mr. Phillips had only enough people to cover critical points around the restricted area. No one expected Iceberg to be here, already inside.

Iceberg climbed on the three-wheeled buggy, gingerly lifting his cast and its now muddy covering over the seat, and pushed the starter. He revved the flat-sounding engine that sent up blue-white coils of exhaust. He knew of one other place inside the restricted area that had the necessary radio equipment to contact his crew, another place that should have been cleared of personnel for the launch.

Spinning the fat tires, he made off overland for the towering Vehicle Assembly Building, a good three miles away.

The ride was bumpy, but no more so than the off-road biking he'd done at the sand dunes south of here during the early months of astronaut training, him and Nicole on the weekends, blazing their own trails, exploring. Their relationship had crashed and burned, but at least Iceberg knew the terrain of the KSC and its surrounding Merritt Island National Wildlife Sanctuary.

The Vehicle Assembly Building loomed larger as he sped for the massive squarish structure. Heading west, he couldn't see the multistory American flag painted on the front; it dwarfed everything around, and beside it was the red-white-and-blue rounded star of the Bicentennial symbol.

From his perspective, the VAB looked like a huge white monument, jutting up alone in the swamplands. It towered high above the flat terrain like a giant's building block on the edge of the wide and sluggish Banana Creek, which was used as a turn basin for barges bearing the shuttle's external fuel tanks. Parallel tracks of multilayered gravel formed the crawlerway, the straight path used to haul the massive launch-prepped orbiters from the VAB out to the pad.

Coming in overland, Iceberg flew from the soft, weed-covered ground onto the concrete parking lot. Iceberg headed for the half-open giant hangar doors that could raise up in sections and slide sideways to allow rocket assemblies to emerge on slow-moving crawler vehicles. The sound of his vehicle puttered like shots from a toy machine gun, but he saw no indication of anyone around to hear him.

He shut the buggy's engine down, then swung off the padded seat, grabbing his pack. He hobbled across the concrete apron toward the cool, shadowy interior of the VAB, a mouse entering a hole in the wall.

The inside of the building was as voluminous as five Empire State Buildings. It echoed like a giant man-made cave as he stepped inside. Metal-gray structures meshed with the cement floor. A forklift at the other end of the building looked like a toy in the distance. The ceiling yawned nearly two hundred feet above him, and the opposite wall was a football field away. If he looked up, he would get dizzy from the myriad catwalks incredibly high above. Iceberg had heard engineers say that clouds sometimes formed at the top of the stratospheric high bay.

Two solid rocket motor engines hung in a preparation carriage, mounted to the tall structure of the Mobile Launcher Platform, ready to be mated to the next shuttle due to come into the assembly bay. The previous orbiter, *Endeavour*, had recently completed its long, slow journey out to launchpad 39B, scheduled for launch not long after *Atlantis*. Already the VAB was prepped for the next orbiter, *Discovery*, currently undergoing reconditioning in the Orbiter Processing Facility.

Business as usual at America's Spaceport, he thought. But a lot of things would change after today.

With his limping jog, Iceberg quickly reached the downstairs command post at the side of the VAB high bay, an office that served as a checkpoint for all shuttle moving operations.

The glass door was locked. Great. At least they didn't have alarms rigged to these internal offices.

He spotted a rack of tools fastened to the wall, each item marked with a code-locator number. He unlatched a long wrench, painted sky-blue for easy finding, and returned to the glass door. Turning his head, he smashed the window out just above the handle, then reached in to open the door from the inside.

Transparent walls around the room gave supervisors an unobstructed view of all shuttle assembly activities inside the bay. The desk held two phones, a radio, check sheet, clipboards, and a stained coffee cup that looked as if it hadn't been washed since Apollo-Soyuz.

As he entered the office, Iceberg saw a radio. Switching it on, Iceberg tuned to the main shuttle comm frequency. Gator's voice came over the speaker, querying about the extended countdown hold and receiving only a double-talk answer.

With a sigh of relief, Iceberg swung a swivel chair around and slumped down, grateful to take weight off his foot. He could count on Gator Green, his best friend and the best damned pilot he had ever known—next to himself, of course.

When the *Atlantis* crew had flown from Houston cross-country to KSC, two per aircraft, Gator had piloted while Iceberg rode behind him in the backseat of the T-38. The crew had roared eastward in a dawn flight to arrive in Florida at mid-morning, landing their four jets on the sparkling runway.

During the flight, the two friends had a chance for plenty of conversation, lightweight banter, and cautious questions until Gator finally asked him about Panther, how she had left the astronaut corps to be a desk jockey. Iceberg had been bitter, while Gator had been quite understanding, even defending Nicole—but then Gator never managed to speak ill of anyone. Iceberg had shut down his own emotions, refusing to understand Nicole's point of view, preferring his own explanations.

The jets had touched down, taxiing forward to meet the small group of news representatives, NASA Security with explosives-sniffing dogs snooping around the news vans, and a few cheering family members and supporters. It seemed to Iceberg a pitifully small crowd. He and the *Atlantis* crew gathered around a microphone for the standard-issue rah-rah speech, then marched off to crew debriefing and, later, isolation in prep for the launch several weeks away.

Iceberg remembered that newly appointed Launch Director Nicole Hunter had been in the crowd that day, standing quietly in the back, making no statements and refusing to meet his eye.

Now, in the VAB, Iceberg thought briefly about trying to get hold of Nicole directly. But she was a hostage in Launch Control, and he couldn't afford to let the terrorists know what was going on. She would just have to trust his instincts.

Picking up the microphone, he punched in one of the private frequencies from memory. No way did he intend to let Phillips know he was out here by using the main comm channel. "Gator, Iceberg. Do you read?" He waited a moment. Nothing. He tried again. "Gator, Iceberg—do you read me? This is urgent."

Still nothing. Crap. He'd hoped at least someone in the crew would be listening to the science channels used by payload specialists to run their onboard experiments. Typically, NASA didn't trust the science geeks on Earth to communicate directly with the astronauts, but the old ways were changing. So if no one was listening now, that meant either the crew didn't know what was going on outside the shuttle, or the payload specialists had switched off those frequencies.

He punched in the main comm frequency. "Gator, Iceberg—Payload Button two." He immediately switched to a prearranged frequency the crew would know from the checklist, but nothing happened. He tried again. "Come on, dammit!"

Seconds later a cautious voice came over the radio. "Iceberg?"

Iceberg felt his heart yammer. *Yes!* He leaned forward in his chair, forgetting the ordeal he had undergone the last half hour. "Gator, I don't have much time."

"Iceberg, what the hell are you doing on this channel? CAPCOM will have a fit! Where are you?"

"Gator, shut up. I've got something important to tell you."

22

ATLANTIS

Gator switched off the onboard radio in cold astonishment. Iceberg's voice had been broadcast over the shuttle's main intercom system to the entire crew, breathlessly asserting that *Atlantis* was being held hostage. It chilled him to realize that the news explained a lot of the strange happenings.

The shuttle's cockpit windows stared up and ahead, straight up into the blue Florida sky—effectively blinding them to anything happening on the ground away from the launchpad.

He looked over as Dr. Marc Franklin snorted. "What's the matter, Marc?" Gator asked. "You don't believe him?"

Franklin looked disgusted. "Lieutenant Commander Green, your friend has gone one step too far in his practical jokes. Don't you think we'd have been able to verify this before his call? How many other channels of information do we have coming into the shuttle?''

''And how many times has CAPCOM refused to answer our questions about this indefinite hold?'' he said defensively. ''If the LCC has been taken over, like Iceberg said—''

''It's a piss-poor joke. That cowboy may be amused by his stupid fighter-pilot pranks, but a stunt like this could cost us the mission—and his career.'' Franklin picked up the checklist, as if it might have an answer for him. ''Since he can't fly himself, he wants to ground us, too.''

Alexandra Koslovsky's voice came from behind and below in her mission specialist's chair. ''This team knows Colonel Iceberg well enough, Dr. Franklin. He understands difference between joking and seriousness.''

Franklin twisted in his seat and frowned down at the pretty cosmonaut as if he couldn't believe what she had said.

''Standard procedure, Marc,'' Gator spoke up. ''We've got to check this out. Iceberg has more respect for this shuttle—and for us—than any other person in NASA. Just check it out.''

''Great,'' muttered Franklin, his voice dripping with sarcasm. ''What's going to happen next—mutiny? We abandon ship because he says 'boo'?''

Gator reached up to change the frequency on the main cockpit comm, drawing a deep breath to keep from making a retort that he would regret. If it had been Iceberg sitting in the left-hand seat, Gator would have given a snappy, smartass answer. But Franklin showed all the signs of someone who was in over his head, taking everything personally and listening to no advice.

Gator said, "It won't hurt to ask a few careful questions, just in case. Isn't it strange that CAPCOM hasn't given us any reason for the hold? They always give a reason, even if it's only to cover their own butts."

"Maybe they're too busy trying to get us *out* of this hold."

Gator gritted his teeth. "That's not the way it's supposed to be done. It's not in the checklist, and it sure as hell was never in the simulator. This isn't a green card with a new problem, Marc."

Franklin looked annoyed. "We'll see about this." He reached up and changed the main radio to CAP-COM. He clicked his microphone even as Gator tried to caution him. Franklin brushed him aside. "CAP-COM, *Atlantis*. Do you copy?"

When Nicole Hunter's voice came back, she sounded strained. "*Atlantis*, we need you to sit tight. We're working on a time-critical problem. We're, uh, having difficulty with the comm and need these channels for the engineers to inspect the system. We'll get back to you as soon as we can."

"Hey!" sputtered Gator. "What the hell is Panther doing speaking for Houston CAPCOM? She can't do that!"

Franklin raised his eyebrows at Gator and clicked on the mike. "Copy that, Launch Control. Please be informed that we have received some . . . uh, spurious transmissions on this frequency. Can you verify any unusual problems at LCC? Unauthorized access, for instance—"

Gator flicked off the microphone and grabbed Franklin's elbow. "Careful. You *know* something's

wrong if Launch Control is speaking directly to us—
CAPCOM would never allow that to happen! What if
Iceberg's right?''

Franklin shook off Gator's hand. "Excuse me,
Launch Control—has there been an unscheduled
change in CAPCOM procedures?''

Nicole Hunter's voice came back slowly over the
speaker. "*Atlantis*, we need this channel open. I repeat, we're holding at T minus twenty and your instructions are not to interfere. Copy that?''

"Sorry to bother you, Launch Control. We've had
a communication from Iceberg that—''

Gator grabbed the mike away from him. "Roger
that, Launch. We'll keep quiet. *Atlantis* out." He
switched off the radio, then turned to Franklin. He
could barely control his anger. "What are you thinking, Commander? Houston controls all communications to the crew, not the LCC. They've been cut off
somehow.''

"She's the Launch Director, and we're supposed to
stay put," Franklin said, stubbornly oblivious. "How
much clearer could she have been?''

"She didn't even answer your questions! None of
them. If everything was all right, Houston would be
going apeshit right now. Something is *wrong*.''

Franklin thought for a second, trying to concoct an
excuse that even he could believe. "You heard her:
There's a communications breakdown. And maybe she
didn't understand what I was trying to say.''

It was Gator's turn to snort. "Give me a break,
Commander. Panther not only understood it, but she
confirmed what Iceberg told us.''

"You're crazy.''

"And you're stupider than hell. *Sir*." His frustration

and anger finally drove away his usual good humor. "I just spoke with Panther about Iceberg not more than two hours ago. She knows how he acts—she almost married the guy, and he was commander of this crew until last week. We know him, too. And you're just being dense." Then he dropped his voice, somewhat cowed by his own words. "No disrespect, sir, but this is an emergency situation."

Franklin looked around the cockpit, as if trying to come to grips with the situation. His face hardened, but his overt anger faded. "You really think this ridiculous story is true?"

Gator felt his heart pound harder than he had imagined it would during the actual launch. "I believe *Iceberg*. That's the important part. The scary thing is—what are we going to do about it?"

23

LAUNCH CONTROL CENTER

Nicole switched off the radio link to *Atlantis*, working to keep her expression calm and emotionless, though a hurricane raged inside her. Showing fear, showing panic, showing any sort of indecision would only provoke these terrorists, and she didn't want to give Mr. Phillips an excuse or make anything easier for him.

Iceberg! Here? She struggled to keep her surprise from showing.

She had known the shuttle crew would immediately suspect something out of the ordinary when she called them directly instead of going through Houston CAPCOM. The precedent of using CAPCOM had been set in the Mercury era, when the astronauts would only communicate with one of their own—a Capsule Communicator. Now she'd have to figure out her next step.

She hoped the *Atlantis* crew wouldn't do anything foolish.

Touching the delicate gold key on its chain around her neck, she tried to focus. Her father had called it the key to her future, able to unlock her dreams. But she wouldn't have a future anywhere if she didn't resolve this disaster somehow. She had to assess the situation, put the pieces together, and make some sort of solution *work*.

"Just how long do you expect the crew to wait, Mr. Phillips?" she said, hoping to distract him. She had caught Franklin's comment, and though she couldn't figure out *how* Iceberg had gotten himself involved, she knew that it was just his style. As usual, she wanted to strangle him for barging in like a bulldozer. He never took ill-considered actions, but he never wavered from his determination either, and his stunts might endanger the lives of everyone.

"They'll just have to wait as long as is necessary," the little man answered, annoyance showing on his face. He tapped his fingertips together and paced around the VIP observation deck. "A great deal of forethought went into this operation, Ms. Hunter—perhaps as much as goes into preparing for a shuttle launch. The *Atlantis* crew wasn't supposed to speak to you about the extended hold until"—he pulled out his PDA and flipped it open to scan down the items on his list—"until about ten minutes from now. Fortunately, as with any NASA launch, we have allowed for problems in our own private countdown.

"I do, however, need to determine exactly how the crew was contacted and alerted as to our presence, and how to keep it from happening again. Clearly, someone has clued them in. Feel free to make any helpful suggestions.''

"I'm afraid you would find my suggestions particularly unhelpful," Nicole retorted, "and anatomically impossible to boot."

"Now, now. Don't let the stress get to you," Mr. Phillips said. He picked up a walkie-talkie and depressed the "transmit" button. "Duncan, come in please. Duncan, are you there?" He waited while everyone else in the VIP deck remained motionless, terrified.

Nicole ransacked her brain for something to do but came up with no solutions. She looked down at the rows of concerned engineers and technicians in the security-locked firing room. The LCC workers were clearly restless, their faces either livid or pale. The preposterous situation had already rattled them, but the call from the *Atlantis* crew had pushed many over the brink.

"Come on, Duncan—answer me," Mr. Phillips said into the walkie-talkie.

Rusty snorted. "Probably out taking a piss. You just can't count on some people."

Mr. Phillips shot a sharp glance at him. "Our Duncan is far too much of a professional to wander away." He tried three more times, then slammed the set down. "Something has happened to him. Most distressing."

Nicole fought to hide her hopes.

She did not see how the ruckus started on the firing floor—but in a moment all the technicians and engineers were shouting, clamoring, waving their clenched fists up at the windows for Mr. Phillips to see, while others pushed toward the security-locked doors where Yvette stood guard with her weapon.

"Oh, now what is it?" Mr. Phillips said.

Yvette came sprinting up. "I have smashed the code lock at the door, Monsieur Phillips. I'm not sure they believe our gunmen are standing outside the emergency exits."

Mr. Phillips shook his head, stroking his lapel. "They seem to have a misconception as to their options," he said. "Ms. Hunter, I defer to your authority. Get on the intercom and tell your people to cease this childishness instantly, or I'll ask Rusty to make an example of someone. You'd like that wouldn't you, Rusty?"

"Definitely, Mr. Phillips. There's plenty to choose from."

Nicole gritted her teeth and resisted for just a second. Mr. Phillips picked up on her emotion but did not give her a chance to express it. He spoke coldly. "Ms. Hunter, if you don't make the announcement this instant, I will show you just how unimportant some of these hostages are to me."

Nicole believed him utterly. She grabbed the microphone. Even with her hands tied here, at least she could prevent other people from getting killed. That had to be her first priority.

"This is the Launch Director. Firing Floor, keep it down! You have to sit quiet or these"—she cleared her throat—"these *gentlemen* will start killing hostages. There's nothing you can do from your stations." She prayed under her breath that they would believe her. Their noise quieted to an uneasy muttering. "Let's just wait it out."

"Very good, Ms. Hunter," Mr. Phillips said, straightening his tie. "I should have recruited you as part of our team. Such an aura of command! It sends shivers down my spine. Ever think of using your talent on Wall Street?'' He smiled at her. She glowered back.

Mr. Phillips started pacing. He seemed deeply disturbed about his missing Duncan but struggled to cover it with aloofness. He tapped a finger against his lip. "Let us consider this—we're controlling all communications with the shuttle, but somehow the crew was contacted in the cockpit. The astronauts are aware of our situation, at least partially. So someone has alerted them from the ground. Correct me if I'm wrong, but that must not be a simple thing to do. Otherwise our astronauts would be getting radio solicitation calls from life insurance salesmen as they await the countdown."

Rusty laughed, but Mr. Phillips didn't revel in the humor. He continued his analysis. "Therefore I must assume that with your superhuman abilities as Launch Director, Ms. Hunter, *you* can determine where that bothersome call originated. I want to know immediately." He stopped his pacing and turned to grip the edge of a table. His fingers tightened, as if he were fighting to keep his composure.

Nicole sat down, purposely sliding away from the banks of phones and computer terminals, and crossed her arms over her chest. Iceberg was a pain in the butt, but she would never set him up for these assassins. "If you think I'm going to lift a little finger to help you, you're—"

Mr. Phillips pounded his fist on the counter, losing his cool in an alarming emotional change. "I have no desire to argue the point! I have a precise timetable to keep."

He shifted his flinty gaze from Rusty to Nicole, past the senator and his aides, to the news cameramen. He smoothed his hair, then spoke in measured tones. "Yvette, would you be so kind as to kill one of the cameramen? Our friend Ms. Hunter seems unconvinced of our resolve."

The big blond woman reached into her waist satchel, rummaging among the clanking sharp-bladed exotic weapons she carried.

The cameramen glanced at each other. Two put down their cameras, rigid with fear. Mr. Phillips eyed them dispassionately. "Oh, go ahead and do the one from channel seven. I never liked channel seven."

The singled-out cameraman blinked, unsure what was going on. With a smile of satisfaction Yvette withdrew a strange, looped blade from her collection— a set of brass knuckles with razor-edged sawteeth that looked like wicked shark fins extending from her fist.

"Wait a minute," Nicole blurted, standing up. "Okay, I believe you—"

Mr. Phillips just sighed. "But I'm afraid *I* don't believe *you*, Ms. Hunter—and I don't want to have to go through this discussion every time I make a simple request." He nodded to Yvette.

With a springy step the blond Amazon stalked toward the cameraman like a predator. The man raised his heavy video cam and backed against one of the narrow viewing windows. "Hey, wait a minute," the cameraman squawked as Yvette approached him with calculated slowness, confidence. "I didn't do anything. Hold it!"

Rusty held everyone else at bay with his two big pistols, smiling as he watched the lithe blond. Yvette's pale blue eyes seemed like tiny disks of frost. She swept her bladed fist back and forth, making a swishing sound.

"Mr. Phillips, I told you I would do it." Nicole bolted up and stepped forward. "Stop this bullying behavior. It's . . ." What would affect him? What would get his attention? "It's *uncivilized*."

He looked at her, his eyebrows raised. "Yes, I suppose it is."

Yvette bent over, her eyes narrowing as she coiled to spring. The helpless man held his video cam as if it were a shield. "Back off!"

"Oh, brother! This takes too long." Rusty released the thumb safety, casually pointed his handgun, and fired. With a quick coughing sound, a single bullet slammed into the reporter's chest, smashing him against the wall. Bright red smears ran down the cinderblock where the bullet had penetrated.

Rusty lunged forward to rescue the heavy video cam as the man slumped, gagging and coughing blood. He snatched the camera from rubbery fingers, then held it up and used the fabric of his jumpsuit to polish away two droplets of blood from the lens. "Whew!" he said. "Expensive equipment."

Yvette, thwarted from her enjoyment, glared at Rusty, then moved in on him instead. The redhead stepped back and brought up his handgun.

Mr. Phillips interposed himself between Yvette and Rusty. "Calm down, both of you," he said. "Rusty, you must not be so impulsive. If I can't count on you to follow orders—explicitly—I will consider cutting you from seven-and-a-half percent down to five."

"Hey, Mr. Phillips! You owe me, after all I've—"

"*Yes*, Rusty, as you never fail to remind me. But you must follow the plan and do as I say. Besides, you're stealing all of Yvette's fun."

"Tell her not to take so long next time," he said

petulantly. "Didn't you say we're on a tight schedule?"

"Yes, we are," Mr. Phillips said. "Yvette, perhaps you should try to enjoy yourself a bit less next time."

"*Oui.*" She glanced at Rusty. "*Next time.*"

Senator Boorman gasped, hyperventilating. He stood but was unable to speak. Nicole felt as if she had turned to ice, suffocating in regrets. She should have argued more, insisted that Mr. Phillips stop—or she should have argued less in the first place, did what the terrorist told her to do. It was the coward's way out—but if she had cooperated immediately, that man wouldn't now be dead. He lay soaked in blood on the floor, as if accusing her.

Andrei Trovkin stood up, then sat down again, simmering enough that his black-rimmed eyeglasses seemed on the verge of steaming up. He gazed at Nicole, then at the others, but managed to restrain himself, though he looked as if he wanted to go berserk.

Nicole slumped back in her chair. She gripped the padded arms to keep from trembling. An internal sound like roaring wind passed her ears, but she could not concentrate. *Think. Think!* How could she get out of this?

She needed to draw on all her skills as a coolheaded negotiator, all the politics she had learned after leaving the astronaut program and entering the cutthroat world of upper management. This negotiation had a prize far more important than simple budgetary victories. Shooting off her mouth had just cost the life of an innocent man. She felt powerless—and she suspected that was exactly what Mr. Phillips wanted.

The little man folded his hands in front of him as if he were patiently praying in front of an audience.

"Now that I have your full attention, Ms. Hunter," he said, "I shall ask you again. Where did the radio call come from? Did it come from a would-be hero on the firing floor below? Who is this Iceberg, and how did he get in touch with *Atlantis*? I need to know, and you must tell me."

"No, the call didn't come from the firing floor." Her shoulders slumped. "Iceberg is the call sign for Colonel Adam Friese, the former commander of this mission—and he is definitely not here," she said dully. "It'll take me a minute to track where the call came from."

"Colonel Friese!" Mr. Phillips exclaimed. "The poor man with the broken ankle?"

"Broken foot," Nicole said, pleased to be able to correct him. With numb fingers she punched into the keyboard and studied one of the monitors at the guest station. Behind the glass wall stood her now-unoccupied Launch Director's station on the firing floor, the chair pointedly empty, but she couldn't go down there now. She had to do what she could to solve the mystery from up here.

Mr. Phillips's intuition was right. Very few communications systems had the ability to reach the cockpit directly. Iceberg couldn't have just picked up a radio and spoken to Gator, though he did know the command frequencies. Given the right transmitting equipment, the correct security protocol, he could reach his former crew....

A message flashed up on her terminal, and Nicole sat bolt upright. Of course, the Vehicle Assembly Building!

Mr. Phillips saw her reaction. "Yes, Miss Hunter? And what answer do you have for me?"

"I . . . uh . . ." she mumbled, her mind whirling.

Mr. Phillips tapped his fingers on the countertop, whistling the theme from the game show *Jeopardy*. He nodded to Yvette, who still clenched the razor-edged blade over her knuckles. Nicole got the point.

"The VAB," she said dully. "The Vehicle Assembly Building. That's where the call came from."

Nicole felt a rush of adrenaline. *Iceberg was inside the secure zone.* The VAB had been evacuated well before the launch, and these terrorists claimed to have secured the perimeter beyond that point. But Iceberg had gotten himself trapped somewhere *inside*. Always where he wasn't supposed to be . . . that was just like him.

She should have known something was up the moment Mr. Phillips tossed the mission patch onto the counter. The name FRIESE embroidered at the top now leaped out at her. She couldn't imagine how Phillips had gotten the old patch, but that didn't matter right now.

She felt a surge of anger, knowing how volatile the dapper little man was. If Iceberg was running around inside KSC, a loose cannon, a maverick, she hoped he didn't screw everything up. Negotiations would be delicate enough.

Then she realized they had very little to lose. Her own tactics weren't doing much good, as the murdered cameraman showed. Iceberg might even be their only hope.

Mr. Phillips grabbed the walkie-talkie again and tuned to a specific frequency. He clicked the "transmit" button and spoke. "Hello, Mory? Mr. Phillips here." He tensed for a moment until an acknowledgment crackled over the speaker. "Good, at least one team member is where he's supposed to be! Would you and Cueball please make your way to the Vehicle Assembly Building? We seem to have a pest, and he has holed himself up there. I would consider it a personal favor if you two would remove him with . . . what is the Hollywood phrase? Ah, yes. With *extreme prejudice.*''

"Acknowledged, Mr. Phillips," came the nasal voice over the speaker.

Nicole clenched her fists but kept her mouth shut, afraid a careless comment might cost another life. Iceberg had gotten himself into a mess, as usual, and he would have to fend for himself.

But he was good at doing that.

Mr. Phillips checked his PDA and read a brief snatch of information. "Colonel Adam Friese, call sign *Iceberg.* Ah! Our former commander has a rather checkered record on file. Seems to be quite competent, but he can barely walk with his foot in a cast that goes up to his knee." He glanced at his watch. "And we have three and a half hours until the gems arrive."

He flipped shut the PDA. "I don't suppose Iceberg will be any problem at all."

24

VEHICLE ASSEMBLY BUILDING

Iceberg sat within the glassed-in command post of the cavernous Vehicle Assembly Building, tensely watching the lower bay door, feeling all alone. As he saw the two men approach, a sense of relief washed over him.

"It's about time, NASA Security." He had wondered how long it would take the space agency forces to sweep past the terrorists. He stood, keeping the weight off his cast.

The two men crept into the VAB, looking from side to side. As they entered, they rotated around a common center, keeping their weapons pointed outward, prepared for a surprise attack.

Iceberg started to limp toward the door when it struck him that these two moved *too* stealthily, too silently. Something didn't seem quite right.

"Why do I get the feeling this isn't the cavalry?"

Maybe it was the fact that they wore mud-streaked camouflage outfits. Or maybe it was just the oversized backpack that held what looked like too much ammunition for a security detail.

He muttered, "They don't exactly look like they're here to help."

He ducked out of the confining command post, not wanting to be there unprotected and alone, on the vast empty floor under High Bay number 3. He hissed in pain as he limped toward the steel-reinforced concrete walls and the elevators that led up to the high bays. *Time to switch plans again,* he thought. He had to get out of sight until he figured out what these two heavily armed men were after.

There didn't seem much question, though, that they were after *him*.

He punched the "open" button, but the red-painted doors of the cargo elevator refused to budge. A loud *clank* echoed from above and the lift started down. Iceberg pushed the button again and again, urging the door to open. "Come on, come on!"

The silhouettes of the two intruders appeared against the big rectangle of outside sunshine from the lower bay doors. Bright industrial lights shone garishly from above. Catwalks and access arms on the Mobile Launcher Platform—used for assembly of the solid rocket boosters and for mating the shuttle's external tank to the orbiter—masked part of the glare.

The VAB operations had ceased following the standard launch-day evacuation, and the sound of the elevator engine and hydraulics seemed as loud as thunder as the elevator continued its descent.

The two shadowy intruders hustled toward High Bay 3.

The cargo elevator doors finally ground open. Iceberg stumbled inside and punched the button for level 3, which would take him away from immediate harm, yet where he could keep an eye on the intruders.

As the elevator lurched upward, Iceberg held the rails inside, keeping weight off his left foot. His head pounded, and his entire body sprouted aches like weeds. This made the NASA astronaut training tortures seem like a Sunday bicycle ride. He hadn't put out this much sweat since trying out for the wrestling team his doolie year at the Air Force Academy.

There might be something to a calm, desk jockey job like Panther's after all.

When the elevator doors opened, Iceberg took one deep breath before he made his way out onto the high walkway. Red metal railings bordered the path. He crept forward, moving slowly so that the motion would not attract the attention of the two enemies below. He held the rail, gritting his teeth, as residual pain thudded through his entire foot; it had probably swollen into the cast.

Looking three levels down to the floor, Iceberg saw the creeping, heavily armed figures. He felt cold sweat break out along his skin. "Chill out," he said to himself.

He narrowed his eyes in the dimness of the vast building, studying the two intruders as they glided into the enclosed low bay, scuttling like plague rats. They must be searching for the elevator.

It would take their eyes a moment to adjust after coming in from the bright Florida sunshine, so Iceberg used that to his advantage. Study the enemy, find his weakness . . . he tried to remember all that Military

Studies crap he hadn't paid attention to when he'd been a cadet. *Think.* Deception. Speed.

Iceberg edged over and studied the two. One man was large and muscular with skin the color of mahogany. His head was completely bald and so shiny it glistened, as if he used furniture polish on his scalp. The other man, who carried the backpack, had sharp narrow features that made him look like a weasel. His cheeks were covered with wispy, wiry hair in a pathetic attempt at a beard. He walked forward with his aquiline nose eerily raised, as if he were sniffing the air.

The open spaces of the VAB were filled with lifting cranes, dangling chains from overhead girders in heavy-duty block-and-tackle arrangements, pumping systems, safety fences. Fluttering yellow plastic tape demarcated an area designated for recent propellant fueling. DANGER—DO NOT CROSS.

In front of him in High Bay 3 stood a pair of cylindrical solid rocket boosters, canisters of propellant twelve feet in diameter that looked like white grain silos. Heavy cranes stacked and mated each booster section on the two-story Mobile Launcher Platform, a technological island that provided a transportable launch base for the shuttle to be hauled out to the launchpad by the slow-moving crawler transporter.

Below, the two terrorists stepped stealthily across the floor. They swept their eyes upward, scanning the high catwalks. The weaselly guy sniffed again. Iceberg remained in the shadows above, knowing they would spot him instantly if he moved.

But Iceberg had never been one to sit around and hide when he could conceive of a course of action. He studied the catwalk beside him, searching for something he could use as a weapon, not just to defend himself but to take an active role.

He spotted only a bench bolted to the floor, a case of disposable plastic safety goggles, and a tool locker. Stepping quietly and trying not to put much weight on his broken foot, Iceberg crept forward. Farther down the catwalk he saw a rack of gas canisters: oxygen, acetylene, and compressed helium. The helium and oxygen were in large metal tanks that were chest high, far too heavy to heave—but one of the blowtorch acetylene tanks was the size of a small scuba tank, easy enough to lift . . . and when accelerated by three stories of height, it just might make a decent bomb. Iceberg had always prided himself on his ability to improvise.

He withdrew the tank and staggered to the rail. Below him the two thugs continued searching possible hiding places in the lower levels, still without calling out or making a sound. The two were quite methodical, working on a grid search pattern. It would be only a matter of time before they came up level by level to flush him out. Iceberg had to act while he had a height advantage.

As they walked under him, he ran his mind through parabolic trajectories, doing a few calculations to determine how far out he had to toss the tank so it would drop straight on the head of one of the men. Just like lobbing an old Mark 5 bomb. He did his best, allowed for their movement below—then heaved the heavy projectile.

He watched it sail out silently, pirouetting in the air as it began to drop like a stone. The containers were pressurized, but thick-walled. He hoped it would hit the ground and blow up, eliminating both men.

The tank struck the concrete less than a foot behind the bald black man.

The metal canister did not explode but ricocheted off the cement with a monstrous *clang*. Both men practically leaped out of their skins. The bald man remained silent, but the weasel scrambled backward, yelling and looking around. He fired short wild bursts of his automatic rifle into the distant walls, where the bullets ricocheted off the concrete and flew into the open high bay. Weasel swung his rifle around, looking for another target. The gunshots still echoed in the enclosed VAB.

With grim satisfaction Iceberg saw a spreading wet spot in the weasel's crotch.

The bald man silently extended his arm, pointing toward the third-level catwalk, indicating Iceberg's hiding place.

Uh-oh, thought Iceberg, backing up. He turned to the waiting elevator, punching the button for the red metal doors to groan open again. He could hear Weasel shouting below to the bald thug.

"Cueball, go up there and get him! I'll come around the other side as soon as I check in. I want to twist that bastard's head off myself." He brushed at his damp pants.

Silently, Cueball hustled off to the metal stairs. Just as the elevator doors ground open, Iceberg heard Weasel grab his walkie-talkie. "Mr. Phillips, this is Mory. We've got him cornered in the VAB." He paused as the muffled voice crackled back. Iceberg couldn't understand the words. "Yes, he's being annoying—but we'll take care of it. Mory out."

Leaning back into the elevator, Iceberg punched the button for the top level of the high bay. He could think of no way to outrun them, but if he could lure them to follow to the highest levels, Iceberg could double back and get down, escape the VAB on the all-terrain buggy.

Iceberg emerged from the top level of the catwalk, and now the floor was very, very far down. It seemed as if he had already reached halfway to orbit by taking an elevator instead of a space shuttle. Unlike a normal building with floors and offices each step of the way, the Vehicle Assembly Building was a giant boxed-in open space, like a hangar.

Iceberg had gained breathing room for the moment, but he didn't know what to do next. The bad guys must have seen him get into the elevator, and they knew he wasn't on floor 3 anymore. Should he try to get their attention somehow, trick them? He crept along the catwalk delicately, trying not to drag his cast.

Suddenly, on the opposite wall of the high bay four floors below him, he saw the muscular bald man, Cueball, stalking down another narrow walkway, his high-powered rifle in hand. The bald man glanced up at the movement and noticed Iceberg above. Their eyes met from across the gulf of open air. Cueball's mouth opened but no sound came out. Iceberg had suspected the man was mute, and now he could not call attention to Mory.

But Cueball aimed with his rifle and quickly popped off two shots. Iceberg dove backward against the wall, ducking down. The bullets missed him by yards, leaving white starflowers where they had ricocheted. But the sound of the gunfire and the spang of impact were enough to tell Mory where Iceberg had hidden.

Iceberg scuttled along. The solid rocket boosters

stood like white pillars in the open space. One of the yellow-painted 250-ton lifting cranes stretched out in the open while other chains, block and tackle, and pulleys dangled from the high ceiling overhead.

He moved back to the elevator. He *should* take the stairs, but the thought of descending all the way back down to ground level with a broken foot seemed almost worse than being shot outright by the terrorists.

As he reached the elevator, though, he saw the indicator lights moving. The hum of machinery brought the lift up to the top floor. Someone was coming to get him. Mory.

Just as the elevator chimed with the car's arrival, Iceberg flattened himself against the wall beside the red-painted doors. His heart pounded. His vision focused to crystal clarity. He saw the open space, the long drop, and the thin dangling chains in front of the safety rail by the elevator.

The metal doors creaked open, and weasel-faced Mory strode out in a crouch, fanning his assault rifle in front of him, ready to take out his target.

Iceberg didn't give him a chance.

With his good foot he shoved off from the wall and launched forward like a torpedo. Iceberg struck Mory's side just as he was turning, and smashed into the lumpy pack—and Iceberg kept going.

Mory let out a cry, and a burst of rifle fire sprayed into the open air—but Iceberg shoved the weaselly man forward into the safety rail with enough impact that the thug's breath exploded out of him. Without pausing to think, Iceberg grabbed one of the dangling chains and whipped it in several loops around Mory's ankle. Iceberg put his shoulder into the shove and knocked the bearded man over the railing.

Mory shrieked in terror as he sailed out into empty space, falling several feet until the thin chain caught. Iceberg heard the crunch of the ankle snapping, as if the chain were a noose around a condemned man's neck.

Mory dangled upside down over the high bay, flailing with his hands to reach the rail, to find some stability. The automatic assault rifle dropped, tumbling in the air. It struck the floor with a loud clatter several seconds later.

"Help!" Mory cried. "You bastard." His face was a bright beet color as he hung suspended. The wet spot at his crotch had darkened.

Iceberg grabbed the chain and hauled Mory closer. The chain tore into Iceberg's hand. The thug reached out, flailing for the safety rail, but Iceberg kept the weaselly man from reaching it. "Who are you? What are you after?"

"Fuck you," Mory said.

Iceberg swung the chain, making the man dangle farther out in the open bay. He grunted from Mory's weight. The weasel wailed in terror from the height and from the pain of the chain wrapped around his snapped ankle.

"How many times are we going to have to do this?" Iceberg panted. "Who are you?"

"Get me down! I'm not telling you anything."

Iceberg leaned over the rail and looked down. He gained purchase against the railing and hauled Mory up another foot, then released the chain.

Mory fell two feet and stopped with a sudden jerk. He screamed.

It took Iceberg a moment to catch his breath before he said, "From this level the Vehicle Assembly Building is five hundred and twenty-five feet high. Imagine the splash pattern you'd make. I can keep quoting you statistics . . . or you can start telling me some answers.''

''All right, all right!'' Mory cried. ''Just get me closer to the rail.''

Iceberg pulled the chain, hand over hand. Slowly he brought his captive near, swinging Mory around—but just then the weaselly man's eyes widened with surprise and relief. Iceberg turned, yanking the man on the chain just as Cueball appeared on the stairwell, firing his high-powered rifle.

Iceberg swung Mory as a shield. Two bullets tore long bloody channels through the weaselly man's side and exited through his rib cage.

Iceberg didn't have any choice but to grab one of the other chains. With his hands wrapped around the links, he swung out over space.

The chain spun in his hands, rattling and vibrating as the block-and-tackle ratcheted. He dropped, swinging toward another level, yelling in his own terror. The chain dropped him, slowly catching with trip mechanisms in the pulley as Iceberg swung to a catwalk three floors down. Smashing into the railing, he let go of the chain.

He fell and rolled onto the catwalk, striking it with his shoulder. His palms were bloody. He winced as he opened and closed his hands.

He squeezed his eyes shut as he exhaled a great painful breath. ''Man, I never want to do that again.'' Iceberg lay trembling, dreading the prospect of getting back to his feet and running—but he knew he had to.

Cueball wouldn't give him a chance to recuperate.

• • •

Up on the top level of the high bay, the big bald man reached out to grab the chain and pulled Mory back toward the rail.

The other man bled profusely from the two gunshot wounds, moaning pitifully. He coughed blood and looked with bleary relief into Cueball's face—but the black man remained expressionless as he struggled to pull the backpack and the Stinger missiles from Mory's shoulders. He tugged, and Mory's ankle gave another sharp snap, evoking a wail of increased pain.

Cueball set his high-powered rifle behind him. He carefully held the launcher, then fit a missile inside. He smiled, showing square white teeth as he admired the new weapon.

Mory groaned once more. Distractedly, Cueball unwrapped the chain from his broken ankle and let his partner drop 525 feet to the floor below.

25

LAUNCH CONTROL CENTER

During the tense moments in the VIP viewing deck, Nicole watched Senator Boorman's demeanor evolve from shock to gradually increasing alertness. She cringed to think what he might do, what ill-advised solutions he might come up with. After witnessing the cameraman's violent murder, the senator now seemed to be turning cold, calculating.

The body of the channel 7 cameraman lay slumped against the wall, sticky with blood—a reminder to them all. Mr. Phillips ignored the corpse as he strutted back and forth, glancing at the various TV monitors that showed the Kennedy Space Center, *Atlantis* on the launchpad, the Vehicle Assembly Building, and the LCC's main firing floor.

Yvette paced restlessly in the confined observation deck like a caged tiger; her leg and arm muscles rippled as she walked. Rusty had been sent below to guard the sealed door to the crowded firing floor.

Senator Boorman drew himself up, finally making his move. "It's time I had a word with you, Phillips."

The dapper man turned, incredulous that the senator had spoken. "That's *Mr.* Phillips to you, Senator. We are not on a first-name basis. A man with your political savvy should understand a bit about respect."

"Excuse me, sir," Boorman amended smoothly. "I apologize. I've considered how I might be able to help you—as you requested. If it will help resolve this situation without further bloodshed, I would be willing to make a few phone calls, check with my political network, and get you what you want. We can end this situation without letting it get more"—he glanced uncomfortably at the dead news cameraman—"more complicated. We all want to get out of here alive."

The senator's gray eyes gleamed, and Nicole felt cold inside. She had far less confidence in his abilities and motivations. He had spent decades politicking, but not much time in the real world facing life-or-death situations.

"I love uncomplicated situations," Mr. Phillips said. "Very well. Yvette, see to it that the esteemed senator gets an outside telephone line." The little man raised his eyebrows. "Show us your brilliant political prowess, Senator. Get me a briefcase full of gems, by hook or by crook, and I'll give you your space shuttle back."

Boorman flared his nostrils but did not reply. Nicole could tell from his expression that Boorman didn't really care whether or not he got the shuttle back; he simply wanted to get out of this intact, no matter what the cost to the space program.

As soon as Yvette nodded to him, Boorman

snatched up a phone like a man with a mission, as if he had stepped into his familiar element once again. His aide pulled out a small black book and looked up telephone numbers for him, muttering them into Boorman's ear as he dialed. The senator sat back in a chair and feigned relaxation, ready to make a deal. As he began chatting into the phone, Nicole got the distinct impression that Boorman had begun to enjoy himself.

She could see why Iceberg hated bureaucrats so much.

Mr. Phillips startled Nicole by speaking close to her ear. His breath smelled strongly of peppermint. "Ms. Hunter, I hope you don't think too ill of me. I have admired your career for some time now. I've known that great things were in store for you once you left the Navy, whether you chose to be an astronaut or to play politics at NASA. From a certain point of view, you and I are really on the same side."

Nicole snorted, wary of Mr. Phillips's game. "What could we possibly have in common?"

He waggled a finger at her. "Tut tut, Ms. Hunter, no need to be rude. We were both present at the disastrous Ariane launch, for example. We're both just trying to make a living."

She narrowed her eyes, squeezing her lips into a moue of disgust. "Why couldn't you just knock over a bank or something?" Then Nicole drew a deep breath and looked at him more curiously. "In fact, why *didn't* you just rob a bank? Why did you pick something so spectacular and so high risk? You know you don't have a chance of pulling it off, with the entire country now gearing up against you."

Mr. Phillips raised a finger. "Ah, but I do have a chance. A chance—and that's all I need. To be truthful, though, I did consider robbing a bank. In fact, I considered many different options. I am, if nothing else, a very meticulous man. After I had decided on the need to undertake such an operation, I sat down and wrote out possible operations, then jotted down detailed lists of pros and cons."

"You're all going to be cons before the day is over," Nicole muttered.

Mr. Phillips gave her a look of long-suffering patience before he continued. "My team and I came up with many possibilities. But how many people remember just a bank robber? Everyone *remembers* an outrageous bandit such as D. B. Cooper—he's become an American legend. I'm not just an ordinary person, and this caper will put me on the cover of every magazine."

His smile carried an air that was at once swelled with ego and coldly calculating. "Besides, the potential payoff was much higher in holding the shuttle hostage. Each oil rig erected in the North Sea, for example, costs the petroleum companies nearly a billion dollars to build—I've seen their expense sheets —but the corporations are willing to make such expenditures because the profit potential is so extreme."

Nicole crossed her arms over her chest. "But an operation like this one must have cost you a fortune just to put together, all the plans, all the weapons, all the thugs. If you're already rich, why risk everything to get more? And don't give me a lame answer that 'one can never have enough money.' "

Mr. Phillips seemed to be enjoying the repartee. "The weapons did cost, but my team members work on commission, just as contingency attorneys in a corporate lawsuit. It isn't easy to get people to work on a percentage basis these days, but they know the potential payoffs, especially for four hours of work. Some of them are in it because they like the excitement, some of them feel they owe me a favor, the others . . . well, they have their own reasons.''

Nicole could imagine a bloodthirsty wildcard like Rusty agreeing to do anything just to get a little excitement in his life.

''Now, given that I wanted to do something spectacular, we could have threatened to destroy the Statue of Liberty, the Hoover Dam, the Washington Monument, Wall Drug in South Dakota. . . .'' Mr. Phillips raised his eyebrows. ''But I'm not a particularly murderous man—all those other possibilities would have risked the lives of thousands of people, but even if I do blow up *Atlantis*, the maximum number of deaths would only be seven, all of them astronauts who knew the risks when they climbed on board. Not to mention a few incidental civilians, such as our reporter friend from channel seven.

''Another item in the pros column—I know high-tech, and I love technology, specifically the space program, perhaps even more passionately than you do. I adore NASA. This operation had a certain appeal to me.''

''You've got a weird way of showing your affection,'' she said with a snort.

He looked at the detonator box, as if admiring its components. ''Perhaps you haven't thought it through, Ms. Hunter. I want to force this country to *value* their space program, their future. There's too much apathy among the public.

''I used to rise at the crack of dawn to watch the live NASA coverage on TV. Not many people get up for a launch anymore—in fact, the news networks usually just have a sound bite,'' he sniffed, ''as if a shuttle launch is 'regular news.'

''But with what I'm doing today''—he gestured with his well-manicured hand around the LCC—''I'm going to make the viewing public put their money where their mouth is. Today, they must decide if their space program is worth anything to them. TAN-STAAFL—are you familiar with that acronym, Ms. Hunter? NASA's full of acronyms.''

She answered slowly, ''There Ain't No Such Thing As A Free Lunch.'' *What is this guy getting at?*

Mr. Phillips beamed, and his lips curled upward. ''Very good—and it's absolutely right. There ain't no such thing as a free lunch. America is going to have to pay to keep their space shuttle. Love it or lose it— don't you agree that's a worthwhile question to pose?''

''And you're betting they'll pay up,'' Nicole said.

Mr. Phillips shrugged. ''As I said, I've got to make a living somehow.''

Nicole narrowed her dark eyes. ''Some of us do it in legal ways.''

Mr. Phillips seemed unaffected by her venom. ''Ms. Hunter, if you've been out in the business world as long as I have, you'd know that legal methods can be just as brutal as any act of terrorism. Ever try to cross a stockbroker? Wall Street is just as much a war zone as the Persian Gulf ever was.''

Senator Boorman hung up the phone, flustered and disturbed. He rubbed his square jaw with one of his large-knuckled hands. His color had gone pale.

''Success, Senator?'' Mr. Phillips asked with cheerful optimism.

Boorman shook his head. "I'm encountering resistance from people on the Hill. Getting so many gems all together in one place is going to be tough. They keep passing me from one person to another. I can't even get hold of the NASA Administrator—the president called him into a National Security Council meeting."

"Welcome to the real world," Nicole muttered.

Boorman lashed out at her. "I'm the head of the Senate Foreign Relations Committee, Ms. Hunter, and this is an emergency situation. Nobody should be putting me on hold."

"Then I suggest you try calling someone else," Mr. Phillips said coldly. "Our countdown clock is ticking." He held up the small black detonator controls. "We don't have much time if we're going to save this shuttle."

"Yeah," Nicole said derisively, "because you care about the space program so much."

Mr. Phillips spoke with an edge to his voice. "I do care, Ms. Hunter—more than you'd ever know. But don't take that to mean I won't blow up *Atlantis*. I've discarded much dearer things to me for less."

He held up one finger and his face pinched with an intensity she had seen before only on the faces of Shakespearean actors. "Listen to me. You've got a weathered old memorial kiosk at complex thirty-four over at the Cape, on the site of the launchpad fire of Apollo One that killed Grissom, White, and Chaffee.

"You've got a sealed Minuteman missile silo out on ICBM Road that holds the recovered wreckage from *Challenger*, cemented shut so that nobody can sell pieces for souvenirs. And just downstairs in the lobby, one wall is filled with plaques for all the missions—only *one* plaque has no landing date. *Challenger*, again. A national wound.

"I've been to your beautiful astronaut's memorial erected at Spaceport USA to honor all those who have died serving in the American space program—and there are plenty of blank spots remaining. Do you really want me to fill in a few new names? Seven more names?" He ticked them off on his hand. "Franklin, Green, Burns, Koslovsky, Orlov, Purvis, Nichi."

Nicole met his gaze coldly. Finally, she shook her head.

"The shuttle is a magnificent machine, a marvel of engineering," said Mr. Phillips. "The astronauts are true heroes—don't force me to make them into martyrs." He stabbed his finger at her. "But I'll do it if you can't cough up my price."

One of the telephones inside the firing floor began to ring, startling everyone with its loud sound even behind the Plexiglas walls. The noise would normally have been drowned out in the bustle of prelaunch activities. Now, though, everyone turned toward the sound. The phone rang a second time.

It was the telephone on the Launch Director's desk.

"It would appear someone is trying to call you, Ms. Hunter," Mr. Phillips said.

"I'm the Launch Director," she answered, feigning disinterest. "It's supposed to be a busy day for me." But her heart pounded with intense fear—could it be Iceberg? She knew Mr. Phillips had sent two killers after him in the VAB.

The phone rang again. No one moved to pick it up. Nicole wondered if she should reach out and punch the button to transfer the call to the observation deck. Finally, after a fourth ring, her eyes locked with Mr.

Phillips's. He nodded briefly. ''Go ahead, answer it.''

She reached out and paused to concentrate on her movements, making sure that her hand didn't tremble. Then she grabbed a headset and depressed the button to transfer the call. ''Hello?'' she said, hoping it was Iceberg, hoping for him to say that he had taken care of the two terrorists and was now coming to rescue everyone in the LCC. That would be just the way he'd do it—in front of all the cameras . . . and get himself killed in the process.

On the phone she heard only silence, then the distant sound of a scuffle, faded shouting. ''Hello?'' she said again, more loudly—then she heard nothing else. Nicole swallowed hard and hung up.

Mr. Phillips watched her intently. ''Yes?'' he asked. ''I suppose it must be your friend Colonel Friese?''

''Wrong number,'' she said.

''Ah,'' he said, clearly disbelieving her. ''Well, at least it wasn't a telephone solicitor.'' Mr. Phillips spun on his heel. ''I'll go see how our friend the senator is doing.'' He stepped away to hover behind Boorman, who was still talking heavily into another phone.

Nicole sat back in a rush, dizzy from adrenaline. Andrei Trovkin turned from his perpetual position of staring out the narrow launch windows toward the distant gantry. He kept his voice low as he spoke to Nicole.

''I feel like helpless baby. How is it that a gang of bullies can cause such enormous problems?'' He shook his head, then scratched his close-cropped brown hair, straightening his black-rimmed glasses. He heaved a heavy sigh. ''We find ourselves trapped in little room like accountants with nothing more important to do. We are outside of loop in grand space program.'' He looked up at the ceiling. ''Ah, to be inside cockpit of *Atlantis* at this moment. You and I, my friend, were both cut out to be brave astronauts—that little man Phillips makes me want to *do* something.''

Nicole looked around, and her eyes met the pale deep-freeze gaze of Yvette as she prowled among the hostages. ''You'll just get yourself killed,'' she muttered to Andrei.

''Unfortunately, you are correct,'' he agreed.

Withdrawing into herself, Nicole pondered the Russian's words. He did have a point—perhaps the two of them were cut out to be astronauts—but she didn't agree with his assessment. She and the ambassador may have started out with the same goals, intent on exploring space, riding rockets into orbit—but Andrei had left the cosmonaut program for medical reasons. Nicole, on the other hand, had *chosen* to step out of the race, walking away from the rigors of training to become a desk jockey rather than following her dreams. She touched the gold key on her necklace. No, she had simply chosen different dreams, but they were still her dreams.

That had been one of the main reasons her relationship with Iceberg had crumbled. They'd once had much in common, but she couldn't compete with him anymore. Iceberg didn't know how to deal with her change of heart. He couldn't fathom it. He was always a bulldozer, insisting on his way or no way. He made Nicole feel she had taken the easy way out—and it stung because she suspected Iceberg may have been exactly right.

She glanced at the video monitor, seeing the close-up of the motionless shuttle on the launchpad. Knowing the crew was in peril caused her insides to knot up. Conflicting thoughts whirled in her head. She could have been there herself. *She* might have been one of the trapped astronauts in the cockpit, waiting for some manager to come to the rescue.

Trovkin reminded her very much of Iceberg, wanting to take action, insisting on tackling any problem with a thick skull and balled fists. She thought about Iceberg battling terrorists by himself in the Vehicle Assembly Building, taking matters into his own hands, fighting impossible odds.

It was exactly the way he liked it.

26

VEHICLE ASSEMBLY BUILDING

Finding impending death to be a great motivator, Iceberg picked himself up from the hard floor of the high walkway, where he had been thrown from the chain. Unfortunately, he saw no convenient rocks to crawl under; he knew he had to move. Now.

Chill . . . cool . . . frosty . . .

He wished he could use one of the VAB's heavy lifting cranes just to help himself stand up. He hadn't felt this bad since he'd gotten the crap beat out of him in boxing class at the Academy. Talk about déjà vu.

As he moved, his entire body let out a silent clamor of pain. "All nerve endings firing quite efficiently, yes sir." He wondered if his body were covered with a thousand small bruises—or just a dozen huge ones.

He had been so careful to contact the *Atlantis* pilot compartment and warn the astronauts there, rather than directly calling the LCC, so as not to tip his hand.

How had these thugs known he was hiding inside the VAB? Maybe Marc Franklin hadn't taken him seriously, and blabbed. What a guy.

Iceberg wished he could have gotten more information from weasel-faced Mory. How many more terrorists did Mr. Phillips have? He had to contact somebody, now that the terrorists knew about him anyway. Nicole would be his first choice. Despite his reluctance, he had nothing to lose—and he needed help as soon as possible.

But right at the moment, Cueball was coming.

Staggering with every step, Iceberg worked his way down the walkway toward one of the cargo elevators again. He waited for the bald man to appear with high-powered rifle in hand. But the red elevator door remained sealed, without the vibration of the cable or a descending car.

Iceberg found an emergency phone near the elevator and picked up the receiver, listening to the dial tone as he panted and fought back the dizziness brought about by stabbing pains in his foot and ankle. His hands dripped blood from where his palms had been scraped open. The buffered aspirins he had taken earlier that morning had given up on him.

He punched in the familiar number for the LCC firing floor. Now that his secret was already blown, he had to let her know what he had done, and what he intended to do. And this might be his only chance. As mission commander, he knew the Launch Director's private extension, of course. How could he remember such a thing as Nicole's phone number, when he was trying to *forget* everything about her? What a waste of brain cells!

The phone rang once, then a second time. He

glanced behind himself, but he could hear nothing. He saw no motion. The VAB stood hushed and expectant, and Iceberg felt very exposed. Cueball must be coming after him in silence.

Iceberg felt his heart thudding. The phone rang again. "Come on, Panther—come on!" he muttered.

Then he heard the hydraulics of the elevator. Cueball was on his way down, coming after him.

Against his ear, the phone rang a fourth time. "Nicole, pick up the phone!"

The elevator dinged. The hydraulics sighed. Iceberg dropped the phone and let it clack against the cinderblocks, dangling on its cord. He grabbed a small red fire extinguisher mounted to the wall.

The elevator door opened, and the burly bald man lurched out with a satchel slung over one shoulder. He held his long rifle in both hands. Sweat glistened on his polished scalp.

Just as Cueball turned toward him, Iceberg hefted the fire extinguisher toward the big man's chest. "Here—catch!"

With a grunt of surprise, the bald man instinctively flinched away from the heavy object, letting his rifle dip.

Iceberg leaped sideways behind Cueball, sliding between the doors of the elevator as they began to glide shut automatically. He felt his adrenaline soaring, barely enough to muffle the pain in his foot cast to a dull thud. Iceberg pounded the button for floor 1. The doors sealed.

"Down, down—come on!" Iceberg said.

He heard a thud as Cueball hit the door with the flat of his hand, and then again with a clang as he battered with the discarded fire extinguisher. But the elevator was already descending, too late for the thug to get at him.

Iceberg breathed rapidly. His foot hurt like a son of a bitch. He didn't want to move at all—but he had to. The elevator reached the bottom of the high bay and opened onto the vast concrete floor cluttered with equipment. But now that he had a head start from Cueball, he had to make his way across the open interior of the VAB, get to the bright outside where he could climb on his all-terrain buggy and roar off across the swamps.

Feets don't fail me now!

With a glance behind him, Iceberg tried to see if the burly mute had climbed into another elevator or was taking the stairs—but he saw nothing, heard nothing. He found that even more frightening.

Hobbling at the best speed he could manage with his cockeyed gait, Iceberg scrambled across the concrete floor, dodging pumps and generators, parked forklifts, big steel bells used as test weights for the lifting cranes. Knowing Cueball's high-powered weapons, he felt the targeting cross crawling over his skin.

Making his way directly for the yawning outer door of the high bay, he hurried for the shelter of the tall Mobile Launcher Platform, on which stood the stacked solid rocket boosters. The sunshine glared brightly on the top of the platform, casting a jungle of shadows. He passed under the flexible yellow barrier tape.

Iceberg struggled along, taking cover in camouflaging shadows and in construction equipment. The VAB's vast open floor seemed as large as Nebraska. But no shots came.

He passed the splattered remains of Mory lying in the middle of an open loading area. The body was crumpled, as if a giant hand had tossed him in a puddle of red paint. A 525-foot drop sure could make a mess of things.

Iceberg focused on the battered automatic rifle Mory had dropped from high above. Squatting, he picked it up and scanned wildly around. His palms felt like shredded sausages, but it was good to have a weapon in his hands.

He laughed at himself, thinking how he had earlier tried to convince himself he wouldn't be getting into any shootouts—no sir, not this ole boy! He'd just wanted to make a phone call to the shuttle cockpit.

From now on, he would be prepared for anything.

Taking the rifle, Iceberg worked his way toward the rectangle of sunlight from the outer bay doors. The way out. The bald thug wouldn't be able to see him hidden inside the steel labyrinth of the Mobile Launcher Platform, but Iceberg couldn't hide here forever. He was hurt and could barely move. Cueball knew where he was.

Ahead, daylight beckoned. Iceberg limped along like a car with two flat tires. Still no gunshots.

Salvatore's three-wheeler waited just outside. He could get to it in only a few minutes.

Finally Iceberg passed out from under the Mobile Launcher Platform. He ducked, increasing his speed because now he was out in the open again, heading for the towering, wide-open doors.

He made an easy target.

His foot was killing him.

Almost home free. He risked a glance back to the dim interior of the VAB, turning to see if he could glimpse the muscular black man. Iceberg spotted movement on one of the catwalks of the high bay three stories up. His stomach dropped.

Cueball hadn't been chasing him after all.

He had been *getting into position.*

On the high walkway the bald thug had set up a missile launcher and loaded it with what looked like an explosive-tipped Stinger. Even from far away, Iceberg could see the man's eyes lock on him. Cueball's silent face broke into a wide grin, showing big teeth.

"Oh, shit—" Iceberg said, as his pain vanished into the background. He turned the commandeered rifle toward Cueball and let off a half dozen rounds. The automatic weapon belched bullets as its momentum drove the stock into his side. He heard a spray of ricochets against metal.

Cueball ducked. Iceberg knew he hadn't hit anything, but he might have bought himself a few seconds.

He lurched forward, stepping on his heavy cast but not caring as he made a beeline out the door. If that missile hit him, he'd need a tombstone instead of a cast.

He collapsed onto the seat of the all-terrain buggy. Grasping the handle, he started the engine and roared off on the fat tires, trying to put as much distance between him and the VAB as possible, make a moving target for the missile.

Iceberg urged the puttering buggy faster. He ducked low as he tore across the concrete parking lot toward the sluggish water, the turning basin used for floating in empty external tanks for the shuttle.

The huge bay doors wouldn't allow him to move far enough out of Cueball's line of sight.

Turning, he saw the bald man swing the launcher up.

Cueball looked through the missile launcher's sight. From this position, he had all the time in the world. Sunlight glared off the metal of the Mobile Launcher Platform. He shifted his aim, saw the tiny man racing away like something from a comedy routine, and overcompensated for the distance.

He fired the missile.

The Stinger shot forward as its propellant ignited. Startled, Cueball jerked the launcher. The missile's heat-seeking sensor spotted the bright reflection of the sun gleaming from the polished hull of the platform. Like a spitting cobra the Stinger spun wild, streaking sideways, curving in a crazy arc until it slammed into the biggest structure in the middle of High Bay 3.

One of the stacked solid rocket boosters.

The Stinger detonated—and ignited 1.1 million pounds of propellant, ammonium perchlorate oxidizer, powdered aluminum fuel, and iron oxide catalyst, designed to burn . . . and burn *hot*.

The resulting explosion was like the *Challenger* accident inside an enclosed building.

27

LAUNCH CONTROL CENTER

The bright fireball of the VAB explosion spread a garish smear across the TV screens in the viewing area. Though the speakers picked up no sound, Nicole winced as if the boom of the incredible detonation had slammed into her.

Within seconds, though, the narrow launch windows shattered, spraying through the open metal louvers. People screamed. Mr. Phillips held up an arm to shield his face and jerked his head aside. The sound of the explosion seemed to go on and on. Then the shock wave passed, rumbling into the distance.

No one spoke. Suddenly weak-kneed, Nicole slumped into her chair breathing heavily, sharply. The stale, air-conditioned atmosphere inside the observation deck felt cold on her teeth, suddenly mixing with the humid outside air that drifted in through the broken windows. A rush of sweat made her silk blouse clammy, sticking to her skin.

Iceberg had been in there at the VAB, going out in a blaze of glory. Idiot! She hated him for his impetuousness, for thinking he could handle any problem head-on and alone.

Now the Vehicle Assembly Building was in flames, gutted in the explosion.

And worse, Iceberg was dead.

Mr. Phillips let his eyelids fall closed in a shudder of amazement. He dropped his arm away from his eyes and stared at the smoke boiling from the VAB. "Exhilarating!" he said, "but also disappointing." He turned to view *Atlantis*. Three miles away from the blast, the shuttle looked unharmed.

His mouth formed a deep scowl, etching lines around his lips. "This is really turning into a mess . . . and it could have been so simple if you all had just followed a few elementary instructions. If you can put a man on the moon, you should be able to meet a simple ransom demand."

He shook his head while staring at the flames roaring out of the mouth of the VAB as the solid rocket fuel burned and burned. "Just look at that. I never meant to cause such grievous damage to this wonderful facility. Think of how much this alone will set back the space program." Mr. Phillips slapped his forehead. "Sometimes it makes me just want to cry."

Andrei Trovkin turned slowly from the narrow viewing window, squaring his broad shoulders and moving like a pot coming to a boil. His fists clenched like battering rams, and his florid face turned crimson with anger. "I could kill you, Mr. Phillips," he said.

Feigning boredom, Mr. Phillips replied, "Yes, and I could have *you* killed. But let's try to avoid that, shall we?" He looked to Yvette, who stood lithe as a switchblade ready to spring open. She grinned, showing perfect teeth on her tanned face.

Standing at his station, ignoring the roiling flames from the VAB and the broken glass scattered on the floor around him, Senator Boorman returned to his telephone conversation. His ponderous voice grew more strident. He wiped the back of his hand across his tall forehead, smearing droplets of perspiration. "If you can't help me, then let me talk to someone who can. I'm Senator Charles Boorman!" He punctuated each word with a pounding of his fist on the countertop.

Boorman caught Mr. Phillips watching him. The senator calmed himself and tried to sound more reasonable as he spoke again into the phone. "Look, the whole world is watching. I'm only concerned for the safety of those poor crew members inside *Atlantis*. Think of how this tragedy is affecting their families. Someone else might get hurt."

Nicole tore her attention away from the VAB fire, bristling at the senator's crocodile tears.

Mr. Phillips folded his arms. "Having problems, Senator? You people have only two and a half hours remaining."

Boorman turned away. His voice thinned out, becoming more of a hiss as he spoke into the phone. "Just yank it out of next year's space program budget, for God's sake! So what if we fly one less mission. Do you really think we'll be able to afford another VAB anyway?" He leaned forward as if trying to climb inside the phone.

Nicole turned back to the conflagration on the screens, thinking of the damage. Through the smoke and flames she could see twisted steel girders and gaping holes where the siding had blown away. The Vehicle Assembly Building had been built with so many steel reinforcements and pilings driven down to bedrock that the building frame had withstood the explosion. Little short of a direct nuclear attack would destroy the entire VAB, but it would take a great deal of time and money to refit. She drew in a breath.

Nothing could bring back Iceberg, though.

28

VEHICLE ASSEMBLY BUILDING

Just as the heat-seeking missile struck the solid rocket boosters, Iceberg drove the ATV headlong to the edge of the turn basin, not slowing. He flung himself off the vehicle and dove into the questionable shelter of the sluggish water as the shock wave belched out of the VAB. He had no place else to run, or hide. He just hoped he could get low enough, duck the worst of the blast.

The fireball roared through the high bay of the VAB like Armageddon. Flames erupted, boiling out the huge open door. The shock wave slammed Iceberg deeper into the warm water—and he stayed under, not knowing how far the flame front would sweep.

The three-wheeled vehicle toppled into the deep mud at the edge of the basin, as if a grizzly bear had slapped it aside.

Iceberg stayed low in the warm water that led to

the curling waterways that connected with the Banana River. So much for keeping his cast dry.

His ears rang from the shock pressure. Desperately needing a breath, he felt the impact of the delayed heat wave roll over him, singeing the short hairs on the back of his neck.

After holding his breath for nearly a minute, he lifted his head and gasped for breath. Hauling himself dripping to his hands and knees on the muddy shore, he looked dully back at the destroyed building.

Even such an explosion was not able to flatten the massively reinforced VAB—but with more than a million pounds of propellant inside each solid rocket booster, plus flammables stored in the high bays, the building's interior raged in an inferno. More than a kiloton of high explosives—and thank God he was far enough away and underwater. Flames shot out every opening and crack, and what was left of the side walls reverberated with the shock. Hot burning debris fluttered down from the sky.

"And I thought my life would get boring once I was pulled from this mission," Iceberg muttered. He waited a few moments before he hauled himself out of the turn basin, dripping. The three-wheeler lay on its side in the mud, and with his injured foot he would never be able to retrieve it.

His confiscated rifle had been submerged, and he doubted it would still function. His cast was soaked through, and would probably begin to fall apart within an hour or so. This whole situation wasn't turning out as well as he had hoped.

Iceberg had just crawled back onto dry land when he heard the sound of yet another blast, from farther away. He jerked his head up, searching for the source of the sharp boom.

A plume of gray-black smoke rose over the swamps not more than a mile away. Iceberg's heart froze as he wondered what else could go wrong. The entire Kennedy Space Center had turned into a war zone!

29

NASA TELEVISION RELAY BLOCKHOUSE

Scrambled nightmares, dark images, and weird impressions interrupted by sudden thunder . . .

The explosion was loud enough to wake the dead—or at least someone in an abyss of drugged sleep. The noise was so tremendous, the shock wave so sharp, and the burned chemical smell so pungent that it slashed through tranquilized stupor and nudged Amos Friese back into semiconsciousness.

His head felt as if it were wrapped in bandages. Each breath seemed like a slow sucking of air through a tiny straw used to stir coffee. His arms and legs felt leaden, tingling, as if some Pygmy had shot him with a curare-tipped blow dart. . . .

Blow dart!

Amos suddenly remembered: a scarlet dart striking him, its sharp point stinging. As he stumbled backward, the dart poked through his bulky sweater, just pricking his skin. He had slapped it off, but not before receiving a sufficient dose to trip him over the cliff into a deep, unconscious paralysis.

Amos groaned, and his voice sounded like another explosion in his head. It took him several tries before he managed to pry his eyelids open. Gray light seeped in. He smelled acidic smoke, chemicals burning, as if an explosive had gone off nearby.

His clothes were clammy with perspiration, the thick sweater wrapped around him like sodden blankets, cold from the blockhouse's excessive air-conditioning. Everything remained fuzzy, out of focus.

He realized that he couldn't see because his glasses had fallen off. No, not fallen off—someone had removed them. He found them folded and neatly—lovingly?—laid on his chest. With numb, clumsy fingers Amos unfolded the eyeglasses and settled them on his face again, blinking until images came into focus at last.

Lying prone, he scanned the video relay station. He spotted cracks in the cement floor that had been painted over and sealed when the old blockhouse had been refurbished. A black beetle toiled awkwardly across the floor.

"Oh man, oh man," Amos said, and propped himself on one elbow. Big mistake. The motion set off bongo drums of pain inside his skull, reminding him of a hangover he'd once had when he went out drinking with his brother. Amos had foolishly tried to keep up with the other fighter pilots, shot for shot—not something he wanted to do more than once.

With the care he usually reserved for bringing up a new computer system, Amos drew himself into a sitting position.

"Hello?" he croaked. "Anybody here?" He heard nothing but the hum of the air conditioner and feedback from the many video monitors on the racks behind him. "Cecelia?" he said.

Holding the edge of the desk, he hauled himself up, swaying dizzily. Straightening his legs, he heard a tiny *clink* on the floor. He saw a red-feathered dart attached to a mostly full hypodermic vial of amber liquid. He had been lucky, he realized. With his thick sweater and his own quick dodge, he had received only a partial dose.

But why had the strangers left him here unattended? Cecelia had mentioned something about the CIA . . . but he doubted that story.

Or were they still around?

On his desk Amos saw his windup orange space shuttle, his jar of jawbreakers, and the cans of now warm Jolt Cola, just the way he had left them.

Then he spotted Cecelia's shoes and her outstretched legs poking from behind her desk.

His heart leaped, and adrenaline slammed him fully awake. They must have tranquilized her, too. Weaving like a drunkard, he worked his way over to her. He held the edge of his own desk, then grabbed a battered swivel chair that threatened to throw him off balance again.

"Cecelia," he gasped, "hey, wake up." He reached her desk; then he thought again of the two "CIA" strangers in their NASA jumpsuits . . . how nervous Cecelia had been.

Now she lay sprawled on the floor in her bright flower-print blouse and black slacks. Her once dusky skin looked waxen. Another scarlet dart protruded from the flesh of her plump neck just above the collarbone.

This time, though, the hypodermic vial was completely empty.

Amos felt his heart sink like a mainframe dropped in water. "Cecelia," he said again, but his voice came out in a hoarse croak. With the remnants of dizziness from his drugged state, and the shock of seeing her like this, his legs turned wobbly. He knelt by Cecelia's side, propped up her head, and brushed her dark hair away from her face. He had always wanted to run his fingers through her hair. . . .

Her big brown eyes remained closed. Amos gently touched her eyelids but received no response. Her skin felt unnatural, like vinyl.

He put his ear next to her nose, sensed no warm exhalation coming from her. After swallowing hard and hesitating more from fear than embarrassment, he laid his head on her breast, listening for a heartbeat.

He found none.

Amos sat with Cecelia's head cradled in his lap. He kept stroking her hair, but it brought him no pleasure. He wanted to say things to Cecelia, to ask her questions and tell her his thoughts, things he hadn't had the nerve to do before. But no words came.

Amos knew the two CIA impostors must have been up to some fiendish job. He felt anger burning through him, enough to drive back his grief. He pictured the cocky freckle-faced redhead, and the blond Amazon woman who had shot him with a blow dart; only through his own blind luck had Amos averted a fatal dose of the drug himself.

But they had taken care of Cecelia. Oh, yes, he could see that.

Suddenly coming to himself, Amos noted again the acrid smoke in the air, like gunpowder—something burning, a sharp chemical flame. He struggled to his feet and saw daylight shining around the blast corridor, where the bunker's heavy shield door had been closed.

He carefully straightened Cecelia's hair, folded her arms across her ample chest, then staggered toward the blockhouse entryway. He passed through a maze-like series of sharp corners built of thick cinderblock designed in the Apollo days to prevent explosive damage from penetrating into the interior.

The bunker's heavy steel door had been twisted outward, as if some great hand had punched it from its hinges. The cement-block walls were also chipped and cracked, smudged with a flash of smoke.

Two burned and bloody NASA security officers had been thrown outside, their uniforms crisped, their entire bodies looking as if stepped on by the force of an explosion.

Someone had booby-trapped the door. The security officers had tried to get into the video relay bunker to rescue Amos and Cecelia—and they had triggered the bomb.

Amos's mind whirled. "Oh, man!" he said. The pieces began to fall into place. Those two impostors had forced Cecelia to bring them here for . . . for what? The blond Amazon had shot both of them with a blowgun, leaving Amos for dead . . . then the two had done something and departed, rigging explosives to take care of anyone who came to investigate.

But the blast had finally been enough to wake him up. "I would have preferred an alarm clock," he said to himself.

He worked his way back to the racks of video monitors. The heavy tranquilizer drugs still made his mind fuzzy, but he had to get with the program—and right now.

Action! Doing *anything* was better than sitting around and doing nothing. That's what his brother would say. He knew Iceberg could have handled this problem in a cinch, but Iceberg was out watching the launch somewhere. He probably didn't even know anything suspicious had happened.

When Amos reached the bank of TV screens on their metal racks, he studied the images in shock. The chronometer showed that *Atlantis* should have already launched, but the countdown had frozen in an indefinite hold. "Oh, man."

On another screen he stared at the smoldering exterior of the Vehicle Assembly Building. Black flames curled out from a portion of the outer wall.

"Oh, man!" he said again, with more energy this time.

On screens displaying the interior of the Launch Control Center, all the firing-floor technicians stood helpless beside their stations, upset, confused—and finally on the image of the VIP observation deck Amos saw Nicole Hunter, indignant and frustrated beside a short but suave-looking man. With them stood the blond Amazon and the cocky redhead, both of whom carried ominous weapons, holding the LCC hostage.

Definitely not CIA.

Amos turned cold. Fumbling, he picked up the phone and punched 9 for an outside line, intending to call 911. But he heard no dial tone. The line was dead. He tried it again. Still nothing. Running his hands over his panel that controlled the relay lines, he flicked a switch. An LED display blinked: all outside transmissions had been cut off.

Amos slumped back in his groaning old chair. Cecelia dead, himself attacked, the video blockhouse booby-trapped, the VAB in flames, and terrorists with guns strutting through the Launch Control Center.

"Oh, man—oh, man!" he said.

He got momentarily frightened. "What if they come back for me?"

And where was Iceberg?

30

ATLANTIS

Gator Green, lying on his back in the pilot's chair and facing the sky, was looking out of the front-side viewing port when he saw a reflection of bright light out of the corner of his eye. Scrambling up, he leaned across the center console C-3 and looked out Franklin's small side viewport. His helmet bounced from his lap, but he paid it no attention.

"Holy shit! Would you look at that!" A brilliant fireball spat from the cube-shaped building, gushing through the VAB high-bay door. A purple afterimage blurred his vision.

Marc Franklin had unstrapped himself and sat on the aft bulkhead with his arms crossed over his orange pressure suit, squatting on the cockpit wall; while the shuttle remained upright on the gantry, it was difficult to look at anything but the open sky above. Alexandra Koslovsky had leaned over the side of her chair to speak down to her comrades on the mid-deck.

The two American payload specialists on the mid-deck, Major Arlan Burns and Dr. Frank Purvis, reacted the same instant Gator blinked from the light. Burns yelled, "Unbelievable! What's going on out there? Look out the side port—you can just see it around the gantry structure."

Gator tried to blink the afterimage away to focus better on the VAB. The red-and-yellow fireball coughed out of the bay doors, and thick black smoke swirled up into the air.

Franklin climbed over and pushed Gator aside for a better view. Alexandra Koslovsky crowded up, standing on her tiptoes to look around the mission commander.

The shuttle vibrated, and a muffled boom rattled the spacecraft as the dissipated blast wave hit them. The shuttle shuddered in its yoke. Taken off guard, Franklin and Alexandra stumbled from their precarious balance at the viewport. Gator reached out to keep the two from falling.

Burns climbed forward and stuck his head through the deck access port. "What the hell is going on? We just had an explosion at the VAB!"

Finally acting like a leader, Franklin turned around and snapped to Gator, "Get on the Guard frequency, Lieutenant Commander. Find out what's going on. Follow the checklist."

"Probably the terrorists Iceberg warned us about," Gator said, dead serious. The NASA simulator instructors would hand out unanticipated problems on "green cards," trying to rattle the crew. Some astronauts could handle it without a checklist, and others, like

Franklin, needed a checklist whenever they ran out of toilet paper.

But this wasn't any green card.

Burns ducked back down into the mid-deck; the payload specialists excitedly spoke with their Russian counterparts. Alexandra knelt on the bulkhead to consult with her comrades below.

Gator was already on the comm channel, trying to get a response from either CAPCOM or the LCC, but no one answered. Gator punched in another frequency, but the LCC took forever to answer. Gator blinked in astonishment at the gruff, frightened response from one of the station chiefs on the firing floor. "*Atlantis*, we have a situation here. Unable to provide details. LCC out."

"Hey, at least let me talk to the Launch Director. This is Lieutenant Commander Green—"

"Ms. Hunter is unavailable at this time. You will be advised. Out."

Alexandra Koslovsky straightened from the mid-deck as Orlov, her gangly Russian cosmonaut partner, climbed up into the shuttle's command deck. They chattered quickly in Russian.

"Okay, Launch Control is assessing the problem," Franklin said, as if the transmission had explained everything. "We need to wait until they make a recommendation. Nothing we can—"

Gator felt exasperated, turning from the radio. "It's not right, Commander. Launch Control should be yammering at the top of their lungs. We're out of touch with CAPCOM in Houston. They're keeping us in the dark, and it's no accident! What's all this baloney about staying off the air and not asking any questions?"

Franklin climbed back toward his commander's seat. "We were ordered to sit tight." He stubbornly grabbed for his heavy-duty seatbelt.

"And Iceberg directly informed us that the LCC had been taken over by a bunch of thugs. Dammit, Franklin—the VAB just blew up, for Christ's sake! And Nicole won't even respond. *Panther*, remember? And she's one of *us*!"

From his partially obstructed view, Gator strained to see any movement around the launch area or the VAB, but it was weirdly still. Flames licked at the blackened exterior of the building, and smoke rose high into the air. No fire crews, no rescue vehicles, no NASA Security.

"Franklin, think! If this was an ordinary launch, people would be going bananas!"

"Give it time. It's only been a few minutes since the explosion—"

"And nothing has happened. That in itself should be telling us to act." He stepped up, weary of Franklin's indecision. Mission Commander or not, there came a time when action and not words made the difference. Gator's eyes shone bright as his own fear pumped him higher. "Iceberg was right. Launch Control has been compromised, and we're hostages here in the shuttle. I have no intention of being a bargaining chip for some wacko—not if I can help it. I think we need to get the hell out of Dodge."

"Excuse please?" said Alexandra.

Cosmonaut Orlov said, "I believe I understand Comrade Gator—"

As Franklin looked at him in astonished disbelief, Gator started for the mid-deck hatch. "Hit the emergency exit baskets. We're sitting on a couple of kilotons of explosives, boys and girls, and I'm not staying around any longer to debate. Launch Control is totally FUBAR.''

Small, relieved cheers rang out from the payload specialists on the mid-deck below. "Emergency egress—it's about time somebody made a decision up there!" Burns stuck his head through the hatch.

Alexandra frowned. "FUBAR?"

"Fucked-Up Beyond All Recognition," Gator translated. "What do they teach you in your English classes? Come on, we're ready to egress."

"Apparently not American English," Alexandra snorted as she started to follow.

Franklin caught Gator's arm as the shuttle pilot made for the hatch. "This terrorist story hasn't been confirmed. We have to make sure we're doing the right thing."

"Commander Iceberg would not lie to us," Alexandra said with unshakable confidence.

Franklin nervously wet his lips and looked around the command deck for a checklist. His stoic demeanor started to crack. "Wait, I'll inform Launch Control that unless we hear from them—"

Alexandra slipped past Gator and made her way through the access hatch to the mid-deck. Sounds came from below as the rest of the crew ran through the egress checklist.

Gator positioned himself above the hatch and said, "Marc, if we tip our hand, we're screwed. Let those terrorists figure it out for themselves."

Franklin persisted as Gator disappeared down the hatch to the mid-deck. "But what if Iceberg is wrong? This is just the kind of stunt—"

Gator looked at him, hard as ebony. "If there aren't any terrorists, Launch Control will start squawking the moment we open the hatch. At least we'll get them off their fat asses and spark some reaction."

31

KENNEDY SPACE CENTER—
RESTRICTED LAUNCH AREA

I **ceberg gritted his teeth** and tried to push away the thudding agony. "Keep cool," he said to himself, then hissed as a spang of pain shot through his broken bones grinding together. Chill . . . frosty . . . The mental litany seemed to be losing its effect.

Iceberg skipped on his good foot and barely touched the ground with his wet cast as he staggered away from the burning VAB. Keep moving, head off for the next target, gotta help. . . .

Even in the mid-morning sun, he could see a second shadow cast in front of him from the flames. Slimy water from the turning basin dripped from his clothes.

Time to move on before the bad guys threw something else at him. He sure as hell hated to walk across the sprawling swampy site, but the three-wheeler lay submerged in the mud of the turn basin. He couldn't very well hitchhike.

With a sinking feeling, Iceberg wondered how much longer he had to do all this alone. Where was NASA Security? He turned toward the far-off launchpad and debated if he should try to help his crew first. Or Nicole. He felt overwhelmed. He couldn't do everything!

"Chill out," he said to himself. "Chill." His heart continued to pound, and the adrenaline scattered his concentration rather than focusing it.

Iceberg knew his crew, knew how they worked together, how much they had trained, each with their mission specialties and areas of research interest—but while the other six had their separate duties on the flight of *Atlantis*, they'd had to learn teamwork as well. And his crew was tight, like the strings on a well-tuned guitar.

Astronauts and cosmonauts had enjoyed running the obstacle courses in the training areas in the Johnson Space Center in Texas, getting themselves ready for their flight. Alexandra Koslovsky had established a friendly rivalry between the Russians and Americans, running their paces through the grueling course. Gator Green whipped Burns and Purvis into shape, while Alexandra pushed the two Russian mission specialists to beat them. Iceberg, as commander, swore that he could surpass the best marks of either team.

Yes, he could trust them to perform well together—but he also couldn't just leave them alone. He had the world's biggest smoke signal going off behind him at the VAB, so Gator knew something was definitely not right. Even Franklin would have gotten it through his thick head by now.

Iceberg grasped Mory's battered assault rifle and hobbled along the damp, thick grass beside the gravel tracks of the crawlerway. The pain from his foot

lanced through him like a son of a bitch every time
he stepped down on his softening cast. He winced, but
kept going away from the burning VAB. He heard
only the distant crackle of fire, and no NASA fire engines.

About a million miles away, he spotted the Armored
Personnel Carrier in the vicinity of the shuttle complex. At least Gator and the rest of the crew would be
helped by the rescue team if they took his advice and
evacuated the shuttle. The astronauts could scramble
out and use the emergency baskets; the APC would
meet them at the blast shelters and whisk them away
from the launch area.

But why wasn't the APC responding to the VAB
fire? All emergency crews should have been rushing
to the huge facility. Surely every military and security
installation in Florida would be aware of what was
going on; NASA had agreements with all the military
bases for security support. Mr. Phillips had made his
ransom demand for the whole nation to see. And the
VAB explosion had provided a signal no one could
ignore. The smoke would have been seen for miles
around on the flat swamplands, from the press stands,
from the state highways.

Yes, Iceberg thought, it would only be a matter of
time before the cavalry arrived. But he had never been
one to sit around waiting.

Trying to ignore his pain, he speeded up his pace.

32

ATLANTIS GANTRY

"Okay, kiddos," **Gator Green** said. "Ready for emergency egress. This is it—no turning back."

He gripped the handle on the shuttle's hatch and positioned himself for better leverage. With *Atlantis* pointed upright on the launchpad, he stood on the middeck bulkhead, using the cockpit's back wall as the floor.

"Go ahead and do it," Franklin ordered, still sounding skeptical. "Our butts are going to be in a sling if you're wrong about this, Lieutenant Commander—but while I'm here we may as well make it a textbook evacuation."

Gator turned the manual handle of the orbiter's thick door, bypassing the automatic systems. All indicator lights around the hatch burned a steady green. He grunted as he pressed the handle. The turning mechanism gave a little, then stuck. He felt a sudden chill. Great—now what? He strained against the handle until it moved with a sudden jerk and then spun freely. He pushed the shuttle's hatch open wide.

Automatic alarms shrieked, drowning out the creaking and snapping of superchilled metal of the external tank and the low rumbling of the gantry hydraulics.

"So much for sneaking out unnoticed," Gator yelled over the din. He motioned for Burns and Purvis to exit first. "Let's go, guys!"

Behind him, Franklin waved the two mission specialists through the thirty-inch hatch. "Lead the way—the cosmonauts will follow. By the numbers, hustle!"

Burns ducked, grabbed the edge, and pushed himself out. The White Room chamber at the end of the access arm was still attached to the hatch.

"Go, go, go!" screamed Gator. "Come on, it's not a fashion show!"

Purvis followed next, bounding through the hatch without touching it.

Gator gestured for the two Russian payload specialists. Orlov and his partner moved with astonishing grace in their orange pressure suits; they reached the White Room before Alexandra even moved up to the hatch. She stooped in front of the hatch, looking flustered.

Just what they needed—a traffic jam at the emergency exit. "Get moving." Though smaller in stature than the muscular female cosmonaut, Gator picked Alexandra up and shoved her through.

Franklin gripped Gator's elbow and tried to urge him on. "I'll take the rear. Commander's privilege."

Gator shook off the shuttle commander's arm. "Experience counts, Franklin. For God's sake, don't try to be a hero—get going."

Franklin started to protest. "I'm the commander, dammit."

"No reason to go down with the ship. I've gone over this drill a dozen more times than you, *sir*. Now get your butt in gear."

Franklin looked as though he were going to continue protesting, but instead he closed his mouth and ducked through the hatch. Gator followed, slipping into the connected White Room chamber. So far so good.

If the creeps had waited another few minutes into the countdown before forcing a halt, the walkway itself would have pulled back, cutting off the emergency baskets. Then the *Atlantis* crew would have really been held hostage. As he sprinted down the access arm, Gator thanked God for small errors.

Then he froze at the sight of a gantry surveillance camera.

Their every move was being broadcast back to Launch Control. And presumably the watching terrorists as well.

33

LAUNCH CONTROL CENTER

The automated surveillance cameras on the gantry of launchpad 39A showed *Atlantis*'s emergency egress hatch popping open. Sensor alarms sounded on the firing floor, sending the trapped engineers and technicians into greater agitation.

Mr. Phillips looked up, startled. Lights blinked red at monitor stations; status symbols reported the unexpected occurrence. This wasn't supposed to be happening, and he found it most annoying, after all the other troubles he had encountered.

"Hey, what's that?" Rusty said. He turned and shouted, "Mr. Phillips, you'd better see this."

On the monitor, the shuttle astronauts, clothed in orange pressure suits, emerged from the orbiter's hatch, climbing through the White Room chamber onto the gantry structure. They moved carefully but efficiently, one at a time, like kids in a fire drill. One by one the astronauts sprinted from the access hatch. The mounted surveillance cameras could not track the figures, but the crewmembers proceeded with a clear sense of urgency.

Since they had not queried the LCC for further instructions before popping the emergency hatch, their actions took Mr. Phillips by surprise. He had expected them to be a bit more obedient. "Ms. Hunter, I thought you told those astronauts to stay in place." He straightened his tie, waiting for her response.

Nicole shook her head, struggling to keep a smug smile off her face. "These are highly trained astronauts, and they have minds of their own. No matter how much you planned to keep them in the dark, they could *see* the explosion at the VAB. They *know* something is definitely wrong, and it's not surprising that they might respond to a changed situation. You couldn't expect them to stay put without giving them any more information."

"Ah, but I can." Mr. Phillips smoothed his jacket. *Control. I have to keep control.* His mind spun through the possibilities, seeing options clearly defined like numbers on a stock-price sheet. Times like these separated the great men from the good.

He flipped open his PDA again, looking at decision trees, contingencies he had outlined on the flow chart of the morning's caper. Two hours left, and he expected to have a king's ransom in his hand.

Years ago he had discovered the intoxicating beauty of cold logic, sound reasoning . . . and its tremendous rewards. He had been forced to bury his feelings then, and do the logical thing; it had hurt at the time, but the lesson he had learned that stark December day in Connecticut, walking away from the mass of IV lines, wires, pumps, and breathing tubes after switching them off had brought him his rightful fortune from his pathetic mother. Just as this decision would bring him an even greater treasure.

He closed his eyes as he gathered strength from his own convictions. He snapped them open. "Though those astronauts are true national heroes, they are half of my collateral . . . and letting them go simply won't do."

He picked up the walkie-talkie and tuned to a specific frequency, punching the "talk" button. "Jacques, this is Mr. Phillips. Are you still in position at the APC?"

After a quick burst of static, Jacques acknowledged, "I am here, Monsieur Phillips."

On the other side of the observation deck, Yvette's water-blue eyes narrowed at the mention of her lover. Mr. Phillips drew his mouth tight. The . . . *ravenous* devotion of those two to each other was incomprehensible to him—as was any amount of deep affection. But then he himself had not been through the hard lives the two magnificently beautiful specimens had endured. What they did in their private hours was none of his business. Yvette and Jacques had never let him down when it counted, and they had gambled everything on his being able to pull off this one caper.

"What are you planning to do?" Nicole Hunter asked. Her voice had a hysterical edge. "Please reconsider—"

Mr. Phillips popped another breath mint into his mouth, ignoring her. "Jacques, would you be so kind as to take out your rifle and *explain* to the *Atlantis* crew that we don't wish for them to leave at this point."

Mr. Phillips could imagine the young blond grinning from ear to ear. "*Oui*, Monsieur Phillips. I understand. Guaranteed bull's-eye."

Four astronauts had already emerged from the crew compartment. They hustled away from the shuttle hatch, crossing the gantry access arm over to the emergency escape baskets. Seconds later Mr. Phillips saw the Belorussian gymnast Alexandra Koslovsky, the grim-faced mission commander Marc Franklin, then the dark, wiry form of the pilot Vick Green hurrying across the metal framework high above the ground.

The Russian liaison, Andrei Trovkin, watched the beautiful cosmonaut standing on the gantry. The ambassador's face grew florid as he lunged to his feet. "I will not allow you to harm her—"

Yvette moved with sinuous grace and amazing speed. In an instant she stood behind the broad-shouldered ambassador with her hand gripped around her razor-edged brass knuckles. She used the side of her fist to pound on the base of Trovkin's neck, careful to keep the shark-tooth blades from slicing his skin, but enough to send him crashing back into his chair, stunned.

"Please remain seated, Monsieur," Yvette said, narrowing her empty ice-blue eyes. "*Merci*."

Mr. Phillips looked oddly at the Russian liaison, puzzled at the sudden outburst; then he glanced back to the TV, noting the slender blond cosmonaut. He thought he remembered a certain detail, something that might be advantageous for later. With rapid strokes of the blunt stylus, he checked his Personal Data Assistant, calling up the file on Alexandra Koslovsky.

"Ah, I see it now, Ambassador Trovkin. So those rumors about you and Comrade Koslovsky must be true. Too bad.'' Mr. Phillips turned to Yvette as the Russian liaison sat seething but helpless in his pain. ''Yvette, my dear, I just hope your precious Jacques doesn't miss his shots and hit the hydrogen tank instead.''

Yvette's nostrils flared in indignation. ''Jacques is an expert sharpshooter, Monsieur Phillips. He will hit the target, nothing else.''

''I suppose we've already had our quota of mistakes for today,'' Mr. Phillips said dryly. ''I'm sure the rest of our plan will come off without a hitch.''

34

ARMORED PERSONNEL CARRIER

Breathing harder as he struggled overland, Iceberg kept his gaze fixed toward his goal—the launchpad. His crew. His shuttle. He saw helicopters hovering on the horizon, security forces held at bay.

Distant alarms sounded on the gantry, and he recognized the emergency evacuation signals, loud blasts used only when the crew intended to make a rapid and unplanned escape from the launchpad.

Good, Gator had finally gotten the message. At least somebody was listening.

He passed a line of low Georgia pines and wild palmettos to spot the rescue Armored Personnel Carrier, at its assigned station only a few hundred yards away. Just sitting there! Why wasn't the APC rumbling toward the launchpad right now, if the astronauts were attempting to evacuate? Dammit, that was the vehicle's sole purpose for being there! The APC crew could roll into action faster than he could with a broken foot and a soggy cast.

Before he could call attention to himself, though, the armored hatch popped open. A lone figure rose out of the interior, unaware of Iceberg's presence as he withdrew a sharpshooter's rifle and braced it on the top of the vehicle. The guy was dressed in a sand-colored camouflage outfit, nonregulation. He stood silhouetted against the yellow-splotched APC like a jet flying across a full moon. He had broad shoulders, white-blond hair that dazzled in the sunlight, and tanned skin.

As Iceberg crouched down into the foliage in disbelief, he watched the uniformed man adjust something at one end of the rifle—a telescopic sight? The blond swung his professional weapon in a slow one-eighty in front, then another full arc to the rear, scanning the area around the shuttle.

Iceberg dropped to the underbrush, hitting his already bruised hands and digging Mory's battered automatic rifle into his shoulder. He bit back the pain. Must be another terrorist! This Phillips character had his people everywhere, swarming like cockroaches.

A roll of sweat formed on Iceberg's forehead. He had to do something, and do it fast. "Cool it," he said to himself like a prayer. "Chill out." But the words no longer gave him strength.

The APC was probably the terrorists' safety valve—a last-ditch defense against any NASA security forces sneaking into the restricted launch area. The blond-haired thug probably had standing orders to take out the shuttle if the astronauts tried to escape. The terrorist had only to fire one well-placed shot into *Atlantis*'s external tank, and the resulting inferno would make the VAB explosion look like amateur night on the Fourth of July.

Iceberg knew he was too far away to get in a good shot with his commandeered assault rifle—he couldn't count on his own accuracy anyway, not with his battered and bedraggled condition. Besides, astronauts weren't chosen for their target-shooting abilities. He just wished he had one of those Sidewinder missiles he used to shoot when he was flying F-15s.

He had to stop the sniper some other way. Iceberg felt his stomach go sour. Cool . . . chill . . . frosty . . . Yeah, right. Gritting his teeth from the pain in his hands, he pushed up, the decision made. If he kept quiet, he could sneak up on the APC . . . he hoped. Move fast, move quiet.

Holding his rifle steady with one hand, he crouched and sprinted for the armored vehicle, tripping through the creepers and thick bushes that played hell with his broken foot, snagging on the wet, clammy cast. He just hoped the moon boot support would hold up long enough for him to do what he had to do.

Iceberg followed the winding track of an overgrown dirt road and the trampled path the APC had crushed on its way into position. He had at least two hundred yards to cover—and no telling how much time. His foot hurt, big-time, but unless he kept moving, his broken bones would be the least of his worries.

Far away, the astronauts continued their evacuation routine, small figures in the distance, high up on the gantry.

The sniper settled down into the APC, keeping only his head and rifle in view out of the armored hatch. He sighted in the shuttle—and fired.

35

ATLANTIS

Gator raced down the crew access arm, leaving the White Room chamber behind him. With the emergency alarms going off and the surveillance camera covering their escape, he didn't want to guess what the terrorists might do.

The crew had to get to the emergency egress baskets and reach safety.

Purvis and Burns had already climbed in the baskets aligned at the edge of the fixed launch structure. Each of the five two-person baskets hung from a long wire that stretched twelve hundred feet down to a wide-mesh catch net and blast-shielded emergency bunker.

"Go, go!" Gator yelled as he ran, waving his arms for the two mission specialists to get going. "Just think of it as an amusement park ride!"

Burns didn't look up as he braced himself against the dangling basket. "Hit it!"

Purvis smashed his arm down on the release lever. The basket jerked once, then started trundling down the long cable with a growing whine, picking up speed.

Marc Franklin stood ready to help the two Russian payload specialists; they scrambled aboard the next basket in line even as Burns and Purvis slid out of sight. The Russians' basket lurched once and started sliding down the wire. Orlov let out a loud, ridiculous whoop as they sped off to safety.

Franklin reached the third basket just before Alexandra Koslovsky. He started to get in but stopped and turned to Gator. "Hurry—you take this one."

Then Gator heard the sound of a bullet *ping* against the metal of the gantry. Another bullet whizzed by, slicing through the air.

"Somebody's using us for target practice!" Gator said. His heart clawed up his throat. If a bullet hit the external tank, the whole launchpad would be consumed by a million pounds of explosive fuel. "Just get on!" he yelled. "I'm right behind you—I'll ride solo."

At the bottom, the first basket slammed into the netting, throwing Purvis free with the impact. Burns managed to hold on; then he scrambled out to drop beside his fellow mission specialist. As the second basket crashed into the wobbly net, the first two astronauts struggled to open the emergency bunker.

From above, Franklin looked around, confused by the echoing gunfire. He started to climb into the basket, then stopped, turning to yell a question back at Gator.

Alexandra, racing full-out, tried to stop her forward momentum as Franklin hesitated getting into the bas-

ket. They collided. Seventy pounds lighter than the
shuttle commander, Alexandra bounced back. She
tried to get her footing but slipped. Her leg slid underneath the lower railing guard that ran along the
walkway.

As she tried to get up, a look of terror crossed her
face. "I cannot move!"

Gator crawled on the metal gantry walkway, trying
to duck from the ricocheting bullets. "Are you all
right?"

She strained to move. "I am stuck."

He knelt to examine her foot. Alexandra had somehow slipped under the metal railing at the edge of the
access arm. Her slender foot was caught between criss-
crossed metal bars. If her foot had only been bigger,
it could not have pushed through. From the angle at
which she lay, it looked impossible to get her out.

Another bullet ricocheted around the fixed metal
structure. Gator flinched instinctively. Franklin
crouched down beside them, out of breath, his eyes
wide. He looked wildly around. "Let's go—the shots
are coming from the APC below." Finally he noticed
Alexandra's twisted position on the metal walkway.

"She's stuck." Gator tried pushing up on her foot,
but Alexandra winced. They had to get out of there,
and get out now. He looked at the cosmonaut. "Can
you turn your leg?"

Alexandra grimaced and tried to reposition herself.
She pushed up on her hands but was unable to turn.
She shook her head. "I cannot move at all."

"Okay, we'll turn you." Gator motioned to Franklin. "Pick her up."

"We'll be targets, plain as day!"

"Shut up and help me lift, Commander," ordered

Gator. "We've got to get her foot free."

Gator reached under Alexandra's arms. Franklin positioned himself at her torso. Gator said, "One, two, lift." Alexandra was light, but with her foot stuck awkwardly under the metal railing, it was unwieldy to lift her. "Now rotate her this way."

Alexandra's clenched lips turned white, but she didn't cry out for them to stop. They just about had her in a position where her foot could come free when another bullet clanged against the superstructure.

"Hurry!" Franklin said, hunching down, nearly losing his grip.

Gator stood up to get in better position when something spun him around. The impact was like a plane crash. It felt as if someone had shoved a hot needle into his back or his side . . . or somewhere. Alexandra slipped out of his arms. He staggered back and opened his mouth—then another bullet hit him.

Gator felt himself falling. Even the floor of the gantry seemed very far away, and surrounded in blackness.

36

LAUNCH CONTROL CENTER

On one of the TV monitors in the VIP observation deck, Nicole watched the orange-suited form of Gator Green jerk like a marionette twitched by an epileptic puppeteer. The shuttle pilot crumpled to the metal walkway as Marc Franklin dove for cover. Gator lay motionless on the gantry, his body obscured by the metal framework.

Nicole gasped in shock. She felt so damned isolated and ineffective here. She whirled to snap at Mr. Phillips. "You bastard! You could have let me talk—"

The little man ignored her and slicked back his hair, then turned to the news cameramen, who kept their lenses trained on the LCC hostages. "Replacing a good pilot is going to be difficult, but luckily the crew is cross trained."

Alexandra Koslovsky struggled where she lay trapped in the superstructure. Even in the silent video image, a bright puff of ricochet showed that gunfire continued to pelt the gantry.

Nicole controlled herself, trying to think of something, anything, that might help. "Look, if you want your little treasure chest full of diamonds, you'd better start showing some good faith. Call off your sniper. Tell him to stop shooting."

Mr. Phillips raised an eyebrow. "Perhaps I'll consider it. Can *you* get the remaining astronauts back in the shuttle?"

Nicole swallowed, knowing the crew was completely out of contact. Gator had been shot—if he wasn't dead already, he needed medical help. Only Franklin and Koslovsky remained on the gantry.

Mr. Phillips squinted down at the monitor as Alexandra struggled to free herself. Franklin crawled over and tried to help her, though he seemed torn between leaving for the escape basket and freeing the trapped Belorussian. A bright shot spanged from the metal less than a foot away from Alexandra's head.

"Oh my, that was a close one," Mr. Phillips said. "But no points for a near miss." He raised his eyebrow, as if expecting laughter from the audience.

Instead, it finally triggered Ambassador Andrei Trovkin to act.

The burly, nearsighted Russian had remained silent since his pummeling by Yvette, apparently cowed. Now, he took everyone by surprise. His face scarlet with rage, Trovkin lunged out of his chair and collided with Mr. Phillips like a steel wrecking ball. "You will die first, little man!" he bellowed in his thick Russian accent.

Trovkin grappled Mr. Phillips to the floor. He sledge-hammered a fist into the other man's stomach, causing the Personal Data Assistant to clatter out of his pocket.

Yvette had already swung into action.

In less than a second the lithe blond woman was across the room, her arms literally ripping Andrei Trovkin from Mr. Phillips as if gravity had been turned off.

Nicole leaped into motion, trying to cross the four steps to Trovkin, but time seemed to slow down. "No!" she shouted. "Wait!"

Yvette slammed the Russian liaison to the floor, knocking one of the rolling chairs away. Digging a knee into the small of his back, she grabbed Trovkin's square chin with her left hand and dragged his head upward. He struggled, but with a flash of speed, Yvette drew her other fist across his throat—the fist bearing the shark-toothed knuckle blade.

Nicole couldn't get there in time.

Yvette sliced so quickly that very little blood even stuck to the razor teeth, but a fan of arterial scarlet sprayed out, bright and foamy. Trovkin's thick neck suddenly gave, as if it had grown an extra hinge. He choked, his arms and legs still twitching and writhing, trying to throw the big woman off him even in the last moments of his life.

Mr. Phillips staggered back to his feet, coughing and trying to regain his composure. He looked in disgust at the blood that had splashed onto his jacket as he brushed himself off.

Yvette stood up from her twitching victim, breathing hard. "That will teach you to behave, Monsieur Trovkin," she panted.

The Russian reached out a bloody hand, but then his fingers curled together. Trovkin's dark eyes blazed at her from behind his askew black-rimmed glasses, still glaring even as they dulled in death.

Nicole dropped to her knees beside the dying ambassador. Everything had happened so fast. She had been negotiating, perhaps even getting Mr. Phillips to concede, to call off the sniper fire on the crew—but then Trovkin had acted. Though she doubted she could have done anything, Nicole still cursed herself for her brief hesitation.

She had lost her edge. If this had been an emergency on a shuttle mission, she could never afford such a delay. A reluctant pause could be fatal for her entire crew—as it had just proved fatal to the cosmonaut liaison.

Senator Boorman looked short of breath, letting the phone dangle in his hand. He loosened his tie and opened his collar, swallowing repeatedly. "My God," he whispered. "He was the Russian liaison!" Boorman sounded as if he had suddenly just realized the fact. "That man was my responsibility."

Mr. Phillips whirled and snapped at him. "Senator Boorman, this isn't a committee action. Shouldn't you be making more phone calls? Get some wheeling and dealing going here, logrolling, calling in favors! Start ransacking a few jewelers' warehouses. The government can obtain whatever it needs in the name of national security."

Boorman jerked as if he had been slapped. He looked to Nicole as if she might provide the answer for him. His face grew slack as if suddenly aware this was not a back-room deal that he could dominate. He turned back to the phone and began dialing.

Sniffing, brushing the front of his jacket, Mr. Phillips picked up his PDA from the floor and flipped open the lid to make sure the device still functioned properly. He tapped the LCD screen with one fingernail, then smiled in satisfaction.

Then he rubbed at the dark red wetness soaking into the fine fabric of his jacket. "Now where am I going to get this cleaned?" He looked down at the body of Andrei Trovkin. "Why can't everyone just follow the rules?"

Nicole could see perspiration on Mr. Phillips's forehead. She kept chastising herself for being unable to save the situation. Trovkin had been very much like Iceberg, charging in headfirst without thinking, solving problems by brute force rather than finesse. The Russian had died for pursuing that way of solving problems, as Iceberg had died in the conflagration of the VAB.

But Nicole's calmer, more personal approach had proven just as ineffective. Her negotiations hadn't succeeded either, and now another person had been killed. At least Trovkin and Iceberg had tried.

Mr. Phillips turned to Yvette. "Move our Russian friend over by Mr. Channel Seven." He glanced around, focusing on Nicole, as if all this were somehow her fault. And, as Launch Director, it *was* her fault—just as the captain of a ship was responsible for the actions of an entire crew.

Yvette dragged the burly cosmonaut liaison's body over against the bloodied corpse of the cameraman. She moved purposefully, as if gaining some erotic excitement out of it.

Mr. Phillips shook his head in disappointment. "Before long, we're not going to have room to store all the bodies unless you people come to your senses."

37

ARMORED PERSONNEL CARRIER

Iceberg ducked behind the shelter of creepers and low Georgia pine, ready to make a limping, agonizing dash the last hundred yards to the Armored Personnel Carrier.

"Oh, great," Iceberg breathed. He felt a pounding in his eardrums as the pressure built within him. He heard the sharp crack of rifle fire, and again, and again—expecting to hear the roar of the shuttle exploding at any moment.

On the distant gantry, Iceberg saw the astronauts scrambling into the emergency escape baskets, the first two away like hang-glider projectiles along the long cables. Even from this distance he could hear a bullet's thin ricochet against the Fixed Service Structure.

Luckily, the noise of the gunfire covered Iceberg's own movements, and he plunged forward at a half-run, hopping on his good foot and lightly touching the ground with his softening cast. Shards of pain ran up his leg. "Hold on just a little longer," he muttered to himself. "And I promise not to walk for a month."

He swung his commandeered rifle free with his raw right hand, still too far away to get a good shot at the sniper. Any botched attempt to shoot from here would only result in the sniper's turning his weapon on Iceberg.

He had to get in closer before his entire crew was massacred. He gritted his teeth at the agony as he lunged forward. It felt as if his leg might give way any second, and he had no way of numbing the pain.

The sniper leaning out of the hatch of the mottled yellow APC seemed immensely pleased with himself as he took aim at *Atlantis*. He was big and muscular, larger than Iceberg. His tanned skin seemed a stark contrast to his blond-white hair. The man took his time, squinting through the rifle's telescopic sight. He squeezed off two more rounds in succession. A coward shooting helpless people from a distance.

Hustling in his agonizing crippled run, Iceberg saw that two of the escape baskets had slammed into the catch-nets and four crewmembers had already scrambled toward the emergency bunker. Maybe they would make it! "Go, you guys—go!"

But his elation was short-lived. The sniper aimed at the high gantry again, squinted for an endless moment through his telescopic sight, and squeezed off another round. The crack of the rifle sounded like a baseball bat hitting a home run.

One of the three remaining astronauts on the access arm spun around, thrown backward. From this distance Iceberg could make out only that the orange-suited astronaut was small, wiry, with dark skin. Gator!

The sniper fired again. The wounded pilot staggered and fell to the metal grating as the others scrambled for cover.

Iceberg saw red, wanting to howl in rage, but somehow he prevented himself from crying out. Like a battering ram, he plowed over the last small rise, across the low wet grass. Streaks of pain raced up his leg like broken glass on fire, but he canceled it. Not now. Sweat rolled off his forehead in the thick mid-morning humidity.

A walkie-talkie at the sniper's waist spoke a series of clear words in a cultured voice Iceberg recognized from Mr. Phillips's announcement on the TV monitor. "Jacques, report please. How is our problem progressing?"

The sharpshooter reached down to depress the "talk" button. "One down, Monsieur Phillips. I will take out the elevator power box so they have no other way to get up or down from the gantry. But please excuse me for now. Jacques out."

On the APC, the sniper, Jacques, leaned forward for another shot.

Reacting more in anger than as cool, detached machinery, Iceberg swept up his automatic rifle as he staggered to a halt. He leveled his weapon and took aim. "Take this, asshole," Iceberg whispered through clenched teeth. He jammed his swollen finger on the trigger. It clicked—

Nothing happened. The battered rifle wouldn't fire.

Iceberg yanked the trigger twice, then another time in anger, but the weapon had failed him.

38

ATLANTIS GANTRY

Bullets whizzed through the air over Dr. Marc Franklin's head. One projectile ricocheted off a thin metal crossbar and bounced against steel girders, passing so close he swore he felt the hot wind of its passage. Another bullet struck and penetrated the elevator power box with a *spang*. Sparks flew from the severed electrical wiring.

Cosmonaut Koslovsky remained trapped in the gantry walkway, twisted in an awkward position from where she had fallen. Her face rippled with pain from her caught foot. She was out in the open, without cover, another helpless target for the terrorist sniper.

Lieutenant Commander Green lay bleeding, motionless.

Leaving Koslovsky and Green, Franklin crawled over to the remaining two emergency baskets, hoping against hope that some technician might have strapped a first-aid kit somewhere. Above him, the remaining two baskets rattled as the long cables thrummed from when the first four crewmembers had successfully slid down. At least the others had made it to the ground and out of harm's way.

Franklin found no first-aid kit, spotting nothing but a small fire extinguisher. Fire extinguisher? Probably placed there to fulfill the requirements of some obscure OSHA rule. The bureaucrats could always plead innocent by following the book, nothing more and nothing less. Just as Franklin himself had always done.

But following the book just might get him killed in this instance, him and his crew. Since he was the only one mobile at the moment, it was Franklin's responsibility to rescue the remaining two members of his crew. He was, after all, the Mission Commander.

Franklin turned back toward Lieutenant Commander Green when he heard the *ping* of a bullet strike the nearest emergency basket. He kept low, crawling on his belly back to where the wounded pilot lay. Another bullet spanged off a girder.

Below him, through the metal grid of the walkway, he saw wisps of white vapor from the venting cryogenic fuels. He scuttled forward, mashing his elbows into the rough grating to speed his way.

If just one of those bullets hit the liquid hydrogen tank, all three of them would be crispy critters in milliseconds.

39

ARMORED PERSONNEL CARRIER

Iceberg tried to shoot again, but the automatic rifle still refused to fire. He wanted to throw the useless weapon across the swamp.

The rifle had dropped from the high bay to the VAB floor, then fallen in the water as Iceberg had dived out of the way of the explosion. Given time, he could have taken the rifle apart, cleaned it, and put it back together; he'd done that enough times in basic cadet training at the Academy.

Well, *given time* he could have called in an air strike to take out the son of a bitch, too. But he had no such luxury.

Jacques kept firing. Now that one of the crewmen was down, the sniper slowed his pace, methodically taking aim to keep from wasting bullets.

Grimly furious, Iceberg plodded the last distance to the APC. He had difficulty seeing straight through the blur of pain. He tried to control his breathing. The heartbeat pounding in his ears grew louder. Twenty yards away. Cool . . . frosty . . . chill . . .

The sniper had only to turn around, see him, fire a round into his chest—

Ten yards. Iceberg grasped the useless rifle by the barrel, like a caveman with a club. He could creep up to the side and surprise the son of a bitch, whop him on the side of the head—

Five yards. Jacques clicked off another round toward *Atlantis*, then reached down to pick up a new magazine casing. He hesitated, as if he had heard something, then jerked his head up and looked around.

Iceberg leaped forward. No time like the present.

Jacques cursed in a string of deep French gutturals as he spotted Iceberg. He stood and fanned his weapon, shooting bullets over the damp grass. Still dashing forward, Iceberg slammed up against the hard, hot body of the APC, where the sniper standing inside the vehicle's hatch could not aim. Projectiles hit the ground with muffled thuds, and then nothing.

Iceberg breathed hard, trying to catch his breath. Cool, cool, he told himself. He heard Jacques curse as he struggled with what sounded like a jammed magazine case.

No time to think—just move. Holding the rifle barrel with his right hand, Iceberg boosted himself on the APC's wide tracks and popped over the top of the armored vehicle, yelling like a banshee.

Jacques frantically tried to reload from a kneeling position, but seeing Iceberg appear like a madman, Jacques struggled out of the hatch. A magazine cartridge of bullets clanked and pattered on the vehicle's armor plates.

"Freeze!" Iceberg yelled, bringing up his automatic rifle as if it still worked. He jabbed the weapon toward the sniper, finger encircling the trigger, bluffing with 100 percent enthusiasm. His heart thundered with adrenaline.

Jacques flicked a glance down at his own unloaded weapon.

"Do it if you want," Iceberg shouted. "This is one of those 'make my day' situations."

Jacques clenched his huge fists and stepped back, obviously calculating the chances of being able to overpower Iceberg. The sniper flicked his gaze toward the sodden, muddy cast on Iceberg's left leg.

"Drop your weapon. Now!" Iceberg stepped forward gingerly on the uneven metal surface. "Or we'll see what a few rounds will do to your skull from a range of two feet." He made his voice cold, vicious. "A teaspoon of your brains might even make it all the way to the launchpad if I get the splatter pattern right."

Jacques spoke with a thick French accent, his tanned face melting into a confident smile. "If you couldn't shoot me from back there, you will not shoot me now, stupid man." Taking a slow step backward, the sniper suddenly lurched for the APC's access hatch as if to reach for another weapon.

Iceberg smashed the butt of his useless rifle into the small of the thug's back. Jacques yelped in pain. Iceberg grabbed the collar of the sniper's camouflage shirt, hauling him back out onto the roof. He swung the rifle as hard as he could and cracked the sniper on the side of the skull. Jacques staggered and Iceberg swung out again.

Jacques went down like a single-engine fighter with a flameout.

"More than one way to use a weapon," Iceberg said.

He prodded the terrorist with his right toe, to make sure the man was out cold; then he slumped down himself, feeling his body shake with the sudden release of tension. "No time for a siesta yet," he told himself, then heaved up to his feet again. At least he had stopped the shooting.

Moving gingerly, hoping that his aches and pains would somehow cancel themselves out, he climbed down inside the APC to scrounge around in the vehicle's emergency equipment.

He smelled blood and the acrid bitterness of gunpowder, then saw the two blood-soaked bodies of the original rescue crew, unceremoniously dumped in the rear compartment. Their glazed dead eyes glinted at Iceberg in the slanted light, as if asking why he had taken so long to get there.

Iceberg stared for a helpless second, then snapped himself back into motion. He had to take care of Jacques before he returned to consciousness. Cold . . . chill . . . frosty . . . He took the emergency kit and climbed back up, hopping from rung to rung on the ladder.

Squatting out in the hot morning sunlight, Iceberg pulled a fireproof line and a utility knife from the emergency kit. It took a few minutes to tie up the sniper, and then a potent whiff from a packet of smelling salts from the kit revived him. Jacques shook his head groggily as he came to.

Iceberg needed a hell of a lot more information before he went charging out to the launchpad, and he didn't have time to play games. Gator had been shot, Nicole was a hostage at the LCC, and *Atlantis* could blow up at any moment. He took out the utility knife, holding it close to the sniper's cheek. The blond man's eyes rolled to the side, trying to see what his captor intended. It would be easy to slash the man's face, to force him into talking. But Iceberg couldn't do that. *That's why we're the Good Guys*, he thought grimly. He just hoped the threat would be strong enough.

Iceberg breathed hard with exertion. "Okay, asshole—what's going on?" Jacques didn't answer.

"Listen to me—you just shot my best friend up there, and I'm not feeling very charitable right now." He pricked the tanned cheek with the tip of the utility knife, drawing blood before he pulled back.

"Last time I tried to interrogate one of your friends—Mory, I think his name was—he ended up with two bullets in the chest and a long fall to the floor of the VAB. I also watched big, bald Cueball go up in flames. And before that I took care of your ponytailed friend at the guard gate. Now I've got you."

Jacques still just glared at him.

Iceberg set his mouth and tightened the ropes around Jacques's wrists. The man grunted with new pain but said nothing. Iceberg twisted his head to glance at the sky. It was still a cloudless day, and the sun was rising higher.

"Just wait until it really gets hot up here," Iceberg said, "and you start to cook on top of this metal frying pan."

Iceberg yanked the walkie-talkie from the sniper's waist. It was time to poke a stick in the hornet's nest. He angrily depressed the "talk" button. "Hello, is anybody out there? I've got your boy Jacques."

Static filled the speaker.

He scowled at the sniper lying bound on top of the APC and spoke into the walkie-talkie. "I'm looking for that scumbag Phillips. Hey, you looked like Geraldo on TV, only with less class." He hoped his taunting would get some sort of reaction. "I've taken out your blond-haired coward here, just like I got rid of your goons at the VAB. The *Atlantis* crew is safe in the emergency bunker—and now I'm coming to get you. You're next, Phillips." The part about the astronauts was not entirely true, but he hoped it would infuriate the little man—and buy Iceberg some time.

The speaker on the walkie-talkie clicked. "Who is this, please? I wasn't aware we had a party line."

"Yeah, it's a party all right." Iceberg smiled at Jacques, who glared back at him. "You can just call me Iceberg."

Phillips came back after only the slightest hesitation. "Ah, this must be the famous Colonel Adam Friese. You seem most enduring. We had thought you were no longer with us."

The cultured voice sounded rattled. Iceberg clicked the radio once more while keeping a steady eye on Jacques, showing no surprise that Phillips knew his name. Maybe he had tortured it out of Nicole. "Hey, I'm laughing at your tough guys, Phillips. What a bunch of amateurs. Cheerio—and hold on tight. I'll be coming for you before the day is done."

Iceberg released the "talk" button. Picking up his broken rifle, he forced another grin—for no other reason than to rattle Jacques.

The sniper sneered at him. "You can't stop us, stupid man. It is all over your television. There are enough explosives on the external tank to take out the entire launchpad complex—and Monsieur Phillips controls the detonator. The access arm was retracted during the countdown, so you cannot reach the bomb I planted. It is *you* who's lost.''

Iceberg's face drained of color. A bomb on the external tank! Trying to control his rage, he picked up Jacques by the ropes and slammed him against the armor, then let him drop back. He shook his head in disgust, reining in his temper. ''You aren't worth it.''

Iceberg picked up his rifle. After seeing the sniper shoot at the astronauts on the gantry, after watching Gator fall, after seeing the bodies of the APC crew murdered in cold blood and stuffed in the back compartment, Iceberg would have shot the bastard himself if he'd had a working gun.

Instead, he hit Jacques on the side of the head with the rifle butt again. He couldn't afford to have the jerk get loose. Blood dribbled from his temple wound, and the sniper lay still.

Iceberg took several deep breaths, then wiped his face with the back of his hand. He glanced toward the shuttle, knowing his time was running out.

''So many terrorists, so little time,'' he said.

40

LAUNCH CONTROL CENTER

Raising his eyebrows at the vehemence of Iceberg's outburst, Mr. Phillips stared at the walkie-talkie. "My, such language from a respected astronaut!" He pursed his lips, hiding his annoyance that the pest was still alive. "Some people just can't control themselves under pressure. I see why he was taken off the *Atlantis* crew."

He glanced over at Nicole Hunter, who was grinning in a childish expression of utter delight upon learning that Iceberg still lived. He scowled. "Don't allow yourself to be so pleased, Ms. Hunter. Just because Colonel Friese has survived so far doesn't mean we can't rectify the situation."

On the countertop, the walkie-talkie remained silent. Nicole didn't say a word, but her continued smug expression made him want to stride over, carrying the step stool with him, so he could climb up and stare at her eye to eye.

Yvette's frost-pale eyes blazed wide, her tanned face flushed with urgency. "Monsieur Phillips, that man has done something to my *brother*." She tucked the saw-bladed knuckle knife into her waist satchel, preparing to leave. "I will . . . punish him."

Mr. Phillips saw the deep furnace of love in Yvette's cold eyes, the rage that shone on her bronzed face. He couldn't afford to have Colonel Friese making more trouble, and they only had another hour and a half to meet the deadline. More important, he would never be able to stop her, no matter what he said, if her lover and brother was in danger. It was better to focus Yvette's energy than to allow her to simmer.

It intimidated him to be left with only trigger-happy Rusty to hold the hostages in the LCC. This wasn't how he had planned it. He thought of poor Duncan assigned to the guard gate, a colleague who had helped the team on other missions, a man who hated authority and hated the establishment. But Duncan no longer answered his radio—perhaps Iceberg had done something to him, as he claimed . . . not to mention the debacle in the Vehicle Assembly Building and the certain deaths of Cueball and Mory. Mr. Phillips hoped NASA Security continued to believe in a veritable terrorist army hidden throughout the KSC site.

On the bright side, with every death of a team member, the respective shares of the shuttle ransom grew larger and larger to the survivors.

Also, seeing Nicole Hunter's dark eyes dart away with a flicker of uncertainty, afraid of what the big blond woman might do to Iceberg, made it all worth while.

He shooed Yvette away with a wave. "Go save your dear Jacques," he said as he watched Nicole, "and make certain the outcome is unpleasant for Iceberg." He held up a finger. "Send Rusty up here as you leave."

Even with only the trigger-happy redhead, Mr. Phillips knew he had the upper hand so long as he held the detonator button. "Don't worry about the rest of those pesky astronauts above on the gantry—no one can reach them now that Jacques took out the elevator."

"*Oui*, Monsieur Phillips. I'll see to Jacques . . . and Iceberg." With her rangy legs, she sprinted out, anxious to save her lover. Yvette always made an extremely effective deterrent.

Mr. Phillips walked to the counter and picked up a phone. He held it up to Nicole. "Ms. Hunter, I need you to contact your security forces. Yvette must have clear passage—*any* problems she encounters will mean an instant response on my part." He held up the detonator button. "Is that clear?"

Nicole nodded stiffly, looked at Andrei Trovkin's body on the floor, and made the call, feeling numb, in shock.

The freckle-faced redhead ran up the half flight of stairs two steps at a time to join Mr. Phillips in the VIP observation deck. He grinned, breathless with his own excitement. He held both handguns out, like a cowboy, and his assault rifle was strapped to his chest.

"A heavier responsibility has fallen on just the two of us, Rusty," Mr. Phillips said with a thin smile. "You and I must baby-sit our friends."

Rusty beamed. "Definitely, Mr. Phillips."

Senator Boorman slumped in his chair like a limp

doll and continued staring at the silent phone, as if mentally willing it to ring. He tossed jittery glances at the two corpses in the corner under the narrow shattered windows, at the glass from the VAB explosion still on the floor.

Mr. Phillips raised his voice. "Senator, have you given up?"

Boorman frantically held up both hands. "I've made all the calls," he said. "I'm waiting. The NSC is discussing it right now. This decision has to go to the highest levels."

Mr. Phillips gave him a cold smile, then snapped open his pocket watch. "Our time is running out. While I do enjoy your company, Senator, you wouldn't believe how many items remain on my list of Things to Do Today."

Nicole Hunter snorted. "Or we could just wait a few minutes while Iceberg takes out the rest of your goons."

Mr. Phillips rounded on her, trying hard to keep his temper in check. But before he could say anything, the senator blurted, "Hasn't your boyfriend already caused enough damage, Hunter? If it wasn't for him, we could have been out of this a long time ago."

Nicole's face turned pale, then flushed in embarrassment. She backpedaled, leaning into her chair. "He's not my boyfriend."

Mr. Phillips drew a sharp breath. He reached inside his jacket for the PDA, flipped open the small screen, and used the stylus to scroll down through the files. There it was, clearly marked. "How could I have missed this before?"

During her time as an astronaut trainee, Nicole Hunter—call sign *Panther*—had engaged in a lengthy, steamy relationship with her fellow astronaut Adam "Iceberg" Friese.

But since Colonel Friese had been taken off the flight manifest, Mr. Phillips had not marked his information files as *priority*. The cross-reference had not been apparent, and now the discovery filled him with a warm glow. "Exhilarating!" he said with a knowing smile.

Nicole avoided his gaze. Now Mr. Phillips had a much stronger bargaining chip the next time the renegade astronaut called. And knowing Iceberg's legendary ego, Mr. Phillips was certain he'd call.

41

ATLANTIS GANTRY

The shooting finally stopped.

When Dr. Marc Franklin reached his injured pilot's side, he was stunned to find the young astronaut still breathing. Franklin heard a thick gurgling in the man's chest. He had been hit twice, once in the shoulder, once low in the chest.

But at least Gator was alive.

Fallen backward on the walkway, Alexandra Koslovsky struggled to release her foot from the metal grating. "I feel stupid."

"Feel stupid later," Franklin said curtly. "Let me think of something here, unless you've got any suggestions."

He considered loading Gator into the escape basket and sending the pilot down the long wire to safety while he, Franklin, worked to get Alexandra loose. But with the other four crewmembers already holed up in the emergency bunker, there would be no one to help the injured man once the emergency net stopped him. Someone had to ride along to take care of him.

That meant the only thing to do was to free Alexandra. Step one. Just like an impromptu checklist.

Franklin crawled up, expecting the sniper fire to begin again at any moment, and started tugging at her leg to help her out. He couldn't fathom how she had ever managed to slip her foot beneath the railing—she must have had her toes pointed straight down like a ballerina. So much for the graceful space walker.

Alexandra gasped as he tugged. She tried to speak, but her ankle seemed to hurt too much. Franklin slowly twisted it around to find any way of freeing her without pushing her leg deeper, but it seemed hopeless.

"You . . . must save yourself," she finally said. "Take Lieutenant Commander Gator with you."

"No."

"At least you will save someone," she said. "Two out of three."

"I said no. I'm the commander of this mission and that's the end of it." Franklin struggled harder. Damn her slim legs, and damn these low metal railings.

Part of Franklin's mind screamed for him to save himself, just as Alexandra had urged, to carry Gator into the basket and ride down to safety. But he couldn't stand the thought of leaving her behind—a part of his crew, which he was supposed to lead. Provide a good example. And throw in the fact that Alexandra Koslovsky was a cosmonaut, and a woman—if Franklin abandoned her up here, NASA would never live it down. *He* wouldn't be able to live with himself.

This should have been a routine mission, another

triumph for the space program. He was qualified, respected; he had trained for all of his duties. But not this! Angry at how the circumstances had conspired against him, Franklin jerked harder on her pinned leg. Alexandra cried out in pain.

By the book, he thought. *Follow the checklists.* Franklin had been trained to minimize his losses, maximize the return. That had been drilled into him in every astronaut training class, though it certainly wasn't the way the much-vaunted Commander Iceberg would have done it.

But then, he didn't worship Iceberg the way the rest of the crew seemed to. Granted, the former commander had tipped them off to the hostage situation, but it had forced the whole crew to react without orders, getting them into this whole mess. He had no idea what delicate negotiations their brash action had screwed up back at the LCC. Now, judging from the other disasters he had seen around the site, smoke trails from other explosions, the sniper shooting at them on the gantry, he supposed Iceberg was still running around, mucking up the situation.

In fact, if Iceberg had followed the rules weeks ago—resting and taking care of himself—instead of showing off with his back flip and breaking his foot, Marc Franklin would be safe right now, watching the launch from elsewhere. *He* would have taken his responsibilities more seriously.

But then, I'm not Iceberg, he thought sourly as he pulled on Alexandra's ankle once again. *Thank God.*

42

NASA Television Relay Blockhouse

Inside the video relay bunker, Amos Friese swallowed the sharp, sour lump in his throat. He felt like a rabbit hiding in a hole, and the forest was filled with prowling wolves.

He straightened the body of Cecelia Hawkins, running his fingertips along the smooth fabric of her floral-print blouse, touching her cold arms as he folded them peacefully in place. He had already closed her half-open dark eyes. That had been the hardest part.

His knees creaked as he struggled to stand. He sucked in a deep breath, searching for courage as he went to ransack the mildew-smelling blockhouse for supplies, for some way to cover Cecelia . . . because that seemed like the appropriate thing to do. He couldn't think beyond that at the moment.

Fighting leftover dizziness, Amos scrounged in storage lockers and found coaxial cables, extra fuses of varying amperages, a tool kit, a fire extinguisher, and an old jar of instant coffee crystals that had fossilized into a strange sedimentary lump. But he came up with nothing that would serve as a covering sheet.

Finally, Amos removed his glasses, then tugged the thick sweater over his head. His hair stuck up in odd tufts, and he straightened it down with the palm of his hand. He took the sweater to Cecelia's body, draping it over her head and chest.

"Sorry, Cecelia," he whispered to her. "It's the best I can do."

Around the corner, the bunker's blast door still hung open from where the booby-trap explosion had rocked it off its hinges. Shards of sunlight lit the outer corridor. He avoided the bodies of the two fallen NASA security men outside, stopping only long enough to make sure both were dead. He couldn't think of anything to do for them.

He couldn't think of anything to do at all. Iceberg would have had the answer, would have swung into action, would have gone looking for solutions or, finding none, he would have created them out of thin air.

Amos wondered if more security would come to rescue him, or if the bad guys would return first. The best thing for him to do would be to go back and watch his video monitors—no, not just watch them, *study* them. Once he understood the entire situation, maybe then he could figure out a way to help NASA.

He felt faint as he slumped into the old government-issue chair. His body rebelled from the aftereffects of the tranquilizer dart, as well as grief over Cecelia's death. His stomach roiled, and he popped one of his fruit-flavored jawbreakers in his mouth, hoping that would settle him down. It didn't, but at least it eased his terror-dry throat.

Just watching the scenes displayed by the surrounding cameras, Amos could see that the entire Kennedy Space Center was in "deep kimchee," as his brother would have said. He had no idea how many terrorists were out there, but anyone could see that the bad guys had the upper hand—at the moment. And, judging by the gantry images on the monitors, Iceberg was out in the thick of things . . . no big surprise there. Iceberg didn't know how to stay put, even with a broken foot.

With the one remaining camera in the Launch Control Center he saw two murdered bodies against the wall in the VIP observation deck. Nicole Hunter seemed to be handling the situation bravely, though she looked flustered, completely out of options. Amos knew exactly how she felt.

He watched the tigerlike blond—Yvette?—set off under orders to go get Iceberg. Here, sitting on the sidelines, Amos desperately tried to figure a way that he could give her some alternatives, or at least help his brother.

Amos had watched the four astronauts from *Atlantis* take the escape wire down and reach the safety of the blast bunker, but Gator Green, Dr. Franklin, and the Russian cosmonaut Koslovsky all remained on the gantry, under sniper fire. Gator was down with a gunshot wound.

With the gantry surveillance cameras, the terrorists in the LCC could also see everything that happened up there. Mr. Phillips, the little guy in charge, had a big advantage because nobody could surprise him. Iceberg could never sneak up there, nor could the astronauts slip away.

Mr. Phillips was able to keep an eye on everything.

But all those images came through Amos's TV relay bunker. Maybe he could do something about that. He allowed himself a small grin as he finally plotted a course of action.

Due to multiply redundant NASA safety procedures, numerous shutdown points existed around the control net inside the restricted launch area. Because so many things could go wrong at any point in the countdown, any authorized person in the loop who witnessed a potentially dangerous problem had the power to call for a stop, to cancel the ignition order and halt the launch.

Amos's relay bunker was one of those shutdown points. The huge responsibility had been awe-inspiring when he first realized it, but it had quickly become just part of the job.

And now Amos had to use it. Iceberg and Nicole and the *Atlantis* crew were counting on him—even though they didn't know it. But he needed to make sure that someone didn't reroute the video feed. He needed to ensure the cut was permanent.

He froze, intimidated by what he was about to do— but Iceberg was out there, with the blond assassin coming after him. And Nicole was being held hostage in the LCC. Gator had been shot, maybe killed. The space shuttle itself was threatened.

Some situations called for drastic action.

It would be up to *him*, Amos Friese, to take this next step.

Rummaging through the bank of fiber-optic cable, Amos yanked out the video connections to launchpad 39A. The surveillance cameras on the gantry went dead. The video transmissions winked out, leaving only static on half the monitor screens. Now the terrorists were blinded.

"Okay, Iceberg," Amos mumbled. "The rest is up to you."

43

Launch Control Center

Still reveling in the knowledge that Iceberg had survived—so far—Nicole glanced at the bank of TV monitors showing *Atlantis* vulnerable and trapped on its launchpad.

The video screens blinked, then all went blank at the same time.

"What the hell?" Rusty yelled. "Hey, Mr. Phillips!" He whipped out both of his handguns and pointed them at the hostages, as if he wanted to shoot someone, anyone, just to blow off a little steam.

Amos, thought Nicole with sudden realization. Had Iceberg's little brother shut down the video feeds from the relay bunker? She drew in a breath but kept the information to herself.

Mr. Phillips's face blanched. He tapped on one of the dead gray monitors with a smooth fingernail, as if that might somehow help. He opened his pocket watch and studied the time. He kept his voice low, cold, threatening. "Explain what has just happened, Ms. Hunter." He snapped his watch closed. "Without delay." He tugged on his tie as he strode toward her. He did not look happy.

Nicole studied the little man. Things were crumbling around him as his deadline approached. Was he losing control? She decided to take a gamble, albeit a small one. "It looks to me like the power went out."

"And why is that?" he asked.

Nicole shrugged. "Maybe Yvette tripped over an extension cord. She was in such a hurry."

"I do not find your attitude amusing, Ms. Hunter." Distractedly, he brushed the front of his jacket, where dried bloodstains still marked a splatter from Trovkin's death. Mr. Phillips straightened his white-and-gold shuttle pin, then took a deep breath to calm himself. "My guess is that it has something to do with your not-so-charming beau, Colonel Iceberg."

He took out the walkie-talkie he had used to contact Jacques at the APC and set it on the counter in front of Nicole. "It's time to call him to the principal's office. If you would do the honors, please, Ms. Hunter? Let us speak with this Iceberg."

She shook her head, tossing her short brown-gold hair from side to side. "He won't listen to you. Iceberg's a very stubborn man."

Mr. Phillips snapped his fingers at the redhead beside him. "Rusty, hand me one of your guns, please." Mr. Phillips held out his hand while staring down Nicole. Rusty slapped one of the pistols into his palm like a medical assistant handing a scalpel to a surgeon.

"I like to think of myself as a patient man, Ms. Hunter, but there are limits—and you have reached them.'' Mr. Phillips brought the pistol to bear against Nicole's forehead, pushing it forward. He moved the last inch slowly, tantalizingly, until the cold barrel pressed directly between her eyes. ''Do you want me to pile *three* bodies in the corner, or is two enough?'' He leaned over and whispered in her ear. ''You see, I've come much too far to put up with any further setbacks. We're butting up against my deadline. Less than an hour to go. This is where—how do you astronauts put it?—the rubber meets the road.''

Nicole felt the hard, deadly circle burning the front of her skull. She froze, too tense even to breathe. It seemed as if her heart had stopped beating. ''You wouldn't kill me yourself,'' she said, trying to keep her voice from shaking. ''You'd have someone else dirty their hands.''

''I'll do it!'' Rusty piped up.

Mr. Phillips hesitated. He pulled back and smoothed his lapels, all the time looking at her curiously. ''You're quite right, Ms. Hunter.'' He turned and held the pistol by its trigger guard, handing it back to the redhead. ''Rusty, take this and shoot Ms. Hunter.''

Grinning wildly, Rusty snatched the pistol away from Mr. Phillips and turned it toward Nicole.

''No, wait . . . wait!'' Her breath quickened.

Mr. Phillips held up a hand to stop Rusty. The red-head frowned in disappointment.

With a trembling hand Nicole reached out to pick up the walkie-talkie. Leering like a playground bully, Rusty pressed the pistol against her head hard enough that it would leave a mark. She tried to ignore the threat, putting the walkie-talkie against her ear and mouth. She clicked the ''talk'' button.

''Iceberg! Iceberg, come in. This is . . . this is Panther. Over.'' She released the button, listening to a hiss of static. It had been a long time since she had used that call sign. It brought back too many memories that she couldn't afford to dredge up. . . .

She repeated her message and waited. She hoped he wouldn't play games, not now. Rusty pressed the pistol even harder. ''Iceberg, this is *Panther*,'' she said. ''Answer, dammit. It's important.''

She was about to try again when his voice crackled back. ''Panther, are you okay?''

She bit her lip to keep it from trembling, then pushed the ''transmit'' button. ''Just having a ball. You know how hectic launch day is.'' She drew a deep breath and extended the walkie-talkie toward him, still holding the ''talk'' button down. ''Mr. Phillips, meet my friend Iceberg.''

Mr. Phillips held his hands behind his back and leaned forward to speak into the walkie-talkie. ''A pleasure, Colonel Iceberg. However, I must tell you we don't appreciate your meddling. If you continue to be a nuisance, you will have to face the consequences. Consequences poor Ms. Hunter will experience.''

Nicole swallowed hard. ''Did you get that, Iceberg? Over.''

The long, silent pause on the walkie-talkie told her just how angry he must be. She knew Iceberg didn't like to feel helpless, didn't like to be reminded that he wasn't in control. He expected to be the center of attention, the problem solver, the great commander— and now he was all alone. And she was here in the LCC, as ineffective as he was.

Finally, Iceberg answered slowly. ''Panther, do you want me to come over and put this guy's chin through his forehead?''

Rusty began to giggle. "Just let him try it!"

Mr. Phillips frowned. "I am not amused by displays of bravado, Rusty—not from this crippled astronaut who thinks he's too important . . . or from you, either."

The redhead looked cowed. "Sorry, Mr. Phillips. You're the boss."

With prompting from Mr. Phillips, Nicole squeezed the "transmit" button again. She spoke as she looked over at the body of Andrei Trovkin. "Iceberg, you can't handle it yourself. You've got a broken foot, and they outnumber you and outgun you. This is not a training exercise. And . . . and I don't want you killed."

Her dread grew with her certainty that he planned to do something stupid. "Iceberg, don't be bullheaded. These people are ready to blow up *Atlantis* if they don't get their way."

He finally answered back, his own frustration and anger directed at her. "Sure, Panther—I'll leave it to you and Boorman. You just keep sitting around discussing the situation. Why don't you all have a *meeting*? That'll solve everything. Talk, talk, talk it over." The words were laced with scorn. "Meanwhile, though, I've got to do whatever I can to help my crew. They're my responsibility—no matter what some penny-ante gangster has in mind."

The transmission cut off momentarily; then Iceberg clicked back. "Oh, I forgot to follow protocol and say 'Over and Out.' " Then Nicole heard only static, stung by his words.

Mr. Phillips walked up to Rusty and with a finger lifted the pistol from Nicole's forehead. He heaved a long-suffering sigh. "I should have read my horoscope this morning. 'Scorpio: Taking large spacecraft hostage may be more inconvenience than it's worth.' " He shook his head.

Senator Boorman, who had kept himself apart from this entire exchange, hung up his own telephone and bolted out of the chair with a smug look on his face. "I got it!" he said, clenching his fist triumphantly, as if this was the best thing he could have imagined in his entire life.

"They'll pay your ransom, Mr. Phillips. The helicopter is on its way, complete with your briefcase full of gemstones—it'll be here within the hour."

44

LAUNCHPAD 39A

Yanking one more time on the rope that bound the unconscious form of Jacques, Iceberg jammed the walkie-talkie onto his own belt clip and tried to ignore his swirling thoughts of Nicole.

Trying to talk reasonably with her drove him crazy, as always. The "new" Nicole wanted to negotiate, map out the implications, reach compromises—rather than just making up her mind to *do* something. But a lot of touchy-feely discussions would not solve the terrorist problem, nor would it rescue his crew.

It was typical of management types—the same people who had brought him artsy-fartsy solutions like Zero Defects, Management By Objective, and TQM would rather sit around the campfire and sing "Kumbaya" than attack the problem head on. He had to charge in. Action not words. Easier to apologize afterward than to ask permission in the first place.

Iceberg took a brief inventory. Jacques's rifle had jammed and remained unloaded, while Mory's battered weapon wouldn't shoot. So much for Iceberg's terrorist-smashing arsenal. He didn't have the time to break down and repair either rifle—but at least he had stopped the sniper fire, and now he could go see about his friend Gator . . . see if he was still alive.

Next stop, launchpad 39A.

If he was in shape, with his foot in perfect condition, Iceberg could make the run in a few minutes. Now, though, if he tried to walk that far, even hopping on one leg, it would take him half an hour.

And that was precious time he didn't have. Iceberg glanced at his watch. According to the broadcast ultimatum, the ransom money was due in fifty minutes. Time to book.

He tumbled the limp form of the blond terrorist into the APC hatch like an old mail sack. "Sorry about this," Iceberg said, "but you'll get over it." Jacques dropped with a painful-sounding thud. Iceberg hoped the blow would knock him out for a little longer.

Moving gingerly, breathing through clenched teeth because of the pain in his bones and muscles, Iceberg eased himself through the APC's hatch. The inside of the vehicle remained hot and dark; it smelled oily, with overtones of gunpowder and blood from the slaughtered rescue crew.

At the moment, though, he couldn't be choosy. Shouldering Jacques's bound form aside, he made his way to the control panel. It felt great to sit down, but now his aches turned to agony as his body had a chance to realize just how much damage it had suffered.

Iceberg looked around and tried to recall the routine.

All astronauts were required to go through APC training, so he set to work powering up the armored rescue vehicle. He reached up to the right and flipped two switches before setting the vehicle in gear.

The diesel engine coughed once, then twice more before dying.

Iceberg slammed his hand against the control panel. "Okay, big guy—what gives?" He tried again, but the engine refused to turn over.

Looking around the cramped area, he found the checklist. "When all else fails . . ." He scanned the instructions until he spotted two steps he'd neglected. The next time he tried to bring the engine up, it started like a charm.

The APC vibrated, and the control area filled with a high-pitched whirring as various diagnostic systems came to life. The exterior video screen flicked on to show an unobstructed view of the shuttle. The entire launch area looked weirdly deserted—as it should have been during the final countdown.

He reached down and shoved the vehicle into gear. The APC lurched forward at a crawl, then shifted into a higher gear. Soon Iceberg bumped across the desolate area at twenty-five miles an hour—which seemed a mindboggling speed after all he'd been through.

"Now this is more like it," Iceberg said. He glanced over at Jacques, out cold. He hoped the sniper was having nightmares.

He drove up to the white concrete pad surrounding the gantry, past a chain-link inner security fence bearing a red-white-and-blue banner that proclaimed GO ATLANTIS! in huge letters.

Iceberg drove around to the elevator side of the launch superstructure and throttled down the APC en-

gine. His watch showed that four minutes had passed—
so far so good. He looked at Mory's automatic rifle in
the seat beside him, then decided to take it anyway.
A good club was better than a bloody fist.

Hauling himself out of the APC, he blinked in the
harsh sunlight. Jacques still lay like discarded garbage
in the dimness of the vehicle, tied up and unconscious,
incapable of causing further harm. Iceberg lowered
himself over the side of the vehicle and started limping
toward the gantry elevator.

The launch complex remained quiet. Too quiet.
Usually, the air was filled with the sound of access
arms swinging out, cranes moving, guard patrols and
technicians milling about. Now, he heard only the
creaking and groaning of the shuttle's cryogenic tanks
and a distant hum of two backup generators.

Four of the *Atlantis* crewmembers had holed up in
the emergency bunker at the end of the escape lines,
far from the flame bucket and launchpad. But Gator
Green and two other crewmembers remained high up
at the shuttle crew level, almost two hundred feet
aboveground.

And he knew Gator had been shot.

Iceberg hobbled to the gantry elevator, using the
broken rifle as a crude walking stick. His damp cast
had started going soft at the edges, losing its support.
He stabbed the elevator button.

Glancing up, he thought the gantry and shuttle
looked like an immense skyscraper overhead. Somewhere even higher was the explosive package Jacques
had boasted about planting.

Iceberg punched the button again for the elevator,
but nothing happened. No sound of hydraulics, no mo-
tors running, no motion whatsoever. No lights winked

on—not even security lights. Stepping back, he scanned the launchpad complex. He heard nothing but the sound of distant generators.

And then it hit him. *Backup* generators. They must have kicked in to keep venting the volatile liquid fuel and oxidizers, providing a minimum of emergency electrical power to keep things from blowing up all by themselves.

But the rest of the launchpad power had been cut.

He stopped, stunned. If those secondary generators had kicked on, that meant there was an electrical short somewhere, a short that could cause a spark to ignite the hydrogen vapor bleeding off from the fuel tank. Had the sniper taken out the elevator power box? And was Mr. Phillips watching him even now?

Iceberg jerked his head up to see the surveillance camera. The light on the camera was off.

Iceberg stepped to the side. The camera didn't follow his motion.

What was going on? Even without the elevator power box, the emergency generator system should be running the video cameras.

Unless someone had physically shut them off. That's the only way it could happen.

Iceberg grinned. It had to be Amos. Phillips would be blinded, unable to see Iceberg or any other rescue efforts on the gantry. Now with the sniper removed from the picture and the cameras switched off, Iceberg was free to act. *Way to go, little bro!*

But, of course, without power the elevators would never work either. And Iceberg had no choice but to climb to level 195 using the winding metal stairs. With a broken foot in a cast that had started to fall apart.

He shuddered, then shook his head to clear his vision. He slung the broken rifle over his shoulders and limped up to the long flight of stairs. Two hundred feet up.

"This is going to be one hell of a long climb," Iceberg said.

Running his hands up the warm metal rails alongside the narrow steps, he pulled himself up, then hopped on his good foot. His biceps bulged with the strain. He'd have to proceed with agonizing slowness, step by step. *Cool . . . chill . . . frosty . . .*

But instead of thinking about the ordeal, Iceberg just did it.

45

LAUNCH CONTROL CENTER

When **Mr. Phillips heard** that the ransom suit-case was on its way, his elation helped him to rebound from the bad news about the blacked-out cameras on the gantry. Up and down, like a bouncing bull market. Exhilarating!

"All good things come to those who wait," Mr. Phillips said with a grin. He could barely suppress his excitement. He strutted to the windows that over-looked the firing floor, feeling in total control. Technicians and engineers sat glumly at their workstations below him; some scowled, others looked up in resignation. Remarkable.

The firing floor looked uncannily like the stock exchange's trading floor after the market took a dive, stunned workers filled with cowed desperation. It was as if interest rates had hiccuped, and first the bonds then the stocks had plummeted ... traders selling short, never quite believing that the science-and-technology sector would rebound. Once again Mr. Phillips felt the satisfying warmth of defeating a technological genie, and this time it was the shuttle program.

The emotional high rivaled that from his early teens when he had finally, cleverly switched off his mother's life-support system, after years of wishing for her to die. He had led a lonely life as a child, waiting and *waiting* for the promise of wealth she would bequeath him upon her death, but technological advances had kept her frail and useless body alive, for years denying him an inheritance and freedom. He had overcome the system then that had kept her from dying—and today he had overcome the system again.

Mr. Phillips turned as Senator Boorman cleared his throat. The senator looked around the VIP room as if seeking approval of his toil and selfless effort in arranging for delivery of the gems, but no one applauded. Judging from his track record, the senator probably expected a substantial campaign contribution—say, a percentage of the ransom.

Mr. Phillips pointed a narrow finger at Boorman. "You'd best make sure the briefcase isn't rigged, no explosive dye packets or other Hollywood gimmicks. I would be quite angry to discover any FBI pranks."

His heart pounded with the thrill, yet he maintained his calm demeanor. Just a short while longer, and all would be triumphant fanfares and infamy in the news media . . . and once again, financial security, but this time for a very long time.

He could deal with that.

Mr. Phillips turned to Rusty. "We must prepare for

our departure. However, there's an uncomfortable loose end that I'd like to see to.''

He straightened his tie and walked to where Nicole had primly seated herself, folding her hands on her navy slacks. The Launch Director waited, a coiled mass of resistance and reluctant cooperation. ''Ms. Hunter, I believe this falls under your area of expertise. I must be able to observe the shuttle and the gantry, to make sure my bargaining chip has not been tampered with in these last, most crucial moments of our transaction. There's no telling what your boyfriend might be doing out there.''

''He's *not* my boyfriend,'' Nicole said.

''That's not my problem,'' Mr. Phillips answered. He held up the detonator box, rubbing his thumb in a light caress over the firing button. ''I want you to get the video back on at the launchpad—immediately, if not sooner.'' He snickered. ''My mother used that phrase a lot. I've always hated it myself.''

Moving stiffly, Nicole turned to the controls in front of her. She played with the computer terminal for a few moments, looked at the meaningless words on her screen as if she didn't think Mr. Phillips knew what was going on. He hated it when people underestimated his intelligence.

She looked up soberly, fingering her gold necklace charm as if it were some sort of talisman. ''I can't do that. The line's been severed. It's physically impossible to bring the cams back on-line unless the cable is repaired. And I can't find the break from here.''

Mr. Phillips shook his head, heaving a long disappointed sigh. ''I don't think so, Ms. Hunter. Apparently I know your own safety lockout systems better than you do . . . or could it be that you're lying to me?''

Nicole pressed her lips into a pale hard line but made no comment.

"I know there are shutdown points at many places in the loop, and I also know that the video can be rerouted from the source. As Launch Director you are capable of determining where this emergency cutoff was thrown. I would like you to do that for me—right now, please.''

Nicole hesitated. Her hands twitched on the keyboard as if she were on the verge of crossing her arms in defiance again. Mr. Phillips rolled his eyes toward the acoustic panels on the ceiling. "So late in the game, everyone in this room is expendable. I would advise that you not force me to prove my resolve yet another time. We've still got a few hostages left.''

That did the trick, and Nicole moved rapidly to check her status board. She used every system as if she had been trained on it. A very well-rounded astronaut, this Ms. Hunter.

"We can see the shutdown didn't occur here in the LCC,'' Nicole said. She swallowed, as if reluctant to give the answer, glancing through the slanted windows toward the crowded technicians still trapped on the firing floor.

Mr. Phillips waited patiently, tapping his fingers together. "Yes? Do tell.'' He glanced toward Rusty. The redhead saw the glance and gave a high laugh.

"It's . . . in the TV relay bunker,'' she said quietly, sounding defeated. "The control point for the security monitoring cameras.''

"Impossible. The bunker's been neutralized.''

Nicole merely shrugged.

Mr. Phillips turned to scowl at Rusty, whose face flushed with surprise, masking his forest of freckles with a ruddy tinge. "That was your department, Rusty. Could this be evidence of sloppy work?"

The redhead frowned deeply, angrily. "The fat bitch was dead! I checked her. And we booby-trapped the door to kill anybody coming in. . . ." He drew a sudden quick breath. "The geek with glasses! Maybe he didn't get a full dose. Yvette said the blowdart would kill him but—"

"*But* somehow it didn't turn out as planned," Mr. Phillips finished, letting his disappointment show through again. He felt suddenly hot, as if the temperature had soared. This would ruin everything.

"Why can't Yvette just use a gun like everybody else?" Rusty grumbled. "Damn showboat."

Mr. Phillips worked at his collar as the heat seemed to grow. Everyone in the room watched him. *Damn*, he had used Yvette to neutralize the bunker, and she had never failed him before. But the signs were all there—this was the most critical part. Without the video he had no way to check on the bomb on the shuttle. Everything depended on this—the ransom, the escape. *Everything*.

He strutted across the room. He didn't like it, but he was forced to play his last card. "Rusty, now you're going to have to go take care of it yourself. I don't like being left alone with our guests here. No telling what misbehavior they might consider, but there's nothing for it. You must go tend to the mess."

He snapped his finger. "Hand me the Beretta. You take another assault rifle out of the car for yourself, but leave the rest of the toys for me. Dump them in the lobby. I have to prepare for the arrival of our helicopter. Now go on, and don't dawdle along the way. We need you back here as soon as possible.''

Rusty looked determined and eager. The redhead's passion more than made up for his lack of foresight. ''I'll get him, Mr. Phillips. You can count on me. Definitely!''

Mr. Phillips nodded absently. ''You do that.'' He wasn't sure if he had sent Rusty out on this mission in the hopes that the young man might become a casualty. He felt he had more than made up for any outstanding obligations he owed Rusty, even if the redhead had helped to establish a new life for Mr. Phillips, back when it had mattered. But as much as he disliked being left alone, being able to see the shuttle was too important for the rest of the plan.

Mr. Phillips cradled the Beretta in his hand and held the detonator in the other. He didn't like to use weapons, which were so loud and heavy and uncertain. He preferred employing other people for that, but he had to be flexible. No plan could be too rigid to account for circumstances.

After Rusty dashed down the LCC steps and out of the building, Mr. Phillips leaned back in a creaking chair and surveyed the hostages in front of him. ''I know you must be considering how to overpower me, and I naturally get rather edgy in situations like this. It's the burden of responsibility, you know—but because the stakes are so high, I will be less understanding if anything, *anything at all*, makes me nervous.''

He swept the pistol across the hostages, most of whom flinched in fear. Only Nicole sat back, meeting his gaze. ''Besides''—he waved the detonator—''I can always blow the shuttle as a last resort. It'll only take me a second.''

He wished he had thought to get a cup of coffee, but by now the pot would be sour and bitter, several hours old. And he had noted that the LCC provided only powdered artificial creamer, which he despised. If they had kept real cream, Mr. Phillips might have made someone get him a cup.

"Let's just sit back and relax for this last half hour, everybody." Mr. Phillips crossed one leg over the other. "I've got an idea. Does anyone know the Yale fight song?"

46

NASA Television Relay Bunker

Sitting on the edge of his creaking chair in the video blockhouse, Amos Friese watched his array of TV monitors, barely restraining a self-satisfied chuckle. By cutting the video feed from the launchpad, he had caused one heck of a lot confusion inside the Launch Control Center! Mr. Phillips certainly found it distressing.

"I hope you find that *exhilarating*, suckers," Amos said. He had thrown a wrench in the terrorists' plans, and now he felt elated—glad to have done something. It was only a small flicker of vengeance for what they had done to Cecelia—but it was better than nothing. Iceberg would have slapped Amos on the back hard enough to knock the wind out of him.

But, unfortunately, the plan backfired on him.

Watching on the LCC monitor, Amos saw Mr. Phillips dispatch the freckle-faced thug to the video relay bunker. The redhead nodded eagerly after receiving his instructions, and ran out of view . . . coming *here*, coming to get him. *Him!*

"Uh-oh," Amos said. As he watched from inside the once safe blockhouse, he felt a hard lump of ice form in the pit of his stomach, spreading fingers of frost through his bloodstream. His nostrils flared as he breathed heavily. "Man oh man, am I in trouble."

Rusty would never settle for a simple tranquilizer dart, as the blond woman had. Because Amos had screwed up their plans, the redhead would want blood—*his* blood, and lots of it.

Amos jumped out of his chair and looked around, seeking help—but he found nothing to assist him. He was inside the restricted launch area, and it was him alone to fight against an overzealous thug with a machine gun.

He had to hide.

Amos looked for nooks or crannies into which he could squeeze his body—then he saw sunlight spilling in through the ruined blockhouse entry and rubble from the booby-trap explosive.

Maybe he could run outside, far from the bunker.

Amos could just run out of the building, take his old Firebird, or maybe even the NASA security vehicle, and drive off—but then he would be painfully obvious and vulnerable on the empty and restricted roads. Rusty was probably already in his own car and would have no trouble chasing after him.

Or he could head out on foot and duck into the dense underbrush. The thickets of palmettos, creepers, and scrub oak would hide him from prying eyes—and he would be left alone to make his peace with the coral snakes and the wild boars and the alligators. This was

Merritt Island National Wildlife Sanctuary, after all.

But then he thought of Iceberg, out there doing what he could to save the day. No, Amos would stay here. Not because of his fear of the wild animals, but because running away meant flat-out surrendering to the bad guys . . . and he just couldn't do that.

These people had already killed Cecelia. They had tried to kill him, threatened to blow up *Atlantis* and its crew, and taken Nicole Hunter hostage. Iceberg was already out fighting his own battles against the thugs, so Amos certainly couldn't just cower in the bushes and wait for help.

He wondered what his brother would have done in this situation. Iceberg would stay and slug it out, of course. He would come out swinging his bare fists if he could find no other weapon—and he would probably take out three or four of the slimeballs before they finally gunned him down.

Amos knew he couldn't succeed doing that. He wasn't a brawny hero-type. *Admit it*, he thought. *I'm a nerd with delusions of grandeur, and would cause no harm whatsoever*. Do not pass Go! Do not collect $200.

He had to use his head. He had time, not much . . . but enough, if he could come up with a kind of plan. And he had an advantage in that he knew Rusty was coming.

His throat went dry, and he considered sucking on another one of the jawbreakers from the big jar on his desk. Instead Amos took out his second can of Jolt Cola, popped it open, and shot it down. It seemed like only seconds before the supercharged drink hit him like a bag of pure sugar.

Wow! That was great. He popped open a third can,

gulped it, and felt the energy surge through his veins. Man oh man did he need that!

As he sipped the last of the cola, Amos thought of his childhood. He and his older brother, Adam—before Adam had adopted his call sign *Iceberg*—had played in the snow-covered mountains around Colorado Springs. The two boys were Air Force brats, their father assigned to the USAF Academy for a few years, before they were hauled off to Dayton, Ohio . . . then Albuquerque, New Mexico . . . then San Antonio, Texas.

Amos remembered playing hide-and-seek in the quiet, cold pine forests of Colorado, wrapped in his insulated winter jacket to keep him from catching a cold. His mother never failed to make sure Amos dressed warmly because his health was always bad.

The two boys would play war, hiding in ambush and then attacking each other with snowballs. But it was always a one-sided battle. Adam knew how to track his little brother, how to find every place the kid went to hide. More often than not, young Amos got a snowball in his face, cold and wet, splattering across his glasses, until he surrendered.

It was all good fun, but Iceberg always won.

Now, in the damp and cold blockhouse, Amos crushed the aluminum can into a satisfying mangled lump of thin metal, but it did little to convince him of his strength. He flexed his fingers. Now, down to business.

He was left to fend for himself, all alone against a well-armed assassin.

And this time Amos would get more than a snowball in his face if he was caught.

47

LAUNCHPAD 39A GANTRY

Feeling as if he had completed a marathon, Iceberg climbed the last fifteen steps to level 195. They were by far the hardest. He could barely keep himself conscious with all the pain, all the exhaustion . . . but if he slipped, he had a long way to fall.

Iceberg shook a drizzle of sweat from his short, dark hair. Pin-sized gnats and voracious mosquitoes buzzed around his head. The hard rifle dug between his shoulder blades, growing heavier by the moment. He was tempted just to shrug it off and let it fall, but even that seemed to take too much effort.

He pulled himself up the endless stairs using the metal railing, keeping the weight off his cracked and soggy cast, lifting his body to balance on one foot before moving to the next step. The dissolving Fiberglas and plaster of Paris inside the cast made a slimy muck around the sensitive skin of his swollen foot—

but he had so many other discomforts that one more didn't make much difference. He just wished he had swallowed a few more buffered aspirin before this whole mess started.

The gantry's crew access arm wasn't more than ten feet from him, but it seemed to stretch away with every step. In the distance, Iceberg saw rows of cars blocking every road into the massive space complex. Whoever this Phillips character was, he had NASA security standing around with their thumb up their ass.

Just a little farther. Grunting, he staggered up the last few metal stairs. He felt his biceps aching, his hands burning, his legs trembling, his foot shouting with pain. Hold out another few feet—

"Colonel Friese? I don't believe it! Good God alive, am I glad to see you!" Dr. Marc Franklin's voice called from above. The disheveled astronaut peered over the edge, amazed. "You could have gotten killed by coming up here like that. Lucky that sniper didn't see you."

It seemed too surreal. Through an exhausted haze Iceberg saw the man who had taken his place commanding the *Atlantis* mission. No, not taken his place, he corrected himself—the man who'd been assigned by NASA to sit in the left-hand seat.

"No need to worry about the sniper anymore," Iceberg said.

Franklin extended his arm. Iceberg instinctively wanted to decline the assistance but shoved aside his misgivings. He had the rest of his crew to rescue and a bomb to disarm. He balanced himself on his good foot and held up a sweat-slicked hand. Franklin grabbed it firmly and helped pull him up onto the wide access arm. "Let's get you safe."

Franklin inspected Iceberg's damaged cast, his battered features. Iceberg sprawled out, exhausted. "Safe?" he said with a groan. "I'd hate to see what you call dangerous." He waved off further mothering. "Where's Gator? I saw him get hit. How is he?"

Franklin shook his head. "He's still alive, but not good. And Koslovsky's got her foot caught under the lower railing by the escape baskets. With Gator down, I can't get her free." He screwed up his face, looking as though he bore the burden for the entire mishap.

"Got to get them out of here," Iceberg said. "You, too. Right away." He tried to stand. Damn, he felt dizzy. He should never have stretched out—it only moved the blood to his head. Franklin reached over to help him walk down the access arm, but Iceberg waved the hand away. "I'm okay."

"Yeah, right, Colonel." Franklin didn't sound convinced. "Looks like you've got everything under control."

Iceberg worked his way down the access arm like an old man trying to walk after a car accident. "You don't know half the story. Let's get to Gator and Alexandra."

The shuttle pilot sprawled on his back, unconscious. Iceberg saw a dark blood splotch on his chest, soaking into the orange jumpsuit. His upper right arm was also crimson. Iceberg knelt beside him. "Hey, Gatorman—can you hear me?" His friend did not respond.

Iceberg looked up at Franklin. "We've got to get him out of here right away. Looks like he's in shock." He wavered slightly as he stood. "Let's free Alexandra; then we can discuss our next step."

"Right."

The trapped cosmonaut lay on her side, nursing her

leg. Her boot was just petite enough to have slipped in the small gap between the floor and the lower railing, and now at an angle she couldn't pull it out. "Can you move it at all?"

She tried to rotate her ankle. "No. But I do not believe I am otherwise injured. Otherwise I would have to wear a cast like you, Colonel Iceberg!"

"Very funny."

Franklin squatted next to him and pointed. "If we both lift and turn, we'll be able to pull her out. Lieutenant Commander Green and I were trying that . . . uh, when he was shot."

"You're right. It needs both of us." Iceberg moved around behind her. "Here. I'll pick her up while you turn her leg." He slipped his hands underneath Alexandra's armpits, gripping the slick orange pressure suit.

Franklin looked at him skeptically. "Sure you can hold her?"

Without answering, Iceberg gained purchase on the flooring, careful not to put additional force on his own bad foot, then grunted as he lifted. Alexandra helped as she could.

Once the cosmonaut was up, Franklin rotated her leg, reaching down between the metal bars. She winced but made no outcry. Blood stained his fingers. "Shift her to the right."

Iceberg grunted and started to move. He put more weight on his cast—a sharp pain shot up his leg. He suppressed a yelp, feeling sweat break out on his forehead, fighting not to collapse.

"That's good. Let me know if I'm hurting you," Franklin said to her.

"Just get me free!" she cried, then hissed something in Russian.

Franklin hesitated, then quickly jerked her lower leg. Alexandra gasped as Iceberg almost toppled backward. "One more time," Franklin said. "I think I've got it." He didn't wait for an answer and tugged at her leg.

She gave a sharp cry. Her booted foot slipped out from the narrow space.

Iceberg staggered back, trying to keep from falling off the gantry. He steadied himself, then let the cosmonaut slump to the metal flooring. Sitting, Alexandra rubbed her ankle through the pressure suit. She staggered to her feet, unmindful of any pain. "We must go from here."

Iceberg turned back for his injured friend. "I'll carry Gator to the emergency baskets—"

Franklin pushed him aside. "*I'll* carry him. You can't even walk."

Iceberg nodded. The replacement commander had a point. "Okay, you and Alexandra get Gator down the emergency basket, then into the bunker. There must be medical supplies there."

"Aren't you going to help us?" Franklin looked at the ragged edge of his composure. "You're not going to stay up here."

Iceberg drew a deep breath. "My turn for bad news—there's a bomb planted up by the oxygen venting hood."

"A bomb?" Franklin's eyes widened. "In addition to that sniper, and these injuries, now we've got to worry about a *bomb*?"

Iceberg craned his neck to look toward the top of the rust-red external tank. The beanie cap hooked to the tip of the tank seemed incredibly high. "The access arm was only partially retracted during the countdown sequence. Wonderful. But I've got to take care of that bomb."

"Have you ever disarmed explosives?" Franklin said incredulously. "Is that one of your many hidden talents? How much extra did NASA train you?"

Iceberg pressed his lips together. "I guess I'm having a lot of new experiences today." His head pounding, he wiped sweat out of his eyes and turned to the shuttle commander. "Look, Franklin, the external tank itself is going to be the real bomb—the terrorists only need to use a few pounds of plastique to set the whole launchpad off. What I intend to do is get those explosives far enough away where they won't cause any damage. Piece of cake."

"But the elevator's dead—how are you going to get up there?"

"What is this, Twenty Questions? Same way I got up here."

Franklin said in exasperation, "You'll never make it. Look at yourself! We need to get down to the emergency bunker, where we'll all be safe."

Iceberg felt his face grow stony. The replacement commander was showing his true colors as a whiner, looking for problems instead of solving them. "I'm going. Now help Alexandra get Gator down to the ground. Save yourself if you want—as long as you save them, too."

He started limping for the ladders on the gantry. He had only another hundred feet to climb.

Only.

And this time it was a metal-runged ladder, not stairs.

Franklin's voice called out. "I can't stop you, can I?".

Iceberg drew himself up. It would be easy to go down in the last basket, rest in the bunker, and ride this out in safety. God knew he'd done enough in this fight. But he'd come too far to let that slimeball Phillips win. Iceberg turned and shook his head. "No, you can't stop me."

Franklin looked up at him, his face filled with uncertainty. "Well, suit yourself." It took him considerable effort, but Franklin said, "And be careful, Colonel. Good luck up there."

Iceberg grudgingly gripped the replacement commander's hand, wincing at the pain in his shredded palm. "Thanks."

Reaching the ladder, he slung the rifle over his shoulder. He patted the walkie-talkie he had gotten from Jacques, then took a deep breath before shifting his mind into neutral. He started pulling himself up. First push up as far as he could on his good foot, then pull with his stinging hands before hopping to the next rung with his broken foot, hoping the damaged cast wouldn't fall apart. Just like one of the NASA torture-training exercises. One rung at a time. Another rung. Another one.

From the other side of the gantry superstructure, he heard an emergency basket release with a clatter, then a high-pitched whine as the basket accelerated down the twelve-hundred-foot-long line.

Now his crew was safe. Finally.

Trying to ignore the sweat that rolled into his eyes, Iceberg hauled himself up, a meter at a time. Even this high, bugs homed in on his droplets of perspiration;

birds swooped around the high levels of the gantry, as if showing off their aerial skills.

His mind went on autopilot, just like on a cross-country flight, allowing time to stream past him. Before he knew it, he would be at the pinnacle of the external tank, keeping company with a bomb. . . .

Finally, he pulled himself over the edge of the gaseous oxygen vent arm, one of the highest points on the gantry. The KSC launch area spread out before him. America's Spaceport—a great tourist attraction, drawing huge crowds to watch each shuttle launch. Iceberg hoped he wouldn't give them an even more spectacular show if he messed up removing the bomb.

Seeing the flat swampland in all directions and the gray-blue Atlantic to the east, he felt alone on top of a skyscraper. Even the launchpad's tall water tower stood below his height now, waiting to dump three hundred thousand gallons of water into the flame trench and launch platform during the first twenty seconds of liftoff.

Part of the gantry rose still higher above and to his left, with a heavy crane arm rotated out of the way and a white-encased lightning rod pointing toward the sky. Below, electrical towers and telephone poles dotted the verdant landscape, looking like matchsticks. The Launch Control Center was a large white building barely visible through the morning's humid haze.

The view gave him enough of an adrenaline high to numb the waves of pain, but not enough to take away his caution. Somewhere down there were the NASA security troops, blindsided by the terrorist siege. A half dozen helicopters were visible, keeping their distance. Mr. Phillips still held Nicole hostage at the LCC.

Iceberg had to take it one step at a time, like a checklist.

"Cool down," he told himself. "Chill out." His crew was safe. Next, he'd take care of the bomb.

Then go get Phillips.

"Break's over," he said, checking his watch. The helicopter bringing the ransom would be due any time now. He just prayed that he had enough time to disarm the explosives first. Once he got his money, Mr. Phillips just might punch the detonator anyway.

He unslung his rifle for greater freedom of movement, setting it on the narrow walkway. Wisps of white vapor curled around the vent ports at the top of the external tank. The rust-red tanks were huge, manufactured in Louisiana and shipped by barge to the Kennedy Space Center—and now, with an explosive device to provide the spark, the tank contained over half a million gallons of liquid hydrogen and oxygen just waiting to mix together and ignite. . . .

As Iceberg started crawling for the top of the tank down the narrow access arm, he heard a noise from the ladder below. He felt a chill. Had a terrorist followed him up here? But how could they have known where he was with the gantry cameras shut off?

He turned around, inching back toward the ladder, ready to defend himself. He could use a second of surprise, grab the intruder, and fling him backward off the high vertical ladder.

Marc Franklin's face appeared, flushed but determined. "Need some help?"

"What the hell are you doing up here? I heard the escape basket—"

Franklin hauled himself onto the vent access arm.

"Face it, Colonel, you can't get rid of that bomb by yourself."

"You're crazy," Iceberg said.

Franklin raised an eyebrow. "Hey, *I* wasn't the one playing Rambo." He started for the shuttle across the access arm, squeezing past Iceberg. "Just shut up so we can both find those explosives."

Iceberg started to retort. Of course he needed Franklin's help, but with the other commander here, it felt as if he had lost control again, putting someone else in charge. Franklin had stepped into his territory before.

On the other hand, Nicole would have told Iceberg—in no uncertain terms—that his reaction was only so much macho bullshit. They didn't have time for a pissing contest over responsibility. He swallowed his pride. But just a little. "Okay, Franklin. Let's move out and inspect the tank. It would be nice if this access arm went out all the way, but we've got to make do. I always wondered if my gymnastics would turn out to be practical after all."

"Right," Franklin said simply, moving forward. He looked down at the battered rifle Iceberg had discarded, but made no comment.

They were nearly twice as high above the ground as they had been on the lower walkway to the crew compartment. Plus, the vent access arm was much narrower, more utilitarian in function, existing only for an oxygen vent hose and a lone technician to reach the very top of the external tank. Grasping the handrails, Franklin leaned over the edge and inspected the red insulated tank.

"Look for anything out of the ordinary," Iceberg said as he scanned the other side of the external tank's bulging hull. With each passing moment he felt the sick dread grow. Franklin was probably right. They didn't have any business up here, trying to play hero.

Chill . . . cool . . . Boy, would he be embarrassed if he set off the explosive himself, blowing them all sky-high.

But if he ran to safety in the emergency bunker, Iceberg would have to wait for somebody else to take care of the situation, twiddling his thumbs while the countdown reached zero and Mr. Phillips pushed the detonator button. Good-bye *Atlantis*.

Iceberg would never be able to live with himself for giving up. They had to find the bomb.

Reaching the tip of the access arm, he noticed a dark red bump on the otherwise smooth shell of the tank. He frowned. The bulge was a similar rust-red color to the rest of the tank, but it had a squarish, too-symmetric look. Like a block of clay. He felt a thrill roll over him. "Hey, Franklin. Look at this."

The replacement commander appeared next to him, leaning out over the railing. Franklin emitted a low whistle. "That's it, I'll bet. Way down there." He gulped, as if summoning courage. "I guess I'll go get it."

Iceberg shook his head. "No, let me. Gymnastics, remember?"

Franklin looked at him, incredulous. "With the condition you're in, you don't look like you could tie your shoe without collapsing." Iceberg bristled, but the replacement commander continued, "Use the walkie-talkie on your belt and call Security. They can get a demolitions expert to walk us through this."

Iceberg put a hand on the walkie-talkie he had taken from Jacques. "I've got the endurance and the balance, Franklin. *You* get on the radio. You're a scientist, not an athlete.''

This was his shuttle, and Franklin was being bull-headed about the whole thing. Iceberg was in better physical shape, better trained, more dedicated than this wimpy scientist-turned-astronaut. He extended the walkie-talkie as if it were a blunt weapon.

Franklin said, ''Don't be so damned independent—were you out sick during 'teamwork training'?''

''What makes sense is to let the best person do the job.''

''That's what I'm telling *you*!'' Franklin looked just as coldly back at him. ''Someone needs to dangle out and pluck that bomb off the external tank, and *I* wasn't running around fighting terrorists all day. The longer you argue about it, the sooner it's going to blow.''

Iceberg set his jaw. Cool . . . frosty . . . chill . . . Man, did this guy piss him off. He took a step forward, then winced, the broken bones in his foot throbbing. He tried to shove the pain away. But it didn't help.

As much as he hated to admit it, Franklin had a point. He had to convince himself that what mattered now was getting the job done. Not *who* did it. It ran against his grain as a type A competitor, but he had to accept it.

Iceberg said gruffly, ''All right, I'll make the call. Just be careful.''

Franklin barely nodded, then eased his way farther along the access arm. ''Right.''

Fuming, Iceberg took the walkie-talkie, intending to punch in the channel for NASA Security—but then he realized that the frequency had been hardwired to Mr. Phillips's private channel. The terrorists could hold their conversations, but Iceberg couldn't switch to anything else. "Oh, dammit!"

The other commander had already climbed over the handrail and was about to reach out toward the rust-colored tank. He looked unbalanced, ready to fall any second. And only the pavement far below would catch him.

48

LAUNCH CONTROL CENTER

Seconds ticked away, trickling into minutes. Nicole watched Mr. Phillips's feigned relaxation quickly wear off as his impatience seized center stage. The little man paced the glass-walled room, kicking his step stool aside as he held his Beretta up in the air.

"What is taking everybody so long?" he said, his voice brittle, his words clipped. He fumbled in his suit jacket and pulled out his pocket watch, though numerous clocks adorned the LCC walls.

"The helicopter will be here momentarily, but I can't see a thing. Why hasn't Rusty got those gantry cameras on again? Why haven't Yvette or Jacques checked in with me?" He looked to Nicole as if she might give her an answer, and she fought hard to keep a satisfied smile from her lips.

"And what is your Iceberg up to?" Screwing his

face up in an expression of hard determination, he grabbed the walkie-talkie again and thrust it toward her. "I don't like this. Here. Contact your boyfriend and tell him to surrender."

Nicole blinked her dark eyes, genuinely astonished. "Iceberg—surrender? And you think he'll listen to *me*? You'd better check his personal file on that computer of yours, Mr. Phillips. You seem to have faulty data."

"I don't buy faulty data." Lifting Rusty's handgun, he pushed it against her temple. She didn't flinch as much this time. "We'll just have to give him a greater incentive to surrender."

Nicole hesitated. If there was any good time to resist the man, this was it. With no one here to back him up, surely someone in the room would be able to overpower him—

Yet, the dead bodies in the corner showed just how far Mr. Phillips was willing to go; he seemed much more jumpy than at the beginning of the siege as all of his plans reached their tensest moments. And no telling how many more might die if she tried anything now.

Her shoulders slumping, she picked up the walkie-talkie. With a shrug to show him that she didn't think his tactics would work, she clicked the "talk" button. "Iceberg, come in. This is Panther, over." She waited a moment, then clicked the mike again. "Iceberg, Panther."

When his ragged voice finally came back over the speaker, Iceberg sounded breathless, exhausted. "I'm kind of busy, Panther."

She tried to sound casual, letting a fake drawl creep into her voice. "Yeah, well things aren't too relaxing here either. We can't see a thing on the surveillance cameras, and that's got certain people a bit upset. The power's been cut to the elevators as well.''

Iceberg answered, his voice rough, panting, ''So I noticed. Look, can we just go out to dinner sometime if you want to chitchat? I'm preoccupied at the moment.''

She swallowed. ''All right, let's do dinner after this is over—Original Fat Boy's in Cocoa Beach. But for now Mr. Phillips wants you to, uh, surrender.''

Iceberg coughed a short laugh into the speaker. ''Surrender? He doesn't know me very well.''

''That's what I told him.''

''Well, did he at least say 'Please' ?''

''No,'' Nicole said, swallowing a thick lump in her throat as he pressed the barrel of the weapon hard enough to leave a bruise on her temple. ''But, um, he is holding a gun to my head. I think he plans to do some redecorating of the LCC if you don't cooperate with him. He's already killed two hostages.''

She heard Iceberg's short intake of breath, and then a long pause. Finally he said, ''Dammit, Panther, I—''

She knew he was fighting for words, so she saved him the embarrassment and cut him off. ''Senator Boorman has already negotiated the settlement. The ransom briefcase is on the way—and Mr. Phillips has got a bad case of terrorist PMS.''

Mr. Phillips jammed the gun against her head in annoyance, but she didn't flinch. ''Right now it's time to throttle back and stand down before anybody else gets killed—including yourself.''

A long silence followed, and Nicole could almost hear him wrestling with his thoughts. She knew he still cared about her, didn't want to see her trapped in such an untenable situation—but Iceberg wouldn't admit his feelings for her, any more than she would admit similar feelings for him.

But she knew he could never give up.

Finally, he spoke in a thick voice. "Panther, I . . . I can't do that."

"You're right," she whispered. Oh God, what have we done?

Mr. Phillips grabbed Nicole's brown-gold hair and pressed the pistol harder still, speaking through clenched jaws; then he shoved her away. "*I* set the priorities here, Ms. Hunter." He snatched the walkie-talkie out of her hand and backed off. He squeezed the "talk" button. "Colonel Iceberg, you don't know what you're up against—"

Iceberg's voice came back loud and clear, cutting off the little man's rant. "Look, I don't have to listen to any more of this bullshit. I'm confident in Panther's negotiating skills—that's what she's good at. Look to her for a solution, not me. But if you hurt her in any way, you're the one who has to face the consequences, Phillips."

"That's *Mr.* Phillips," he said with an edge to his voice.

But Iceberg's transmission blanked, leaving only static.

"What happened? Why did he switch off the radio?" he demanded, glaring at Nicole.

She bit her lip, wondering what the little man would do now. "Knowing Iceberg, he probably did far worse than just switch it off."

49

Holding on to the railing, Iceberg watched the walkie-talkie sail out into open air, tumbling, growing smaller as it dropped. It had felt so good to hurl Mr. Phillips's voice far away from him. "I hate tedious conversations."

The radio fell for a full four seconds before it impacted on the launchpad pavement and exploded into dark shrapnel.

Dangling at the end of the vent arm as he tried to reach the camouflaged plastic explosive on the external tank, Marc Franklin let his mouth gape open. "Are you crazy?"

It took Iceberg a moment to answer, still too wound up by Phillips's intrusion, the threat to Nicole. His anger began to boil over, but he tried to think straight. "We're better off on our own."

Franklin slid back under the handrails to the access

arm. "But what are we going to do? We don't have a checklist on how to disarm this thing—if we can even reach it!"

Iceberg turned to him. It was a gamble, but one they had to take. "I'm betting the bomb isn't too sophisticated, just a block of plastique with some sort of radio receiver as a detonator. The slimeball didn't have time to rig any complex booby traps. He was too visible to everyone on the launchpad."

"But what if you're wrong?"

Iceberg drew in a breath. From what Nicole said, the ransom money was on its way. And the only other option was to hole up like a scared bunny in the emergency bunker—if that wacko Phillips didn't detonate the bomb before they got there. "Got a better idea?"

They stared at each other for a moment; then Franklin moved to the railing. "Okay, but I need you to help me, or I can't get to it."

Iceberg followed, biting back his pride. "Show me what I have to do."

Franklin squatted, pointing to the external tank. "You'll need to crawl out there and hold my arm while I swing out. It's just outside my reach if I have to hang on to the railing."

"I've got longer arms," said Iceberg. "I can make it, I think."

"Don't start that again—look at your palms. You'll have a hard enough time holding me."

Iceberg flexed his hands, which were scraped raw from the chains in the VAB, and still hurting from pulling himself up the rungs of the access ladder. He took a deep breath. Chill . . . "You're right. Let me get into position."

Leaving Franklin behind, he worked his way under

the guardrail and inched out. He studied how the other man would get to the boxy device. If the partially retracted vent access arm had been in place, it would have been a simple step to reach down and pluck it off the tank's insulation.

No such luck.

Up here, Iceberg seemed to be a thousand miles high, clutching a rickety scaffold. With him holding on to Franklin, they would have to swing out, away from the access arm over a dizzying height, like the Flying Wallendas.

He blinked the vertigo away, still trying to drive thoughts of Nicole and her own precarious situation out of his mind. Mr. Phillips had rattled him, but he couldn't be shaky, not now. Steady, cool, chill, frosty . . .

He shifted position and braced himself where he could carry Franklin's weight. Now or never. "Okay, Franklin," he said without looking back. "I'm in position. Let's get this show over with."

Then Marc Franklin let out a scream of agony.

Iceberg whirled, lost his balance, and grabbed frantically for the metal rail. He watched in horror as a muscular, tanned woman—her hair as pale as Jacques's—lunged forward to stab Franklin a second time in the back with a long thin stiletto as sharp as an icepick.

Her face was set in a grim, inhuman smile. She ripped the long blade upward as if she were gutting a fish. Franklin's blood sprayed in all directions, splattering downward in arcs of scarlet rain as she shoved the body aside like a discarded carcass. She held the knife up, letting blood run down the slender blade, over the hilt, and onto her hand.

"Oh shit," Iceberg said, struggling to get into a defensive position.

"Ah, *merde*," she replied with a smile.

She must have been six feet tall and looked even taller as she strode toward him with a rolling, catlike gait. From the other side of the guardrail, she sprang for Iceberg and slashed at his head.

He ducked, reeling backward, battling for balance on the narrow metal arm. The stiletto whipped through the air with a thin whistle, missing his throat by a centimeter.

Iceberg gripped the bar and pulled his feet up, forgetting about his cast, about the pain, about everything but smooth, fast motion. He used the guardrails like parallel bars at a gymnastics meet. He rocketed his legs underneath, swinging as hard as he could as he rotated his body.

He hit the Amazon's right kneecap with a perfect, full-force impact. He heard and felt a satisfying crunch of bone and cartilage. He hoped that he had at least damaged her more than he had damaged himself.

Her head and upper body whipped forward, but Iceberg's momentum knocked her back. She jackknifed to a sitting position on the access arm, but somehow she retained her grip on the thin, curved blade.

Iceberg grimaced, closing his eyes with the reverberating agony from the impact. He couldn't pass out now. Keep moving. Frosty . . . Iceberg tumbled over the railing, hopping back to the main access arm. He breathed deeply and tried to regain his focus.

The woman hissed so loudly it became a snarl. Her ice-blue eyes flashed at him in a fury that overwhelmed her own pain as she struggled, using one hand to haul herself to her feet. Reeling and overbalanced on one leg, she held her weapon loosely in an underhand grip, a professional knife-fighting position.

Iceberg hopped backward as he watched her. She crouched and crept forward, like a cat. She stabbed out, feinting, as if her smashed kneecap meant nothing to her. He tottered away, anticipating her move.

"Colonel Iceberg," she said coolly in a French accent. "You do not look like an iceberg now—more like a snowflake."

Taking advantage of his surprise that she knew his name, the woman nicked his cheek with the tip of her knife, drawing a long red line of blood, part Franklin's, part his own.

He saw she was playing with him. That feint had been meant to wound, not kill. Foolishly, considering the circumstances, she wanted to keep slashing him, make him die from a thousand cuts rather than kill him outright.

Iceberg hopped back on one foot, anticipating her next thrust, but she stung him in the face again. He felt his warm blood trickle down his cheek. Iceberg ignored the laceration. He'd have to concentrate, throw her off balance, maybe take out her other knee. His commandeered rifle lay at the other end of the access arm, far out of reach—not that it would have helped him much.

He wiped the blood away with a swipe of his hand and continued backing toward the narrow end of the access arm. "What do you want?"

"I want your life, bastard. You've met my dear brother Jacques. Did you enjoy beating him? Tying him up? I think you gave him a nasty concussion."

She lunged again, disoriented from her own smashed knee. "I'm going to enjoy killing you."

The dead-end of the access arm was behind him somewhere, not ten feet away. The woman's eyes brightened as she saw that she had him trapped. She tossed her knife from one hand to the other, toying with him. "Where are your fans now, Colonel Iceberg? No one is here to save you."

At least she was talking. He held out an arm behind him, trying to feel for the guardrail. He'd have to time things perfectly—he didn't have anything to lose.

His knuckles brushed against the metal bar.

A smile grew on the woman's face. Tiny spatters of blood from her wild knife slashes dotted her tanned cheeks. "I am going to make this painful, Colonel Iceberg—"

She pounced, fully extending her upper body, taking all the weight off her injured knee.

Iceberg dropped, pushing his feet under her, bringing them up as he fell backward. He grunted as his feet caught her stomach. She looked surprised as the wind was knocked out of her. She doubled up, bending forward.

Iceberg kept rolling, using his angular momentum as she started to fall. He flipped her up and took advantage of her weight as well as his own. Good old gymnastics. With a final heave with both legs, he sent her flying over the top of him, beyond the railing. "Up and over!" he said.

Screaming, she plunged down, down, out of sight.

Heaving, ready to retch, Iceberg crawled to the side, catching sight of the woman as she hit the curved side of the external tank and bounced. Seconds later her doll-like body caromed off the gantry structure, dangled for a second, then splattered on the concrete pad nearly a hundred yards below.

Iceberg breathed heavily. He pulled his leg up, then yelped. Sweating, he figured he'd probably rebroken his foot, or maybe just his ankle this time. Maybe both.

He crawled over to Marc Franklin and stretched him out. Blood still oozed from the long, gaping wound in the other man's back. His ribs and spine had been ripped open, and he no longer breathed. His orange jumpsuit was soaked with crimson blood. His head rolled lifelessly to the side.

Catching his breath, Iceberg crawled over and reached up to the railing. Blackness surrounded him, and he just wanted to collapse, to forget everything. But he had to keep moving, stop thinking.

One step at a time. Cool, chill, frosty . . .

The bomb remained his biggest priority.

He heard a helicopter flying in the distance. Squinting, he identified it as an Air Force chopper, an MH-60, not one of the NASA security types that had been shot down earlier that morning. It chattered through the air in a beeline toward the Launch Control Center.

The ransom, coming in for Phillips.

Iceberg looked down at the block of explosives still attached to the external tank. The access arm was far away from it, and he'd have to swing out, holding himself with one hand in order to grab the smooth casing. He was all alone, with no one to help him.

He didn't have any other choice.

With a last glance back at Marc Franklin's body, Iceberg drew in a breath to steady himself, then climbed over the railing. The bomb sat just beyond his reach.

Keep moving. Don't think about it.

The sound of the distant helicopter grew louder. He didn't have much time. He just prayed the surveillance cameras remained shut down. Otherwise Phillips would see him and push the detonator button.

50

NASA TELEVISION
RELAY BUNKER

Amos hid inside the cramped metal tool locker, shivering with fear. The clammy air smelled of rust, grease, and plastic, coaxial cables and ammonia-based glass cleaner. He took shallow breaths, since breathing made him move ... and if he moved, he might make a noise ... and he didn't want to make any noise at all.

He wondered how long he would have to stay hidden. Rusty should be coming any time now, armed and dangerous, ready for blood.

It was miserable crammed inside the locker, but it was better than being dead. Amos gripped the fire extinguisher like a safety blanket.

Though the caffeine from the Jolt Colas had begun to sing through his veins, his mouth was dry again, no matter how furiously he sucked on the jawbreaker tucked against his cheek, like a chipmunk hoarding a prized nut.

A prize nut, Amos thought. *That's me*. He reconsidered running out to the dense underbrush, hiding in the swamps where the terrorists would never find him.

He heard a distant, muffled sound, an automobile engine that fell silent. The thump of a car door slamming.

Too late.

Amos swallowed hard and listened hard. His heart pounded too loudly. His breathing was like a hurricane in his ears, accompanied by the roar of blood rushing through his eardrums.

From the doorway he heard the redhead's sarcastic voice as he stumbled upon the two victims of the booby-trap explosion. "Whoa, having a blast, guys?" Rusty laughed. "Definitely!"

Amos held himself rigid, not making a sound. He heard footsteps, a chair shoved aside, the clack of something metal—a gun, a big gun—bumping against metal shelves.

"Yoo-hoo!" Rusty called. "Come out, come out, you little geek! I know you're in there."

Amos wondered if he actually expected an answer.

He heard prowling movements out in the main chamber of the bunker. The thick walls blocked outside sounds and reflected the tiny noises, amplifying them.

His glasses began to steam up. Amos strained to see through the razor-edge line of light through the crack in the locker door.

Shadows moved about, flickering in a weird strobe-light effect across his line of sight. The old blockhouse was small enough that it would be only a matter of time before Rusty found him. *Man, oh man!* he thought, afraid even to whisper the words.

His hiding place didn't seem at all like a good idea right now, and his weapons were utterly pathetic. He wanted to laugh and cry at the same time. Maybe he should just give up and ask Rusty for a quick death. The freckle-faced terrorist would squash him like a bug.

The air conditioner kicked on with a roar. Amos heard Rusty bump against the furniture as if suddenly startled; the thug must be tense as well. Rusty had to be wondering just what Amos had up his sleeve.

From what Amos had seen on the TV monitors, Iceberg had made a good accounting of himself, and several of the other bad guys were dead. How could they know that Amos had far less skill than his big brother?

"Aww, isn't that sweet!" Rusty said in a voice thick with scorn. "Almost makes the fat bitch look like sleeping beauty. Maybe I should give her a kiss and see if she wakes up."

Amos, livid, fought to restrain himself. He remembered the teasing that other kids habitually inflicted upon the skinny brainy kid. It made no difference which city they lived in; his father's Air Force assignments had taken them from one end of the country to the other, and the bullies were always the same.

Amos could endure the tauntings. He always had, even if now it was directed against Cecelia. He pictured the evil freckle-blotched creep bending over her, puckering his rubbery lips like slabs of sliced raw meat . . . or worse, pawing all over her cold, rigid body.

Often, his big brother had come to his rescue—but

Iceberg couldn't always be there. No doubt Iceberg would have launched himself out and ripped the thug's head off his shoulders and plopped it right into his twitching hands like a fresh cantaloupe . . . but Amos had to move at the right time. It was his only chance.

Rusty moved around, hitting equipment, clumsy and full of bravado. "Well, I guess the geek buggered off. I suppose I'll have to go now."

Amos heaved a faint sigh of relief. But even as the sound left his lips, he realized Rusty's voice had been too loud, too calculated—as if the redhead meant to flush him out.

Suddenly the locker doors were ripped open with a rattle of metal, flooding Amos's hiding place with light. "Peekaboo!" Rusty crowed, wearing a huge grin.

Amos shoved the nozzle of the fire extinguisher forward like a tightly coiled spring suddenly released. He squeezed the trigger and gave Rusty a long, loud blast of cold white foam right in the eyes.

Then, without hesitation, he slammed the extinguisher hard on Rusty's right shin. He ducked and slipped under the killer's arm, diving past him.

Shrieking with surprise and howling in pain, Rusty let out a reflexive chainsaw blast with his assault gun. Amos scampered to the other side of the relay bunker.

Rusty roared, blinded, drilling the metal tool locker with so many holes that it looked like a cheese grater.

"Over here, carrot head!" Amos called, and then ducked under the safety of one of the bulky government-surplus desks.

Rusty swiveled toward the sound and let out another spray of bullets, sweeping from side to side like a man with a sprinkler hose. Shots took out the wall of TV monitors and video control panels. Cathode-ray tubes imploded, sparks flew, and smoke curled into the air. Bullets ricocheted, zinging around the concrete interior of the blockhouse.

The sound was deafening. Amos reached up to pull over his desk for more protection, but the jar of round jawbreakers toppled off, shattering; the candies bounced and skittered over the painted cement just in front of Rusty.

"Hey, you've shot everything else—but you missed me! What a klutz!" Amos shouted into the din.

Rusty lumbered forward as fast as he could charge, limping because of his smashed shin. The sounds of the crackling electrical fires drowned Amos's movement as he crept to one side. The fire-suppression sprinklers in the ceiling turned on, spraying everything with water.

Rusty lunged like a maddened bull, shooting off another quick burst—then he lost his footing on the carpet of bouncing jawbreakers. He stumbled forward, off balance in a drunken ballet, yowling, swinging his machine gun around—and he tripped on Cecelia's body sprawled on the floor.

Amos stood stock-still, watching in astonishment as Rusty went down like a felled tree, clipping the side of his head on the bulky desk. The redhead landed face-first so hard that even over the sparking electronics and hissing sprinklers, Amos could hear Rusty's teeth *click* together as his chin smacked the cement floor.

Trembling with disbelief over his victory, Amos stood above the unconscious freckle-faced terrorist, fists clenched against his hips and breathing hard. "Don't call me a geek," he said.

Amos bent down to check, making sure that Rusty was indeed out cold. He whispered into the redhead's ear, "Next time, mess with somebody your own size—you might have a better chance."

51

LAUNCH CONTROL CENTER

Through the blown-out windows of the LCC, Nicole could hear the helicopter approach, a fluttering machine hum that brought a relieved grin to Mr. Phillips's face. "Isn't that a wonderful sound?" He stood up to his full height of no more than five feet. "Like sleigh bells at Christmas."

Nicole looked up at him. "Or the sound of a cell door slamming and the clink of a key being thrown away forever."

Mr. Phillips shrugged. "To each his own."

He waved Rusty's pistol around, making eye contact with every one of the hostages. "Unfortunately," he said, "my team is now scattered around the space center in positions that make it less convenient for an easy pickup. Since nothing would be accomplished by spreading the blame around, suffice it to say that none of it is my fault, and all of it is yours."

Nicole let her anger twist itself into sarcasm, as much as she thought she could get away with, one small step back from open defiance. "Why don't you just take the money and run? Screw the rest of your team."

Mr. Phillips considered what Nicole had said. "If I must, I will take the diamonds for myself—but I would rather not leave my colleagues in the lurch. They were willing to work on a percentage basis, and we've been through a lot together. We're a team."

"You deserve each other," Nicole said.

He narrowed his eyes at her. "You may consider me a bad man, Ms. Hunter—but I'm an *honorable* bad man."

"I suppose that makes all the difference," Nicole said.

Senator Boorman leaned over to hush her, his usually plodding voice now high-pitched. "We're almost out of this—after all my work negotiating, don't ruin it!"

With a crackle over the open radio channel, the helicopter pilot checked in. "This is Air Force helicopter Charlie niner-three on approach, bearing ransom briefcase." The pilot's voice was soft and uninflected, evened out by the muffled chatter of helicopter engines. "I am nearing the Launch Control Center and awaiting specific instructions for rendezvous."

Senator Boorman stood up from his seat and reached for the radio, as if he were in charge. His square-jawed face smiled confidently, but Mr. Phillips stopped him. "That won't be necessary, Senator."

Boorman's expression grew stormy. "Let me talk to the pilot. This was my deal."

"Yes," Mr. Phillips replied, "but I trust Ms. Hunter's capabilities more than I trust your own. No offense,'' he said, his tone clearly implying a great deal of offense.

Mr. Phillips handed the radio to Nicole, and she grabbed it out of his hand. She could think of no further effective resistance, no way to fight against him. And this close to the end of the crisis, she didn't dare give him an excuse to kill anyone else.

"Tell the pilot to land in the LCC parking lot, just outside the main doors," he said crisply. "We'll meet him momentarily."

Nicole did as Mr. Phillips asked, and the pilot acknowledged without further comment.

The little man sighed, then smiled, raising his eyebrows. "There. See how simple things can be?" Outside, the throbbing chopper noise grew louder. "Exhilarating!"

Mr. Phillips pointed his pistol straight up and fired one round into the acoustic ceiling tiles. "Since I'm unassisted, I'm afraid I must do this in a more traditional manner," he said. "Due to logistical difficulties, I'll be taking only two hostages with me." He swept his gaze across the gathered people in the VIP observation deck. "I think my choices are obvious. The rest of you, into the side room. Quickly, now! Ms. Hunter and Senator Boorman, would you accompany me, please?"

Nicole let herself settle more heavily in her chair, resigned. She had known this would happen. Boorman, though, seethed as if he could stand no more of the indignity. The remaining hostages hurried into the side room, which Mr. Phillips locked.

Mr. Phillips picked up the radio transmitter himself and broadcast on the open band. "Attention NASA.

My name is Mr. Phillips . . . the man holding your shuttle hostage?'' he said, as if they wouldn't remember who he was. ''I'd like to request that you clear the skies for our departure. That includes your chase helicopters and tracking aircraft. Our helicopter has arrived, and we must be on our way.

''I have Launch Director Nicole Hunter and Senator Charles Boorman as my companions to ensure my safety. Oh, and don't forget that I have my finger on the detonator button that could make quite a mess of *Atlantis*.''

He clicked off, then directed the pistol at his two high-profile hostages. ''Now then, you two—shall we go meet the helicopter?''

52

ARMORED PERSONNEL CARRIER

Jacques groaned, and his eyelids fluttered open. The pain in his head wouldn't go away. The sunlight made him squint, and when he shut his eyes again, he saw the pain as red fingers pressing against his eyeballs, squeezing his temples, digging into his back.

He wanted to kill somebody. Anyone would do.

He started coughing. His throat was dry. The pain overwhelmed him again, and he felt like giving up, closing his eyes and dying—

Images of his sister Yvette swirled around him, his beloved Yvette, with her silky soft thighs, full breasts, moist and sensuous lips. . . . Somehow she was with him.

And then he remembered. Colonel Adam Friese. Iceberg. The astronaut with a broken foot.

Jacques forced his eyes open. He lay outside the

Armored Personnel Carrier, carefully situated in the shade cast by the vehicle. The launchpad complex soared high above him; he must be right at the base of the gantry. He saw no one around.

Jacques struggled to an elbow. His hands and wrists hurt, as though he had been bound. He spotted some nylon rope lying twisted on the ground next to him, its ends neatly severed with a sharp knife. He briefly remembered someone cutting him free—Yvette? He shook his head. But how? She was still at the LCC with Mr. Phillips. He was too groggy to remember details—but she had looked like an avenging angel.

It must have been Yvette. He had never seen anything so beautiful, not even in dreams.

Pulling himself upright, he had to grab onto the APC to keep himself steady. Where was his lover, if she had come here to rescue him? What had happened to that sadistic Iceberg?

Jacques searched the complicated metal labyrinth of the Fixed Service Structure cradling *Atlantis*. As far as he could tell from his position, the gantry was deserted.

Jacques staggered around the vehicle, swaying with dizziness, fumbling for his walkie-talkie. He would give Mr. Phillips a call, warn him about Iceberg's meddling. But the radio was gone, stolen.

He stopped as he heard a scream from above him. High above. He held his hand up to shield his eyes, squinting—then he saw the falling figure plunge from the gantry's topmost access arm, the gaseous vent hood where he had planted the bomb.

Time seemed to elongate as he focused on the shape of a falling human being—a woman. She hit the side of the external tank and bounced. The screaming stopped, and the body tumbled.

Even from this distance he recognized Yvette. He had spent enough time studying her body, her curves, her soft skin, her hard muscles.

She struck the gantry and continued to fall, a broken doll.

It couldn't be! Yvette was with Mr. Phillips, safe back at the Launch Control Center. Unless Iceberg had somehow managed to destroy the plan, and Yvette had been sent to stop him.

"No!" he screamed.

Yvette's body impacted the concrete pad on the far side of the gantry with a popping sound like a grapefruit hit with a baseball bat. The noise carried across the silent, shut-down launchpad complex.

Jacques pushed away from the APC and staggered toward the gantry, shaking his head, insisting that it had to be some kind of mistake. He reached the elevator and punched the button. Nothing. He angrily pulled the emergency override switch, but again nothing happened. The machinery remained dead. Then he remembered that he had shot out the controls himself.

Jacques turned to the winding access stairs that ran all the way up the gantry, hundreds of meters above him. He tried to step up and almost fell. He caught himself by hanging on to the narrow metal steps, but a wave of dizziness caused him to collapse back down against the concrete.

His eyes filled with tears. His skull pounded, probably with a severe concussion. He was too weak to reach his beloved Yvette. Not strong enough even to go to her.

He remembered the times she had been at his side,

when she would soothe him, pull him to her breast, and run her hands through his pale blond hair. He remembered when he would turn to her, after he had given his body to those men—old men, fat men, or just men bored with their wives—and he had brought home the money that would get the two of them through another day. Yvette would always be there, and she would make love to him for hours to erase the pain that wouldn't go away. . . .

And now, he couldn't even reach her side.

Jacques dropped to his knees, sobbing. The concrete radiated heat, the humidity soaked his clothes with sweat, but his grief throbbed around him in waves. He stared up at the gantry, the monumental white beast of the shuttle, gleaming as the sun reflected off its surfaces.

If Iceberg had thrown Yvette off the top access arm, then he must have discovered the bomb. A tremor shook through him like an earthquake. He should never have mentioned the bomb. Iceberg would never have found it, and Yvette would not have had to climb the hundreds of stairs to stop him—where she had met her death.

Without his precious Yvette, he had no reason for living. They'd been together all their lives, from the orphanage to when Mr. Phillips had rescued them from the streets. Continuing without her was incomprehensible to him. Just as her death had been.

Jacques staggered back toward the APC, where he hoped to find his sharpshooter's rifle. The man who had murdered his sister must not escape. Jacques could not allow it.

53

Once more, Iceberg scrutinized the colored block of plastique attached to the external tank. He didn't have much time. What if Mr. Phillips decided to blow the shuttle anyway once his suitcase full of gems arrived? It would certainly distract any pursuers on his tail.

The mid-morning sun beat down, and the humidity grew thicker with each passing second, making it difficult to breathe. Iceberg's clothes clung to his body. The soft, crumbling cast made his left leg feel like a nightmare from the knee to his toes, barely held together by the moon boot covering. His stinging hands were slippery with sweat and fresh blood, and he tried to dry them on his pants one at a time as he held the railing with his other hand.

A cold shower would have felt marvelous at the

moment. A cold beer even better. Instead, he was stuck with cold reality.

He tried to imagine he was back at the Academy at Colorado Springs, getting ready for a gymnastics meet: all alone in a huge, hollow gym, with no one watching.

No mistakes. Total concentration. This was it.

Iceberg drew in a breath. He grasped the railing with his left hand and flexed his fingers. *Three, two, one*—he swung out, levering himself away from the narrow access arm with his aching biceps until he dangled over empty space. No spotters or padded mats below to catch his fall.

Don't look down. Cool, chill, frosty . . .

He made a grab for the plastic explosive. The puttylike brick was only inches away, tantalizing, just out of reach. He held out his fingers and strained, grunting, trying to unpop his joints so that he might somehow extend them another centimeter. . . .

Exhausted and discouraged, he swung back to safety on the access arm. He panted, groaning deeply. He saw no way to reach the device—his arms weren't long enough, and the bomb had been placed too low, now that the access arm had swung partway back during the countdown.

He thought about using the rifle he had brought, but the reddish substance would be soft, with nothing solid to hook onto. He would have to do it by hand. Somehow.

Catching his breath, Iceberg tried again. He moved as far from the access arm as he could, his fingers barely gripping the railing. He gained half an inch, but he'd need another two—and two inches didn't come easy.

There had to be another solution. Just as he had been taught in pilot training, if one procedure doesn't work, don't focus on it; keep your head out of the cockpit and try another procedure. Keep trying until something works.

Or until the plane crashes.

He stood back against the railing, looking for another way to tackle the problem. Maybe if he lay flat on the access arm and anchored himself by wrapping his legs around the lowest rail. . . . His body protested at the mere thought, but he clamped his teeth together and did it anyway.

Moving onto his stomach, he pushed out until his chest extended over the platform where the external tank dropped off. He saw the concrete nearly three hundred feet below him. The blond woman had made quite a splash—and Iceberg had no desire to join her.

He let himself hang down, legs crossed, body screaming in all-too-familiar pain. Iceberg bent his knees, reaching backward toward the tank. He was low enough, but he needed another half foot.

He heard the stuttering sound of the distant helicopter landing at the LCC. Perspiration flowed off his forehead. *Phillips*, he thought. Iceberg wouldn't have more than a few minutes until the terrorist would be far enough away to detonate the shuttle and get off scot-free.

Iceberg still couldn't reach—unless he hooked his bad foot over one of the support posts on the railing. That would do it.

Cold needles of sweat stung him as he thought of the agony he would have to endure. He'd have to support his body with the broken bone in his foot. He wasn't sure he could even remain conscious long enough to remove the explosives.

But if he passed out, at least he wouldn't notice the long fall—or worse yet, the sudden stop at the bottom.

Any other day he'd have hesitated, but with the sound of the helicopter at the LCC, Iceberg gritted his teeth and scooted out, putting more and more weight on his cast. White-hot swords shot up his leg, but he tried to keep focused on the bomb. Rescuing *Atlantis*. He imagined the bones resnapping, jutting through his skin—

His fingertips touched the rectangular block. He tried to get his hands around the soft, smooth corners. Finally, he dug his fingers in, got a grip, and pulled—

The bomb stuck to the external tank.

He felt himself sliding from the access arm over-head and clamped his legs together like a vise. He nearly fainted from the new wash of agony, and he didn't know how much longer he'd be able to hold on.

Iceberg lurched out and grabbed the bomb, cursing it with a long string of imaginative insults. He pulled, using his hard cast as an anchor—and the weakened cast cracked. Pain flashed like a supernova in his head.

But the plastique block tore free of the tank, leaving adhesive strips behind.

Iceberg jammed his eyes shut and arched his back, trying to force himself back up to the platform, feeling muscles strain to the ripping point in his abdomen and legs. The cast weakened, softened by water, abused by rough treatment.

He heaved himself back around, and finally col-lapsed on the narrow metal access arm.

Gulping deep breaths of the stifling air laced with the chemical smells around the launchpad, Iceberg gingerly placed the device on the platform. His foot felt as if it were going to burst. Right now, amputation seemed as good an answer as any.

Colors of nausea and dizziness washed over his eyes as he pried open the painted plastic top. A small radio receiver was embedded next to an array of wires. Iceberg felt his heart sink. He hoped one of them wouldn't be a fail-safe device that would detonate the bomb if he messed with it.

He had convinced himself that the bomb wouldn't be so sophisticated.

He thought he heard the helicopter's engines start to pick up in intensity over at the LCC. Iceberg wet his lips. Mr. Phillips, with his diamonds and rubies in hand, could blow the shuttle at any instant.

54

LAUNCHPAD 39A

Jacques climbed back out of the Armored Personnel Carrier, swinging his high-powered rifle for balance. It had taken him too long—precious minutes—just to get inside the APC, secure his weapon, clear the jammed cartridge, and reload it.

Now he was ready to kill.

His side ached, his head felt as if it would explode from the pain. His vision blurred, his skull pounded. He almost certainly had a concussion.

And Yvette was dead.

Jacques knew that if he had been just a little quicker when Iceberg had surprised him in the first place, all of this would never have happened. He could have shot the rest of the shuttle crew, massacring them in their emergency bunker if he had to, and the launchpad area would still be secure. Mr. Phillips would even now be swooping in with his escape helicopter, along with Yvette and the ransom money, to take him away.

But he didn't care about the money. Not anymore.

Jacques crawled on his hands and knees on the top of the APC. He positioned himself for an unobstructed view of the shuttle. The metal hinge on the vehicle's entry hatch dug into his back, providing more than enough support for what he had to do. More than enough.

It wouldn't be hard. Hitting the shuttle's external tank with the rifle from this distance should ignite the highly volatile fuel. Jacques would ensure that his sister's death had not been in vain, even if that bastard Iceberg somehow managed to defuse the bomb. At this point, the bomb itself was irrelevant.

Squinting through the telescopic sight, he scanned the gaseous oxygen access arm again but could see no one high above. The gantry seemed abandoned.

As he took careful aim, Jacques remembered the admonishment Mr. Phillips had given him: *The cryogenic tank has an aluminum exterior, so you will be shooting though the skin of the external tank as well as much insulation.*

He wished he had armor-piercing rounds. The small-caliber bullets would have difficulty penetrating the insulation, the outer skin, and then the inner tank. It might require several direct hits.

But Jacques knew from the model he had studied where the most vulnerable spots were located. Mr. Phillips had briefed them thoroughly, drilled them over and over.

Jacques tried to find the tank's stress points in his sights. Only a single bullet had to penetrate. "Just one tiny hole," he said. "Just a spark."

He drew the rifle up and settled back for some target practice.

55

LAUNCHPAD 39A, *ATLANTIS* GANTRY

With no better alternative, Iceberg grasped the detonator wires.

Maybe he would be blown to bits in the next five seconds. He'd never hear or see the twenty pounds of explosives going off in his hands. He would be vaporized before his brain could process the information, or send a flicker of pain.

But if he didn't do anything, and do it now, Mr. Phillips would set off the bomb anyway.

Iceberg closed his eyes as he yanked the wire out, disconnecting the radio receiver from the block of plastic explosives. The wire leads came free of the claylike substance with a faint sucking sound.

Nothing happened.

Which meant he was still alive—and the bomb was disarmed.

Iceberg stood, shaking from the experience,

drenched in sweat. Although his mind comprehended that he was safe, just looking at the remains of the bomb made him ill. Best leave it alone, he thought. The experts could dispose of the rest later. For now, the device was neutralized.

He wiped his raw, sweaty hands on his pants and decided not to wait around, not with the way this day was going.

Gripping the railing, he limped toward the metal ladder, not looking forward to the ordeal of another descent. Cool, wispy fumes that smelled like wet dust circled around him; the cryogens must be bleeding out like crazy in the rising morning heat. The shuttle should have soared into orbit hours ago.

Struggling past Marc Franklin's body, Iceberg paused to stare down at the fallen mission commander. He swallowed a lump in his throat. The space program had had its share of martyrs, from the astronauts who had died in the Apollo 1 fire, to the *Challenger* crew, to the innumerable test pilots and trainees who had perished for each step of progress. But no one should have to die like this.

"Sorry, Marc," he muttered. "We should have checked our six."

He plucked up the battered rifle again and slung it over one shoulder, as if it were an old friend. Reaching the edge of the ladder, Iceberg punched the button to see if the elevator power had come back on—but no such luck. At least the video cams were still out of service. Amos must still be hanging in there, keeping the terrorists blinded. "Thanks, little brother," he muttered, then started the agonizing descent.

Going down was a hell of a lot easier than struggling up. He could drop two or three rungs at a time, and all he had to do was to support his weight with his aching arms and land on his good foot. Shifting into autopilot mode again, he proceeded carefully, not counting the rungs, not thinking, not looking down.

He finally reached the crew level.

Two of the five emergency baskets remained anchored. It would be a wild ride, but he could hole up in the emergency bunker with the remainder of his crew. He had to check on Gator, make sure the wounded pilot was doing better. Now, at last, he could rest. . . .

Like a long-distance runner reaching a much-anticipated finish line, Iceberg crawled into the nearest basket, collapsing into the flexible cage. Almost there. Stay cool, frosty. . . . He placed his rifle next to him. His arm felt as heavy as a redwood tree as he lifted it to smash down the release lever.

The metallic *spang* of a sniper's bullet took him completely by surprise.

"Not again!" he cried, ducking into the basket.

Another bullet struck, but this time the *clang* came from against the massive external tank.

Looking below, he spotted the APC at the bottom of the gantry. He caught a fleeting movement on top of the armored vehicle, someone sitting by the hatch, his head sporting a shock of white hair.

Jacques! The sniper had gotten free somehow!

A third bullet crashed against the rust-red tank. And Iceberg realized that Jacques wasn't shooting at him.

Jacques was intentionally trying to hit the external tank!

Iceberg smashed down the lever, and the emergency basket disengaged from the dock. With a high-pitched whine the basket catapulted down the wire. He sped away, picking up speed as he flew toward the emergency bunkers. He felt as if rocket engines were shoving him along.

Iceberg gripped the basket's rim and watched the gantry recede as he continued to accelerate. The shuttle looked hazy and pristine through the humidity.

Below, Jacques continued shooting.

The hydrogen in the external tank was extremely volatile. Visions of the *Hindenberg* explosion raced through his head. If Jacques bored through the tank, the fireball would engulf him in a second before he could ever reach the emergency bunker.

The ground rushed toward him. The safety net at the bottom looked incredibly flimsy. He braced himself, keeping his head rigid against the basket's padded backboard. He pushed his arms against the seat, waiting for the impact.

Another shot rang out.

Iceberg slammed against the back of the basket, swept up in the catch-net as he crashed to the ground.

Without an instant's delay to recover from the shock, he clambered over the side, kicking out with his good leg. He rolled to the ground and pushed up, gritting his teeth at the pain. So, what was another broken bone or two?

He heard the distant thuds of bullets as Jacques continued shooting.

Iceberg almost collapsed, but he forced himself to go on. Any hesitation and he'd die. He threw himself against the vaultlike door of the emergency bunker, and bounced back.

It didn't open.

He worked at the lever, frantically trying to get in. Was it jammed? The tightness in his stomach almost crippled him. Why wouldn't it open? He used the butt of his rifle to pound on the door.

Suddenly, the heavy hatch opened from the inside, and Alexandra Koslovsky grabbed at him. "Colonel Iceberg! Come in quickly!"

At the APC, Jacques shot his rifle one more time.

This time, the bullet struck home.

56

Jacques saw the bullet strike, and he *knew* he had found the mark.

He never heard the sound. His brain could not process the events that took place in less than a thousandth of a second. Insulation sprayed out as the bullet broke through the aluminum wall of the external tank.

Spark.

Ignition.

Fueled by tons of liquid oxygen in the cryogenic tank just above the hydrogen, the fireball engulfed the entire pad. In a second, a flaming storm of terrifying strength vaporized and melted the majority of the gantry.

Atlantis blazed.

Before Jacques could blink, the shock wave from the explosion imploded him, pulverizing his bones, crushing his internal organs like a meat mallet.

Then the fireball swallowed him up, blasting the Armored Personnel Carrier aside and torching the rest of launchpad 39A.

Inside the emergency bunker, Iceberg collapsed. Alexandra Koslovsky and Major Arlan Burns slammed the door shut just as the ground started moving.

Less than a second later they were all slammed to the bunker floor as a shock wave rocked the building. A deafening white-noise roar thundered through the enclosed shelter, deafening despite the heavy fortification and insulation.

The lights blinked and went out, leaving the *Atlantis* crew in suffocating darkness.

But the noise outside went on and on.

57

LAUNCH CONTROL CENTER

The huge explosion of *Atlantis* on the launchpad was so spectacular that, even three miles away, it bathed the LCC in bright yellow-and-orange light. The fireball roared upward and outward with equal speed, as if the terrorists had dropped an atomic bomb on Kennedy Space Center.

It took several seconds for the distance-damped boom to rattle the shutters of the observation deck. Nicole felt the brief overpressure wave pass through the windows that had already shattered in the explosion of the much closer VAB.

If Nicole had had any sense, if her reactions had been as finely tuned and high strung as an astronaut's were *supposed* to be, she could have lunged sideways and tackled Mr. Phillips in that instant, ending the whole situation. But for a brief eternity it seemed that no one could move, no one could respond with more than openmouthed astonishment, their faces flat, gaping in horror and disbelief. Even Senator Boorman seemed profoundly affected.

Mr. Phillips stared at the detonation control box in his left hand, as if it had betrayed him. "But I didn't push the button! I didn't push it!"

Nicole suddenly came to her senses, and she coiled, ready to spring. Something had gone wrong, and Mr. Phillips was screwed. His plan had fizzled. The little man could salvage nothing now . . . and he knew it.

Before Nicole could move, though, the terrorist snapped his pistol around and fired into the Plexiglas observation walls that angled out into the upper firing floor. He shot out the static-filled video monitors and blasted one of the telephone banks in front of him. The observation deck filled with smoke, shards, sparks, and screams. The gunshots killed all thoughts of resistance.

Mr. Phillips grabbed Nicole's arm, yanking her in front of him next to Boorman. "Quickly now. Time to go, so don't dawdle." He buried the Beretta in the small of her back, and she heard the sound of him quickly reloading. "I believe in happy endings, don't you?"

He pushed Nicole forward. She and the senator stumbled down three flights of stairs into the lobby. Behind them she still heard the quiet sounds of terror mixed with relief as the other hostages found themselves still alive, sobbing, babbling . . . possibly even free. From the yells and rattling sounds inside the sealed-off firing room, Nicole suspected it might be only a matter of moments before the rest of the technicians managed to batter their way out—but it would be too late.

Downstairs, through the LCC lobby windows, she spotted the Air Force helicopter that had just landed on the hot asphalt out front. With its rotors still turning, it appeared to have been shielded from the blast by the Launch Control Center itself.

The sky was china blue, and the sun pounded down—a great day for a space launch. But everything had gone wrong.

In the lobby Mr. Phillips dashed over to one of the padded blue chairs beside a scale model of the VAB. He reached down to pull up a canvas satchel. "Ah, thank you, Rusty," he said. At Nicole's blank expression, Mr. Phillips said lightly, "Two more of those Stinger missiles. Just in case we run into further difficulties." Her heart sank. "They're really quite versatile weapons."

The little man's flushed face sparkled with perspiration. He seemed to have passed beyond his ability to maintain a cool demeanor and had fallen into some sort of manic routine. "Contingency plans, contingency plans!" Cradling the satchel of tiny missiles under one arm, he gestured with the pistol. "Out you go to the parking lot. Our ride is waiting for us."

The helicopter had settled onto an open space on the blacktop. The rotor blades still spun slowly, like an aborigine's bolo. Boorman instinctively bent low and shuffled forward in a ducklike run across the short distance to the waiting helicopter. Nicole followed, prodded from behind by Mr. Phillips's gun.

She tried to look for NASA security, but they were either well hidden or not around. Close behind her Mr. Phillips's polished shoes slapped the pavement—as if concerned that snipers might take him out as he rushed toward his escape craft. No shots rang out, though.

Senator Boorman climbed into the helicopter and squeezed into the back; Nicole quickly followed. Still holding the pistol on them, Mr. Phillips grabbed the passenger side of the open-framed helicopter and hauled himself in. A lone pilot sat inside the cockpit wearing a helmet and a dark green flight jacket. His expression was unreadable behind mirrored sunglasses.

Mr. Phillips turned his pistol on the pilot. "Are my pretty gems in here?"

With a leather-gloved hand, the pilot indicated a reinforced briefcase on the passenger's seat. "Right there, just what you asked for."

"Looks like the right size," Mr. Phillips said. He hauled it forward with a grunt. "My, it's heavy!" He snapped it open and stared at stacks and stacks of small plastic packets that contained glittering gems of various hues and colors. He ran his fingers through the packets, glancing at gem after gem. His lips curved upward in a grin, like a man ransacking a pirate's treasure.

Nicole said from the back, "I thought you were going to use your loupe and your gemology expertise to check all the gems. Go ahead—we've got plenty of time." *Where was Security?*

He frowned at her. "Oh no, that was just a bluff." He looked over at the pilot. "Do I have your personal word of honor that all the ransom is there, as I requested?"

The pilot looked surprised by the question. "Yeah, it's there."

"Good," Mr. Phillips said, clicking the briefcase shut again. "Thank you. That will be all." He pointed the pistol and shot the pilot twice in the chest.

Nicole cried out in utter shock, while the flabbergasted senator sat beside her, his big-knuckled hands hanging like wrecking balls at his sides.

"But what?" Boorman said, his mouth opening and closing like a fish out of water. "What . . . why—?"

Mr. Phillips looked coldly at him. "I would think the distinguished gentleman could be a bit more articulate." He bent down quickly, savagely, to yank the zipper of the pilot's jacket. Opening it up, he revealed that the pilot carried a concealed pistol and an FBI badge-wallet in his pocket. "Just can't trust anyone these days."

Twisting his shoulder in a Quasimodo motion, Mr. Phillips slung the satchel of missiles and launcher tube into the back passenger compartment. He reached to grab the pilot's bloodied green jacket and pushed the body out of the seat, dumping the dead man unceremoniously onto the parking lot.

Nicole felt numb until, unbidden, a derisive laugh came from her lips. "Now how are you going to get away, Phillips?" she said, intentionally leaving off the "Mr." "You don't even have a pilot."

"I wouldn't leave such a critical detail to chance, Ms. Hunter." He smiled at her. The oiled strands of his hair were now out of place, protruding in spiky dark wires. His suit looked very rumpled. "*You* will be my pilot."

Nicole tried to control her shock. "Me? I can't fly a helicopter. I'm the Launch Director. I'm just a manager, a desk jockey—"

"You underestimate yourself." Mr. Phillips yanked out the charcoal-gray PDA from his pocket, but he didn't bother to flip open the screen. "As I told you before, I do *not* buy faulty data. You may be an administrator now, but you were rated to pilot this helicopter during your Naval aviator training. You are going to fly us out of here yourself.''

When she didn't answer he smiled. ''We had a saying on the trading floor: 'In science, you can afford to be wrong as long as you're not stupid; in business, you can afford to be stupid as long as you're not wrong.' I, Ms. Hunter, am neither stupid nor wrong. So get moving. Now.''

She sat like a statue, knowing he was right and knowing he had her exactly pegged. Flying this thing was like riding a bicycle—she might be rusty, but she'd never forget how. She couldn't say anything to argue with him.

At gunpoint, she squeezed to the front, sat in the left-hand seat of the helicopter, and grasped the controls.

58

LAUNCHPAD 39A,
EMERGENCY BUNKER

Iceberg lifted his head when the ground-splitting noise stopped. He sat speechless in shock, but one of the other crewmembers shouted, halfway between a scream and a wail of despair. The two Russian mission specialists chattered furiously with each other.

Burns slumped back down onto the bunker floor. "Damn, they blew it up anyway!"

A red emergency light glowed above the heavily reinforced door; the air-recirculation system chugged in the background, running off batteries stored in a deep cache beneath the thick concrete floor.

Iceberg coughed, unable to believe what he had heard. He hung his head in his hands. *Atlantis* was destroyed, even after he had disarmed the bomb! Sometimes, life just wasn't fair.

Alexandra still gripped him tightly, as though unwilling to give up the sanctuary of having another hu-

man being so close. Iceberg squeezed her arm, and
she loosened her grip. She didn't say a word.

The bunker was cool and refreshing after the last
four crazy hours—a refuge from the outside insanity.
Iceberg didn't venture to speak, knowing that once he
did, he'd have to return to the real world of friends
dying and futures shattered.

Atlantis had exploded after all, destroyed in a fireball that had nearly engulfed him as well. He wanted
to stagger back outside to stare at the holocaust—but
he knew that for a while the launchpad would remain
a hellish inferno, swirling with toxic fumes. For the
moment they were stuck in the bunker, helpless.

"Gator's still unconscious." Arlan Burns's voice
broke the silence. He stood behind them, the red emergency light casting deep shadows across his face.
"What about Dr. Franklin?"

Iceberg shook his head. "He didn't make it."
Franklin's body would have been incinerated in the
shuttle explosion, a fitting funeral for an astronaut, he
supposed.

Burns nodded stiffly. Alexandra moaned, and the
other crewmembers murmured in disbelief. "This is
just too much," said Purvis, the other payload specialist. "Just too much."

At the moment it felt as if Iceberg had never left
his crew at all. They all waited for him to speak, to
tell them what to do.

Grunting, Iceberg attempted to stand. An avalanche
of pain nearly bowled him back over, but he held on
to Alexandra for support. Burns stepped over to him
and draped Iceberg's other arm around his shoulder.
"Come on, let's go see Gator." The three hobbled
over to the injured pilot.

Stretched out on the floor, Gator Green groaned softly. He kept his eyes shut and his head lolled to the side. Purvis knelt by the pilot, looking helplessly at an open first-aid kit. "I did what I could, stopped the bleeding a little—but we have to get him to a doctor. Fast."

Iceberg nodded, drawing in cold breaths, trying to focus his concentration. "Yeah, that would be a fine idea. If we could get out of here."

Purvis called from the front. "Hey, Iceberg—the alarm light's off. Do you really think it's okay to evacuate?"

"Let's get that door open," Iceberg said. "I suppose NASA isn't going to waste any time sending rescue choppers out here." He shook his head in dismay. With *Atlantis* gone, the terrorists didn't have much of a bargaining chip left.

Except Nicole.

The other two cosmonauts turned the sealing mechanism and pushed open the heavy bunker door. Hot air and sunlight spilled in, filled with chemical smoke and crackling flames from the launchpad. A smoke alarm in the ceiling began to shrill.

"I had planned on being in orbit by now," Burns said, staring stunned at the bunker wall.

Iceberg coughed as the door opened wider. His eyes hardened as he looked out at the destruction.

The explosion had destroyed most of the Fixed Service Structure and obliterated *Atlantis*. Black-and-gray smoke boiled into the sky, and flames still licked the wreckage of the gantry. An orange cloud drifted out to sea. A sharp, acidic smell rolled into the bunker. It made the VAB inferno look like a Boy Scout campfire.

"And Phillips still wins in the end," Iceberg said

bitterly. He clenched his raw fists, feeling helpless. But what about Nicole?

He heard the faint chopping of helicopters, growing louder. Sirens warbled in the background.

His stomach tightened. Part of him wanted to slam the heavy vault door closed, shut out the rest of the world. All he wished to do was sit back in the cool, dark sanctuary and wait for the rescue squad to get them out. He'd done enough.

Except he couldn't leave a job half finished. He couldn't stand to think of Phillips flying off with the ransom money after all.

And what about Nicole?

59

ESCAPE HELICOPTER

Nicole settled into the pilot seat of the helicopter, shunting aside any feelings for the dead FBI man who had been in the same spot only moments before. Specks of his blood dotted the controls and the curved windshield.

Despite his cultured appearance, Mr. Phillips couldn't disguise the fact that he was a butcher at heart.

She closed her dark eyes and then opened them again, trying to reset her thoughts and slow her breathing. Time to think like an aviator again. She reached down; the cockpit vibrated with a hypnotic, powerful sensation as the rotors powered up again. As Nicole gripped the control stick, she let all the old feelings, the old confidence, flood back into her. She had to step even closer to the edge, push her abilities.

It had been a long time since she'd flown an aircraft. Too long.

Mr. Phillips settled into the front seat beside her, while Senator Boorman hunched in back, cowering next to the gem-filled briefcase and the satchel containing the missiles and shoulder-mounted launcher tube.

"Everybody buckle your seatbelts," Mr. Phillips said, shifting the pistol from one hand to the other as he fastened the strap. "We don't want to be unsafe."

He moved the pistol from Nicole to Senator Boorman. "I wish the rest of my team members had been able to come along, but that didn't prove feasible. They will have to fend for themselves. Not to worry, though—they're quite resourceful."

Nicole increased the throttle, and the blades spun up to a roar. In the pilot's seat again . . . in control, like a rodeo cowboy on a wild bronco. Any other time it would have been . . . *exhilarating*, as Mr. Phillips might have said.

She had flown fixed wings a great deal during her short Naval career and had been checked out in helicopters, but that was years ago. Iceberg had scorned her for spending the last few months flying a desk rather than pushing her reflexes to the edge.

She pulled back on the stick, and the helicopter edged forward as it rose into the air, like a ballet dancer performing a graceful leap. She compensated, and the craft ascended slowly with a downwash of air from the prop blades. She started slipping a little too much to the side. Nicole's heart pounded in time with the engines. She felt the gold key at her neck hit against her skin. The good luck charm didn't seem to be working very well today.

In the back Senator Boorman leaned forward. He breathed deep with fear, making his words thick and slurred, difficult to understand against the background chatter of the copter's blades. "Just cooperate with him. It's almost over." Perhaps, after seeing so much blood, the senator had realized how *useless* he was to Mr. Phillips. "Think of our lives. We *have* to survive. We've both got important work to do."

Nicole turned her chin to the right, glancing over her shoulder. She wondered if Phillips had brought Boorman along just to annoy her. "Let's work on one important thing at a time, Senator. Save the speeches. I've got to fly this aircraft, and I'm a little out of practice."

"Thank you for your cooperation, Ms. Hunter," Mr. Phillips said with a polite smile. "Please proceed straight east toward the ocean. I'll give you directions as we go along."

Tight-lipped, she tilted the rotors, curving away from the parking lot and out across the wide-open Kennedy Space Center. "Why are we heading out to the water?"

"What, do you think I'll give away my entire plan?"

"It would help me to follow your instructions better."

They left the Launch Control Center behind, picking up speed. In the distance they could still see the conflagration at launchpad 39A.

Mr. Phillips smiled. "Very well. Let me give you a scenario. Imagine if you will that I have reached an agreement with a certain foreign country, one with a small yet capable navy, one willing to send a submarine into the waters just off the coast of Florida. Perhaps we could fly low over the waves, reach a rendezvous point where the submarine will meet us.''

''So what . . . what'll happen to Ms. Hunter and myself?'' Boorman asked, leaning forward. ''Are we going to be hostages aboard the sub, too?''

Mr. Phillips sighed. ''While I enjoy your company, Senator, I think you've overstayed your welcome. I would not want to be cooped up in a tiny underwater craft with you. You and Ms. Hunter could get to know one another floating out on the water in an inflatable life raft. I'm sure the Cape Canaveral Air Force Station will be combing the waters for us anyway.''

''Excellent compromise, Phillips!'' Boorman agreed so readily that Nicole found it embarrassing. ''Sounds like a good resolution to this plan. Everyone's happy.''

Nicole wanted to say that *she* wasn't happy. Many people were dead. *Atlantis* had blown up. The Vehicle Assembly Building was severely damaged, and the bad guy was getting away with a huge ransom of jewels. But most of all, she didn't believe Phillips would let them live.

No, she thought, this was not a good way to end the situation.

60

A **military helicopter appeared** over the concrete roof of the emergency bunker, circling away from the smoke. It hovered above the ground, then bumped to a landing fifty feet away. The heavily armed MH-53J was outfitted more to secure the scene than to act as an ambulance for the injured.

Iceberg stood like a lost, beaten soldier, the useless, broken rifle hanging from his shoulder. He watched a second rescue helicopter circle the devastation, an Air Force MH-60 rescue bird with the latest emergency medical technology. The rest of the *Atlantis* crew stood at the doorway, shell-shocked, staring as the rescue helicopter nosed toward the bunker.

Ten parajumpers ran from the security helicopter, ducking their heads, leaving the pilot and co-pilot behind in the cockpit. One of the parajumpers carried a pair of white suitcases, each marked with a red cross;

the others held automatic weapons. The armed jumpers stalked around the complex, securing the area from any terrorists lurking there who might have survived the explosion itself.

The trooper with the first-aid kit called out as he approached, "Colonel Friese? Thank God you're alive. What's the casualty situation?"

Iceberg nodded stiffly. "We're all here, except for Dr. Franklin. He . . . he didn't make it. We've also got a badly hurt crewman who needs immediate attention. Gunshot wounds from sniper fire."

The rescue jumper pushed past Iceberg into the bunker with no more than a cursory glance. Iceberg allowed himself to relax. So it was over. All the running around, trying to get to the *Atlantis* crew. And it ended like this; talking to a kid probably just out of rescue school.

The second helicopter landed. More paramedics boiled out, rushing toward the bunker. Iceberg heard sirens in the background, a fire truck, ambulances, and other rescue vehicles. About time.

The all-out response meant that Phillips must have gotten away, leaving NASA unhampered.

He heard no other aircraft in the sky. The Air Force should have scrambled everything from all the bases in the southeastern United States. Mr. Phillips wouldn't stand a chance up against one of the F-16s from around here, not with their look-down tracking radar. But the terrorist and his hostages could be miles away by now. Where to—Cuba? The Cayman Islands? Some pirate hideout in the Caribbean?

While the rest of the *Atlantis* crew assisted the rescue troops, Iceberg hobbled toward the nearest helicopter, the security chopper, to get away from the frantic bustle. He scanned the sky, raising a hand to his forehead to block the sun. He saw another helicopter flying alone, streaking low across the swampy wildlife refuge as it headed out to sea.

He hoped it was tracking Phillips . . . but the terrorist bastard must be long gone. With Nicole.

Iceberg finally reached the security copter, swaying from pain and dizziness as he tried to keep weight off his bad foot. He probably looked as if he had been run over by a truck . . . no, an entire fleet of trucks. Maybe he could spend a week on the beach after this was all over.

The pilot jumped out of his craft, the visor still down on his helmet. "Here, sir, let me help you!" He wore captain's bars on his dark green Nomex flight suit. He spoke loudly to be heard over the whine of the thrumming engines. "Shoot, you look pretty beat up, Colonel—sure you're okay? Are we going to be flying out any wounded? The rescue helicopter has full facilities."

Iceberg leaned against the side of the aircraft, ready to collapse, wanting to get inside, to be away from this site of devastation. The co-pilot hopped down and joined them. "Howdy, Colonel. Need any help?"

Iceberg motioned with his head to the bunker. "The crew might need some."

"I'll check it out." He turned and trotted for the bunker.

The pilot gave Iceberg a hand, helping him up into the cockpit, looking at the battered automatic rifle. "Can I take your weapon, sir? Uh, shouldn't you be over at the ambulance chopper?"

Iceberg shook his head as he slumped down into the co-pilot's seat like a piece of luggage. "This'll be fine.'' The rescue helicopter looked very far away right now. ''I don't think I could make it all the way over there, Captain. Just tell me what's going on. Are the hostages from the LCC all right? Did they catch the bastard behind all this?''

The captain chewed his gum, popping it in tiny bubbles. ''Things were really crazy. We heard the terrorist leader shot his original pilot, then forced Senator Boorman and Ms. Hunter to go with him. He's got a few Stinger missiles and a launcher, and he's threatened to shoot down anyone who follows him. We flew in low so nobody would see us—right over the treetops.''

''So Panther's got the stick,'' Iceberg muttered. Figured. What the hell else could go wrong today?

The young man took a deep breath, turning his helmet to look regretfully at the frantic activity, the tower of smoke still roiling up from the gantry. Iceberg saw flashing lights half a mile away from approaching ground rescue equipment.

''Nobody pursuing the guy?'' Iceberg said in disbelief, forcing himself to sit upright.

The pilot shook his helmeted head. ''We've got orders to stand down so as not to set him off, sir. NASA's cleared the skies. We almost didn't even get this rescue mission approved.''

Iceberg pointed at the lone helicopter flying away from Kennedy. Barely visible, it was skimming low over the ocean. ''Then who's in that copter?''

''No idea, sir. Probably another mission.''

Right, thought Iceberg—but he knew. That was Phillips, flying low, just as the rescue team had. The tracking teams would never pick him out of the ground clutter unless someone followed him visually—and right now. "Let me use your radio," he growled, reaching toward the control panel.

"Hey, slow down, Colonel." The pilot put out a hand to stop Iceberg. He popped his gum. "Cape Canaveral cleared us in only under radio silence."

Iceberg bristled. "Listen, Captain—if we don't stop Phillips *now*, we'll never see him or the good senator alive again." *Not to mention Nicole.*

The captain's gum popped faster. He looked around the sky. Iceberg couldn't see the captain's eyes through the darkened shade. "Sorry, Colonel. I've got my orders." His voice took on a patronizing tone. "You need medical attention, not more excitement. Don't worry, sir—I'm sure somebody's got the situation under control."

Iceberg cursed silently. All this and they were *still* dropping the ball—probably fighting among the agencies as to who had the tracking responsibility while Phillips slipped away.

He motioned back toward the bunker and softened his voice, intentionally looking ready to collapse at any moment—it wasn't a difficult act to perform. It took his remaining strength to remain calm. "All right, Captain. Our first priority is to get my injured crewmember out of here. I think your buddies might need a hand in the bunker with a stretcher. My pilot was hurt pretty bad."

"I really shouldn't abandon you here alone, sir. And I'm not allowed to leave my aircraft."

Rotorheads! Iceberg thought. "No need to go out of visual range, Captain," he said, "but I'd feel a lot better if you could verify for me that my crew is okay. Your co-pilot may need some help." He sagged in the seat with a groan. "Be sure you hurry back and tell me. Maybe bring one of those medics over here." He winced in pain that wasn't at all faked. "If they can spare a few minutes."

The captain looked uncertainly toward the activity. "Please don't touch anything in the cockpit, Colonel. Remember, no radio transmissions."

"I won't touch a thing. Now get moving."

The pilot glanced at the emergency crew running across the flat grass to the emergency bunker. "Yes, sir. Back in half a minute" He dashed off.

As soon as the captain had stepped away, Iceberg strapped in and reached down to throttle up the main rotor. "Like riding a bicycle," he muttered. "Never forget how to do this." He breathed a sigh of thanks for the helicopter time NASA had shoved down his throat. Back then, being a "rotorhead" had seemed a fate worse than death for a fighter pilot. Now it proved a useful skill.

But flying the craft would still be quite the challenge, especially working the pedals with his injured foot. He wondered if he was going to get a medal for this—or a court martial.

The duped pilot stopped abruptly halfway to the bunker. He spun around and shouted something. Iceberg started the rear rotor. The pilot sprinted back toward the chopper, red-faced and angry.

Out of the corner of his eye Iceberg caught a glimpse of an ambulance roaring down the road through the grassy swampland. Four large fire trucks followed behind it, as well as two dark Broncos. NASA Security.

Iceberg glanced over the helicopter controls and satisfied himself that things looked airworthy. No time for the full-fledged checklist.

At the bunker, a security paratrooper shouted to the rescue troops and came charging toward the helicopter, holding his automatic weapon in front of him. The rest of the stunned *Atlantis* crew watched Iceberg in shock.

The pilot ran full-out, only a few steps from the copter. ''Sir, take your hands off the controls—*now*!''

Making his decision in a flash, Iceberg swung out the battered rifle he had taken from the VAB. The pilot had no way of knowing it couldn't fire a shot. ''Back off, son! I've had a bad day, and my fuse is damned short!''

The pilot pulled up so abruptly he had to catch himself to keep from falling over backward.

Iceberg didn't give him time to think. The rotors caught. He reached down to engage the throttle. ''Here goes.''

The helicopter moved forward, then sideways. Iceberg compensated as it lifted off the ground and brought the nose down. The rotors bit the air, and finally he rose like an elevator.

The two NASA security vehicles raced ahead of the rescue vehicle, tearing across the grass toward the smoldering launch pad and skidded to a stop at the bunker. Uniformed personnel poured out, bristling with weapons.

Iceberg reached down for the radio but stopped before he picked up the microphone. He didn't want to receive any orders he'd have to ignore. No use swatting the hornet's nest once it had fallen from the tree. He had more important things to do.

Wheeling the helicopter around, Iceberg pushed the throttles to the max and set out for the ocean, after Phillips.

61

ESCAPE HELICOPTER

The helicopter skimmed over the tangled swampland of the Kennedy Space Center and the Merritt Island National Wildlife Refuge: a strange combination of untamed wilderness and high-tech space-launch facilities. They headed toward the strip of sand that formed Canaveral Beach and the low, steamy line of the ocean.

Nicole swallowed, not knowing how far they were going or how this journey would end. She looked toward the passenger seat and narrowed her dark eyes. "Phillips isn't even your real name, is it?"

The little man laughed and then stroked his hair back in place with one palm. "Of course not," he said, "but the name should be familiar to you." He raised an eyebrow, but she didn't answer. He sighed in disappointment, and she was glad to disappoint him. "General Sam Phillips was in charge of the space shuttle program at its inception—quite an important man in moving our nation to the next phase of space exploration. Considering my plan, it's quite an ironic alias, don't you agree? 'Phillips'?''

She stared straight ahead as she flew. "Actually, I was thinking more of a pointy-headed screwdriver."

Mr. Phillips suddenly squirmed in his seatbelt to look behind their craft, scowling as he stared out the open door of the passenger side. Wind whistled through the airy carriage of the helicopter.

Nicole also looked behind her—and saw the black insect shape of another helicopter roaring after them. An MH-53J, a military craft, in hot pursuit. Her own craft shot past the strip of beach as the sun reflected from the waves, then continued out over open ocean.

"I said we weren't to be followed," Mr. Phillips said. "Why does everyone have such a problem following instructions today?"

"They're crazy," Boorman said. "They're going to get us all killed. They wouldn't risk that."

"At least they're persistent," Nicole said.

Mr. Phillips frowned. "I wish they'd bother someone else."

The cockpit radio crackled, but Nicole knew even before the words came that this wasn't NASA Security. The voice caused shivers up her spine.

"Land the helicopter, Phillips," Iceberg said. "It's over. You can't get away."

Mr. Phillips ground his teeth together. He turned to Nicole. "Your Iceberg is quite a pain in the ass."

Nicole nodded. "I absolutely agree with you."

Iceberg's transmission continued. "Set the helicopter down, Panther. Phillips won't harm you—he needs you to fly the helicopter. Do you hear me?"

She picked up the handset. "How could you tell it was me? Is it my flying style?"

"Yeah, I recognized a talented pilot who's a bit rusty."

She felt a surge of confidence. "Maybe I'll get the chance to practice a bit more."

"Your Iceberg is quite astute about my not being able to kill you at the moment," Mr. Phillips said. "Maybe I should shoot the good senator instead."

Nicole threw a glance to the back as Mr. Phillips swung his pistol toward Senator Boorman. Boorman's eyes widened as he fell back against his seat, raising his hands to shield himself.

But Mr. Phillips turned back to the front. "No, I'd be doing everybody a favor. That's probably what your Iceberg wants me to do, anyway." He gestured quickly with his pistol. "He's close behind us. Turn around and head back inland. You can't evade him over the open ocean. There are no obstacles."

"Where should I go, then?" she said, stubbornly indecisive. "You're the one with the map."

Mr. Phillips peered out the open side of the helicopter. "Head down the Cape to the old gantries and the swamps. I'm giving you the chance to demonstrate that you're a better pilot than he is. Romantic competition—how wonderful."

His face became hard. "Understand one thing, Ms. Hunter—if your boyfriend captures us, I intend to take you all down with me. You, him, and the senator." He waved his pistol in the same tiresome threat. "It would behoove you to do some fancy flying."

Nicole pressed her lips together and kept quiet, trying to calculate how she might somehow thwart his plans.

She shot overland, cruising south away from the roiling flames and smoke on the shuttle launchpad. She headed toward a group of tall structures to the south on a narrow spit of land, big black cubes stacked like industrial building blocks for the Titan rocket program. The Solid Motor Assembly Building and the Solid Motor Assembly and Readiness Facility, named—with NASA's usual penchant for brilliant acronyms—the SMAB and the SMARF.

Nicole circled tightly around the monolithic buildings, but Iceberg's helicopter stuck close behind her. She roared past the black wall of the SMAB, up over the flat roof where she could look down at the ventilation ducts, the guardrails. Normally the solid motor facilities would have been filled with workers—but the entire complex stood far too close to the shuttle pad for safety, and had been evacuated for launch day.

Farther down the spit of land, the active Titan launch gantries towered above the swamps and the sluggish Banana River, looking like open-air superstructures of government buildings with high aspirations and insufficient funding. A tall white rocket stood linked to the gantry for an Air Force launch scheduled to go up in two weeks.

"What is this, Panther—catch me if you can?" Iceberg said over the radio.

"More like hide-and-seek," Nicole answered quickly as her craft streaked much too close to the open metal gantry and the conical tip of the Titan rocket protruding above the dark girders. "I've got no choice."

She jerked the stick sharply to one side, tilting her helicopter as if it were an amusement park ride. In the back Boorman squawked as if he were about to become an amateur skydiver, grabbing for any handhold. Mr. Phillips lurched, sliding partway off his seat toward the open passenger side, but his seatbelt held him in place. He gripped the arm of his chair.

"It won't work, Ms. Hunter," Mr. Phillips said.

"I can try, can't I?"

"I need an airsickness bag," Boorman moaned.

The clean white sides of the Titan rocket curved close to them like a smokestack. The gantry looked like a nest of metal arms waiting to snatch their helicopter out of the sky. The slightest ding on the rotor blades would turn them into fiery shrapnel. Nicole had seen enough explosions for one day. She felt cold sweat seeping out of her pores, drenching her rayon suit; her focus was honed to razor sharpness.

It was an adrenaline high she had not experienced in nearly a year.

Iceberg spiraled the opposite direction around the rocket and came out in front of them, swooping down so that Nicole had to pull up severely to avoid the backwash of his rotor blades.

"I've got an idea," Mr. Phillips said. "Head down the Cape and out into the open swamps."

The little man reached behind him to fish for his satchel of small missiles. He hauled the package to the front, tucking the pistol in his lap and rummaging in the sack. He pulled out one of the javelin-like missiles, then worked to assemble the launcher tube. Cramped in his seat, he swiveled the cylindrical launcher from side to side so that he came close to smacking Nicole in the face.

"Watch out if you don't want us to crash," she said.

"Excuse me." Mr. Phillips finished assembling the

launcher and then leaned forward in his seat, extending the tube out the open side of the helicopter. "Just fly steady and fly low."

From the back Boorman cried, "Oh my God! He's going to shoot the helicopter. He's going to kill all of us!"

Nicole clamped her jaws together. She felt inclined to shoot Boorman herself if he didn't shut up and let her concentrate.

Below, Georgia pine hunched over sandy soil; the entire landscape was a carpet of greenery—weeds, grass, creepers. She skimmed low over sinuous drainage canals that dead-ended in a network of slow creeks that connected the ocean with the Cape and the wide channel of the Banana River. Nicole increased speed to gain distance from Iceberg, giving him a better chance, but he followed tight behind her.

"Here I go, still chasing your tail, Panther. I thought we'd gotten over all this stuff."

She grabbed the radio. "Iceberg, I'm supposed to shake you somehow so Mr. Phillips doesn't have to fire a missile at you. Any suggestions?" She hoped he might take the hint, that he might let them slip away so they all had a better chance of surviving . . . but then, Earth might also cease to rotate. It was just as likely a scenario as Iceberg giving up.

Mr. Phillips looked up from the launch tube. "That's enough chitchat on the radio, Ms. Hunter."

Up ahead she saw a tall metallic forest of aerodynamic structures on display, what the Kennedy Space Center lovingly called the "Rocket Garden."

Mr. Phillips peered through the curved windshield of the helicopter. "Ah, complex twenty-six," he said, "the Air Force Space Museum." He smiled. "I tried to visit it once, but apparently it's only open to the public on infrequent days, so I've never seen it.''

"Well, take a good look," Nicole said. "We're going to fly close—per your instructions."

The flat area had once been the launch site for Alan Shepherd's Redstone rocket, the United States's first manned launch in 1961. The cracked asphalt around it encircled several low blockhouses, abandoned control bunkers that had been used for the original launches.

She tore her helicopter around the display areas, flying tight around a Thor Able on display and weaving past other rocketry artifacts that stood like metal trees: a Pershing Missile, a Polaris, a Nike Ajax winged like a Flash Gordon rocket. The tallest structure was the restored Redstone gantry from Shepherd's flight, painted red and standing like an elevator shaft that had been ripped out of a skyscraper and erected upright on the concrete.

The two helicopters weaved around the rockets on display, playing tag in a forest of technological relics.

"Oh, this is doing no good," Mr. Phillips said, jabbing the end of his missile launcher out of the helicopter and trying to take better aim. "Get away from these distractions. Fly south into the open swamp, but stay away from the Canaveral Air Force Base. I don't want any trouble from fighter planes and even more helicopters."

Wrenching the stick, Nicole guided the craft away from the rocket garden and headed out to the sprawling open swamp again. Mr. Phillips saw a clearing near rivulets of water, tufts of pampas grass, and palmettos. "There," he pointed, "set down *there*. I need just a few seconds." When Nicole hesitated, Mr. Phillips jabbed his pistol into her ribs. "I don't want to argue."

Nicole pressed her lips together and nodded. After gaining some distance ahead of Iceberg, she brought the helicopter toward the ground.

Mr. Phillips leaned forward, pointing his launcher up into the sky, searching for a good target. He aimed toward the approaching chattering machine—and Iceberg was flying right into the trap.

62

MERRITT ISLAND NATIONAL WILDLIFE REFUGE

The helicopter lurched on its skids as it settled to the damp ground. Nicole chose the best landing spot she could find in the tangle of underbrush. She hoped the surrounding trees would block Mr. Phillips's shot.

The helicopter canted at a slight angle, but the little man braced himself as he propped the rocket launcher against his knees. He tracked Iceberg's oncoming craft with his flinty eyes. Every few seconds he'd glance back into the cockpit.

Nicole watched the man as he simultaneously tried to position the launcher and keep a hand on his pistol. "There's no need to do this, Mr. Phillips," Nicole said. "Let me talk to Iceberg. I'm sure I can—"

"You're taking away all my fun," he said. He slid the missile into the tube and craned his neck, twisting around to get the right angle.

Iceberg's helicopter roared overhead, its engine like stroboscopic thunder. Nicole looked up past the edge of the curved windshield, watching as the copter's shadow passed and then circled back. Iceberg bore down on them.

In the back of the cockpit, Senator Boorman's voice was shrill. "He's going to shoot him out of the sky!"

Turning in his seat, Mr. Phillips aimed his pistol with his other hand and jabbed it toward the senator. "Mr. Boorman, you're making it extremely difficult for me to concentrate. I'm going to shoot you if you don't control yourself."

"You're going to shoot us anyway," the senator wailed.

"Don't encourage me," Mr. Phillips said, giving a calmer but colder glare in Nicole's direction. "I would also be very unhappy if *you* decided to do anything unwise, Ms. Hunter."

Iceberg roared overhead, bearing down. *What the hell does he think he's doing?* Nicole thought. Was he going to crash on top of them?

Mr. Phillips turned back to his missile launcher, squinting through the aiming circle. "Steady . . . steady . . ." His finger tensed on the trigger.

Nicole gripped the control stick, frantically wondering what she could do. Phillips would shoot her if she did anything to defy him. But at least it would save Iceberg. Was he worth dying for?

Nicole was just about to grab the throttle and make the helicopter buck when behind her Senator Boorman suddenly lunged for the wide-open doorway opposite Mr. Phillips. He leaped out the back of the helicopter with a splash into the swamp. Nicole jerked the control stick.

The helicopter joggled from side to side, throwing off Mr. Phillips's aim—just as he depressed the firing button.

The Stinger whistled out, but the shot went wild, arching high and down toward the swamp. The dart-shaped explosive struck a hummock and detonated, transforming a clump of palmettos into a fireball. The thunderous report scared up a group of flamingos that flapped their broad pink wings as they catapulted into the air.

Mr. Phillips snarled. He twisted around to see Boorman running across the marsh, slogging in his wing-tipped loafers through the brown water and mud. The senator ran all-out, crashing in blind panic through creepers and scrub brush. Mr. Phillips brought his pistol around, intending to shoot across the cockpit of the helicopter—but then he controlled himself and snorted with disgust toward the man's receding form. "Let us hope the alligators eat him," he said.

Focusing on the task at hand, Mr. Phillips reached back into the satchel and withdrew his last missile and fitted it into the launching tube. "Second time's the charm," he said.

Iceberg's helicopter came around again, and Nicole couldn't figure out what the big ox had in mind. She knew he was rash and impulsive, but this behavior was nothing short of suicidal. Was he doing it out of some sense of obligation to her? She would have preferred it if he just kept himself alive. Iceberg had already seen the first missile launched at him—but now he was coming back, as if asking for it.

"No, Iceberg," she whispered. "Go away." Was he more interested in stopping Phillips, or saving her?

Or was he just seeing red and bulldozing his way forward?

Mr. Phillips spoke out of the corner of his mouth as he propped his elbow again. "Your Iceberg seems to be under the impression that he can *do* something about this situation."

"It's typical of him," Nicole whispered. "He's never concerned with the fact that the odds are totally against him."

Mr. Phillips grunted, intent on aiming the launcher tube. "Please move away from the controls, Ms. Hunter. I can still see you."

Nicole leaned back. She knew Iceberg was a crack pilot—but not in a helicopter. She had to pray that he could do something to evade the missile as it flew toward him—and once he had launched the second rocket, Mr. Phillips would have nothing but a few bullets in his pistol. He was at the ragged end of his precious plan.

While the little man was preoccupied, though, and as Iceberg's helicopter bore down on them, Nicole saw another chance—something the terrorist wouldn't expect at all. And though it wouldn't help her this instant, it gave her hope, a bargaining chip.

As Mr. Phillips crouched over the launcher tube, Nicole reached with her left foot, probing behind the pilot's seat until her toe snagged the handle of the briefcase full of precious gems.

She watched the dapper little man intently, holding her breath. He tracked with the launcher tube as his lips curved upward in a grin. Finally he let out a long sudden sigh and pressed the firing button.

As the rocket hissed out of the launching tube, Nicole used that moment to drag her foot forward, pulling the briefcase with her, and nudging it over the edge out the pilot's side.

The heavy case tumbled out of the helicopter and fell into the swamp.

Nicole whipped her gaze to the right, staring out the cockpit windshield to see the accelerating missile buzz into the ceramic blue sky on a tail of fire and smoke.

The dartlike Stinger spiraled upward, silently now with the distance, as Iceberg's own MH-53J aircraft moved toward it. The two were on a collision course. Mr. Phillips had aimed well.

But at the last instant Iceberg wrenched his copter to one side, sliding down in the sky. He dropped by a good thirty yards so that the missile roared overhead and detonated just above his rotor blades.

The explosion was close, too close. Like an invisible hand, the blast slammed Iceberg's helicopter—already on a downsweep—farther down.

Nicole saw him lose control, go into a spin. The aircraft seemed to flare out, struggling to remain aloft, but then it crumpled to the ground in the distance, bouncing once.

Mr. Phillips tossed the empty rocket launcher tube over the side, useless now that he had no more missiles. He straightened himself in his seat once again, brushing off his rumpled suit jacket.

"Exhilarating," he said, then carefully buckled his seatbelt. Impatiently, he gestured for Nicole to take off. "Quickly now."

The helicopter heaved itself off the marshy ground and into the sky once more. Nicole gripped the control stick so tightly her knuckles whitened. She imagined it was Mr. Phillips's throat, and squeezed harder.

"It's been fun, but this is getting tiresome. Carry

on back out to the ocean. I want to be flying low over the water as soon as possible.''

He drew a deep breath, smoothed his jacket, and folded his manicured hands neatly in his lap. ''After all of today's hassles, I am very much looking forward to a nice vacation for the rest of my life.''

63

TYNDALL AIR FORCE BASE, FLORIDA

A flight of four F-16C Falcons roared down the runway at Tyndall Air Force Base, near Panama City. Though the F-16s carried a full load of Gatling guns and two air-to-air heat-seeking missiles—more than enough to bring down the helicopter the terrorist had commandeered—they were under strict orders not to shoot because of the two hostages. It wouldn't do to have the Chairman of the Senate's Foreign Relations Committee end his tenure as an incandescent fireball, along with NASA's Launch Director.

The fighter pilots lit their afterburners, throwing fire and exhaust thirty feet behind them. Airborne, they reached their cruising altitude of twenty thousand feet within minutes, leaving the Gulf Coast of Florida and heading inland.

Switching on their Forward-Looking Infrared Radar, they flew in a loose trail formation, following each other a mile apart across the Florida peninsula. With the FLIR they could track the escaping helicopter and lock onto their target from miles away—if they could narrow down the general area for the search pattern. Using scrambled communications, they gave a five-minute estimated time of arrival.

Farther northwest on the Florida panhandle, a flight of two F-15Es took off from Eglin Air Force Base, carrying sophisticated tracking packages that had previously been developed to counter Soviet military threats during the Cold War. Now they would be put to other uses.

The F-15Es gave an ETA of twenty minutes.

Before long, they all expected to converge on the terrorist's escape helicopter.

CINCCENTCOM—Commander-in-Chief of Central Command—was headquartered at McDill AFB in Tampa, across the Florida peninsula from Kennedy Space Center. Technically responsible for U.S. national security interests for Africa and the Middle East, CINCCENTCOM had the closest military command structure available for the defense of Kennedy Space Center. The other CINCs protested when CINCCENTCOM was given the task to apprehend the fleeing terrorist, but geographic location won out over other considerations; too much time had been wasted already on this response.

The four-star general had at his disposal an awesome array of warplanes, naval ships, and ground troops. One of his predecessors had commanded the five hundred thousand troops used during the Gulf War. Now he had to handle one escaping criminal.

CINCCENTCOM moved forward in his chair in the command's ready room. The carpeted, air-conditioned chamber was outfitted with computer monitors recessed into the long wooden table and covered with glass plates. As a half dozen grim-faced men and women stood behind the general in attendance, the computers synthesized and color-coded radar and FLIR data before splashing it on the huge wall screen, which displayed only a small part of Florida in incredible detail. With all the sophisticated weaponry converging on Cape Canaveral, a small, slow-moving blip on the screen drew all their attention.

CINCCENTCOM did not look happy. "How are we tracking the helicopter?"

A young Air Force major stood behind the general, at his left, her black hair in a tight bun pinned neatly out of the way. She would be the only Air Force liaison until her boss, a two-star general, arrived.

"We're getting the feed from NORAD in Colorado Springs, General," she said. "The radar is from two sources, a ground unit at Patrick AFB south of Kennedy, and some Over-the-Horizon-Backscatter information coming in from Virginia.

"Unfortunately, until our fighters arrive in the area, we won't have any airborne data. Special Operations Command is preparing to divert its C-130 that carries FLIR, but it will take a while until they can get there. Some NASA security helicopters are already up, but they won't be able to do any tracking since they can't outfly our bad guy. He's got too much of a head start." She pointed at the large screen. "Right now we're masking out all other air traffic so you can see where we've determined the helicopter must be heading."

The slow-moving blip headed steadily out to sea.

CINCCENTCOM drummed his fingers on the wooden table. "What about AWACS? Do we have any planes available to track this thing other than fighters?"

The young Air Force major checked a crib sheet she had scribbled just minutes prior to entering the command center, studying the data for the Airborne Warning and Command System. "We're using one AWACS for monitoring drug traffic in the Caribbean, but that would take an hour to get up here. Do you want me to do that for you?"

CINCCENTCOM flicked his eyes back to the broad status screen. The FLIR and radar data from the approaching fighters started to converge on the slow-moving blip as it headed across the water. Within minutes he'd have overlapping coverage of the escaping helicopter from the air.

Suddenly, the blip vanished from the screen.

The general spun his chair around. "What just happened?"

The young major stepped forward and studied a monitor. "The helicopter dropped out of sight from our ground-based radar. Could be he's gone down in the Atlantic."

"Put the rest of the air traffic back up. Display it all."

The screen flickered as it filled with radar tracks of commercial airliners, small private planes, and the helicopters around Kennedy Space Center. CINCCENT-COM growled, "So where's our target?"

"It dropped too low for the ground-based radar, sir," the Air Force major said. "The over-the-horizon ground clutter can't handle it."

"So he's rendezvousing with a boat or a sub," said the general simply.

The young Air Force major hesitated. "Either that, sir, or he's landed in the ocean."

CINCCENTCOM settled back in his chair. "Get those fighters out there and send me a visual. We're not going to have him slip through our fingers. That bastard blew up our space shuttle!"

"Yes, sir." She sent out the order even as the general finished speaking.

64

ESCAPE HELICOPTER

Under Mr. Phillips's guidance, Nicole held the helicopter steady, flying at full throttle straight out over the Atlantic. The aircraft screamed so low over the waves she could smell spray through the open sides of the helicopter. The backwash from the rotor blades flattened the greenish-blue swells of the Atlantic, and a fine mist dusted the curved windshield.

"How far am I supposed to go?" she said.

"Just proceed for a few more minutes. You're doing fine."

Nicole kept her gaze intent on the unbroken waves. She spotted no vessel, no rendezvous submarine, not even a fishing boat or pleasure craft. "So where's this submarine? Maybe your friends decided not to show up."

Mr. Phillips reached into his jacket and took out his

pocket watch, flipping open the lid. "So anxious to get rid of me, Ms. Hunter?"

"Yes," she said. "Yes I am."

He snapped his watch shut and casually stuffed it back into his breast pocket before turning to her. A smile curved his lips. "As a matter of fact, there is no submarine . . . but we should have disappeared on all the screens by now." He made a circular motion with his fingers. "Go on, double back. Turn us around and head toward land again. But keep it so low our runners get wet."

"This is crazy!" Nicole pulled the helicopter in a sweeping turn, finally letting loose some of her temper. "You've just stolen millions and millions of dollars, and everyone is looking for you. What are you going to do now?"

He grinned as if she had set him up perfectly. "Why, I'm going to Disneyland! Disney *World*, actually."

If she hadn't already thought as much, Nicole would have decided that Mr. Phillips had gone completely insane. "But what about the submarine? What are you talking about?"

Mr. Phillips loosened his tie and unbuttoned the top of his dress shirt. He spread the fabric apart to reveal another garment underneath, a garish floral print of blue and pink and green—a cheesy Hawaiian shirt.

He removed his jacket, then struggled out of his dress shirt. "Tourist disguise," he said, raising his eyebrows as if waiting for her to congratulate him on his cleverness. "I'm also wearing Bermuda shorts—plaid, of course—but I'll remove my pants at a less embarrassing moment, if you don't mind."

They rushed above the waves, arrowing back toward land. The shoreline was a blurry green-and-tan line growing larger in the morning's haze. "But . . . why Disney World?" she said, completely baffled.

Mr. Phillips rubbed his hands together, then loosened his garish Hawaiian shirt, fluttering the fabric to get himself some air. He looked much more comfortable, a stranger in casual clothes. "It's quite ingenious, actually. While everyone is searching miles and miles of empty ocean, crisscrossing, knowing they must have missed something—you and I will be heading overland to Orlando. Even if the spotters do manage to track us and figure out who we are, we'll be all finished before they can come after us."

"But I don't get it," she said. "I thought you were trying to escape."

Mr. Phillips laughed. "So I will. You will land me smack in the middle of the most densely populated spot in the southeastern United States—the Walt Disney World parking lot! Of course the helicopter will cause quite a ruckus, but I'll just vanish into the crowd, another tourist with a suitcase. Thanks to our timing"—he glanced at his pocket watch and smiled— "we are going to arrive right in the midst of the gate-opening fiasco, the craziest time of the day. You don't think one man alone can just evaporate in the middle of all that? They'll never find me."

"You've got to be kidding."

His eyes became cold. "Certainly not. The parking lots in the Magic Kingdom alone hold twelve thousand cars, and over thirty thousand people go into the parks every day, most of them right around now. I just love trivia."

"You're such a trivial man—no wonder," she retorted. He scowled at her but wasted no further energy on banter.

They broke past the beach, but Nicole kept the helicopter just above the treetops as they flew over the wild swamps filled with lush greenery, matted trees, and drainage ditches, a primeval world.

Mr. Phillips chuckled and turned to toss his suit jacket in the back of the cockpit when he suddenly froze. He spun about to look behind him, scanning the empty passenger compartment.

But he spotted no ransom briefcase.

"What!" he squawked. He leaned over the back of the seat, peering down as if he could ransack the cockpit with his eyes. He swished with his manicured hands but felt nothing. "My treasure!"

Nicole said nonchalantly, "Admission prices are a little high at Disney World these days, Mr. Phillips. You seem to be a bit strapped for cash."

Mr. Phillips scrambled to unbuckle his seatbelt, hyperventilating in wordless rage and alarm. He climbed over the seat into the back where the senator had crouched as a hostage. He dug under the seats, practically excavating the tiny passenger area—but the gem-filled briefcase was gone.

"Boorman!" he screamed. Nicole stayed mute, letting the little man think the senator had run off with the ransom. "I want my jewels back!" Livid, he grabbed the seat beside Nicole, raging. He stood at his full height, not even needing to duck in the low cockpit.

Then they both heard a loud throbbing noise from below that grew to a deafening roar.

Mr. Phillips poked his head out the open passenger side. Nicole glanced over to see Iceberg's battered chopper roaring up from underneath, barely holding together in the aftereffects of the missile detonation. He appeared out of nowhere, closing the gap between them as if they were about to collide in the air. Her heart leaped.

"What is that man doing here?" Mr. Phillips cried.

Over the cockpit radio, Iceberg's voice spoke to Nicole. "Hey, Panther! You always wanted to be on top. You're cleared hot for an evasive maneuver."

Her face grim, Nicole jerked the stick to one side, abruptly tilting her aircraft.

The helicopter lurched, taking Mr. Phillips by surprise. He lost his grip on the edge of the passenger chair, and he whirled in one last frozen instant, staring at her with those flinty eyes that had once been filled with cold mirth but now held only terror.

He flailed his hands, and his mouth opened—but no words came out. He lurched forward and slipped. His fingers caught for just an instant—then he plunged overboard, falling out into open air with a thin cry of surprise.

He had time to thrash his arms only once until he fell headfirst into the blurring blades of Iceberg's helicopter, roaring up from below. Mr. Phillips exploded into a mist of red spray and chunks of flesh that vanished into a rapidly dissipating scarlet rain.

"Exhilarating," Nicole said.

Iceberg's helicopter nearly flipped from the impact on the tip of his blades. The little man's body had damaged the rotor. The helicopter wobbled, out of control like a bucking horse, and started to go down. Nicole's heart froze as she saw Iceberg fight in the cockpit—his jaw set, his face stony. The helicopter lurched in the air, and she paced him, trying to help and trying to stay out of the way.

Finally, only a few meters above the treetops, Iceberg regained control. The engine stuttered, then caught firmly again, and he gained altitude. He rose up grinning, flying parallel to her, waving across at her from his own cockpit.

Nicole slumped back in her pilot's seat, exhausted, looking down. "At least you went out with a splash, Mr. Phillips," she said to herself.

She thought the little man would have appreciated the joke.

65

NASA TELEVISION
RELAY BUNKER

By the time NASA security teams finally arrived at the television relay bunker, Amos Friese already had the situation well in hand.

Holding the deadly assault rifle he had pried from Rusty's fingers, he stood watch, pacing back and forth on the painted concrete floor. With all the video monitors shot out, Amos had no way of knowing what else had gone on during the retaking of Kennedy Space Center, but he intended to hold his bunker against whatever foes might come against him.

As he had proven with the redheaded terrorist, the bad guys had better think twice before they challenged Amos Friese again.

While Rusty was out cold, Amos had used a utility knife to cut several electrical cords from the backs of the now useless monitors and wrapped them around the thug's freckled wrists and ankles. He enjoyed tying the man hand and foot, trussing him like a pig. It seemed fitting.

For good measure Amos also wrapped the man's hands with a thick layer of cellophane tape from the dispenser on his desktop, but Amos didn't know how well that would hold.

When Rusty eventually returned to consciousness, he had struggled, working himself into painful exhaustion. The redhead had quickly learned the futility of grumbling threats and curses, once Amos stuffed an old cleaning cloth in the prisoner's mouth. The grimy rag was saturated with solvent to clean dust off desks and TV screens, and must have tasted awful.

Rusty continued to glare at him, making Amos quite pleased.

His face haggard, his clothes torn from the ordeal, Amos stood watching his captive. Even with the loud air conditioner still on, he found himself perspiring so much that he tore a strip from another cleaning rag and wrapped it around his forehead to keep the salty droplets from running into his eyes.

When the NASA security troops broke into the blockhouse, they stared at the two men, rapidly assessing the situation and wisely realizing that they had better not mess with Amos.

The lead man, a tall, thin Hispanic security officer with very close-cropped dark hair and a chin shaven so clean it was like glass, nodded down at the seething redheaded terrorist. "Just this one, sir?"

Without taking his gaze from his captive, Amos nodded. "Yep, one prisoner. The only one left." Something in his eyes and hardened features kept the guards from asking more.

"According to our intelligence, this is the only

member of the terrorist team to survive."

"Good," Amos said coldly. "Maybe I could be the one to interrogate him."

Rusty tried to say something behind the gag in his mouth, but the words came out only as gurgling grunts. Amos thoroughly enjoyed the light of terror in the redhead's eyes.

A fourth security officer jogged in after inspecting the wreckage of the doorway. He noted the sweater-draped woman on the floor. "Looks like three bodies," he reported, "two NASA security from a booby-trapped door, plus this one."

As the guards moved to pick Cecelia up from the floor, Amos turned to them. "Be careful with her," he said.

"We will, sir," said the clean-shaven security man.

Amos reluctantly let them remove the machine gun from his grip. His arms and hands felt numb. The adrenaline rush was better than slamming down a six-pack of Jolt Cola in an hour. He hoped that his brother had made out as well.

In fact, he decided he might even challenge Iceberg to a rematch of that snowball fight. . . .

66

KENNEDY SPACE CENTER

Flicking the controls in the helicopter's cockpit, Iceberg pushed the wipers to high as he tried to get rid of the remnants of spattered blood from the windshield, a grim reminder of Mr. Phillips's demise.

He was lucky that his main rotor blades hadn't broken apart with the little man's sudden weight. This copter had been through quite a pounding already in one morning, but the blades must have just nicked the man with the tip. It was enough.

He followed Nicole's craft, keeping her in sight half a mile in front of him as they flew back to the Launch Control Center, War Zone Central, he thought. The Florida coast looked a mottled green and brown, contrasting with the deep blue ocean farther east. A nice, peaceful place for a paradise vacation. . . .

The smoldering launchpad still belched fire and smoke, a funeral pyre for the space shuttle *Atlantis*.

Iceberg knew the whole world had been watching the crisis. The blasé public had tragically been reminded of the vulnerability of the space program, that flying into orbit would never be a ho-hum bus ride.

Somehow, Iceberg didn't think the death of *Atlantis* meant the end of the space program. Maybe something so dramatic would finally make Joe Six-pack realize its value. NASA cost the country a minuscule percent of the federal budget, yet delivered more than any comparable government program. Commercializing space was the last great hope for the nation's future, and maybe this disaster would rally the public behind it.

Iceberg could barely make out fire trucks and emergency vehicles parked in a semicircle around the concrete pad. The smoke billowed into the atmosphere like a smoldering volcano. But launchpad 39B and its intact gantry still stood tall in the Florida swamps. *Endeavour* waited to launch.

As he flew, Iceberg felt utterly exhausted. His ankle throbbed, his muscles ached, his palms were still raw, and he felt as though he had been used as a dummy in a series of crash tests.

His radio clicked. It was Nicole's voice on an open channel. "KSC, this is Panther in one of two Air Force helicopters approaching the restricted launch area. Request immediate clearance and permission to land at the Launch Control Center. Reporting loss of one terrorist. No other casualties. Acknowledge."

"Roger that, Panther!" came an excited voice over the radio. "Terrorist lost?"

"Total loss," Iceberg said into the microphone. "This is Colonel Friese, flying wing. We are both safe.

Senator Boorman is unharmed, but he's going to need a pickup out in the swamps. Over.''

The voice acknowledged. "Proceed to Launch Control. You know the landing area—and congratulations on getting back here. We've all been following the events.''

Nicole's voice came back. ''Please have medical personnel available at the landing site—I think Iceberg's going to need a few painkillers. Maybe finally he'll hold still long enough to get treatment.''

Iceberg wearily clicked the button on his microphone twice to indicate he agreed.

As they flew in over the Banana River, the Kennedy Space Center looked more and more like a battlefield. Smoke from the destroyed VAB still curled into the air like a greasy fingerpainting. Several burning vehicles lay strewn on the cleared roadways. A flight of F-16s flew high CAP—Combat Air Patrol—in a holding pattern high overhead; a lumbering C-130 flew in an oval racetrack with its forward-looking infrared sensors deployed..

Kennedy Space Center would never be the same. It had been a victim of a bloody attack, but the astronauts and the space program had been victorious, though at a terrible cost.

At lower altitudes, the air boiled with military helicopters, some bearing NASA markings, others with COAST GUARD or AIR FORCE written on the sides. A menacing-looking MH-60 helicopter, guns poking from its nose and air-to-ground missiles hanging from its stubby wings, swooped in to keep watch over them as they approached the LCC. Iceberg hoped the pilots weren't trigger happy. He'd had enough of playing GI Joe for a while.

The Launch Control Center's parking lot was packed with cars, flashing emergency lights, ambulances, and people milling around. Military trucks and surly-looking security guards with weapons lined the road leading to the Admin area. The press stands to the south of the LCC were jammed with TV cameras, all turned toward their approaching choppers.

The only good that Iceberg latched onto was knowing that, with the Russian *Mir* station waiting for supplies, NASA would have to get the next shuttle up without delay. The urgency would prevent them from sliding into years of paralysis, as had happened after the *Challenger* accident. He supposed *Endeavour*—already in place on launchpad 39B—would be frantically refitted for the *Mir* resupply mission. Maybe now the U.S. would take spaceflight more seriously, build on the shuttle's legacy, and invest in true "leapfrog" technologies such as Single-Stage-to-Orbit spacecraft.

Military police cleared the landing zone as Nicole and Iceberg flew their helicopters in. Two ambulances waited at the periphery, lights flashing.

Pulling back on the stick, Iceberg signaled for Nicole to land before touching down beside her. He felt the skids settle onto the pavement with a bounce. A half dozen men and women ducked their heads and ran out to his copter. He released the rotors and cut the engine, slumping back in his seat. Maybe now he could take a nap—except the pain had tripled in the last few seconds, now that he knew he could slump into exhaustion.

NASA security officers rushed out of the LCC, heading for ambulances and emergency vehicles. Several sheet-wrapped bodies came out on stretchers.

Other uniformed personnel worked together to escort the remaining trembling hostages to safety. Engineers and station managers from the firing floor milled about, angry, excited, like a swarm of ants.

Iceberg swung stiffly out of the burn-stained cockpit, stepping gingerly on his one good foot, keeping off his crumbling cast. He winced and nearly collapsed from the pain. Perhaps it would be a good idea if he waited for a helping hand. . . .

With the rotor still running, Nicole leaped out of her helicopter. She ducked down and raced over to Iceberg, nearly bowling him over with a large hug, which she covered up as an effort to help him to stand. They embraced for a few seconds longer than was necessary, then stepped slowly apart.

Nicole looked at him for a moment. "Thanks, Iceberg." Then, seeming embarrassed, she said, "I knew you'd be too stupid to give up."

Through his elation, Iceberg still felt as if something was missing. He looked around. "I need to see my crew," he said.

He had always insisted on being the star of the show—but now the team of astronauts had found themselves in a deep bind without him. They had fended for themselves, despite his efforts to help. Iceberg realized that the others did matter—but that he couldn't always be there for them.

Before Nicole could answer about the crew, Iceberg staggered again in amazement. "And Amos! Oh God, my brother, Amos. Is he okay?"

Nicole nodded, flashing him an impish grin. "Yeah, I checked on the radio before I landed. Amos had a few adventures of his own. He's on his way to the LCC. I think you'd be proud of him, Iceberg."

"Of course I'm proud of him," he said, puzzled that she'd even mention it. "He's my own brother." Nicole pressed her lips together, silent. Iceberg sighed, and his shoulders slumped. "I guess there's no 'of course' about it. It isn't obvious. Maybe I didn't tell him often enough that I'm proud of the things he does. Amos is a good video jockey, you know, maybe the best there is. He understands gadgets better than anything I can comprehend."

Nicole nodded carefully. Iceberg put his arm around her shoulder and leaned on her. They started walking to the LCC.

Nicole said, "And you don't know the half of it— all by himself, he captured one of the terrorists, who's been babbling like a parrot ever since, trying to make a plea bargain with anyone close enough to listen. He is the only one left alive of the bunch."

The emergency personnel approached. Two women and a man, dressed in the white shirts of paramedics, carried first-aid gear. They jogged up, out of breath. As they drew near, Nicole waved them off. "I'll get Iceberg inside. You just leave him to me." Nicole and Iceberg made their way through the growing crowd to the LCC.

"Thanks for keeping your cool in the Launch Control Center." Iceberg had difficulty finding the right words as they walked.

She shook her head grimly. "A lot of people died under my watch. Two of them right in front of my eyes."

"Yeah, and if you had tried a crazy stunt—like *I* would have—there'd be a lot more bodies, half the people on the firing floor, maybe. I'm not sure anyone else could have pulled that off, that kind of cool control. You really made a difference, Panther.''

Nicole turned her head and smiled back at him. ''So the Iceberg begins to melt.''

He shrugged his broad shoulders. ''Maybe . . . just a little.'' He leaned more weight on her as they shuffled to the LCC.

She lowered her dark eyes, then ran a finger through her short, fluffy hair to loosen the sweat-dampened strands. ''I have to admit this morning was more . . . ah, *exhilarating* than I've had in a long time. I remember my aviator days, my astronaut training. It was tough but rewarding.''

She swallowed. Iceberg squeezed her shoulder as they walked, remembering how good it felt to hold her.

Nicole continued, ''I had been having my doubts about leaving the 'real work' as an astronaut and 'selling out' to administration and politicking. Those are your words, you know.'' She was quiet for a moment, then looked up at him. ''But I'm *good* at this, Iceberg. I shouldn't have to feel guilty because I'm cut out for something different.'' She touched the gold key on the necklace she wore. ''These are my dreams and my decisions, and I don't need to follow anybody else's plans but my own.''

''Especially when some jerks keep getting on your case about it,'' Iceberg said with a self-deprecating smile. ''Must have been tough to deal with that Phillips guy.''

''It's been tough dealing with you too, sometimes.''

A van pulled up, bearing the *Atlantis* crew back to a secure area. Gator had already been hauled off by helicopter to the base hospital at the Cape Canaveral Air Force Station.

The crew—*his* crew—staggered out of the van, still in their orange pressure suits. NASA personnel swarmed around them. Still leaning on Nicole's shoulder, Iceberg grinned at them all. Burns and Purvis spotted him and pushed through the crowd. The rest of the crew followed. The group had spent so much time training together, rehearsing this mission, never expecting the ordeal they would actually endure.

The last to leave the van, Alexandra Koslovsky moved slowly as if she were an old woman with rheumatism. He wondered if her foot had been seriously injured. She blinked at the clear sky, standing tall.

After speaking quietly with the rest of his crew, Nicole helped Iceberg shuffle over to Alexandra. The Russian cosmonaut stood like a soldier waiting to report. "Thank you for your assistance in rescuing me, Colonel Iceberg," she said, seeing his beaten appearance. "I am happy to report that Lieutenant Commander Gator's injuries do not appear to be life-threatening, and we expect him to survive and recover."

Nicole squeezed Alexandra's hand. "I'm so sorry about Andrei," she said. "I was there with him. I wish I could have done something to prevent it. He died a hero."

Alexandra nodded, her face a still sculpture. Then, like a shock wave rippling across her skin, emotion briefly filtered through her cold mask until she covered it up again. She returned a brisk nod. "And I must apologize for the death of Mission Commander Franklin. Both men died bravely." She shook her head before continuing. "But unfortunately both men are still dead."

Hearing the sudden sharpness in her words even in

this sad situation brought the point home to Iceberg. He knew exactly what she meant.

Ambassador Andrei Trovkin, the big bearlike Russian, had done exactly what Iceberg would have done himself—and Trovkin had died for it. Sometimes balls-to-the-wall action was called for . . . but sometimes it was better to keep your head and just wait. All his life, Iceberg had had difficulty telling the difference between those two situations.

"I'm glad you didn't end up dead, Iceberg," Nicole said, "though you sure tried hard enough to get yourself killed."

He hugged her back. "I'm a slow learner, but I'm persistent."

Later, inside her own office in the LCC, Nicole opened the charcoal-gray Personal Data Assistant she had recovered from the suit jacket Mr. Phillips had tossed in the back of her helicopter. She already knew some of the answers, but perhaps this contained more details.

Iceberg and Amos sat beside her, watching and waiting. The medics hovered outside the door, desperate to haul Iceberg off to a hospital—but he wanted some answers first. Nicole hadn't argued. This was probably the only way to get him to sit still for a while, and it felt good to be comfortable next to him after so many months of brooding tension between them.

Though the computerized device was small and handheld, its hard disk was crammed with information, useful data she could unlock to determine just what had driven the dapper little man to such a bizarre plan. It would take months to unravel it all, but some of the details might be close to the surface, where Mr. Phillips could gloat over them.

She handed the PDA over to Amos. "You're the expert, Amos," Nicole said. "He told me his name wasn't Mr. Phillips."

"Thanks." Amos set right to work, using the blunt plastic stylus to call up file after file. Nicole leaned over and squinted at the murky liquid crystal display, studying the information.

NASA security marched through the LCC halls, trying to put a lid back on the situation. The FBI milled throughout the building. It would only be a matter of minutes before NASA Headquarters, the White House, Congress, and all the security forces in the free world would start clamoring for attention. Not to mention the reporters.

"This is the real stuff here," Amos said. "His name was Thomas Carrington Benchley Jr. Man oh man, what an ego."

Nicole stared down at the letters on the PDA screen. "Typical."

Amos said, "I'll cross-check his personal files." He tapped with the stylus, opening up one journal entry after another. Memos, logs, strident letters to investment companies. "We'll need to verify the leads, but it's a good guess he didn't expect anyone else to find this information. His mother died when he was young and left him with quite an inheritance. Looks like he was an upper-class kid, an only child."

Iceberg leaned back in his creaking government chair, wincing in pain. "No surprise there."

From NASA security, she had already heard part of Rusty's story—that "Phillips" was once a high-powered rogue trader on Wall Street who had dumped everything into initial public offerings of high-tech industries and aerospace, hoping for that big breakthrough . . . but his money went faster than the breakthrough came. He had lost his shirt on those investments and got screwed in bad trades, big-time.

Publicly, he had lost the whole family fortune, two hundred million dollars. His wife and kids were now eating Chef Boyardee and eking out a Spartan lifestyle, barely getting along on what little insurance he left them. Nicole bet they didn't have fond memories of their dad.

But he had made other illegal deals, other contingencies, so that he came out with a golden nest egg . . . and a whole new identity.

Iceberg heaved a deep breath. "Good thing he wasn't any more successful at the new career than he was in the old one."

Amos chuckled. "Well, his bank account isn't getting any bigger today."

Nicole laughed out loud. "That's for sure. They'll find that suitcase of gemstones as soon as they track down Senator Boorman out in the swamps."

A rap came at the door. "Ms. Hunter, we really need to get Colonel Friese to the hospital."

"How long are those medics going to make me stay in an uncomfortable bed with sheets that smell like bleach?" Iceberg said.

Nicole smothered a grin. "Not long enough."

Amos straightened his round-lensed glasses and winked at Nicole. "Hey, if you're going to be eating hospital food for a few weeks, how about we all sneak out for some Fat Boy's barbecue? Then, while he's stuffed and satisfied, the medics will be able to operate on him without him feeling the pain!"

Iceberg leaned forward and tried to punch his little brother on the shoulder, but his joints were too stiff and sore to even make a fist. He fell back against his seat and groaned, finally unable to function. Amos and Nicole laughed as the medics came in to take Iceberg away.

67

MERRITT ISLAND NATIONAL WILDLIFE REFUGE

The millions of hungry creatures in the swamp made a deafening racket. Thousands of individual voices, each one disgusting or frightening or threatening in its own way: whining bugs, croaking frogs, biting insects, buzzing gnats. Water trickled and splashed. Creatures moved through the underbrush, large ones, dangerous ones, unseen predators.

Senator Boorman clung to the rough bark of the tree. Spanish moss dangled just out of reach, infested with all-too-large spiders. Ants crawled on his hands and legs. He had given up trying to brush them off, because other things preoccupied him.

He had climbed to what he hoped was safety in the dense branches of a Georgia pine, bothered by sharp evergreen needles and sticky resin that clung to his clothes and the palms of his hands. Boorman thought of multicolored coral snakes slithering through the branches . . . large and deadly Florida panthers just waiting for a free lunch . . . long-tusked wild boars that were so prevalent they left ripped-up patches of grass all across the site.

Boorman was wet, exhausted, hungry, and caked with mud and swamp slime . . . in short, utterly miserable. And the pine tree he had climbed in desperation was not actually very tall after all.

Two enormous bull alligators waited in the grassy area that surrounded the gnarled tree, their backs lumpy with ridges, their skin black as demons of night.

Both gators yawned wide, showing the pinkish insides of their cavernous gullets, flashing enough wicked teeth to line all the freeways in Nebraska. They had treed him on his headlong flight, but they refused to go away. The snorting alligators continued circling the trunk . . . waiting, smelling their quarry above.

Boorman swallowed. He hoped rescue would come soon.

He searched the sky, squinting. The sun was bright, and the air was clear—but he saw no circling helicopters, no search parties beating the bushes to find him and take him away from all this.

They *had* to know where he was. They had to come find him. Somebody would come.

He knew they would want to rescue him. He *hoped* they would rescue him. He was a United States senator, after all.

Boorman looked down again and clung to the tree so tightly that the bark hurt his hands. Those alligators down there appeared to be getting hungrier every minute.

He looked up to the sky again and waited.